PRAISE FOR THE NOVELS OF

LaVyrle Spencer

"Spencer is a winner and the reader is no loser."
—*San Antonio Express-News*

"Spencer, famous for her heartrending slices of Americana,
delivers the goods again."
—*Publishers Weekly*

"You will never forget the incredible beauty
of LaVyrle's gifted pen."
—*Affaire de Coeur*

"A gifted storyteller."
—*The Birmingham News*

"A superb story."
—*Los Angeles Times*

"A journey of self-discovery and reawakening."
—*Booklist*

"Superb!"
—*Chicago Sun-Times*

"A beautiful love story . . . emotional."
—*Rocky Mountain News*

"Touching."
—*The Chattanooga Times*

LaVyrle Spencer

Morning Glory

BERKLEY BOOKS, NEW YORK

THE BERKLEY PUBLISHING GROUP
Published by the Penguin Group
Penguin Group (USA) Inc.
375 Hudson Street, New York, New York 10014, USA
Penguin Group (Canada), 90 Eglinton Avenue East, Suite 700, Toronto, Ontario M4P 2Y3, Canada
(a division of Pearson Penguin Canada Inc.)
Penguin Books Ltd., 80 Strand, London WC2R 0RL, England
Penguin Group Ireland, 25 St. Stephen's Green, Dublin 2, Ireland (a division of Penguin Books Ltd.)
Penguin Group (Australia), 250 Camberwell Road, Camberwell, Victoria 3124, Australia
(a division of Pearson Australia Group Pty. Ltd.)
Penguin Books India Pvt. Ltd., 11 Community Centre, Panchsheel Park, New Delhi—110 017, India
Penguin Group (NZ), 67 Apollo Drive, Rosedale, North Shore 0632, New Zealand
(a division of Pearson New Zealand Ltd.)
Penguin Books (South Africa) (Pty.) Ltd., 24 Sturdee Avenue, Rosebank, Johannesburg 2196,
South Africa

Penguin Books Ltd., Registered Offices: 80 Strand, London WC2R 0RL, England

MORNING GLORY

This is a work of fiction. Names, characters, places, and incidents either are the product of the author's imagination or are used fictitiously, and any resemblance to actual persons, living or dead, business establishments, events, or locales is entirely coincidental. The publisher does not have any control over and does not assume any responsibility for author or third-party websites or their content.

PRINTING HISTORY
G. P. Putnam's Sons hardcover edition / February 1989
Jove mass-market edition / March 1990
Berkley trade paperback edition / February 2009

Berkley trade paperback ISBN: 978-0-425-22928-6

The Library of Congress has cataloged the G. P. Putnam's Sons hardcover edition as follows:

Spencer, LaVyrle.
    Morning glory/LaVyrle Spencer.—1st American ed.
      p. cm.
    I. Title.
PS3569.P4534M6   1989   88-28166 CIP
813'.54—dc19
ISBN 0-399-13413-1

PRINTED IN THE UNITED STATES OF AMERICA

10   9   8   7   6   5   4

Special thanks ...

To Marian Smith Collins and Bob Collins for their help with the Calhoun setting and the law ...

To Gunnery Sgt. Richard E. Martelli, United States Marine Corps, for sharing his invaluable knowledge of Marine history ...

And to Carol Gatts, midwife and beekeeper, for keeping old traditions alive and for letting us glimpse them ...

To my favorite authors,
TOM & SHARON CURTIS,
who by their writing
have taught, entertained and inspired.
With deepest admiration.

Morning Glory

Prologue

1917

The train pulled into Whitney, Georgia, on a leaden afternoon in November. Clouds churned and the first droplets of rain pelted like thick batter onto the black leather roof of a waiting carriage. Both of its windows were covered with black. As the train clanged to a stop, one shade was stealthily lifted aside and a single eyeball peered through the slit.

"She's here," a woman's voice hissed. "Go!"

The carriage door opened and a man stepped out. He, like the carriage, was garbed in black—suit, shoes and flat-brimmed hat worn level with the earth. He glanced neither right nor left but strode purposefully to the train steps as a young woman emerged with a baby in her arms.

"Hello, Papa," she said uncertainly, offering a wavering smile.

"Bring your bastard and come with me." He turned her roughly by an elbow and marched her back to the carriage without looking at her or the infant.

The curtained door was thrown open the instant they reached it. The young woman lurched back protectively, drawing the baby against her shoulder. Her soft hazel eyes met the hard green ones above her, framed by a black bonnet and mourning dress.

"Mama ..."

"Get in!"

"Mama, I—"

"Get in before every soul in this town sees our shame!"

The man gave his daughter a nudge. She stumbled into the carriage, scarcely able to see through her tears. He followed quickly and grasped the reins, which were threaded through a peekhole, yielding only a murky light.

"Hurry, Albert," the woman ordered, sitting stiff as a grave marker, staring straight ahead.

He whipped the horses into a trot.

"Mama, it's a girl. Don't you want to see her?"

"See her?" The woman's mouth pursed as she continued staring straight ahead. "I'll have to, won't I, for the rest of my life, while people whisper about the devil's work you've brought to our doorstep."

The young woman clutched the child tighter. It whimpered, then as a jarring crash of thunder boomed, began crying lustily.

"Shut it up, do you hear!"

"Her name is Eleanor, Mama and—"

"Shut it up before everyone on the street hears!"

But the baby howled the entire distance from the depot, along the town square and the main road leading to the south edge of town, past a row of houses to a frame one surrounded by a picket fence with morning glories climbing its front stoop. The carriage turned in, crossed a deep front yard and pulled up near the back door. The mother and child were herded inside by the black-garbed woman and immediately a dark green shade was snapped down to cover a window, followed by another and another until every window in the house was shrouded.

The new mother was never seen leaving the house again nor were the shades ever lifted.

CHAPTER
1

August 1941

The noon whistle blew and the saws stopped whining. Will Parker stepped back, lifted his sweat-soaked hat and wiped his forehead with a sleeve. The other mill hands did the same, retreating toward the shade with voluble complaints about the heat or what kind of sandwiches their wives had packed in their lunch pails.

Will Parker had learned well not to complain. The heat hadn't affected him yet, and he had neither wife nor lunch pail. What he had were three stolen apples from somebody's backyard tree—green, they were, so green he figured he'd suffer later—and a quart of buttermilk he'd found in an unguarded well.

The men sat in the shade of the mill yard, their backs against the scaly loblolly pines, palavering while they ate. But Will Parker sat apart from the others; he was no mingler, not anymore.

"Lord a-mighty, but it's hot," a man named Elroy Moody complained, swabbing his wrinkled red neck with a wrinkled red hanky.

"And dusty," added the one called Blaylock. He hacked twice and spit into the pine needles. "Got enough sawdust in my lungs to stuff a mattress."

The foreman, Harley Overmire, performing his usual noon

ritual stripped to the waist, dipped his head under the pump and came up roaring to draw attention to himself. Overmire was a sawed-off runt with a broad pug nose, tiny ears and a short neck. He had a head full of close-cropped dark hair that coiled like watch springs and refused to stop growing at his neckline. Instead, it merely made the concession of thinning before continuing downward, giving him the hirsute appearance of an ape when he went shirtless. And Overmire loved to go shirtless. As if his excessive girth and body hair made up for his diminutive height, he exposed them whenever the opportunity arose.

Drying himself with his shirt, Overmire sauntered across the yard to join the men. He opened his lunch pail, folded back the top of his sandwich and muttered, "Sonofabitch, she forgot the mustard again." He slapped the sandwich together in disgust. "How many times I got to tell that woman it's pork plain and mustard on beef!"

"You got to train 'er, Harley," Blaylock teased. "Slap 'er upside the head one time."

"Train her, hell. We been married seventeen years. You'd think she'd know by now I want mustard on my beef." With his heel he ground the sandwich into the dry needles and cursed again.

"Here, have one o' mine," Blaylock obliged. "Bologna and cheese today."

Will Parker bit into the bitter apple, felt the saliva spurt so sharply it stung his jaws. He kept his eyes off Overmire's beef sandwich and Blaylock's spare bologna and cheese, forcing himself to think of something else.

The neatly mowed backyard where he'd ransacked the well. Pretty pink flowers blooming in a white enamel kettle sitting on a tree stump by the back door. The sound of a baby crying from inside the house. A clothesline with white sheets and white diapers and white dishtowels and enough blue denim britches that one pair wouldn't be missed, and a matching number of blue cambric shirts from which he'd nobly taken the one with a hole in the elbow. And a rainbow of towels, from which he'd selected green because somewhere in the recesses of his memory was a woman with green eyes who'd once been kind to him, making him forever prefer green over all other colors.

The green towel was wet now, wrapped around the Ball jar. He folded it aside, unscrewed the zinc lid, drank and forced himself not to grimace. The buttermilk was sickeningly sweet; even the wet towel hadn't managed to keep it cool.

With his head tilted back against the bole of the pine tree, Parker saw Overmire watching him with beady mustardseed eyes while stretching to his feet. The jar came down slowly. Equally as slowly, Parker backhanded his lips. Overmire strutted over and stopped beside Will's outstretched feet, his own widespread, firmly planted, his beefy fists akimbo.

Four days Will Parker had been here, only four this time, but he knew the look on the foreman's face as if the words had already been spoken.

"Parker?" Overmire said it loud, loud enough so all the others could hear.

Will went stiff, slow-motion like, bringing his back away from the tree and setting the fruit jar down by feel.

The foreman pushed back his straw hat, let his forehead wrinkle so all the men could see how there was nothing else he could do. "Thought you said you was from Dallas."

Will knew when to keep his mouth shut. He wiped all expression from his face and lifted his eyes to Overmire's, chewing a piece of sour apple.

"You sayin' that's where you're from?"

Will rolled to one buttock as if to rise. Overmire planted a boot on his crotch and pushed. Hard. "I'm talkin' to you, boy!" he snapped, then let his eyes rove over his underlings to make sure none of them missed this.

Parker flattened both palms against the earth at the sudden jolt of pain. "I been there," he answered stoically.

"Been in Huntsville, too, haven't you, boy?"

The strangling sense of subjugation rose like bile in Parker's throat. Familiar. Degrading. He felt the eyes of the men measuring him above their half-formed, prepotent grins. But he'd learned not to talk back to that tone of superiority, and especially not to the word "boy." He felt the cold sweat break out on his chest, the sense of helplessness at the term calcu-

lated to make one man look small, another powerful. With
Overmire's boot exerting pressure, Will repressed the awful
need to give vent to the loathing he felt, sealing himself in
the cocoon of pretended indifference.

"They only put the tough ones in there, ain't that right,
Parker?" Overmire pushed harder but Will refused to wince.
Instead, he clamped a hand on the ankle, forcing the dusty
boot aside. Without removing his eyes from the foreman, Will
rose, picked up his battered Stetson, whacked it on his thigh
and settled the brim low over his eyes.

Overmire chuckled, crossed his burly arms, and fixed the
ex-convict with his beady eyes. "Word came down you killed
a woman in a Texas whorehouse and you're fresh out for it.
I don't think we want your kind around here where we got
wives and daughters, do we fellows?" He let his eyes flick to
the men briefly.

The fellows had quit rummaging through their lunch pails.

"Well, you got anything to say for yourself, boy?"

Will swallowed, felt the apple skin hitting bottom. "No, sir,
except I got three and a half days' pay comin'."

"Three," Overmire corrected. "We don't count no half days
around here."

Will worked a piece of apple peel between his front teeth.
His jaw protruded and Harley Overmire balled his fists, getting ready. But Will only stared silently from beneath the
brim of his sorry-looking cowboy hat. He didn't need to
lower his eyes from Overmire's face to know what his fists
looked like.

"Three," Will agreed quietly. But he hurled his apple core
out beneath the pines with a fierceness that made the men
start their rummaging again. Then he scooped up his towel-
wrapped jar and followed Overmire into the office.

When he came back out the men were huddled around the
time board. He passed among them, sealed within a bubble of
dispassion, folding his nine dollars into his breast pocket,
staring straight ahead, avoiding their self-righteous expressions.

"Hey, Parker," one of them called when he'd passed. "You
might try the Widow Dinsmore's place. She's so hard up

she'd probably even settle for a jailbird like you, ain't that right, boys?"

Jeering laughter followed, then a second voice. "Woman like that who'll put her card up in a sawmill's bound to take anything she can git."

And finally, a third voice. "You shoulda stepped a little harder on his balls, Harley, so the women around here could sleep better nights."

Will headed off through the pines. But when he saw the remains of someone's sandwich, left amid the pine needles for the birds, hunger overcame pride. He picked it up between two fingers as if it were a cigarette, and turned with a forced looseness.

"Anybody mind if I eat this?"

"Hell, no," called Overmire. "It's on me."

More laughter followed, then, "Listen, Parker, y'all give crazy Elly Dinsmore a try. No tellin' but what the two of you might hit it off right nice together. Her advertisin' for a man and you fresh outa the pen. Could be there's more'n a piece o' bread in it for y'!"

Will swung away and started walking. But he balled the bread into a hard knot and flung it back into the pine needles. Stalking away, he shut out the pain and transported himself to a place he'd never seen, where smiles were plentiful, and plates full, and people nice to one another. He no longer believed such a place existed, yet he escaped to it more and more often. When it had served its purpose he returned to reality—a dusty pine forest somewhere in northwest Georgia and a strange road ahead.

What now? he thought. Same old bullshit wherever he went. There was no such thing as serving your time; it was never over. Aw, what the hell did he care? He had no ties in this miserable jerkwater burg. Who ever heard of Whitney, Georgia, anyway? It was nothing but a flyspeck on the map and he could as easily move on as stay.

But a mile up the road he passed the same neatly tended farm where he'd stolen the buttermilk, towel and clothes; a sweet yearning pulled at his insides. A woman stood on the back porch, shaking a rug. Her hair was hidden by a dishtowel, knotted at the front. She was young and pretty and wore a pink apron, and the smell of something baking drifted out and made Will's stomach rumble. She raised a hand and waved and he hid the towel on his left side, smitten with guilt. He had a wrenching urge to walk up the drive, hand her her belongings and apologize. But he reckoned he'd scare the hell out of her if he did. And besides, he could use the towel, and probably the jar, too, if he walked on to the next town. The clothes on his back were the only ones he had.

He left the farm behind, trudging northward on a gravel road the color of fresh rust. The smell of the pines was inviting, and the look of them, all green and crisp against the red clay earth. There were so many rivers here, fast-flowing streams in a hurry to get to the sea. He'd even seen some waterfalls where the waters rushed out of the Blue Ridge foothills toward the coastal plain to the south. And orchards everywhere—peach, apple, quince and pear. Lord, what it must look like when those fruit trees bloomed. Soft pink clouds, and fragrant, too. Will had discovered within himself a deep need to experience the softer things in life since he'd gotten out of that hard place. Things he'd never noticed before—the beginning bloom on the cheek of a peach, the sun caught on a droplet of dew in a spiderweb, a pink apron on a woman with her hair tied in a clean white dishtowel.

He reached the edge of Whitney, scarcely more than a widening in the pines, a mere slip of a town dozing in the afternoon sun with little more moving than the flies about the tips of the chicory blossoms. He passed an ice house on the outskirts, a tiny railroad depot painted the color of a turnip, a wooden platform stacked with empty chicken crates, the smell of their former occupants rejuvenated by the hot sun. There was a deserted house overgrown with morning glory vines behind a seedy picket fence, then a row of occupied houses, some of red brick, others of Savannah gray, but all with verandas and rocking chairs out front, telling how many people lived in each. He came to a school building closed for the summer, and finally a town square typical of most in the south, dominated by a Baptist church and the town hall, with other businesses scattered around, interspersed by vacant lots—a drugstore, grocery, cafe, hardware, a blacksmith shop in front of which stood a brand-new gas pump topped by a white glass eagle.

He stopped before the office of the town newspaper, absently gazing at his reflection in the window. He fingered the few precious bills in his pocket, turned and glanced across the square at Vickery's Cafe, pulled his hat brim down lower and strode in that direction.

The square held a patch of green grass and a bandstand wreathed by black iron benches. In the cool splash of shade beneath an enormous magnolia tree two old men sat, whittling. They glanced up as he passed. One of them nodded, spat, then returned to his whittling.

The screen door on Vickery's Cafe had a wide red and white tin band advertising Coca-Cola. The metal was warm beneath Will's hands and the door spring sang out as he entered the place. He paused a moment to let his eyes adjust to the dimness. At a long counter, two men turned, regarded him indolently without removing their elbows from beside their coffee cups. A buxom young woman ambled the length of the counter and drawled, "Howdy. What can I do for y', honey?"

Will trained his eyes on her face to keep them off the row of plates behind the counter where cherry and apple pie winked an invitation.

"Wondered if you got a local paper I could look at."

She smiled dryly and cocked one thin-plucked eyebrow, glanced at the lump of wet green terrycloth he held against his thigh, then reached beneath the counter to dig one out. Will knew perfectly well she'd seen him pause before the newspaper office across the street, then walk over here instead.

"Much obliged," he said as he took it.

She propped the heel of one hand on a round hip and ran her eyes over the length of him while chewing gum lazily, making it snap.

"You new around these parts?"

"Yes, ma'am."

"You the new one out at the sawmill?"

Will had to force his hands not to grip the folded paper. All he wanted was to read it and get the hell out of here. But the two at the counter were still staring over their shoulders. He felt their speculative gazes and gave the waitress a curt nod.

"Be okay if I set down a spell and look at this?"

"Sure thing, help yourself. Can I get ya a cup of coffee or anything?"

"No, ma'am, I'll just . . ." With the paper he gestured toward the row of high-backed booths, turned and folded his lanky frame into one of them. From the corner of his eye he saw the waitress produce a compact and begin to paint her lips. He buried his face in the *Whitney Register.* Headlines about the war in Europe; disclosure of a secret meeting between President Roosevelt and Prime Minister Churchill, who'd drafted something called the Atlantic Charter; Joe DiMaggio playing another in his long string of safe-hit games; *Citizen Kane,* starring Orson Welles, showing at someplace called The Gem; the announcement of a garden party coming up on Monday; an advertisement for automobile repair beside another for harness repair; the funeral announcement of someone named Idamae Dell Randolph, born 1879 in Burnt Corn, Alabama, died in the home of her daughter, Elsie Randolph Blythe on August 8, 1941. The want ads were simple enough to locate in the eight-page edition: a roving lawyer would be in town the first and third Mondays of each month and could be found in Room 6 of the Town Hall; someone had a good used daybed for sale; someone wanted a husband . . .

A husband?

Will's eyes backtracked and read the whole ad, the same one she'd tacked up on the time board at the mill.

WANTED—A HUSBAND. Need healthy man of any age willing to work a spread and share the place. See E. Dinsmore, top of Rock Creek Road.

A healthy man of any age? No wonder the millhands called her crazy.

His eyes moved on: somebody had homemade rag rugs for sale; a nearby town needed a dentist and a mercantile establishment an accountant.

But nobody needed a drifter fresh out of Huntsville State Penitentiary who'd picked fruit and ridden freights and wrangled cattle and drifted half the length of this country in his day.

He read E. Dinsmore's ad again.

Need healthy man of any age willing to work a spread and share the place.

His eyes narrowed beneath the deep shadow of his hat brim while he studied the words. Now what the hell kind of woman would advertise for a man? But then what the hell kind of man would consider applying?

The pair of locals had twisted around on their stools and were overtly staring. The waitress leaned on the counter, gabbing with them, her eyes flashing often to Will. He eased from the booth and she sauntered to meet him at the glass cigar counter up front. He handed her the paper, curled a hand around his hat brim without actually dipping it.

"Much obliged."

"Anytime. It's the least I can do for a new neighbor. The name's Lula." She extended a limp hand with talons polished the same vermilion shade as her lips. Will assessed the hand and the come-hither jut of her hip, the unmistakable message some women can't help emanating. Her bleached hair was piled high and tumbled onto her forehead in a studied imitation of Hollywood's newest cheesecake, Betty Grable.

At last Will extended his own hand in a brief handshake accompanied by an even briefer nod. But he didn't offer his name.

"Could you tell me how to find Rock Creek Road?"

"Rock Creek Road?"

Again he gave a curt nod.

The men snickered. The smile fell from Lula's sultry mouth.

"Down past the sawmill, first road south of there, then the first road left offa that."

He stepped back, touched his hat and said, "Much obliged," before walking out.

"Well," Lula huffed, watching him walk past the window. "If he ain't a surly one."

"Didn't fall for your smile now either, did he, Lula?"

"What smile you talkin' about, you dumb redneck? I didn't give him no smile!" She moved along the counter, slapping at it with a wet rag.

"Thought y' had a live one there, eh, Lula?" Orlan Nettles leaned over the counter and squeezed her buttock.

"Damn you, Orlan, git your hands off!" she squawked, twisting free and swatting his wrist with the wet rag.

Orlan eased back onto the stool, his eyebrows mounting his forehead. "Hoo-ee! Would y' look at that now, Jack." Jack Quigley turned droll eyes on the pair. "I never knew old Lula to slap away a man's hand before, have you, Jack?"

"You got a right filthy mouth, Orlan Nettles!" Lula yelped.

Orlan grinned lazily, lifted his coffee cup and watched her over the brim. "Now what do you suppose that feller's doing up Rock Creek Road, Jack?"

Jack at last showed some sign of life as he drawled, "Could be he's goin' up to check out the Widow Dinsmore."

"Could be. Can't figger what else he'd of found in that newspaper, can you, Lula?"

"How should I know what he's doin' up Rock Creek Road? Wouldn't open his mouth enough to give a person his name."

Orlan loudly swallowed the last of his coffee. "Yup!" With the back of a hand he smeared the wetness from the corners of his mouth over the rest of it. "Reckon he went on up to check out Eleanor Dinsmore."

"That crazy old coot?" Lula spat. "Why, if he did, he'll be back down in one all-fire hurry."

"Don't you just wish, Lula . . . don't you just wish?" Orlan chuckled, bowed his legs and backed off the stool, then dropped a nickel on the counter.

Lula scraped up her tip, dropped it into her pocket and

dumped his coffee cup into a sink beneath the counter. "Go on, git out o' here, you two. Ain't givin' me no business anyway, sittin' there soppin' up coffee."

"C'mon, Jack, what say we sashay up to the lumber mill, do a little snoopin' around, see what we can find out."

Lula glared at him, refusing to break down and ask him to come back and tell her what he learned about the tall, handsome stranger. The town was small enough that it wouldn't take her long to find out on her own.

By the time he found the Dinsmore place it was evening. He used his green towel to wash in a creek before going up, then hung it on a tree limb and set the fruit jar carefully beneath it. The road—if you could call it that—was steep, rocky and full of washouts. Reaching the top, he found himself sweating again but figured it really didn't matter; she wouldn't take him anyway.

He left the road and approached through the woods, standing hidden in the trees, studying the place. It was a mess: chicken dung, piles of rusting machinery, a goat chewing his cud on a back stoop that looked ready to drop off the house, outbuildings peeling, shingles curled, tools left out in the weather, a sagging clothesline with a chipped enamel kettle hanging from one pole, remnants of a weedy garden.

Will Parker felt as if he fit right in.

He stepped into the clearing and waited; it didn't take too long.

A woman appeared in the doorway of the house, one child on her hip, another burrowing into her skirts with a thumb in its mouth. She was barefoot, her skirt faded, its hem sagging to the right, her blouse the color of muddy water, her entire appearance as shabby as her place.

"What can I do for you?" she called. Her voice sounded flat, wary.

"I'm lookin' for the Dinsmore place."

"You found it."

"I come about the ad."

She hitched the baby higher onto her hip. "The ad?" she repeated, squinting for a closer look.

"The one about the husband." He moved no closer, but stayed where he was at the edge of the clearing.

Eleanor Dinsmore kept a safe distance, unable to make out much of him. He wore a curled cowboy hat pulled low over his eyes, stood with his weight—what there was of it—on one bony hip with his thumbs hitched in his back pockets. She made out scuffed cowboy boots, a worn blue cambric shirt with sweat-stained armpits and faded jeans several inches too short for his lanky legs. There was nothing to do, she guessed, but go on out there and take a look at him. Wouldn't matter anyhow. He wouldn't stay.

He watched as she picked her way around the goat, down the steps and across the clearing, never taking her eyes off him, that young one still riding her hip, the other one tagging close—barefoot, too. She came slow, ignoring a chicken that squawked and flapped out of her path.

When she stood no more than ten feet before him she let the baby slip down and stand by himself, braced against her knee.

"You applying?" she asked smilelessly.

His eyes dropped to her stomach. She was pregnant as hell.

She watched, waiting for him to turn heel and run. Instead, his eyes returned to her face. At least she thought they did from the slight lifting of his hat brim.

"I reckon I am." He stood absolutely still, not a nerve flinching.

"I'm the one placed the ad," she told him, so there'd be no question.

"Figured you were."

"There's three of us . . . nearly four."

"Figured there were."

"The place needs work."

She waited, but he didn't say he figured it did, didn't even glance sideways at all the junk in the yard.

"You still interested?" she asked.

She'd never seen anyone could stand so still. "I reckon so." His britches were so loose she expected them to drop over his hipbones any second. His gut was hollow. But he had wiry arms, the kind that look as strong relaxed as flexed, with veins standing out in the hollows where the flesh was palest. He might be thin, but he wasn't puny. He'd be a worker.

"Then take your hat off so's I can see you one time."

Will Parker wasn't fond of removing his hat. When he'd been released from prison his hat and boots were the only things they'd returned to him. The Stetson was oily, misshapen, but an old friend. Without it he felt naked.

Still, he answered politely, "Yes, ma'am."

Once the hat was off he stood without fidgeting, letting her get a gander at his face. It was long and lean, like the rest of him, with brown eyes that looked as if he worked hard to keep the expression out of them. Same with his voice; it was respectful but flat. He didn't smile, but his mouth was good, had a nice shape to the upper lip with two definite peaks, which she liked. His hair was a dirty blond, the color of a collie, shaggy at the back and around his ears. The front was plastered against his brow from his hatband. "You could use a haircut," was all she said.

"Yes, ma'am."

He put his hat back on and it hid his eyes again, while from beneath its shadow he took in the woman's worn cotton clothes, the sleeves rolled to the elbows, the soiled skirt where her belly was fullest. Her face might have been pretty, but looked old before its time. Maybe it was just the hair, flying around like goose grass from whatever moored it at the back of her neck. He took her for thirty, maybe, but thought if she ever smiled it might take five years off her.

"I'm Eleanor Dinsmore . . . Mrs. Glendon Dinsmore."

"Will Parker," he returned, curling a hand around his hat brim, then catching his thumb in a back pocket again.

She knew right off he was a man of few words; that'd suit her just fine. Even when she gave him the chance he didn't ask questions like most men would. So she went on asking them herself.

"You been around here long?"

"Four days."

"Four days where?"

"Been workin' at the sawmill."

"Workin' for Overmire?"

Will nodded.

"He's no good. You're better off workin' here." She glanced in a semicircle and went on: "I been here all my life, in Whitney."

She didn't sigh, but she didn't need to. He heard the weariness in her words as she scanned the dismal yard. Her eyes returned to him and she rested one knobby hand on her stomach. When she spoke again her voice held a hint of puzzlement. "Mister, I've had that ad up at the sawmill for over three months now and you're the first one fool enough to come up that hill and check it out. I know what this place is. I know what I am. Down below they call me crazy." Her head jutted forward. "Did you know that?"

"Yes, ma'am," he answered quietly.

Her face registered surprise, then she chuckled. "Honest, ain't you? Well, I'm just wondering why you ain't run yet, is all."

He crossed his arms and shifted his weight to the opposite hip. She had the shoe on the wrong foot. Once she found out about his record he'd be marching down that road faster than a roach when the light comes on. Telling her was as good as putting a shotgun in her hands. But she was bound to find out eventually; might as well get it over with.

"Maybe you should be the one runnin'."

"Why's that?"

Will Parker looked her square in the eyes. "I done time in prison. You might's well know it, right off."

He expected quick signs of withdrawal. Instead Eleanor Dinsmore pursed her mouth and said in an ornery tone, "I says to take that hat off so's I can see what kind of man I'm talkin' to here."

He took it off slowly, revealing a countenance wiped clean of all emotion.

"What'd they put you in there for?" She could tell by the nervous tap of his hat brim on his thigh that he wanted to put it back on. It pleased her that he didn't.

"They say I killed a woman in a Texas whorehouse."

His answer stunned her, but she could be as poker-faced as

he. "Did you?" she shot back, watching his unflinching eyes. The control. The expressionlessness. He swallowed once and his Adam's apple bobbed.

"Yes, ma'am."

She submerged another jolt of surprise and asked, "Did you have good reason?"

"I thought so at the time."

Point-blank, she asked, "Well, Will Parker, you plan on doing that to me?"

The question caught Will by surprise and tipped up the corners of his lips. "No, ma'am," he answered quietly.

She stared hard into his eyes, came two steps closer and decided he didn't look like a killer, nor act like one. He was sure no liar, and he had a workingman's arms and wasn't going to gab her head off. It was good enough for her.

"Okay, then, you can come on up to the house. They say I'm crazy anyway, might's well give 'em something to back it up." She picked up the baby, herded the toddler along by the back of his head and led the way toward the house. The toddler peeked around to see if Will was following; the baby stared over its mother's shoulder; but the mother herself turned her back as if to say, do what you will, Will Parker.

She walked like a pelican, swaying with each step in an ungainly fashion. Her hair was dull, her shoulders round and her hips wide.

The house was a tacky thing, atilt in several directions at once. It looked to have been built in stages, each addition blown slightly off level by the prevailing wind of the moment. The main body listed northeast, an ell west and the stoop east. The windows were off square, there were tin patches on the roof, and the porch steps were rotting.

But inside it smelled of fresh bread.

Will's eyes found it, cooling on the kitchen cupboard beneath a dishtowel. He had to force his attention back to Eleanor Dinsmore when she put the baby in a high chair and offered, "How about a cup of coffee?"

He nodded silently, venturing no further than the rag rug at the kitchen door. His eyes followed as she fetched two cracked cups and filled them from a white enamel pot on the iron cookstove while the blond child hid in her skirts, hindering her footsteps.

"Leave off now, Donald Wade, so I can get Mr. Parker his coffee." The child clung, sucking his thumb until at last she reached down to pick him up. "This here is Donald Wade," she said. "He's kind of shy. Hasn't seen many strangers in his life."

Will remained by the door. "Howdy, Donald Wade," he said, nodding. Donald Wade buried his face in his mother's neck while she sat down on a scarred wooden chair at a table covered with red flowered oilcloth.

"You gonna stand by that door all night?" she inquired.

"No, ma'am." He approached the table cautiously, pulled out a chair and sat well away from Eleanor Dinsmore, his hat again pulled low over his eyes. She waited, but he only took a pull on his hot coffee, saying nothing, eyes flickering occasionally to her and the boy and something behind her.

"I guess you're wondering about me," she said at last. She smoothed the back of Donald Wade's shirt with a palm, waiting for questions that didn't come. The room carried only the sound of the baby slapping his hand on the wooden tray of the high chair. She rose and fetched a dry biscuit and laid it on the tray. The baby gurgled, took it in a fat fist and began gumming it. She stood behind him and regarded Will while repeatedly brushing the child's feathery hair back from his forehead. She wished Will would look at her, would take that hat off so they could get started. Donald Wade had followed her, was again clinging to her skirts. Still feathering the baby's hair, she found Donald Wade's head with her free hand. Standing so, she said what needed saying.

"The baby's name is Thomas. He's near a year and a half old. Donald Wade here, he's going on four. This one's going to be born just shy of Christmas, close as I can reckon. Their daddy's name was Glendon."

Will Parker's eyes were drawn to her stomach as she rested a hand on it. He thought about how maybe there was more than one kind of prison.

"Where's their daddy?" he inquired, lifting his eyes to her face.

She nodded westward. "Out in the orchard. I buried him out there."

"I thought—" But he stopped.

"You got a strange way of not sayin' things, Mr. Parker. How's a body supposed to make up a mind when you keep closed up so?" Will studied her, finding it hard to let loose after five years, and especially when she stood with her children at guard. "Go on, then, say it," Eleanor Dinsmore prodded.

"I thought maybe your man run off. So many of 'em are doin' that since the depression."

"I wouldn't be lookin' for no husband then, would I?"

His glance dropped guiltily to his coffee cup. "I reckon not."

"And anyway, Glendon woulda never dreamed of runnin' off. He didn't have to. He was so full of dreams he wasn't here anyways. Always miles away dreamin' about this and that. The two of us together, we had lots of dreams once." The way she looked at him, Will knew she harbored dreams no longer.

"How long's he been dead?"

"Oh, don't you worry none, the baby is his."

Will colored. "I didn't mean that."

"Course you did. I watched your eyes when you first come up here. He's been dead since April. It was his dreams killed him. This time it was the bees and his honey. He thought he'd get rich real fast making honey out in the orchard, but the bees they started swarmin' and he was in too much of a hurry to use good sense. I told him to shoot the branch down with a shotgun, but he wouldn't listen. He went out on a branch, and sure enough, it broke, and so did he. He never would listen to me much." A faraway look came into her eyes. Will watched the way her hands lingered in the baby's hair.

"Some men are like that." The words felt strange on Will's lips. Comfort—either getting it or giving it—was foreign to him.

"We sure were happy, though. He had a way about him." Her expression as she spoke made Will sure it had once been

Glendon Dinsmore's hair through which she'd run her fingers that way. She acted as if she'd forgotten Will was in the room. He couldn't quit watching her hands. It was another of those soft things that got him deep in the gut—the sight of her leafing through the baby's airy hair while the child continued with its biscuit and made gurgling sounds. He wondered if anyone had ever done that to him, maybe sometime long before he had memory, but he had no conscious recollection of ever being touched that way.

Eleanor Dinsmore drew herself back to the present to find Will Parker's eyes on her hands.

"So, what're your thoughts, Mr. Parker?"

He glanced up, refocused his eyes. "It don't matter about the kids."

"Don't matter?"

"I mean, I don't mind that you've got them. Your ad didn't say."

"You like kids then?" she asked hopefully.

"I don't know. Never been around 'em much. Yours seem nice enough."

She smiled at her boys and gave each a love pat. "They can be a joy." He couldn't help wondering at her reasoning, for she looked tired and worn beyond her years, having the near-three she did. "Just make sure, Mr. Parker," she added, " 'cause three's a lot. I won't have you layin' a hand on them when they're troublesome. They're Glendon's boys and he woulda never dreamed of layin' a hand on them."

Just what did she take him for? He felt himself blush. But what else was she supposed to think after what he'd revealed out there in the yard?

"You got my word."

She believed him. Maybe because of the way his eyes lingered on Baby Thomas's hair. She liked his eyes, and they had a way of turning soft when they'd light on the boys. But the boys weren't the only consideration.

"It's got to be said," she went on. "I loved Glendon somethin' fierce. It takes some time to get over a man like that. I wouldn't be lookin' for a man 'less I had to. But winter's comin', and the baby, too. I was in a fix, Mr. Parker. You understand, don't you?"

Will nodded solemnly, noting the absence of self-pity in her voice.

"Another thing." She concentrated on Thomas's hair, stroking it differently, distractedly, her cheeks turning pink. "Having three babies under four years old, well—don't get me wrong—I love 'em something fierce, but I wouldn't want any more. Three's plenty to suit me."

Lord a-mighty, the thought hadn't crossed his mind. She was almost as sorry-looking as her place, and pregnant to boot. He needed a dry bed, but preferably not one with her in it.

When she glanced up, Will Parker glanced down. "Ma'am ..." His voice croaked. He cleared his throat and tried again. "Ma'am, I didn't come up here lookin' for ..." He swallowed, glanced up, then sharply down. "I need a place is all. I'm tired of movin'.."

"You moved a lot, have you?"

"I been movin' since I remember."

"Where'd you start from?"

"Start from?" He met her eyes, puzzled.

"You mean you don't remember?"

"Texas someplace."

"That's all you know?"

"Yes, ma'am."

"Maybe you're lucky," she commented.

Though he shot her a glance, the remark went unexplained. She merely added, "I started from right down there in Whitney. Never moved farther than from the town to the top of this hill. I reckon you've been around, though."

He nodded silently. Again, she found herself pleased by his brusqueness, his lack of curiosity. She thought she could get along quite well with a man like him.

"So you're lookin' for a dry bed and a full plate is all."

"Yes, ma'am."

She studied him a moment, the way he sat on the edge of his chair, taking nothing for granted, the way he kept his hat brim pulled low as if protecting any secret she might read in his eyes. Well, everybody had secrets. Let him keep his and she'd keep hers. But she sure as shootin' wasn't going to strike up an agreement with a man whose eyes she hadn't even seen in the clear light. And besides, suppose *he* didn't want *her.*

He was a vagrant ex-con; she poor, pregnant and unpretty. Who was the bigger loser?

"Mr. Parker, this house ain't much, but I'd appreciate it if you'd take your hat off when you're in it."

He reached up slowly and removed the hat. She lit the kerosene lantern and pushed it aside so they need not look around it.

For long moments they studied each other.

His lips were chapped and his cheeks gaunt, but his eyes were true brown. Brown as pecans, with blunt black lashes and a pair of creases between well-shaped brows. He had a nice knife-straight nose—some might even call it handsome—and a fine mouth. But so sour all the time. Well, maybe she could make it smile. He was quiet-spoken—she liked that. And those arms might be skinny, but they'd done their share of work. That, above all, mattered. If there was one thing a man would have to do around here it was work.

She decided he'd do.

She had fine-textured skin, strong bones and features that, if taken one by one, weren't actually displeasing. Her cheekbones were slightly too prominent, her upper lip a little too thin, and her hair unkempt. But it was honey-brown, and he wondered if with a washing it might not turn honeyer. He shifted his study to her eyes and saw for the first time: they were green. A green-eyed woman who touched her babies like every baby deserved to be touched.

He decided she'd do.

"I wanted you to see what you'd be gettin'," she told him. "Not much."

Will Parker wasn't one for fancy words, but this much he could say: "That's for me to decide."

She didn't fluster or blush, only pushed herself out of the chair and offered, "I'll get you more coffee, Mr. Parker."

She refilled both their cups, then rejoined him. He wrapped

both hands around the hot cup and watched the lamplight play on the surface of the black liquid. "How come you're not afraid of me?"

"Maybe I am."

His glance lifted. "Not so it shows."

"A person doesn't always let it show."

He had to know. "Are you?"

In the lanternlight they studied each other again. All was quiet but for Donald Wade's bare toes bumping a rung of the chair and the baby sucking his gooey fingers.

"What if I said I was?"

"Then I'd walk back down the road the way I came."

"You want to do that?"

He wasn't used to being allowed to speak his mind. Prison had taught him the road to the least troubles was to keep his mouth shut. It felt strange, being granted the freedom to say what he would.

"No, I don't reckon so."

"You wanna stay up here with the whole bunch of them down there thinking I'm crazy?"

"Are you?" He hadn't meant to ask such a thing, but she had a way of making a man talk.

"Maybe a little. This here what I'm doing seems crazy to me. Doesn't it to you?"

"Well . . ."

She sensed that he was too kind to say yes.

At that moment a pain grabbed Will's gut—the green apples catching up with him—but he wished it away, telling himself it was only nerves. Applying for a job as a husband wasn't exactly an everyday occurrence.

"You could spend the night," she offered, "look the place over in the morning when the light is up. See what you think." She paused, then added, "Out in the barn."

"Yes, ma'am." The pain wrenched him again, higher up this time, and he winced.

She thought it was because of what she'd said, but it'd take some time before she'd trust him in the house nights. And besides, she might be crazy, but she wasn't loose.

"Nights are plenty warm. I'll make you a shakedown out there."

He nodded silently, fingering the brim of his hat as if anxious to put it back on.

She told her older son, "Go fetch Daddy's pillow, Donald Wade." The little boy hugged her shyly, staring at Will. She reached for his hand. "Come along, we'll get it together."

Will watched them leave, hand in hand, and felt an ache in his gut that had nothing to do with green apples.

When Eleanor returned to the kitchen, Will Parker was gone. Thomas was still in his high chair, discontented now that his biscuit was gone. She experienced a curious stab of disappointment—he'd run away.

Well, what did you expect?

Then, from outside she heard the sound of retching. The sun had gone behind the pines, taking its light with it. Eleanor stepped onto the sagging back stoop and heard him vomiting. "You stay inside, Donald Wade." She pushed the boy back and closed the screen door. Though he started crying, she ignored him and walked to the top of the rotting steps.

"Mr. Parker, are you sick?" She didn't want any sickly man.

He straightened with an effort, his back to her. "No, ma'am."

"But you're throwing up."

He gulped a refreshing lungful of night air, threw back his head and dried his forehead with a sleeve. "I'm all right now. It's just those green apples."

"What green apples?"

"I ate green apples for lunch."

"A grown man should have more sense!" she retorted.

"Sense didn't enter into it, ma'am. I was hungry."

She stood in the semidark, hugging Glendon Dinsmore's pillow against her swollen stomach, watching and listening as another spasm hit Will Parker and he doubled over. But there was nothing more inside him to come up. She left the pillow on the porch rail and crossed the beaten earth to stand behind his slim, stooping form. He braced both hands on his knees, trying to catch his breath. His vertebrae stood out like stepping-stones. She reached out a hand as if to lay it on his back, but thought better of it and crossed her arms tightly beneath her breasts.

He straightened, muscle by muscle, and blew out a shaky breath.

"Why didn't you say something?" she asked.

"I thought it'd pass."

"You had no supper, then?"

He didn't answer.

"No dinner either?"

Again he remained silent.

"Where did you get them apples?"

"I stole them off somebody's tree. A pretty little place down along the main road between here and the sawmill with pink flowers on a tree stump."

"Tom Marsh's place. And good people, too. Well, that'll teach you a lesson." She turned back toward the steps. "Come on back in the house and I'll fix you something."

"That's not necessary, ma'am. I'm not—"

Her voice became sharper. "Get back in the house, Will Parker, before your foolish pride pushes your ribs right through your thin skin!"

Will rubbed his sore stomach and watched her mount the porch steps, treading near the edges where the boards were still good. The screen door whacked shut behind her. Inside Donald Wade stopped crying. Outside, night peepers started. He glanced over his shoulder. The shadows lent a velvet richness to the dusky clearing, disguising its rusted junk and dung and weeds. But he remembered how sorry it had looked by daylight. And what a wreck the house was. And how worn and lackluster Eleanor Dinsmore looked. And how she'd made it clear she didn't want any jailbird sleeping in her house. He asked himself what the hell he was doing as he followed her inside.

CHAPTER
2

She left him sitting in the kitchen while she put the boys to bed. He sat eyeing the room. The cabinets consisted of open shelves displaying cookpots and dishes beneath a workbench crudely covered with cracked linoleum. Between the nails that held it on, chunks were missing. The sink was old, chipped and stained, with a single short pipe to drop the runoff into a slop pail underneath. There was no pump. Instead, a dipper handle protruded from a white enamel water pail beneath which the linoleum held a sunburst of cracks. The floor was covered with linoleum of a different pattern, but it showed more black backing than green ivy design. The ceiling needed washing. It was gray with soot above the woodstove. Apparently someone had had dreams of resurfacing the walls but had gotten only as far as tearing off the old plaster on a wall and a half, leaving the wooden slats showing like the bones of a skeleton. Will found it surprising that a room so ramshackle could smell so good.

His eyes moved to the bread and he forced himself to sit and wait.

When Eleanor Dinsmore returned to the kitchen he made sure his hat was on the tabletop instead of on his head. With an effort he rose from the rung-back chair, bolstering his stomach with one arm.

26

"No need to get up. You rest while I get something started."

He let his weight drop back while she opened a wooden trapdoor in the floor and disappeared down a set of crude, steep steps. Her hand reappeared, setting a covered kettle on the floor, then she emerged, climbing clumsily.

When she reached for the ring on the trapdoor he was waiting to lower it for her. Her startled look told Will she wasn't used to men doing it for her. It had been a long time, too, since he'd performed courtesies for a woman, but he found it impossible to watch a pregnant one struggling up a cellar hatch without offering a hand.

For a moment neither of them knew what to say.

Finally she glanced away, offering, "I appreciate it, Mr. Parker." And when he'd lowered the trapdoor behind her, "Never had a man openin' and closin' doors for me. Glendon, he never learnt how. Makes me feel a little foolish. Anyway, I thought I told you to set. Your belly's bound to be hurtin' after you brought them apples up for another look."

He grinned at her homey turn of speech and returned to the chair, watching as she added wood to the stove and put the kettle on to heat.

"I'm sorry about what happened out there in the yard. I guess it embarrassed you."

"It's a purely natural act, Mr. Parker." She stirred the contents of the pot. "Besides, I don't embarrass easy." She set the spoon down and gave him a wry smile. "And leastways, you did it *before* you tasted my cooking."

She gave him a cajoling grin and got one of his rare ones in return. He tried to recall if he'd ever known a woman with a sense of humor, but none came to mind. He watched her move around in an ungainly, swaying way, placing a hand to her roundness when she reached or stooped. He wondered if she really was crazy, if he was, too. Bad enough taking a strange woman for a wife. Worse taking one who was pregnant. What the hell did he know about pregnant women? Only that in his time he might have left a few of them behind.

"You'd probably feel better if you washed up some," she
suggested.

In his usual fashion, he neither moved nor replied.

"There's the basin." She gestured, then turned away, busying herself. He threw a longing glance at the basin, the soap,
the white towel and washcloth hanging on nails at the front
of the sink.

After a minute she turned and asked, "What's the matter?
Stomach hurt too bad to get up?"

"No, ma'am." He wasn't accustomed to freedom yet,
didn't believe it fully. It felt as if anything he reached for
would be snatched away. In prison a man learned early to
take nothing for granted. Not even the most basic creature
comforts. This was *her* house, *her* soap, *her* water. She
couldn't possibly understand what prizes they seemed to a
man fresh out.

"Well, what is it?" she demanded impatiently.

"Nothing."

"Then help yourself to the teakettle and washbasin."

He stretched to his feet, but moved cautiously. He crossed
behind her and found a clean white washbasin in the sink,
and on the nail, the clean white towel and washcloth. So
white. Whiter than anything he remembered. In prison the
washcloths had been puce green and had grown musty smelling long before clean ones were issued.

Eleanor peered over her shoulder as he filled the washbasin, then dipped his hands into the cold water. "Don't you
want it warmed up?" He glanced back over his shoulder. His
eyes, when they weren't carefully blank, were questioning
and uncertain.

"Yes, ma'am," he answered. But when he'd shaken off his
hands and turned he made no move toward the teakettle. She
plucked it off the stove and poured the warm water for him,
then turned her back, pretending to go back to work. But she
glanced surreptitiously over her shoulder, confounded by his
strange hesitancy. He flattened both palms against the bottom
of the basin and leaned forward with his head hung low.
There he stood, stiff-armed, as if transfixed. What in the
world was he doing? She tipped sideways and peeked around

him—his eyes were closed, his lips open. At last he scooped water to his face and gave a small shudder. Lord a-mercy, so that was it! Understanding swamped her. She felt a surge of heat flush her body, a queer sympathetic thrill, a gripping about her heart.

"How long has it been?" she asked quietly.

His head came up but he neither turned nor spoke. Water dripped from his face and hands into the basin.

"How long since you had warm water?" she insisted in the kindest tone she could manage.

"A long time."

"How long?"

He didn't want her pity. "Five years."

"You were in prison five years?"

"Yes, ma'am." He buried his face in the towel—it smelled of homemade lye soap and fresh air, and he took his time savoring its softness and scent.

"You mean the water's cold in there?"

He hung up the towel without answering. The water had been cold all his life—creeks and lakes and horse troughs. And often he dried himself with his shirt, or on a lucky day, the sun.

"How long you been out?"

"Couple of months."

"How long since you ate a decent meal?"

Still silent, he closed two buttons on his shirt, staring out a filmy window above the sink.

"Mr. Parker, I asked you a question."

On a crude shelf to his left a small round mirror reflected her image. What he saw mostly was obstinacy.

"A while," he replied flatly while their mirrored eyes locked.

Eleanor realized he was a man who'd accept a challenge more readily than charity, so she carefully wiped all sympathy from her voice. "I should think," she admonished, stepping close behind him, holding his gaze in the mirror, "a man that's been roughing it might need a touch of soap." She reached around him, picked up a bar of Ivory and plopped it into his hand, then rested her own on her hips.

"You're not in prison anymore, Mr. Parker. Soap is free for the taking here, and there's always warm water. Only thing I ask is that when you're through you spill it out and rinse the basin."

Staring at her in the mirror, he felt as if an immense weight had lifted from his chest. She stood in the pose of a fighter, daring him to defy her. But beneath her stern façade, he sensed a generous spirit. "Yes, ma'am," he returned quietly. And this time before leaning over the welcome warm water, he shrugged out of his shirt.

Holy Moses, was he thin. From behind she eyed his ribs. They stuck out like a kite frame in a strong wind. He began spreading soapsuds with his hands—chest, arms, neck and as far around his trunk as he could reach. He bent forward, and her eyes were drawn down his tan back to where a white band of skin appeared above the line of grayed elastic on his underwear.

She had never seen any man but Glendon wash up. Grandpa was the only other male she'd ever lived with and he certainly hadn't bared himself to any female. Staring at Will Parker while he performed his ablutions, Eleanor suddenly realized she was watching a very personal thing, and turned away guiltily.

"Washcloth's for you—use it." She left the room to give him privacy.

She returned several minutes later to find him shiny faced, buttoning up his shirt. "Got this." She held up a yellow toothbrush. "It was Glendon's, but I'll clean it with soda if you don't mind using it secondhand."

He did, but ran his tongue over his teeth and nodded. She fetched a cup, spooned in soda and filled it with boiling water from the teakettle. "Person oughta have a toothbrush," she declared, stirring with Glendon Dinsmore's.

She handed it to Will along with a can of toothpowder, then stood and watched while he dumped some in his palm.

Will didn't like being watched. He'd been watched for five years and now that he was out he ought to be able to do his private business without feeling somebody's eyes on him. But even with his back turned, he felt her scrutiny all the while he used her husband's toothbrush, savoring the toothpowder that was so sweet he wanted to swallow it instead of spitting it out. When he finished, she ordered, "Well, set yourself down at the table."

She served him vegetable soup, hot and fragrant, thick with okra and tomato and beef. His hands rested beside the bowl while he fought the compulsion to gobble it like an animal. His stomach seemed to roll over and beg, but he hesitated, savoring not only the smell but the anticipation, and the fact that he was allowed as much time as he wanted—no bells would ring, no guards would prod.

"Go ahead . . . eat."

It was different, being told by her instead of the guards. Her motives were strictly friendly. Her eyes followed his head as he dipped the spoon and lifted it to his lips.

It was the best soup he'd ever tasted.

"I asked how long since your last meal. You gonna tell me or not?"

His glance flickered up briefly. "A couple of days."

"A couple of days!"

"I stopped in a restaurant in town to read the want ads but there was a waitress there I didn't particularly care for, so I moved on without eating."

"Lula Peak. She's a good one to avoid, all right. She been chasin' men since she was tall enough to sniff 'em. So you been eating green apples a coupla days, have you?"

He shrugged, but his glance darted briefly to the bread behind her.

"There's no disgrace in admitting you've gone hungry, you know."

But there was. To Will Parker there was. Just emerging from the jaws of the depression, America was still overrun with tramps, worthless vagrants who'd deserted their families and rode the flatcars aimlessly, begging for handouts at random doorsteps. During the past two months he'd seen—even ridden with—dozens of them. But he'd never been able to bring himself to beg. Steal, yes, but only in the most dire straits.

She watched him eat, watched his eyes remain downcast nearly all the time. Each time they flicked up they seemed drawn to something behind her. She twisted in her chair to see what it was. The bread. How stupid of her. "Why didn't you say you wanted some fresh bread?" she chided as she rose to get it.

But he'd been schooled well to ask for nothing. In prison, asking meant being jeered at or baited like an animal and being made to perform hideous acts that made a man as base as his jailers. To ask was to put power into the sadistic hands of those who already wielded enough of it to dehumanize any who chose to cross them.

But no woman with three fresh loaves could comprehend a thing like that. He submerged the ugly memories as he watched her waddle to the cabinet top and fetch a knife from a crock filled with upended utensils. She scooped up a loaf against her hip and returned to the table to slice off a generous width. His mouth watered. His nostrils dilated. His eyes riveted upon the white slice curling softly from the blade.

She stabbed it with the tip of the knife and picked it up. "You want it?"

Oh, God, not again. His hungry eyes flew to her face, taking on the look of a cornered animal. Against his will, the memory was rekindled, of Weeks, the prison guard, with his slitty, amphibian eyes and his teeth bared in a travesty of a smile, his unctuous voice with its perverted laughter. "You want it, Parker? Then howl like a dog." And he'd howled like a dog.

"You want it?" Eleanor Dinsmore repeated, softer this time, snapping Will back from the past to the present.

"Yes, ma'am," he uttered, feeling the familiar knot of helplessness lodge in his throat.

"Then all you got to do is say so. Remember that." She dropped the bread beside his soup bowl. "This ain't jail, Mr. Parker. The bread ain't gonna disappear and nobody's gonna smack your hand if you reach for it. But around here you might have to ask for things. I'm no mind reader, you know."

He felt the tension drain from him, but he held his shoulders stiff, wondering what to make of Eleanor Dinsmore, so dictatorial and unsympathetic at times, so dreamy and vague at others. It was only the painful memories that had transported him—she wasn't Weeks, and she wouldn't make him pay for picking up the food.

The bread was soft, warm, the greatest gift he'd ever received. His eyes closed as he chewed his first bite.

They flew open again when she grunted, "Humph!"

Puzzled, he watched her turn her back and move across the room to fetch a crock full of the most beautiful lemon-bright butter in the world. She came back and held it just beyond his reach.

"Say it."

He swallowed. His shoulders stiffened and the wary look returned to his face. His voice came reluctantly. "I'd like some o' that butter."

"It's yours." Unceremoniously she clapped it down, then herself, across from him. "And it didn't hurt you one little bit to ask for it, did it?" She brushed off her fingers and admonished, "Around here you ask, 'cause things are in such a mess it's the only way you'll find it most of the time. Well, go ahead, butter your bread and eat."

His hands followed orders while his emotions took additional moments to readjust to her quicksilver mood changes. As he bent over his soup, she warned, "Watch you don't overdo it. Best if you eat slow till your stomach gets used to decent food again."

He wanted to tell her it was good, better than good, the best he remembered. He wanted to tell her there was no butter in prison, the bread there was coarse and dry and certainly never warm. He wanted to tell her he didn't remember the last time he'd been invited to sit at somebody's kitchen table. He wanted to tell her what it meant to him to sit at hers. But compliments were as foreign to him as crocks of butter, so he ate his bread and soup in silence.

While he ate she brought out her crocheting and sat working on something soft and fuzzy and pink. Her wedding ring—still on her left hand—flashed in the lanternlight in

rhythm with the hook. Her hands were nimble, but work-
worn, and the skin looked like hide. It appeared all the
tougher when contrasted against the fine pink yarn as she
payed it out from one callused finger.

"What you watchin'?"

He glanced up guiltily.

She adjusted the yarn and smiled. The smile transformed
her face. "Never seen a woman crochet before?"

"No, ma'am."

"Makin' a shawl for the baby. This here's a shell design."
She spread it out on her knee. "Pretty, ain't it?"

"Yes, ma'am." Once again he was assaulted by yearning, a
sense of things missed, a desire to reach out and touch that
soft pink thing she was creating. Rub it between his fingers
as if it were a woman's hair.

"I'm makin' it in pink cause I'd sure like a girl this time.
A girl'd be nice for the boys, don't you think?"

What did he know about babies—girls, boys, either one?
Nothing except they scared him to death. And girls? He'd
never found girls to be especially nice except maybe when
they were older, when a man was sinking his body into them.
Then, for a few minutes, while they stopped harping or
threatening or tormenting, maybe they were nice.

Mrs. Dinsmore's silver hook flashed on. "Baby'll be needing a warm blanket. This old house gets plenty cold in the
winter. Glendon, he always meant to fix it up and seal up the
cracks and such, but he never got around to it."

His eyes lifted to the walls with the missing plaster.

"Maybe I could seal up the cracks for you."

She glanced up and smiled, unrolling more slack from the
basket on the floor. "Maybe you could, Mr. Parker. That'd
sure be nice. Glendon, he meant well, but somehow there was
always something new he was going to try."

No matter what her mood, when she spoke the name
Glendon a softness crept into her voice, a smile, too, whether
there was one on her face or not. Will supposed there'd never
been a woman in the world who'd looked so sentimental
when speaking his name.

"Would you like some more soup, Mr. Parker? A little might be okay."

He ate until his stomach felt hard as a baseball. Then he sat back, rubbed it and sighed.

"You sure can pack it away." She tucked her piece of handiwork into the basket and stood up to clear the table.

He watched her move across the kitchen, thinking if he lived to be two hundred he'd never forget this meal, nor how nice it had felt to sit and watch her work fine pink yarn into a shell design and believe that tomorrow when he woke up, he might not have to move on.

She carried Glendon Dinsmore's pillow and quilt and led the way to the barn. He found himself again performing uncustomary courtesies, carrying the lantern, opening the screen door, letting her walk first through the littered yard.

The moon had risen. It rode the eastern trees like an orange pumpkin bobbing on dark water. The chickens were roosting—somewhere in the junk, undoubtedly. He wondered how she ever found eggs.

"I tell you what, Mr. Parker," she told him as they walked through the moonlight, "tomorrow morning when you look the place over you might decide it's not such a good idea to stay. I sure wouldn't hold you to it, no matter what you said when you first come up here."

He watched her waddle along in front of him, hugging her husband's patchwork quilt against her stomach.

"Same goes for you, Mrs. Dinsmore."

Just before they reached the barn she warned, "Be careful, there's a pile of junk here."

A pile? That was a laugh. She sidestepped something made of black spiked iron and opened the barn door. Its unoiled hinges squeaked. Inside there were no animals, but his nose told him there had been.

"Guess this barn could do with a little cleaning," she noted while he raised the lantern over his head and surveyed the circle of light.

"I can do that tomorrow."

"I'd be grateful. So would Madam."

"Madam?"

"My mule. This way." She led him to a wall-mounted ladder. "You'll sleep up there."

She would have begun climbing but he grabbed her arm. "Better let me go first. That ladder doesn't look too dependable."

He slipped the lantern over his arm and started up. When his foot took the third rung it splintered and dumped him flush against the wall, where he dangled like a puppet with a broken string.

"Mr. Parker!" she shrieked, grabbing his thighs while he pedaled for a toehold.

"Get back!"

She leaped back and held her breath as the lanternlight swung wildly. At last he found a solid rung, but tested the rest before putting his weight on each. She pressed a hand to her heart, watching him climb until he safely reached the loft with his elbows. "Lord, you gave me a fright. Be careful."

His head disappeared into the dark square above, then the lantern went up with him, gilding the underside of his hat brim. Only when he stood on solid planking did he look back down. "You're a fine one to talk. If I would've come down I'd have taken you right with me."

"I reckon this old ladder's about as rickety as everything else around here."

"I can fix it tomorrow, too." He raised the lantern and checked the loft. "There's hay." He disappeared and she listened to his footsteps thud overhead.

"I'm sorry about the smell in here," she called.

"It's not as bad up here. This'll be fine."

"I would've cleaned it if I'd known I'd be havin' overnight company."

"Don't worry. I slept in much worse in my day."

He reappeared, knelt, and set the lantern at his knee. "Can you toss up the bedding?"

The pillow went up perfectly. The quilt took three tries. By the third, he was grinning. "Ain't got much for muscles, have you?"

It was the first lighthearted thing he'd said. She stood with her fists on her hips, gazing up at him while he held the patchwork quilt. It might not be so bad having him around if he'd lighten up this way more often.

"Oh, ain't I? I got those up there, didn't I?"

"Just barely."

The grin softened his face. The cockiness sharpened hers. For the first time they began to feel comfortable with each other.

He flopped to his belly and hung over the edge of the hatch. "Here, you take the lantern."

"Don't be silly. I been walkin' in this barnyard since before you owned that thing you call a cowboy hat."

"What's wrong with my cowboy hat?"

"Looks like it's been through a war."

"It's my own. It and my boots." He waggled the lantern. "Here, take it."

So that was why he kept that sorry-looking thing on his head all the time.

"Take it yourself," she said, and disappeared from sight. He knelt on his haunches and listened for her footsteps, but she was barefoot.

"Mrs. Dinsmore?" he called.

"Yes, Mr. Parker?" she called from the opposite end of the barn.

"You mind my asking how old you are?"

"Be twenty-five on November tenth. How about you?"

"Thirty or so."

Silence, while she digested his answer. "Or so?"

"Somebody left me on the steps of an orphanage when I was little." Will hadn't told that to many people in his life. He waited uncertainly for her reaction.

"You mean you don't know when your birthday is?"

"Well . . . no."

The barn grew silent. Outside a whippoorwill called and the frogs sang discordantly. Eleanor paused with her hand on the latch. Will knelt, gripping his thighs.

"We'll have to pick you out a birthday if you decide to stay. A man should have a birthday."

Will smiled, imagining it.

"G'night, Mr. Parker."

"G'night, Mrs. Dinsmore." He heard the barn door squeak open and called again, "Mrs. Dinsmore?"

The squeaking stopped. "What?"

Five seconds of silence, then, "Much obliged for the supper. You're a good cook." His heart thumped gladly after the words were out. It hadn't been so hard after all.

In the dark below she smiled. It had been good to see a man at her table again.

She made her way to the house, prepared for bed and eased into it with a sigh. As she straightened, a faint cramp caught her low across the stomach. She cradled it, rolling to her side. She had chopped wood today, though she knew she shouldn't have. But Glendon had scarcely managed to get the day-to-day tasks done, let alone stockpiling for tomorrow. The seasoned wood needed splitting, and next year's supply should be cut so it could start to dry. Besides the wood, there was always water to carry. So much. And there'd be more when the new baby came and she'd have two of them in diapers.

She stretched out on her back and rested a wrist on her forehead, picturing the veins along the inside of Will Parker's arms, the cluster of wiry muscles. She remembered how hard his legs had been when she'd touched them as he hung on the ladder.

Stay, Will Parker. Please stay.

In the hayloft, Will sank his head into a pillow made of real feathers and stretched out on a soft handmade quilt. His belly was full, his teeth were clean, his skin smelled of soap. And somewhere out there was a mule, and beehives and chickens and a house with possibilities. A place where a man could make a go of it with a little hard work. Hell, hard work came easy.

Just give me a chance, Eleanor Dinsmore, and I'll show you.

He remembered her standing barefoot in the yard with her two boys, her stomach round as a watermelon, eyeing him warily. He remembered the detached look on her face when she'd questioned him and the momentary flash of shock when he told her about Huntsville. She was probably mulling it over right now, having second thoughts about keeping a jailbird around. And by morning she'd have decided he was too much of a risk. But in the morning he'd show her. First thing, before she had a chance to put him off the place he'd show her he intended to earn his keep.

CHAPTER

3

Lula Peak lived in the tiny bungalow on Pecan Street where she'd grown up. While her mother was alive the furnishings had been adequate, if old. Now, however, the kitchen sported a spanking new Frigidaire electric refrigerator, a bathroom with hot and cold running water and in the living room a new Philco radio.

At eight o'clock that night the Philco and Lula were both tuned to Atlanta, both blasting out "Oh, Johnny, Oh." Dressed in a slinky red-orange wrapper, Lula tilted toward the bathroom mirror, scavenging with the tips of a tweezer for any wayward hair with the audacity to be growing beyond the periphery of her pencil-thin eyebrows.

Oh, Johnny, oh, Johnny, how you can love . . .

She stopped her fruitless search and ran her palms up her silkcovered arms as she'd seen Betty Grable do in the movies.

Oh, Johnny, oh, Johnny, heaven's above . . .

She made a moue at her reflection in the mirror, then shimmied and dipped her knees, letting her palms brush the sides of her breasts. The satin rubbed seductively over her nipples and they popped up like balloons taking air. Lula loved getting hot, either by herself or with someone else—didn't matter which. But to really cool down, she needed a man. Lula always needed a man, and Whitney didn't have enough of them. When Lula itched, she needed scratching. And Lula itched all the time.

She plucked up a bottle of Evening in Paris cologne and spun twice while dabbing it on, watching her face flash across the bathroom mirror. After a third spin she balanced one high-heeled foot on the toilet seat, then touched some of the cologne to the thick thatch of blond hair revealed by the gaping gown. She dropped the foot to the floor, then ran her hand down her belly while giving the mirror a sultry kiss, leaving the imprint of vermilion lipstick on the cold glass.

"Lula, what the hell's goin' on in here?" Harley Overmire bellowed from her living room. "Music's so goddamn loud any bum coulda walked in here and you wouldnt'a even known it."

"Harley-honey, is that you?" The music suddenly dimmed and Lula came flying out of the bathroom, pouting. "Harley, turn that back up! That's my favorite song!" She darted to the Philco—a flash of white limbs and flaming silk—and cranked it up.

Oh, Johnny, oh, Johnny, oh . . .

Harley immediately turned it down. "Lula-honey, I didn't come over here to get my eardrums broke."

"Oh, yeah? Then what did you come for, Harleykins?"

Lula turned the radio to a thunderous volume.

Oh, Johnny . . .

She swung toward him, her expression sultry as she pressed the sides of her ample breasts, accentuating the deep cleavage as she stalked him and slipped one white leg through the break in the garish satin wrapper. Her painted lips pouted voluptuously as she sidled close and rubbed herself against him, straddling one of his thighs.

Harley's eyes became hooded, his lips dropped open with lascivious expectation as he lifted his knee against her.

"Ooh-hoo-hoo, Lula-baby, sugar-pie, you sure know how t' do it to a man."

"You bet I do, kiddo, and you'd like it right now, wouldn't you?"

He gripped her hips with both hands. "I'm here, ain't I, baby?"

She took his hands and transferred them to her breasts. "Feel that? I got gumdrops just thinkin' about you. Wanna know what else happened when I thought about you, Harleykins?"

"Yeah," Harley growled, low and lusty, manipulating her pelvis. "What?"

They ground against each other in earnest. Harley's root had sprung up like a mushroom after two weeks of rain. She grasped his neck and put her lips to his ear and whispered something coarse, for good measure.

He laughed gutturally and said, "Oh, yeah? Let's see," then reached for the thatch of blond hair and slipped a finger inside her.

"Ooh-hoo-hoo, Lula-baby, you need your damper turned down, and how."

She unbuttoned his shirt and pushed it off till it hung from his waist, all the while riding his hand, which was braced against his thigh. She looped both arms around his neck, nipped his ear, licked the inside of it and suggested, "What I need is one of them new electric fans that turns back and forth. I seen one down in a hardware store in Atlanta last time I visited my sister Junie." She eased down and ran her lips across his chest, then splayed her hands on the black curly hair. "Mmm . . . I love my men hairy. Gets me itchin' somethin' awful."

Harley was nearly at the bursting point already. "Honey, I ain't made of money, you know."

She bit his nipple, then tugged it until he yelped and jerked back, nursing it. She gazed into his eyes, her face feigning innocence as she gyrated against him. "I bet your wife's got one o' them electric fans already, hasn't she, Harley?"

"Come on, Lula, let's go to bed. I'm hurtin', honey."

"What about that fan?"

"Maybe next payday."

She pouted her vermilion lips and ran one finger down her damp cleavage. "Next payday's too late. Why, it's been so hot, I just can't hardly sleep nights at all." She wiped her collected sweat beneath his nose.

"Lula, be reasonable. I already give you that Frigidaire and the Philco and had that closet made into a bathroom for you. I had to do some fancy explainin' to Mae about where the extra money went."

Abruptly she gave him a shove and flounced away from him, throwing her hands in the air. "Mae, Mae, Mae! I swear that's all I hear from you, Harley Overmire! Well, if you won't get me that electric fan, I know somebody who will. Why, just today Orlan Nettles was in the cafe and all I'da had to do was crook my little finger and it woulda been him here tonight instead of you. I'll bet you five dollars Orlan never did it the way I had in mind to do it with you tonight."

"You thought of a new way?" Harley was pure miserable by this time.

With her back turned, she inspected her painted nails. "It was a good one, too."

The music on the Philco had changed to "Paper Doll." It continued blasting as he came up behind her and clamped his teeth on her neck, reached around front and started convincing her again. But Lula had coercion down to an art. She dipped her knees and got the most out of Harley's strokes, but she could remain unyielding till she got what she wanted, and it was always more than just an orgasm. If she was going to live the rest of her life in this little jerkwater town, she'd live it in luxury, by God. The fan and the bathroom and the Philco were just the beginning. She intended to have a Ford, and a carpeted front room and an R.C.A. Victor phonograph before this was over.

Behind her, Harley was breathing like a winded horse. What he had inside his pants felt like it belonged to a horse, too. She reached back to help Harley make his decision.

He groaned against her neck and said, "Okay, Lula-honey, I'll get you the fan."

"Tomorrow, Harleykins?" she purred.

"Tomorrow. I'll think of somethin' I got to run down to Atlanta for."

Lula didn't expect something for nothing. The change in

her was immediate and inspired. She swung around and began removing Harley's clothes, licking his chest, fondling
him while backing him toward the kitchen.

"What's your favorite kind of sandwich, Harleykins?"

He stumbled over a pantleg and laughed. "Roast beef and
mustard."

"Mmm . . . roast beef and mustard. You like mustard, do
you, Harley?" She knew he liked mustard. She knew everything about Harley Overmire and used every scrap of knowledge to best advantage.

"Damn right, and Mae, she's always forgettin' to put it
on."

"That's the trouble with Mae," Lula purred, pushing his
boxer shorts to the floor. "Mae doesn't know what a man
likes. But I do." Harley chuckled, thinking he'd get Lula the
biggest damn fan in the city of Atlanta. "And where should
a man eat his roast beef and mustard sandwich, Harleykins?"
She stroked him till he felt hard and pulsing as a jackhammer.

"At the kitchen table?" *Oh, merciful heavens,* he thought.
This is gonna be good.

"That's right, honey-lamb. I got cold roast beef in my new
Frigidaire, just waitin' for you, and all the mustard you want,
and I'm gonna serve 'em both to you on the kitchen table,
and afterwards you and me're gonna climb in that beautiful
new bathtub and run some of that luscious hot water from my
brand-new water heater, and we're gonna put some Dreft in
there and get lost in the bubbles, and everytime you open
your lunch pail up at the mill and see a roast beef sandwich
without mustard, you're gonna remember who it is that treats
you right—aren't you, Harleykins?"

They spent forty minutes on the kitchen table, and the
things Lula did with that mustard would have sold millions of
bottles, had the manufacturer had the ingenuity to suggest
such uses.

Later, in Lula's shiny new porcelain tub, she ran her bare
toes up Harley's hairy chest. His eyes were closed and his
beefy arms rested on the wide edge.

"Harley?"

"Hm?"

"A stranger came into the cafe today."

"Hm." He sounded disinterested.

Two minutes passed in silence while Lula patiently rested with her eyes closed. She was bright enough to know that if she asked, she'd arouse his suspicion. But if Harley thought he alone could scratch her itch, he was sadly mistaken.

"Don't get many strangers through here," she murmured in due time, as if half asleep.

Harley lifted his head. "Tall guy? Wiry? Wearin' a battered cowboy hat?"

"Yeah, that's the one," she replied dreamily, following with a throaty chuckle. "Hey, Harley, how come you always know everything before I can tell you?"

He chortled and laid his head back. "You got to get up pretty early in the mornin' to put one over on old Harley."

"He just read the paper and moved on."

"Prob'ly lookin' at the want ads. I fired him from the mill today."

"What'd he do wrong?"

"Done five years in Huntsville State Pen for killin' a whore in some whorehouse down there."

Lula's foot hit the water with a splash as she sat bolt upright. "My God, Harley, he didn't!" Her blood ran fast at the mere idea of being in the same room with a man like that. "Lord, we women won't be safe on the streets."

"That's what I told him. Parker, I said, we don't want your kind around here. Pick up your pay and git."

So his name was Parker.

"Good for you, Harley." She lay back and stroked his genitals with her heel. Beneath the bubbly water they were sleek. She began growing aroused again, touching Harley, but picturing the tall, taciturn cowboy who'd said so little and had hidden beneath the brim of his hat. Still waters, she thought, and felt her heart begin to race. Going to bed with a man like that would be the ultimate excitement; she imagined it in vivid detail—the danger, the challenge, the sexual drive behind a man who'd been cut off from women for five years. Lord a-mighty, it would be one she'd never forget.

"Bet I know somethin' you don't know, Harley." She let her toes climb his chest like an inchworm.

"What?"

"He went up to see crazy Elly Dinsmore about that ad she run."

"What!" The water slopped over the edge of the tub as Overmire shot up.

"I know damn well he did 'cause first he asked to see the paper, then he sat and read it, then he asked how to find Rock Creek Road, and when I told him he headed off in that direction. What else would he be goin' up there for?"

Overmire roared with laughter and fell back in the water. "Wait'll I tell the boys about this. Jesus, will they laugh. Crazy Elly Dinsmore . . . ha, ha, ha!"

"She really is crazy, isn't she?"

"As a bedbug. Advertisin' for a husband. Christ."

"Course, what could you expect after she was locked up in that house all her life?" Lula shivered.

"I went to school with her mother, you know. Course, that was before she dropped her whelp and they locked her up."

"You did?" Lula sat up and reached over the edge of the tub for a towel. She stood and began drying herself. Harley did the same.

"She stared at the wall a lot, and drew pictures all the time. Once she drew a picture of a naked man on a windowshade. The teacher didn't know it was there and when she pulled it down the class went crazy. Course, they never proved it was Lottie See drew it, but she was always drawin', and who else'd be crazy enough to do a thing like that?"

Harley stepped from the tub and began drying his legs. Suddenly he stopped and stared at the hairless insides of his thighs. "Damn it all, Lula, how'm I gonna explain these mustard stains to Mae?"

Lula explored the evidence, giggled and turned to the mirror, tightening one of the combs that held her upsweep. "Tell her you got the yellow jaundice."

Harley guffawed and slapped her fanny. "Hey, Lula, you're all right, kid." Abruptly he sobered. "You're sure tonight was okay to do it—I mean, you couldn't get pregnant or anything, could you?"

Lula grew piqued. "You're a little late askin', aren't you, Harley?"

"Jesus, Lula, I depend on you to tell me if I need to use anything."

She dabbed Evening in Paris behind her ears, between her thighs. "How dumb do you think I am, Harley?" She capped the bottle and slammed it down. He was always asking the same question, as if she were too ignorant to use a calendar. She'd answered it scores of times, but it always left her feeling empty and angry. So, she wasn't his wife. So, she couldn't have his babies. Who'd want 'em? She'd seen his kids and they were stubby, ugly little brats that looked like bug-eyed monkeys. If she was ever going to have a kid, it sure as hell wouldn't be his. It'd be somebody's like that Parker's, somebody who'd give her handsome, brown-eyed darlings that other women would envy.

The thought of it gripped her with a sense of urgency. She was thirty-six already and no marriage prospects in sight. She'd live the rest of her life in this stinking little dump where she'd probably die, just like her mother had. And when she got so old Harley didn't want to do it on the kitchen table anymore—or couldn't, for that matter—he'd retire to his rocking chair on the front veranda with his precious, boring Mae. And all those homely little monkeys of his would turn out *more* homely little monkeys and old Grampa Harley'd be happy as a tick on a fat sheep.

And she—Lula—would be here alone. Aging. Going to fat. Eating beef and mustard sandwiches by herself.

Well, not if she could help it, Lula vowed. Not if she could by God help it.

CHAPTER
4

Eleanor awakened to a pink sunrise creeping over the sill and the sound of an ax. She peeked across her pillow at the alarm clock. Six-thirty. He was chopping wood at six-thirty?

Barefoot, she crept to the kitchen window and stood back, studying him and the woodpile. How long had he been up? Already he'd split a stack waist-high. He had tossed his shirt and hat aside. Dressed only in jeans and cowboy boots, he looked as meaty as a scarecrow. He swung the ax and she watched, fascinated in spite of herself by the hollow belly, the taut arms, the flexing chest. He'd done some splitting in his time and went at it with measured consistency, regulating his energy for maximum endurance—balancing a log on the stump, standing back, cracking it dead center and cleaving it with two whacks. He balanced another piece and—whack! whack!—firewood.

She closed her eyes—lordy, don't let him leave—and rested a hand on her roundness, recalling her own clumsiness at the task, the amount of effort it had taken, the length of time.

She opened the back door and stepped onto the porch. "You're sure up with the chickens, Mr. Parker."

Will let the ax fall and swung around. "Mornin', Mrs. Dinsmore."

48

"Mornin' yourself. Can't say the sound of that ax ain't welcome around here."

She stood on the stoop in a white, ankle-length nightgown that exaggerated her pregnancy. Her hair hung loose to her shoulders, her feet were bare, and from this distance she looked younger and happier than she had last night. For a moment Will Parker imagined he was Glendon Dinsmore, he really belonged here, she was his woman and the babies inside the house, inside her, were his. The brief fantasy was sparked not by Eleanor Dinsmore but by things Will Parker had managed to miss in his life. Suddenly he realized he'd been staring and became self-conscious. Leaning on the ax, he reached for his shirt and hat.

"Would you mind bringin' in an armload of that wood so I can get a fire started?" she called.

"No, ma'am, don't mind at all."

"Just dump it in the woodbox."

"Yes, ma'am."

The screen door slammed and she disappeared.

He hated to stop splitting wood even long enough to carry it into the house. In prison he'd worked in the laundry, smelling the stink of other men's sweat rising from the steaming water as he tended the clothes in a hot, close room where no sunlight reached. To stand in the morning sun while the dew was still thick, sharing the lavender circle of sky with dozens of birds that flitted from countless gourd birdhouses hung about the place—ahh, this was sheer heaven. And gripping an ax handle, feeling its weight slice through the air, the resistance as it struck wood, the thud of a piece falling to the earth—now that was freedom. And the smell—clean, sharp and on his knuckle a touch of pungent sap—he couldn't get enough of it. Nor of using his muscles again, stretching them to the limit. He had grown soft in prison, soft and white and somehow emasculated by doing women's work.

If the sound of the ax was welcome to Mrs. Dinsmore, the feel of it was emancipation to Will Parker.

He knelt and loaded his arm with wood—good, sharp, biting edges that creased his skin where his sleeve was rolled back; grainy flat pieces that clacked together and echoed across the clearing. He piled it high until it reached his chin, then higher until he couldn't see over it, testing himself again. This was man's work. Honest. Satisfying. He grunted as he stood with the enormous load.

At the screen door he knocked.

She came running, scolding, "What in heaven's name're you knockin' for?"

"Brought your wood, ma'am."

"I can see that. But there's no need to knock." She pushed the screen door open. "And y' got to learn that around here y' can't stand on that rotting old porch floor with a load so heavy. It's likely t' take you right through."

"I made sure I walked near the edge." He felt with the toe of his boot, stepped up and crossed the kitchen to clatter the wood into the woodbox. Brushing off his arms, Will turned. "That oughta keep you for—" His words fell away.

Eleanor Dinsmore stood behind him, dressed in a clean yellow smock and matching skirt, brushing her hair into a tail. Her chin rested on her chest, and a checkered ribbon was clamped in her teeth. How long had it been since he'd seen a woman putting up her hair in the morning? Her elbows—pointed toward the ceiling—appeared graceful. They lifted the hem of her smock, revealing a crescent of white within the cutout of her skirt. She snatched the ribbon from her teeth and bound the hair high and tight. Lifting her head, she caught him gawking.

"What're you staring at?"

"Nothing." Guiltily, he lurched for the door, feeling his face heat.

"Mr. Parker?"

"Ma'am?" He stopped, refusing to turn and let her see him blushing.

"I'll need a little kindling. Would you mind breaking off a few smaller pieces?"

He nodded and left.

Will had been unprepared for his reaction to Mrs. Dinsmore. It wasn't *her*—hell, it could have been any woman and his reaction would probably have been the same. Women were soft, curvy things, and he'd been without them for a long, long time. What man wouldn't want to watch? As he knelt to tap kindling off a chunk of oak, he recalled the checkered ribbon trailing from her teeth, the white flash of underwear beneath her smock, and his own quick blush.

What the hell's the matter with you, Parker? The woman's five months pregnant, and plain as a round rock. Get that kindling back in there, and find somethin' else to think about.

She'd scolded him once for knocking, but returning with the kindling, he paused again. Even before prison, there had been few doors open to Will Parker, and—fresh out—he was too accustomed to locks and bars to open a woman's screen and walk right in.

Instead of knocking, he announced, "Got your kindling."

She glanced up from the bacon she was slicing and called, "Put it right in the stove."

He not only put it in the stove, he built the fire. Such a simple job, but a pleasure. In all his life, he'd never owned a stove. It had been years since he'd had the right to one, even one owned by somebody else. He took care laying the kindling, striking the match, watching the sticks flare. Savoring. Taking as much time as he pleased, realizing time was no longer controlled by someone else. When the kindling had a hearty start, he added a thick log, and though it was a warm morning, extended his palms toward the heat.

Building a fire in a stove was just another morning chore to Eleanor. Watching him enjoy the job made her wonder about the life he'd lived, the comforts he hadn't had. She wondered what was going through his mind as he stared at the flames. Whatever it was, she'd probably never know.

He turned from the stove reluctantly, dusting his hands on his thighs. "Anything else?"

"You could fill that water pail for me."

From behind he scanned her yellow outfit—yellow as a buttercup—and the tail of hair bound by the checkered ribbon. She had donned an apron styled like a pinafore, tied loosely at the back. Studying the bow in the shallows of her spine, he experienced again the wrenching sense of home that had been denied him all his life, and along with it a queer reluctance to approach her. But the water pail was at her elbow, and deliberately stepping close to a woman—any woman—since doing time for killing one made him constantly expect her to leap aside in fright. He made a wide berth around her and, reaching, muttered, "Scuse me, ma'am."

She glanced up and smiled. " 'Preciate your buildin' the fire, Mr. Parker," she offered, then returned to her slicing.

Crossing the room with the water pail, he felt better than he had in years. At the door, he stopped. "I was wonderin', ma'am . . ."

With the knife in the bacon she looked back over her shoulder.

"You milk that goat out there?" He thumbed toward the yard.

"No. I milk the cow."

"You have a cow?"

"Herbert. She's probably down by the barn by now."

"Herbert?" A corner of his mouth quirked.

She shrugged while humor lit her face. "Don't ask me how the name got on her. She's always been Herbert and that's what she answers to."

"I could milk"—his grin spread—"Herbert for you if you tell me where to find another pail."

She completed the slice and wiped her hands on her apron, fixing a teasing grin on her mouth. "Well, my, my . . ." she drawled. "Is that a smile I see threatenin' the man's face?"

He allowed it to remain as they openly regarded one another, finding that the morning had brought changes they each liked. Seconds passed before they were smitten by self-consciousness. He glanced away. She turned to fetch him a galvanized pail.

"There's a milk stool standin' against the south side o' the barn."

"I'll find it."

The screen door slammed and she crossed to it, calling, "Oh, Mr. Parker?"

He pivoted in the path. "Ma'am?"

She studied him through the screen.

He had a pair of the nicest lips she'd ever seen, and they were downright pretty when they smiled.

"After breakfast I'm gonna cut that hair for you."

The grin mellowed and reached his eyes. "Yes, ma'am," he said softly with a touch on his hat brim.

As he turned downyard with the pail swinging at his side, he wondered when he'd been happier, when life had looked more promising. *She was going to keep him!*

Herbert turned out to be a friendly cuss with big brown eyes and a brown and white hide. She and the goat seemed to be pals, exchanging a hello of noses. The mule was out behind the barn, too, with its eyes half closed, facing the wall. Will chose to milk the cow outside instead of in the smelly barn. He tied her to a fencepost, stripped off his shirt and hunkered on the stool while the heat of the sun pelted his back. It seemed he couldn't soak up enough of it to make up for the five years' dearth. Beside him the goat watched, chewing its cud. The cow chewed too—loud, grinding beats. Comfortable. In time Will's milking matched the rhythm of Herbert's jaws. It was soothing—the warm bovine flesh against his forehead, the warmer sun, the homely sound, and the heat building up the length of his arms. In time his muscles burned—satisfying, honest heat generated by his own body toiling as a body ought. He increased his speed to test his mettle.

While he worked, the hens came out of their night roosts, one by one, clucking throatily, walking as if on sharp stones, exploring the grass for snails. He eyed the yard, imagining it clean. He eyed the chickens, imagining them penned. He eyed the woodpile, imagining it chopped, ranked and filed. There was one hell of a lot to do, but the challenge fired him with eagerness.

A mother cat showed up with three taffy-colored kittens, a trio of clowning puffballs with tails straight as pokers. The mother curled against Will's ankle and he paused to scratch her.

"What's your name, missus?" She stood on her hind legs, braced her forefeet on his thigh, begging. Her fur was soft and warm as she jutted against his fingers. "You feedin' those three, huh? Need a little help?" He found a sardine can inside the doorway of the barn and filled it, then watched the four of them eat, one of the babies with a foot in the can. He chuckled . . . and the sound of his own laughter was so foreign to his ears it made his heart hammer. He tilted his head back and squinted at the sky, letting freedom and happiness overcome him. He chuckled again, feeling the wondrous thrust of the sound against his throat. How long since he'd heard it? How long?

When he delivered the milk to the house he smelled bacon frying from twenty feet down the yard. His stomach growled and he paused with his hand raised to knock on the screen door.

Inside the kitchen, Eleanor lifted her head and their gazes caught.

He dropped the hand and opened the door, taking the risk and finding it easy, after all.

"Met the animals," he announced, setting the pail on the cupboard. "Mule's a little stuck-up, compared to the others."

"Well, bless my soul," Eleanor remarked. "A regular speech."

He backed off, rubbing his hands on his thighs self-consciously. "I'm not much for small talk."

"I've noticed. Still, you might try it out on the boys."

The pair was up, dressed in wrinkled pajamas. The older one looked up from where he was entertaining the young one on the floor with five wooden spools. He stared at Will.

"Howdy, Donald Wade," Will ventured, feeling awkward and uncertain.

Donald Wade stuck his finger in his mouth and poked his cheek out.

"Say good morning, Donald Wade," his mother prompted.

Instead Donald Wade pointed a stubby finger at his brother and blurted out, "That's Baby Thomas."

Baby Thomas drooled down the front of his pajamas, stared at Will and clacked two spools together. To the best of Will's recollection he had never spoken to a person so young. He felt foolish waiting for an answer and didn't know what to do with his hands. So he stacked three spools in a tower. Baby Thomas knocked them over, giggled and clapped. Will looked up and found Eleanor watching him, stirring something on the stove.

"I laid out Glendon's razor for you, and his mug and brush. You're welcome to use them."

He rose to his feet, glanced at the shaving equipment, then at her. But already she'd turned to her cooking, giving him a measure of privacy. He'd been shaving with a straightedge and no soap, hacking his skin all to hell; the mug and brush would be as welcome as the hot water, but he paused before moving toward them.

He'd just have to get used to it: they were going to share this kitchen every morning. He'd have to wash and shave and she'd have to comb her hair and cook breakfast and tend her babies. There were bound to be times when he'd have to brush close by her. And she hadn't jumped away so far, had she?

"Excuse me," he said at her shoulder. She glanced at the mug and shifted over without missing a beat in stirring the grits, letting him reach around her for the teakettle.

"You sleep all right last night?"

"Yes, ma'am."

He filled the cup and the washbasin, whipped up a froth of shaving bubbles and lathered his face, back to back with her.

"How do you like your eggs?"

"Cooked."

"Cooked?" She spun around and their eyes met in the mirror.

"Yes, ma'am." He tilted his head and scraped beneath his left jaw.

"You mean you're in the habit of eating 'em raw?"

"I been known to."

"You mean straight out of some farmer's hen house?"

He shaved away, avoiding her eyes. She burst out laughing, drawing his reflected glance once again. She laughed long, unrestrainedly, resting an arm on her stomach, until his eyes—black as walnuts above the white shaving soap—took on a hint of amusement.

"You think it's funny?" He rinsed the razor.

She sobered with an effort. "I'm sorry."

She sounded anything but sorry, but he found her amusement did pleasant things to her face. Outlining a sideburn, he said, "Farmers tend to blame it on the foxes, so nobody comes lookin'."

She studied him a while, wondering how many miles he'd drifted, how many hen houses he'd raided, how long it would take him to lose that distance he maintained so carefully. For the moment she'd created a crack in it, but inside he was rolled up like a possum.

She found herself enjoying the smell of shaving soap in the house again. His face emerged, one scrape at a time, the face she'd be looking at across her table for years to come, should he decide to stay. She was surprised to find herself fascinated by it, by the shape of his jaw, the clean line of his nose, the thinness of his cheeks, the darkness of his eyes. When he glanced up and found her still studying him, she spun back toward the stove.

"Fried soft, hard or scrambled?"

His hands fell still at the question. In prison they were always scrambled and tasted like damp newspaper. My God—to be given a choice.

"Fried soft."

"Soft it'll be."

While he washed up and combed his hair, he listened to the spatter as the eggs hit the pan, a sound he'd seldom heard, living in bunkhouses and boxcars as he had for much of his free life. Sounds. In his life he'd heard a lot of rumbling wheels and other men snoring. Clanging bars, male voices, washing machines.

Behind him the boys jabbered and giggled, and the wooden spools clattered to the floor. The stovelids clanged. The ashes collapsed. A log thudded. The teakettle hissed. A mother said, "Time for breakfast, boys. Jump up on your chairs now."

The smells in this kitchen were enough to make a man drown in his own saliva. In prison the two prevailing smells were those of disinfectant and urine, and food there seemed to have as little smell as it did taste.

When they sat down to breakfast, Will openly stared at the

wealth of food on his plate: three eggs—three!—done to a turn. Grits, bacon, hot black coffee and toast with boysen-berry jam.

She saw his hesitation, saw him rest his hands on his thighs as if afraid to reach out again.

"Eat," she ordered, then began chopping up an egg for Baby Thomas.

As he had last night, Will ate in a state of disbelief at his good fortune. He was half done before realizing she was only picking at a piece of dry toast. His fork-hand paused.

"What's the matter?" she inquired. "Somethin' cooked wrong?"

"No. No! It's . . . why, it's the best breakfast I ever had in my life, but where's yours?"

"Food don't agree with me this early in the morning."

He couldn't imagine anyone not eating if food was plenti-ful. Had she given him her share, too?

"But—"

"Women get that way when they're expectin'," she explained.

"Oh." His eyes dropped to her belly, then quickly aside.

Why, I swear, she thought. *That man's blushin'!* For what-ever reason, the thought pleased her.

After breakfast she sat him on a chair in the middle of the kitchen and tied a dishtowel around him, backward. Her first touch sent shivers down his calves. He listened to the scissors snip, felt the comb scrape his skull and closed his eyes to sa-vor each movement of her knuckles against his head. He shuddered and let his hands go limp on his thighs, covered by the dishtowel.

She saw his eyes drop closed.

"Feel good?" she asked.

They flew open again. "Yes, ma'am."

"No need to stiffen up." She nudged his shoulder gently. "Just relax."

After that, she worked in silence, letting him absorb the pleasure undisturbed.

His eyelids slid closed again and he drifted beneath the

first gentle woman's touch he'd experienced in over six years. She brushed the tip of his ear, the back of his neck, and he was lulled into his private, soft place. Lord, lord . . . it was good . . .

When the haircut was done she had to wake him.

"Hm?" He lifted his head, then jerked awake, dismayed at finding he'd dozed. "Oh . . . I must've—"

"All done." She whisked the dishtowel off and he rose to peer into the tiny round mirror next to the sink. The hair was slightly longer above his right ear than above his left, but overall the haircut was a great improvement over the close shearing he'd received in prison.

"Looks good, ma'am," he offered, touching a sideburn with his knuckles. He looked back over his shoulder. "Thank you. And for breakfast, too."

Whenever he thanked her she brushed it off as if she'd done nothing. Sweeping the floor, she didn't look up. "You got a healthy head of hair there, Mr. Parker. Glendon's was thin and fine. Always cut his, too." She waddled to the side of the room for a dustpan. "Enjoyed doin' it again. Enjoyed the smell of the shavin' soap around the house again, too."

She had? He thought he'd been the only one to enjoy those things. Or perhaps she was being kind to put him at ease. He found himself wanting to return the favor.

"I can do that," he offered as she bent to collect his streaky brown hair from the floor.

"It's as good as done. Wouldn't mind, however, if you took over the chore of feeding the pigs."

She straightened and their eyes met. In hers he saw uncertainty. It was the first thing she'd asked him to do, and not too pleasant. But what was unpleasant to one man was freedom to Will Parker. She'd fed him, lent him her husband's razor, shared her fire and her table and had put him to sleep with a comb and scissors. His lips opened and a voice inside urged, *Say it, Parker. You afraid she'll think you ain't much of a man if you do?*

"That haircut was the best thing I've felt for a long time."

She understood perfectly. She, too, had spent so much of

her life in a loveless, touchless world. Odd, how a statement so simple formed a sympathetic bond.

"Well, I'm glad."

"In prison—"

Her eyes swept back to his. "In prison, what?"

He shouldn't have started, but she had a way about her that loosened his jaws, made him want to trust her with the secrets that hurt most. "In prison they use these buzzy little clippers and they cut off most of your hair so you feel—" He glanced away, reluctant to complete the thought, after all.

"You feel what?" she encouraged.

He studied his own hair lying on the dustpan, remembering. "Naked."

Neither of them moved. Sensing how hard it had been for him to admit such a thing, she wanted to reach out and touch his arm. But before she could, he took the dustpan and dumped it in the stove.

"I'll see after the pigs," he said, ending the moment of closeness.

Donald Wade agreed to show Will where the pigs were, and Eleanor sent them out with a half-pail of milk and orders to feed it to them.

"To the pigs!" Will exclaimed, aghast. He'd gone hungry most of his life and she fed fresh milk to the pigs?

"Herbert gives more than we can use, and the milk truck can't get in here, what with the driveway all washed out. Anyway, I don't want no town people nosing around the place. Feed it to the pigs."

It broke Will's heart to carry the milk out of the house.

Donald Wade led the way, though Will could have found the pigpen with his nose alone. Crossing the yard, he took a better look at the driveway. It was sorry, all right. But Mrs. Dinsmore had a mule, and if there was a mule there must be implements to hitch to it. And if there were no implements, he'd shovel by hand. He needed the driveway passable to get the junk hauled out of here. Already he was assessing that junk not as waste but as scrap metal. Scrap metal would soon bring top dollar with America turning out war supplies for

England. The woman was sitting on top of a gold mine and didn't even know it.

Not only was the driveway sad; the yard in broad daylight was pitiful. Dilapidated buildings that looked as if a swift kick would send them over. Those with a few good years left were sorely in need of paint. The corncrib was filled with junk instead of corn—barrels, crates, rolls of rusty barbed wire, stacks of warped lumber. Will couldn't tell what kept the door of the chicken coop from falling off. The smell, as they passed, was horrendous. No wonder the chickens roosted in the junkpiles. He passed stacks of machinery parts, empty paint cans—though he couldn't figure out where the paint might have been used. The goat's nest seemed to be in an abandoned truck with the cushion stuffing chewed away. Lord, thought Will, there was enough work here to keep a man going twenty-four hours a day for a solid year.

Bobbing along beside him, Donald Wade interrupted his thoughts.

"There." The boy pointed at the structure that looked like a tobacco-drying shed.

"There what?"

"That's where the pig mash is." He led the way into a building crammed with everything from soup to nuts, only this time, usable stuff. Obviously Dinsmore had done more than collect junk. Barterer? Horse trader? The paint cans in here were full. The rolls of barbed wire, new. Furniture, tools, saddles, a newspaper press, egg crates, pulley belts, canepoles, the fender of a Model-A, a dress form, a barrel full of pistons, Easter baskets, a boiler, cowbells, moonshine jugs, bedsprings . . . and who knew what else was buried in the close-packed building.

Donald Wade pointed to a gunnysack sitting on the dirt floor with a rusty coffee can beside it. "Two." He held up three fingers and had to fold one down manually.

"Two?"

"Mama, she mixes two with the milk."

Will hunkered beside Donald Wade, opened the sack and smiled as the boy continued to hold down the finger. "You wanna scoop 'em for me?"

Donald Wade nodded so hard his hair flopped. He filled the can but couldn't manage to pull it from the deep sack. Will reached in to help. The mash fell into the milk with a sharp, grainy smell. When the second scoop was dumped, Donald Wade found a piece of lath in a corner.

"You stir with this."

Will began stirring. Donald Wade stood with his hands inside the bib of his overalls, watching. At length he volunteered, "I can stir good."

Will grinned secretly. "You can?"

Donald Wade made his hair flop again.

"Well, good thing, 'cause I was needin' a rest."

Even with both hands knotted hard around the lath, Donald Wade needed help from Will. The man's smile broke free as the boy clamped his teeth over his bottom lip and maneuvered the stick with flimsy arms. Will's arms fit nice around the small shoulders as he knelt behind the boy and the two of them together mixed the mash.

"You help your mama do this every day?"

"Prett-near. She gets tired. Mostly I pick eggs."

"Where?"

"Everywhere."

"Everywhere?"

"Around the yard. I know where the chickens like it best. I c'n show you."

"They give many eggs?"

Donald Wade shrugged.

"She sell 'em?"

"Yup."

"In town?"

"Down on the road. She just leaves 'em there and people leave the money in a can. She don't like goin' to town."

"How come?"

Donald Wade shrugged again.

"She got any friends?"

"Just my pa. But he died."

"Yeah, I know. And I'm sure sorry about that, Donald Wade."

"Know what Baby Thomas did once?"

"What?"

"He ate a worm."

Until that moment Will hadn't realized that to a four-year-old the eating of a worm was more important than the death of a father. He chuckled and ruffled the boy's hair. It felt as soft as it looked.

I could get to like this one a lot, he thought.

With the hogs fed, they stopped to rinse the bucket at the pump. Beneath it was a wide mudhole with not even a board thrown across it to keep the mud from splattering.

Naturally, Donald Wade got his boots coated. When they returned to the house his mother scolded, "You git, child, and scrape them soles before you come in here!"

Will put in, "It's my fault, ma'am. I took him down by the pump."

"You did? Oh, well . . ." Immediately she hid her pique, then glanced across the property. When she spoke, her voice held a quiet despondency. "Things are a real fright around here, I know. But I guess you can see that for yourself."

Will sealed his lips, tugged his hat brim clear down to his eyebrows, slipped his hands flat inside his backside pockets and scanned the property expressionlessly. Eleanor peeked at him from the corner of her eye. Her heart beat out a warning. *He'll run now. He'll sure as shootin' run after getting an eyeful of the place in broad daylight.*

But again he saw the possibilities. And nothing on the good green earth could make him turn his back on this place unless he was asked to. Gazing across the yard, all he said, in his low-key voice was, "Reckon the pens could use a little cleanin'."

CHAPTER
5

They went for a walk when the midmorning sun had lifted
well above the trees—a green and gold day smelling of deep
summer. Will had never walked with a woman and her children before. It held a strange, unexpected appeal. He noticed
her way with the children, how she carried Baby Thomas on
one hip with his heel flattening her smock. How, as they set
off from the porch, she reached back for Donald Wade, inviting, "Come on, honey, you lead the way," and helped him off
the last step. How she watched him gallop ahead, smiling after him as if she'd never before seen his flopping yellow hair,
his baggy striped overalls. How she locked her hands beneath
Thomas's backside, leaned from the waist, took a deep pull of
the clear air and said to the sky, "My, if this day ain't a
blessin'." How she called ahead, "Careful o' that wire in the
grass there, Donald Wade!" How she plucked a leaf and
handed it to Thomas, then let him touch her nose with it and
pretended it tickled her and made the young one giggle.

Watching, Will became entranced. Lord, she was some
mother. Always kind voiced. Always finding the good in
things. Always concerned about her boys. Always making
them feel important. Nobody had ever made Will feel important, only in the way.

He studied her covertly, noting more clearly the bulk of her belly, outlined by the baby's leg. Donald Wade had said she gets tired. Recalling the boy's words, Will considered offering to carry the baby, but he felt out of his depth around Thomas. He'd be no good at getting his nose tickled or making chit-chat. Besides, she might not cotton to a stranger like him handling Glendon Dinsmore's boys.

They went around to the back of the house where the dishtowel flapped on a line strung between teetering clothes-poles that had been shimmed up by crude wood braces. Beyond these were more junkpiles before the woods began—pines, oaks, hickories and more. Sparrows flitted from tree to tree ahead, and Eleanor followed with her finger, telling the boys, "See? Chipping sparrows." A brown thrasher swept past and perched on a dead limb. Again she pointed it out and named it. The sun glinted off the boys' blond heads and painted their mother's dress an even brighter hue. They walked along a faint double path worn by wheels some time ago. Sometimes Donald Wade skipped, swinging his arms widely. The younger one tipped his head back and looked at the sky, his hand resting on his mother's shoulder. They were so happy! Will hadn't come up against many happy people in his day. It was arresting.

A short distance from the house they came upon an east-facing hill covered by regular rows of squat fruit trees.

"This here's the orchard," Eleanor announced, gazing over its length and breadth.

"Big," Will observed.

"And you ain't seen half of it. These here are peach. Down yonder is a whole string of apples and pears . . . and oranges, too. Glendon had this idea to try orange trees, but they never did much." She smiled wistfully. "Too far north for them."

Will stepped off the path and inspected a cluster of fruit. "Could have used a little spraying."

"I know." Unconsciously she stroked the baby's back. "Glendon planned to do that, but he died in April and never got the chance."

This far south the trees should have been sprayed long before April, Will thought, but refrained from saying so. They moved on.

"How old are these trees?"

"I don't know exactly. Glendon's daddy planted most of them when he was still alive. All except the oranges, like I said. There's apples, too, just about every kind imaginable, but I never learned their names. Glendon's daddy, he knew a lot about them, but he died before I married Glendon. He was a junker, too, just like Glendon. Went to auction sales and traded stuff with anybody that came along. No reason to any of it, it seemed." Abruptly, she inquired, "You ever tasted quince? Those there are quince."

"Sour as rhubarb."

"Make a luscious pie, though."

"I wouldn't know about that, ma'am."

"Bet you'd like to try one, wouldn't you?"

He gave her a sideward glance. "Reckon I would."

"Could use a little fat on them bones, Mr. Parker."

He leveled his eyes on the quince trees and tugged his hat brim so low it cut off his view of the horizon. Thankfully, she changed the subject.

"So where'd you eat 'em, then?"

"California."

"California?" She peered up at him with her head cocked. "You been there?"

"Picked fruit there one summer when I was a kid."

"You see any movie stars?"

"Movie stars?" He wouldn't have guessed she'd know much about movie stars. "No." He glanced at her. "You ever seen any?"

She laughed. "Now where would I see movie stars when I never even seen a movie?"

"Never?"

She shook her head. "Heard about 'em from the kids in school, though."

He wished he could promise to take her sometime, but where would he get the money for movies? And even if he had it, there was no theater in Whitney. Besides, she avoided the town.

"In California, the movie stars are only in Hollywood, and

it gets cold in parts where there are mountains. And the ocean's dirty. It stinks."

She could see she had her work cut out for her if she was to get that pessimism out of him. "You always so jolly?"

He would have tugged his hat brim lower, but if he did he'd be unable to see where he was walking. "Well, California isn't like what you think."

"You know, I can't say I'd mind if you'd smile a little more often."

He tossed her a sullen glance. "About what?"

"Maybe, Mr. Parker, you got to find that out for yourself." She let the baby slip from her hip. "Lord, Thomas, if you ain't gettin' heavier than a guilty conscience, I don't know. Come on, take Mommy's hand and I'll show you somethin'."

She showed him things Will would have missed: a branch shaped like a dog's paw—"A man could whittle forever and not make anything prettier," she declared. A place where something tiny had nested in the grass and left a collection of empty seed pods—"If I was a mouse, I'd love livin' right here in this pretty-smellin' orchard, wouldn't you?" A green katydid camouflaged upon a greener blade of grass—"Y' got to look close to see he's makin' the sound with his wings." And in the adjacent woods a magnolia tree with a deep bowl, head-high, where its branches met, and within that bowl, a second tree taken root: a sturdy little oak growing straight and healthy.

"How'd it get there?" Donald Wade asked.

"How d' you think?"

"I dunno."

She squatted beside the boys, gazing up at the piggyback trees. "Well, there was this wise old owl lived in these woods, and one evenin' at dusk he came by and I ast him the same thing. I says to him, how'd that li'l old oak tree get t' growin' in that magnolia?" She grinned at Donald Wade. "Know what he told me?"

"Uh-uh." Donald Wade stared at his mother, mystified. She dropped to her rump and sat like an Indian, stripping bark from a stick with her thumbnail as she went on.

"Well, he said there was two squirrels lived here, years

ago. One of 'em was a hard worker, spent every day totin'
acorns into that little pocket in the tree up there." She pointed
with the stick. "The other squirrel, well, he was lazy. Laid on
his back on that limb over there" —she pointed again, to a
nearby pine—"and made a pillow out of his tail and crossed
his legs and watched the busy squirrel gettin' ready for winter. He waited until there was so many nuts they was about
to start spillin' over the edge. Then when the hardworking
squirrel went off to look for one last nut, the lazy one scrambled up there and ate and ate and ate, until he'd ate every last
one of 'em. He was so full he sat on the limb and let out a
burp so almighty powerful it knocked him off backwards."
She drew a deep breath, braced her hands on her knees and
burped loudly, then flopped back, arms outflung. Will smiled.
Donald Wade giggled. Baby Thomas squealed.

"But it wasn't so funny, after all," she continued, gazing at
the sky.

Donald Wade sobered and leaned over her to look straight
down into her face. "Why not?"

"Because on his way down, he cracked his head on a limb
and killed himself deader'n a mackerel."

Donald Wade smacked himself in the head and fell backward, sprawled on the grass beside Eleanor, his eyelids closed
but twitching. She rolled up and took Thomas into her lap.
"Now when the busy little squirrel come back with that one
last nut between his teeth, he climbed up and saw that all his
acorns were gone. He opened his mouth to cry and the last
acorn he brung up, why, it fell into the nest beneath the nut-
shells the greedy squirrel had left." Donald Wade, too, sat up,
his interest in the story aroused once again. "He knew he
couldn't stay here for the winter, 'cause he'd already gathered
up all the nuts for miles around. So he left his cozy nest and
didn't come back till he was old. So old it was hard for him
to climb up and down the oak trees like he used to. But he
remembered the little nest in the magnolia where it had been
warm and dry and safe, and he climbed up there to see it
again, just for old times' sake. And what do you think he
found?"

"The oak tree growin' there?" the older boy ventured.

"That's right." She finger-combed Donald Wade's hair off his brow. "A sturdy little oak with enough acorns that the old squirrel never had to run up and down a tree again, 'cause they was growin' all around his head, right there in his warm, cozy nest."

Donald Wade popped up. "Tell me another one!"

"Uh-uh. Got to go on, show Mr. Parker the rest of the place." She pushed to her feet and reached for Thomas's hand. "Come on, boys. Donald Wade, you take Thomas's other hand. Come on, Mr. Parker," she said over her shoulder. "Day's movin' on."

Will lagged behind, watching them saunter up the lane, three abreast, holding hands. The rear of her skirt was wrinkled from the damp grass, but she cared not a whit. She was busy pointing out birds, laughing softly, talking to the boys in her singsong Southern fashion. He felt a catch in his heart for the mother he'd never known, the hand he'd never held, the make-believe tales he'd never been told. For a moment he pretended he'd had one like Eleanor Dinsmore. Every kid should have one like her. *Maybe, Mr. Parker, you got to find that out for yourself.* Her words echoed through his mind as they moved on, and Will found himself glancing back over his shoulder at the oak tree growing out of the magnolia, realizing fully what a rare thing it was.

In time they came to a double flank of beehives, grayed, weathered and untended, dotting the edge of the orchard. He searched his mind for any knowledge of bees, but found none. He saw the hives as a potential source of income, but she gave them wide berth and he recalled that her husband had died tending the bees, was buried somewhere out here in the orchard. But he saw no grave and she pointed none out. In spite of the way Dinsmore had died, Will felt himself drawn to the hives, to the few insects that droned around them, and to the scent of the fruit—wormy or whole—as it warmed beneath the eleven o'clock sun. He wondered about the man who'd been here before him, a man who maintained nothing, finished nothing and apparently never worried about either. How could a man let things run to ruin that way? How could a man lucky enough to own things—so many things—

care so little about their condition? Will could count in ten seconds the number of things he'd ever owned: a horse, a saddle, clothing, a razor. Lengthening his stride to catch up with Eleanor Dinsmore, he wondered if she was as hopeless a dreamer as her husband had been.

They came to a pecan grove that looked promising, hanging thick with immature nuts, and in the lane over the next hill a tractor, which blocked their way.

"What's this?" Will's eyes lit up.

"Glendon's old Steel Mule," she explained while Will made a slow circuit around the rusting hulk. "This was where she stopped running, so this is where he left 'er." It was an old Bates Model G, but of what vintage Will couldn't be sure—'26 or '27, maybe. At the front it had two wide-set steel wheels, and on each side at the rear three wheels of telescoping size surrounded by tracks with lugs. The lugs were chewed, in some places missing. He glanced at the engine and doubted it would ever make a sound again.

"I know a little about engines, but I think this one's shot for good."

They moved on, reaching the far end of the property, turning back toward the house on another path. They passed stubbled fields and patches of woods, eventually topping a rise where Will stopped dead, pushed back his hat and gaped. "Holy smokes," he muttered. Below lay a veritable graveyard of iron stoves, rusting in grass tall enough to bend in the wind.

"A bunch of 'em, huh?" Eleanor stopped beside him. "Seemed like he'd haul another one home every week. I said to him, 'Glendon, what're you going to do with all them old stoves when everybody these days is changin' to gas and kerosene?' But he just kept hauling 'em in here whenever he heard of someone changin' over."

There had to be five hundred of them, as bright orange as the road to Whitney.

"Holy smokes," Will repeated, lifting his hat and scratching his head, imagining the chore of hauling them out again.

She glanced at his profile, clearly defined against the blue sky, with the hat pushed back beyond his hairline. Did she

dare tell him about the rest? Might as well, she decided. He'd
find out eventually anyway. "Wait'll you see the cars."

Will turned her way. After all he'd seen, nothing would be
a surprise. "Cars?"

"Wrecks, every one of 'em. Worse'n the Steel Mule."

Hands on hips, he studied the stoves a long moment. At
length he sighed, tugged down his hat brim and said, "Well,
let's get it over with."

The cars lay immediately behind the band of woods surrounding the outbuildings—they'd come nearly full circle
around the place—and created a clutter of gaping doors and
sagging roofs in the long weeds. They approached the windowless wreck of an old 1928 Whippet. Wild honeysuckle
climbed over its wire wheels and along the front bumper. On
the near runningboard a bird had made its nest against the lee
of the back fender.

"Can I drive it?" Donald Wade asked eagerly.

"Sure can. Wanna take Baby Thomas with you?"

"Come on, Thomas." Donald Wade took his brother's
hand, plowed through the grass and helped Thomas board.
The two clambered up and sat side by side, bouncing on the
tattered seat. Donald Wade pumped the steering wheel left
and right, making engine noises with his tongue. When
Eleanor and Will approached, he whipped the wheel even
more vigorously. Imitating his brother, Thomas stuck out his
tongue and blew, sending specks of saliva flying onto a cob-
web strung across the faded black paint of the dashboard.

Eleanor stood beside the open door and laughed. The more
she laughed, the more the boys bounced and blew. The more
they bounced and blew, the more animatedly Donald Wade
worked the steering wheel.

She crossed her arms on the window opening, bent forward
and propped her chin on a wrist. "Where y'all goin', fellers?"

"Atlanta!" squealed Donald Wade.

" 'Lanta!" parroted Thomas.

"Atlanta?" teased their mother. "What y'all think y're
gonna do clear over there?"

"Don' know." Donald Wade drove hell-bent for leather, the
old wheel spinning in his freckled hands.

"Care to give a pretty lady a ride?"

"Can't stop—goin' too fast!"

"Hows 'bout if I just jump on the runnin' board while you whiz by?"

"Okee-dokee, lady!"

"Ouch!" Eleanor jumped back and grabbed her foot. "You run over my toe, young feller!"

"Eeeeech!" Donald Wade's stubby foot slammed the brake pedal to the floor as he came to a screeching halt. "Git in, lady."

Eleanor acted affronted. She put her nose in the air and turned away. "Don't reckon I care to, now you run over my toes that way. Reckon I'll find myself somebody drives less reckless than you. But you might ask Mr. Parker here if he needs a lift to town. He's been walkin' some and he's probably plum tuckered, ain't you, Mr. Parker?" She squinted up at him with a crooked smile.

Will had never played such games before. He felt conspicuous and unimaginative, while they all watched him, waiting for a reply. He frantically searched his mind and came up with a sudden stroke of genius. "Next time, boys." He lifted one scuffed boot above the grass. "Just got this here new pair of boots and I gotta get 'em broke in before the dance Saturday night."

"Okee-dokee, mister. *Bbvvrr-n-n-n!*" More spit accompanied the engine noise, and more laughter from Eleanor Dinsmore. She and Will stood in the dappled light from a wide oak, in grass and honeysuckle to their knees, and Will felt himself becoming a child again, experiencing delights he hadn't known the first time around. The day was warm and smelled green, and for the moment there seemed no need to rush or plan, to wish or regret. It was enough to watch two blond tykes drivin' down to Atlanta in a 1928 Whippet.

Eleanor's laughter faded, but her smile remained as she studied Will. He leaned against the side of the car with his weight on one foot, arms crossed loosely over his chest. The sunlight lit the tip of his nose. On his lips was a genuine smile. "Well, now, would you lookit there," she said softly.

He glanced up and found her studying his mouth. So she'd

done it; she'd made him smile. It felt as revitalizing as a full belly, and he neither dimmed nor hid it, but rained it on Eleanor Dinsmore.

"Feels good, don't it?" she asked quietly.

His brown eyes softened as they appreciated her green ones. "Yes, ma'am," he replied quietly.

Smiling up at him, noting the pleasure in his eyes, Eleanor thrilled at the realization that she and the boys had succeeded in putting it there. Heaven's sake, what a smile did to Will Parker's face—eyes hooked down at the corners, lids lowered to half-mast, lips softened, the emotionlessness gone. *I could get along with this man quite easy, now I know I can get him to smile.*

His smile traveled from her mouth to her rounded stomach, a tarrying trip. She remained unflinching under his steady regard, wondering what he was thinking. "For life" was a long time. Let him look, let him decide. She'd do the same. She had never cared one way or the other about how people looked. But Will Parker, relaxed and smiling, made a fetching sight, no question about it. Only after the thought struck did she grow uneasy beneath his perusal. His gaze lifted and, meeting hers, made Eleanor blush inside.

"You know, Mrs. Dinsmore—"

Thomas's scream interrupted. Will glanced over his shoulder. "What the—"

Donald Wade screamed—pained and panicked.

Will snapped around and shouted, "Jesus Christ, get them out of there!" He lunged toward the car and hauled Donald Wade out by one arm. "Run! Get away from here! Bees!" Half a dozen of them buzzed around Will's head. One stung him on the neck, another on the wrist, as he reached for a yowling Thomas. By the time he withdrew from the car, the insects swarmed everywhere. Ignoring the stings that fell on him, he swatted the bees off Thomas with his cowboy hat. Eleanor and Donald Wade took off at a run, but just as Will caught up to them Donald Wade tipped over, face first, screaming. Will scooped him up and kept running. His legs were longer than Eleanor's and he soon outdistanced her. Halting uncertainly, he turned back. Behind him, she struggled along at an awkward gait, supporting her stomach with one hand, fanning the air about her head with the other. The bees had thickened and set up an angry hum.

"Mrs. Dinsmore!" he called.

"Take them and run!" Eleanor hollered. "Don't wait for me!"

Will saw the terror in her eyes and paused in indecision.

"Go!" she screamed.

One landed on Thomas's arm. He screamed and began thrashing wildly on Will's arm. Will turned and barreled up the lane, with the boys bellowing and bouncing. When he'd outrun the swarm, he paused, panting, and spun just in time to see Eleanor stumble and go down on her face. His heart seemed to jump into his mouth. He dropped the boys in the middle of the lane and ordered, "Wait here!" Then he was pounding back to her, ignoring the howls behind him. He ran harder than ever before in his life, toward the woman who rolled over slowly and pushed herself up. On one hip she sat, eyes closed, rocking, clutching her stomach. *Oh, Jesus, sonofabitch, Christalmighty*—Will prayed in the only way he knew how—*don't let her be hurt!* He skidded to a halt on one knee, reaching for her.

"Mrs. Dinsmore . . ." he panted.

Her eyes opened. "The boys—are the boys all right?"

"Mostly scared." He took off his hat and flapped angrily at two buzzing bees that hovered about her head. "Git out of here, you sons a bitches!" From up the path the screams continued. Will threw an uncertain glance at the boys, then at Eleanor, fighting panic. He took her by the arms and forced her back. "Lay down here a minute. The bees are gone."

"But the boys—"

"The boys got a few bites, but let 'em howl for a minute. Here now, you lay back like I said." She stopped resisting and wilted to the earth. He stuffed his hat under her. "Here, you put your head on this."

She rested but small pains arced through her abdomen.

"You hurt anything when you fell?" Will asked anxiously, kneeling beside her, wondering what he was supposed to do if she started losing the baby out here in the middle of this weed patch. He watched her stomach lifting and falling in panting beats, wondered if he should touch it, test it. But for what? He sat on one heel, hands resting uncertainly on his thighs.

"I'm okay. Please . . . would you just see after the boys?"

"But you're—"

"I'll just lay here a while. You take the boys up to the well and plaster some mud on their bee stings quick as you can. It'll cut the swelling."

"But I can't just leave you here."

"Yes, you can! Now do as I say, Will Parker! Them bee stings could kill Thomas if he got enough of them, and I already lost their daddy to the bees—don't you understand!" Her eyes filled with tears and Will reluctantly got to his feet. He glanced toward the pair, still sitting abjectly in the middle of the lane, bawling their heads off. He glanced at their mother and pointed authoritatively at her nose.

"Don't you move until I get back." Then he was off at a run again. A moment later he rescued the two squalling boys and trotted on.

"Maa-maaaaw! I want my maa-maaw!" Donald Wade had several welts on his face and hands. One ear was scarlet and puffed. He ground his fists into his eyes.

"Your mama can't run as fast as I can. Hang on and we'll put somethin' cool on them bites."

Baby Thomas was running from all ports and had bites all over, including a mean-looking cluster on his neck. They'd already begun swelling. At the thought of what could happen, should they be swelling as much on the inside as they were on the out, Will made his legs pump harder. He tried to think rationally, to remember if he'd seen where Mrs. Dinsmore kept her bread knife. A picture of the long silver blade flashed through his mind and he imagined having to slip it into Baby Thomas's windpipe, through that soft, pink baby skin. His stomach tumbled at the thought. He wasn't sure he could do it. *Goddammit, don't let this kid choke, you hear me!*

Don't think of it, Parker, just keep runnin'! As long as he's screaming like a banshee he ain't strangling.

Baby Thomas yowled all the way back to the yard. Will hit the mud patch by the pump doing seven miles an hour. His left foot flew west, his right east, and a moment later he landed on his seat with a splat. There he sat with two bawling boys. A bubble formed in Baby Thomas's right nostril. Tears rolled down Donald Wade's cheeks, wetting the bee stings. Will reached up and pulled Donald Wade's fist down.

"Here, don't rub 'em." He sat in the cold, slimy mud and started dabbing it on both boys at once. Thomas fought him tooth and nail, jerking his head back, pushing at Will's hands. But in time the visible welts were covered. The howling subsided to jerky sobs, then the jerky sobs to breathy chuffs of wonder as it dawned on the boys that they were sitting beneath the pump, being plastered with mud. Will unhooked Donald Wade's suspenders, turned his bib down and his shirt up. He treated several stings on his back and belly, then removed the baby's shirt and did likewise.

"They got you, all right," Will confirmed, examining for any he might have missed.

"Are they all right?"

Will's chin snapped up at the sound of Eleanor's voice. She stood at the edge of the puddle, holding his flattened hat in her hand. "I thought I told you to stay put till I could get back to you."

"Are they all right?" she repeated.

"I think so. Are you?"

"I think so."

"Mama . . ." The baby reached toward her, but Will held him in place.

"You sit here a minute, sport. You'll get your mama all muddy."

Suddenly Eleanor's face crinkled and a chuckle began deep in her throat. Will shot her a glare.

"What you laughin' at?"

"Oh, mercy, if you could see the picture you three make." She covered her mouth and doubled forward, laughing. "It just struck me."

Sudden anger boiled up in Will. How dare she stand there cackling when he'd just had five good years scared out of

him! When his heart was knocking so hard his temples hurt!
When he sat with the mud oozing up through his only pair of
jeans! And all because of her and her boys!

"There ain't a damn thing funny, so stop your crowin'!"
He planted both boys on their feet as if they were spades and
he was done shoveling. Clumsily he extracted himself from
the mud and stood bowlegged, like a toddler with full diapers. All the while she giggled behind her hand. Giggled, for
chrissake, when she could be standing there at this very minute having a miscarriage!

He got madder. His head jutted forward. "You crazy,
woman?"

"I reckon I am," she managed through her laughter.
"Leastways, they all say so, don't they?"

Her good humor only intensified his choler. Incensed, he
pointed. "You git up to the house and—and—" But he didn't
know what to advise. Hell, what was he, a midwife?

"I'm going, Mr. Parker, I'm going," Eleanor returned jaun-
tily. She punched out the dome of his hat and plopped it on
her own head, where it fell past her ears. "But how could I
pass by without noticing you sitting there in the mud?" She
reached down for Baby Thomas and Will barked, "I'll take
care of them! Just get up there and see to yourself!"

She turned away, chuckling, and waddled up the path.

Damn woman didn't have the sense God gave a box of
rocks if she didn't realize she should be flat on her back, resting, after the fall she'd taken. It'd take some getting used to,
living with a single-minded woman who laughed at him every chance she got. And didn't she know what a scare she
gave him? Now that it was over, his knees felt like a pair of
rotting tomatoes. That, too, made him mad. Getting watery-
kneed over somebody else's woman, and a stranger to boot!
None too gently, he called after her, "How long does this
mud have to be on 'em?"

From up the path she called, "Ten minutes or so should do
it. I'll fix somethin' to help the itching." She dropped his hat
on the porch step and disappeared inside.

Will removed the boys' shoes and let them play in the
mud. He himself felt twenty pounds heavier with so much

goo hanging off his backside. Now and then he glanced at the house, but she stayed inside. He didn't know if he wanted her to come out or not. Confounded woman, standing there laughing at him while he was trying to calm down her howling kids. And nobody wore his hat. Nobody!

At the house, Eleanor set to work smashing plantain leaves with a mortar and pestle. You really don't know a person till you see him mad. So now she'd seen Will Parker mad, and even riled he was pretty mellow—a good sign. What a sight he'd made, sitting in that mudhole with his dark eyes snapping. If he stayed, years from now they'd laugh about it.

She looked up and saw a sight that made her hands fall still. "Well, would y' look at that," she murmured to herself. Will Parker came stalking toward the house with her two naked sons on his arms. Their rumps looked pink and plump against Parker's hard brown arms, their hands fragile on his wiry shoulders. He had a long-legged stride, but moved as if hurry were a stranger to him. His head was bare, his shirt unbuttoned with the tails flapping, and he scowled deeply. What a sight to see her boys with a man again. Strangers scared them, but in less than a day they had taken to Will Parker. And in the same length of time she'd seen all she needed to be convinced he'd do all right at daddyin', whether the boys were his own or not. He'd be gentle with them. And caring.

She watched from the shadows of the kitchen as he approached the house and paused uncertainly at the foot of the porch steps. She stepped out, noting that his pants and shirttails were dripping.

"Y'all washed in that cold well water?"

"Thought you'd be laying down." His voice still hinted at displeasure.

"I had a pang or two but there's nothin' serious wrong."

"Shouldn't you see a doctor or something?"

"Doctor," she scoffed. "What do I need with a doctor?"

"I could walk to town, see if we could get one out here."

"Town ain't got no use for me, I ain't got no use for it. I'll get along just fine."

Lord a-mercy, she was five months pregnant and she

hadn't seen a doctor? His eyes dropped to the dish she held. "What's that?"

"Crushed plantain leaves for the bites. But we better dry the boys off first. You mind doin' one while I do the other?"

She was gone inside the house before Will could reply. A moment later she returned with two towels, tossed one to Will and sat on the bottom step with the other. While she dried Donald Wade, Will found himself balancing on the balls of his feet with Thomas between his knees. Another first, he thought, awkwardly drawing the child closer. Thomas was pink and gleaming and his little pecker stuck out like a barricade at a railroad crossing. He stared straight into Will's eyes, silent. Will grinned. "Got to dry you off, short stuff," he ventured quietly. This time he didn't feel as ignorant, talking to the little guy. Thomas didn't yowl or fight him, so he figured he was doing all right. He soon learned that babies do little in the way of helping at bath time. Chiefly, Thomas stared, with his lower lip hanging. He had to have his arms lifted, his fingers separated, his body turned this way and that. Will dried all the cracks and crannies, going easy where the bites were worst. Thomas's neck was so small and fragile-looking. His skin was soft and he smelled better than any human being Will had ever been near. Unexpected pleasure stole over the man.

He glanced up and discovered Eleanor watching him.

"How you doin'?" She smiled lazily.

"Not bad."

"First time?"

"Yes, ma'am."

"Never had any o' your own?"

"No, ma'am."

"Never married?"

"No, ma'am."

They fell silent, rubbing down the boys. The mellowness inspired by the task spilled over in Will and softened his annoyance with the woman.

"You scared the hell out of me, you know, falling like that."

"Scared the hell out of myself." Her lazy smile continued.

"Didn't mean to bark at you that way."

"It's all right. I understand." After a pause, she added, "Reckon you're a little shivery in those wet britches yourself."

"They'll dry."

Thomas stood complacently between Will's knees, and Will had no warning until he felt something warming the cold denim on his inner thigh. He glanced down, yelped and leaped to his feet. Baby Thomas unconcernedly bowed his legs and continued relieving himself in a splattering yellow arc.

"Mercy, Thomas, look what you've done!" Eleanor pushed Donald Wade aside and came up off the step. "Oh, mercy, Mr. Parker, I'm sorry." She dropped a self-conscious glance to Will's thigh. "Baby Thomas, he ain't trained yet, you see, and sometimes—well, sometimes—" She fumbled to a stop and turned pink. "I'm awful sorry."

Will stood with feet widespread, surveying the damage. "Like you said, they were wet anyway."

"I'd be happy to wash them for you, and I'll get you something of Glendon's to wear till they're dry," she offered.

He lifted his head and their eyes met. Hers were dismayed, his bemused. A smile began tugging at one corner of his mouth, a smile as slow as his walk, climbing one cheek until an attractive crescent dented it. He snickered. Inside him the laughter built until it erupted. And as Eleanor's chagrin turned to relief, she joined him.

They stood in the sun laughing together for the first time, with the naked children gazing up at them.

When it ended a subtle change had transpired. Their smiles remained while possibilities drifted through their minds.

"So," he said at length, "is this how you initiate all the men who come up here to answer your ad?" he teased drolly.

"You never know what to expect when you got two this little."

"I'll remember that next time."

"I'll get them clothes of Glendon's and you can take a pail of warm water to the barn."

"Appreciate it, ma'am."

For the moment neither of them moved. They stood rooted by surprise and curiosity, now that they'd seen each other in a new light. Her face radiated more than the reflection of her yellow dress. He thought about reaching up and touching it, thought about what her skin might feel like—maybe soft like Donald Wade's and warm beneath the sun. Instead, he bent to retrieve his hat from the step and settled it on his head. From the safety of its shadow he told her, "I've decided to stay, if you still want me."

"I do," she said directly.

The thrill shot straight to his vitals. For as long as he could remember, nobody had wanted Will Parker. Standing in the sun with one foot on her porch steps and her bare children at his feet, he vowed he'd do his best by her or die trying. "And as far as marrying goes, we'll put that off till you feel comfortable. And if it's never, well, fine. I'll be happy in the barn. How's that?"

"Fine," she agreed, flashing him a brief, nervous smile. He wondered if her insides were stirring like his. He might never have known had she not at that very moment dropped her gaze and fussily checked the hair at the back of her neck.

Well, I'll be damned, Will thought. *I'll be ding-dong double damned.*

CHAPTER
6

That first week Will Parker was there Eleanor hardly saw him except at mealtimes. He worked. And worked and worked. Sunup to sunrise, he never stopped. Their first morning had established a routine which they kept by tacit agreement. Will chopped wood, carried it in and made a fire, then filled the water pail and left to do the milking, giving her privacy in the kitchen. She'd be dressed by the time he returned, and would start breakfast while he washed up and shaved. After they'd eaten, he fed the pigs, then disappeared to do whatever tasks he'd set for himself that day.

The first two things he did were to make a slatted wooden grid for beneath the pump and to fix the ladder to his hayloft. He cleaned the barn better than Eleanor ever recalled seeing it—cobwebs, windows and all—hauled the manure out to the orchard and spread the gutters with lime. Next he attacked the hen house, mucking it out completely, fixing some of the broken roosts, putting new screen on the door and the windows, then sinking posts to make an adjacent pen for the chickens. When it was done, he announced that he could use a little help herding the birds inside. They spent an amusing hour trying to do so. At least, Eleanor found it amusing. Will found it exasperating. He flapped his cowboy hat and cursed when a stubborn hen refused to go where he wanted her to.

Eleanor made clucking noises and coaxed the hens with corn. Sometimes she imitated their strut and made up tales about how the hens came to walk that way, the most inventive one about a stubborn black cricket that refused to slither down a hen's throat after it was swallowed. Chickens weren't Will's favorite animal. Goddamn stupid clucks is what he called them. But by the time they got the last one into the hen house, Eleanor had teased a reluctant smile out of him.

Will got along well with the mule, though. Her name was Madam, and Will liked her the moment he saw her wide hairy nose poking around the barn door while he was doing the evening milking. Madam smelled no better than the barn, so as soon as it was clean, Will decided she should be, too. He tethered her by the well and washed her down with Ivory Snow, scrubbing her with a brush and rinsing her with a bucket and rag.

"What the devil are you doing down there?" Eleanor called from the porch.

"Giving Madam a bath."

"What in blazes for?"

"She needs one."

Eleanor had never heard of an animal being scrubbed with Ivory Snow! But it was the durndest thing—Glendon had never been able to do a thing with that stubborn old cuss, but after her bath, Madam did anything Will wanted her to. She followed him around like a trained puppy. Sometimes Eleanor would catch Will looking into Madam's eye and whispering to her, as if the two of them shared secrets.

One evening Will surprised everyone by showing up at the back porch with Madam on a hackamore.

"What's this?" Eleanor stepped to the door, followed by Donald Wade and Baby Thomas.

Will grinned and hoped he wasn't about to make a fool of himself. "Madam and me . . . well, we're goin' to Atlanta and we'll take any passengers who want to come along."

"Atlanta!" Eleanor panicked. Atlanta was forty miles away. What did he want in Atlanta? Then she saw the grin on his lips.

"She said she wanted to see a Claudette Colbert movie," Will explained.

Suddenly Eleanor understood. She released a peal of laughter while Will rubbed Madam's nose. Foolery wasn't easy for him—it was apparent—so she appreciated it all the more. She stood in the doorway with a hand on Donald Wade's head, inquiring, "Anybody want a ride on Madam?" Then, to Will, "You sure she's safe?"

"As a lamb."

From the porch Eleanor watched as Will led the smiling boys around the yard on Madam's back, that back so broad their legs protruded parallel with the earth. Donald Wade rode behind Thomas with his arms folded around the baby's stomach. Surprisingly, Baby Thomas wasn't frightened. He clutched Madam's mane and gurgled in delight.

In the days following that ride, Donald Wade took to trailing after Will just as Madam did. He pitched a fit if Eleanor said, no, it was time for a nap, or no, Will would be doing something that might be dangerous. Nearly always, though, Will would interject, "Let the boy come. He's no trouble."

One morning while she was mixing up a spice cake the pair showed up at the back porch with saws, nails and lumber.

"What're you two up to now?" Eleanor asked, stepping to the screen door, stirring, a bowl against her stomach.

"Will and me are gonna fix the porch floor!" Donald Wade announced proudly. "Ain't we, Will?"

"Sure are, short stuff." Will glanced up at Eleanor. "I could use a piece of wool rag if you got one."

She fetched the rag, then watched while Will patiently sat on the step and showed Donald Wade how to clean a rusty sawblade with steel wool and oil and a piece of soft wool. The saw, she noticed, was miniature. Where he'd found it she didn't know, but it became Donald Wade's. Will had another larger one he'd cleaned and sharpened days ago. When the smaller saw was clean, Will clamped the blade between his knees, took a metal file from his back pocket and showed Donald Wade how a blade is sharpened.

"You ready now?" he asked the boy.

"Yup."

"Then let's get started."

Donald Wade was nothing but a nuisance, getting in Will's way most of the time. But Will's patience with the boy was inexhaustible. He set him up with his own piece of wood on the milking stool, showed him how to anchor it with a knee and get started, then set to work himself, sawing lumber to replace the porch floor. When Donald Wade's saw refused to comply, Will interrupted his work and curled himself over the boy, gripping his small hand, pumping it until a piece of wood fell free. Eleanor felt her heart expand as Donald Wade giggled and looked up with hero-worship in his eyes. "We done it, Will!"

"Yup. Sure did. Now come over here and hand me a few nails."

The nails, Eleanor noticed, were rusty, and the wood slightly warped. But within hours he had the porch looking sturdy again. They christened it by sitting on the new steps in the sun and eating spice cake topped with Herbert's whipped cream.

"You know"—Eleanor smiled at Will—"I sure like the sound of the hammer and saw around the place again."

"And I like the smell of spice cake bakin' while I work."

The following day they painted the entire porch—floor in brick red, and posts in white.

At the "New Porch Party" she served gingerbread and whipped cream. He ate enough for two men and she loved watching him. He put away three pieces, then rubbed his stomach and sighed. "That was mighty good gingerbread, ma'am." He never failed to show appreciation, though never wordily. "Fine dinner, ma'am," or "Much obliged for supper, ma'am." But his thanks made her efforts seem worthwhile and filled her with a sense of accomplishment she'd never known before.

He loved his sweets and couldn't seem to get enough of them. One day when she hadn't fixed dessert he looked let-down, but made no remarks. An hour after the noon meal she found a bucket of ripe quince sitting on the porch step.

The pie—she'd forgotten. She smiled at his reminder and

glanced across the yard. He was nowhere to be seen as she picked up the bucket and headed inside and began to mix up a piecrust.

For Will Parker those first couple of weeks at Eleanor Dinsmore's place were unadulterated heaven. The work— why, hell—the work was a privilege, the idea that he could choose what he wanted to do each day. He could cut wood, patch porch floors, clean barns or wash mules. Anything he chose, and nobody said, "Boy, you supposed to be here? Boy, who tol' you to do that?" Madam was a pleasurable animal, reminded him of the days when he'd done wrangling and had had a horse of his own. He flat liked everything about Madam, from the hairs on her lumpy nose to her long, curved eyelashes. And at night now, he brought her into the barn and made his own bed beside her in one of the box stalls that were cleaned and smelled of sweet grass.

Then came morning, every one better than the last. Morning and Donald Wade trailing along, providing company and doting on every word Will said. The boy was turning out to be a real surprise. Some of the things that kid came up with! One day when he was holding the hammer for Will while Will stretched wire around the chicken pen, he stared at an orange hen and asked pensively, "Hey, Will, how come chickens ain't got lips?" Another day he and Will were digging through a bunch of junk, searching for hinges in a dark tool shed when a suspicious odor began tainting the air around them. Donald Wade straightened abruptly and said, "Oh-oh! One of us farted, didn't we?"

But Donald Wade was more than merely amusing. He was curious, bright, and worshiped the shadow Will cast. Will's little sidekick, following everywhere—"I'll help, Will!"— getting his head in the way, standing on the screwdriver, dropping the nails in the grass. But Will wouldn't have changed a minute of it. He found he liked teaching the boy. He learned how by watching Eleanor. Only Will taught different things. Men's things. The names of the tools, the proper way to hold them, how to put a rivet through leather, how to brace a screen door and make it stronger, how to trim a mule's hoof.

The work and Donald Wade were only part of what made his days blissful. The food—God, the food. All he had to do was walk up to the house and take it, cut a piece of spice cake from a pan or butter a bun. What he liked best was taking something sweet outside and eating it as he ambled back toward some half-finished project of his choice. Quince pie—damn, but that woman could make quince pie, could make anything, actually. But she had quince pie down to an art.

He was gaining weight. Already the waistband on his own jeans was tight, and it felt good to work in Glendon Dinsmore's roomy overalls. Odd, how she volunteered anything at all of her husband's without seeming to resent Will's using it—toothbrush, razor, clothes, even dropping the hems of the pants to accommodate Will's longer legs.

But his gratitude was extended for far more than creature comforts. She'd offered him trust, had given him pride again, and enthusiasm at the break of each new day. She'd shared her children who'd brought a new dimension of happiness into his life. She'd brought back his smile.

There was nothing he couldn't accomplish. Nothing he wouldn't try. He wanted to do it all at once.

As the days passed, the improvements he'd made began tallying up. The yard looked better, and the back porch. The eggs were easy to find since the hens were confined to the hen house and, slowly but surely, the woodpile was changing contours. As the place grew neater, so did Eleanor Dinsmore. She wore shoes and anklets now, and a clean apron and dress every morning with a bright hair ribbon to match. She washed her hair twice a week, and he'd been right about it. Clean, it took on a honey glow.

Sometimes when they'd meet in the kitchen, he'd look at her a second time and think, *You look pretty this morning, Mrs. Dinsmore.* But he could never say it, lest she think he was after something more than creature comforts. Truth to tell, it had been a long, long time, but always in the back of his mind lingered the fact that he'd spent time in prison, and what for. Because of it, he kept a careful distance.

Besides, he had a lot more to do before he'd proved he was worth keeping. He wanted to finish the plastering, give the house a coat of paint, improve the road, get rid of the junk cars, make the orchard produce again, and the bees ... The list seemed endless. But Will soon realized he didn't know how to do all that.

"Has Whitney got a library?" he asked one day in early September.

Eleanor glanced up from the collar she was turning. "In the town hall. Why?"

"I need to learn about apples and bees."

Will sensed her defiance even before she spoke.

"Bees?"

He fixed his eyes on her and let them speak for him. He'd learned by now it was the best way to deal with her when they disagreed.

"You know about libraries—how to use 'em, I mean?"

"In prison I read all I could. They had a library there."

"Oh." It was one of the rare times he'd mentioned prison, but he didn't elaborate. Instead, he went on questioning. "Did your husband have one of those veiled hats, and things to tend bees with?" He didn't know a lot, but he knew he'd need certain equipment.

"Somewhere."

"Think you could look around for me? See if you can find 'em?"

Fear flashed through her, followed quickly by obstinacy. "I don't want you messin' with those bees."

"I won't mess with 'em till I know what I'm doing."

"No!"

He didn't want to argue with her, and he understood her fear of the bees. But it made no sense to let the hives sit empty when honey could bring in cold, hard cash. The best way to soften her might be by being soft himself.

"I'd appreciate it if you'd look for them," he told her kindly, then pushed back from the dinner table and reached for his hat. "I'll be walkin' into town this afternoon to the library. If you'd like I can take whatever eggs you got and try to sell them there."

He took a bucket of warm water and the shaving gear down to the barn and came back half an hour later all spiffed up in his own freshly laundered jeans and shirt. When they met in the kitchen, her mouth still looked stubborn.

"I'm leaving now. How about those eggs?"

She refused to speak to him, but thumbed at the five dozen eggs sitting on the porch in a slatted wooden crate.

They were going to be heavy, but let him carry them, she thought stubbornly. If he wanted to go sellin' eggs to the creeps in town, and learning about bees, and getting all money-hungry, let him carry them!

She pretended not to watch him heft the crate, but her curiosity was aroused when he set it back down and disappeared around the back of the house. A minute later he returned pulling Donald Wade's wooden wagon. He loaded the egg crate on board only to discover the handle was too short for his tall frame. She watched, gratified when with his first steps his heels hooked on the front of the wagon. Five minutes later—still stubbornly silent—she watched him pull the wagon down the road by a length of stiff wire twisted to the handle.

Go on, then! Run to town and listen to every word they say! And come back with coins jingling in your pocket! And read up on bees and apples and anything else you want! But don't expect me to make it easy on you!

Gladys Beasley sat behind a pulpit-shaped desk, tamping the tops of the library cards in their recessed bin. They were already flat as a stove lid, but she tamped them anyway. And aligned the rubber stamp with the seam in the varnished wood. And centered her ink pen on its concave rest. And adjusted her nameplate—Gladys Beasley, Head Librarian—on the high desk ledge. And picked up a stack of magazines and centered her chair in the kneehole. Fussily. Unnecessarily.

Order was the greatest force in Gladys Beasley's life. Order and regimentation. She had run the Carnegie Municipal Library of Whitney, Georgia, for forty-one years, ever since Mr. Carnegie himself had made its erection possible with an endowment to the town. Miss Beasley had ordered the initial titles even before the shelves themselves were installed, and had been working in the hallowed building ever since. During those forty-one years she had sent more than one feckless assistant home in tears over a failure to align the spine of a book with the edge of a shelf.

She walked like a Hessian soldier, in brisk, no-nonsense steps on practical, black Cuban-heeled oxfords to which the shoemaker had added a special rubber heel which buffered her footfalls on the hardwood floors of her domain. If there was one thing that ired Gladys worse than slipshod shelving, it was cleats! Anyone who wore them in *her* library and expected to be allowed inside again had better choose different shoes next time!

She launched herself toward the magazine rack, imposing breasts carried like heavy artillery, her trunk held erect by the most expensive elastic and coutil girdle the Sears Roebuck catalogue had to offer—the one tactfully recommended for those "with excess flesh at the diaphragm." Her jersey dress—white squiggles on a background the color of something already digested—hung straight as a stovepipe from her bulbous hips to her club-shaped calves and made not so much as a rustle when she moved.

She replaced three *Saturday Evening Post* magazines, tamped the stack, aligned it with the edge of the shelf and marched along the row of tall fanlight windows, checking the wooden ribbing between the panes to be sure Levander Sprague, the custodian, hadn't shirked. Levander was getting old. His eyesight wasn't what it used to be, and lately she'd had to upbraid him for his careless dusting. Satisfied today, however, she returned to her duties at the central desk, located smack in front of double maple doors—closed—that led to wide interior steps at the bottom of which were the main doors of the building.

Overdue notices—bah!—there should be no such thing. Anyone who couldn't return a book on time should simply be disallowed the privilege of using the library again. That would put an end to the need for overdue notices, but quick. Gladys's mouth was puckered so tightly it all but disappeared as she penned addresses on the penny postcards.

She heard footfalls mounting the interior steps. A brass knob turned and a stranger stepped in, a tall, spare man dressed like a cowboy. He paused, letting his eyes scan the room, the desk, and her, then silently nodded and tipped his hat.

Gladys's prim mouth relaxed as she returned the nod. The genteel art of hat doffing had become nearly obsolete—what was the world coming to?

He took a long time perusing the place before moving. When he did, there were no cleats. He went directly, quietly, to the card catalogue, slid out the *B*'s, flipped through the cards and studied them for some time. He closed the drawer soundlessly, then scanned the sunlit room before moving between the oak tables to nonfiction. There were library patrons who, ill at ease when alone in the vast room with Miss Beasley, found it necessary to whistle softly through their teeth while scanning the shelves. He didn't. He selected a book from the 600's—Practical Science—moved on to select another and brought them straight to the checkout desk.

"Good afternoon," Gladys greeted in a discreet whisper.

"Afternoon, ma'am." Will touched his hat brim and followed her lead, speaking quietly.

"I see you found what you were looking for."

"Yes, ma'am. I'd like to check these out."

"Do you have a card?"

"No, ma'am, but I'd like to get one."

She moved with military precision, yanking a drawer open, finding a blank card, snapping it on the desktop off the edge of a tidily trimmed fingernail. The nail was virgin, Will was sure, never stained by polish. She closed the drawer with her girded torso, all the while holding her lips as if they were the mounting for a five-karat diamond. When she moved, her head snapped left and right, fanning the air with a smell resembling carnations and cloves. The light from one of the big windows glanced off her rimless glasses and caught the rows of uniform silver-blue ringlets between which the warp and woof of her skull shone pink. She dipped a pen in ink, then held it poised above the card.

"Name?"

"Will Parker."

"Parker, Will," she transposed aloud while entering the information on the first blank.

"And you're a resident of Whitney, are you?"

"Yes, ma'am."

"Address?"

"Ahh . . ." He rubbed his nose with a knuckle. "Rock Creek Road."

She glanced up with eyes as exacting as calipers, then wrote again while informing him, "I'll need some form of identification to verify your residency." When he neither spoke nor moved, her head snapped up. "Anything will do. Even a letter with a canceled postmark showing your mailing address."

"I don't have anything."

"Nothing?"

"I haven't lived there long."

She set down her pen with a long-suffering air. "Well, Mr. Parker, I'm sure you understand, I cannot simply loan books to anyone who walks in here unless I can be assured they're residents. This is a municipal library. By its very meaning, the word *municipal* dictates who shall use this facility. *Of a town*, it means, thus this library is maintained *by* the residents of Whitney, *for* the residents of Whitney. I wouldn't be a very responsible librarian if I didn't demand some identification now, would I?" She carefully placed the card aside, then crossed her hands on the desktop, giving the distinct impression that she was displeased at having her time and her card wasted.

She expected him to argue, as most did at such an impasse. Instead, he backed up a step, pulled his hat brim low and studied her silently for several seconds. Then, without a word, he nodded, scooped the books against his hip and returned to the nonfiction side where he settled himself on one of the hard oak armchairs in a strong shaft of sunlight, opened a book and began reading.

There were several criteria by which Gladys Beasley judged her library patrons. Cleats, vocal volume, nondisruptiveness and respect for books and furniture. Mr. Parker passed on all counts. She'd rarely seen anyone read more intently, with less fidgeting. He moved only to turn a page and occasionally to follow along with his finger, closing his eyes as if committing a passage to memory. Furthermore, he neither slouched nor abused the opposite chair by using it as a footstool. He sat with his hat brim pulled low, elbows on the table, knees lolling but boots on the floor. The book lay flat on the table where it belonged, instead of torqued against his belly, which was exceedingly hard on spines. Neither did he lick his finger before turning the page—filthy, germ-spreading habit!

Normally, if people came in and asked for a paper and pencil, Miss Beasley gave them a tongue-lashing instead, about responsibility and planning ahead. But Will Parker's deportment and concentration raised within her regret for having had to deny him a borrower's card. So she bent her own standard.

"I thought perhaps you might need these," she whispered, placing a pencil and paper at his elbow.

Will's head snapped up. His shoulders straightened. "Much obliged, ma'am."

She folded her hands over her portly belly. "Ah, you're reading about bees."

"And apples. Yes, ma'am."

"For what purpose, Mr. Parker?"

"I'd like to raise 'em."

She cocked one eyebrow and thought a moment. "I might have some pamphlets in the back from the extension office that would help."

"Maybe next time, ma'am. I got all I can handle here today."

She offered a tight smile and left him to his studies, trailing a scent strong enough to eat through concrete.

It was mid-afternoon. The only things moving in town were the flies on the ice cream scoop. Lula Peak was bored to distraction. She sat on the end stool in an empty Vickery's Cafe, grateful when even her brassiere strap slipped down and she had to reach inside her black and white uniform to pull it up. God, this town was going to turn her into a cadaver before she even kicked the bucket! She could die of boredom right here on the barstool and the supper customers would come in and say, "Evenin', Lula, I'll have the usual," and not even realize she was a goner until thirty minutes later when their blue plate specials hadn't arrived.

Lula yawned, leaving her hand inside her uniform, absently rubbing her shoulder. Being a sensual person, Lula liked touching herself. Sure as hell nobody else around this miserable godforsaken town knew how to do it right. Harley, that dumb ass, didn't know the first thing about finesse when he touched a woman. Finesse. Lula liked the word. She'd just read it in an article on how to better yourself. Yeah, finesse, that's what Lula needed, a man with a little finesse, a *better* man in the sack than Harley-Dumb-Ass-Overmire.

Lula suppressed a yawn, stretched her arms wide and thrust her ribs out, swiveling idly toward the window. Suddenly she rocketed from the stool.

Christ, it was him, walking along the street pulling a kid's wagon. She ran her eyes speculatively over his lanky form, concentrating on his narrow hips and swaying pelvis as he ambled along the town square and nodded at Norris and Nat McCready, those two decrepit old bachelor brothers who spent their dotage whittling on the benches across the street. Lula hustled to the screen door and posed behind it. *Look over here, Parker, it's better than them two boring old turds.*

But he moved on without glancing toward Vickery's. Lula grabbed a broom and stepped into the sun, making an ill disguised pretense of sweeping the sidewalk while watching his flat posterior continue around the square. He left the wagon in the shade of the town hall steps and went inside.

So did Lula. Back into Vickery's to thrust the broom aside and glance impatiently at the clock. Two-thirty. She drummed her long orange nails across the countertop, plunked herself onto the end stool and waited for five minutes. Agitated. Peeved. Nobody was going to come in here for anything more than a glass of iced tea and she knew it. Not until at least five-thirty. Old Man Vickery would be madder than Cooter Brown if he found out she'd slipped away and left the place untended. But she could tell him she'd run over to the library for a magazine and hadn't been gone a minute.

Deciding, she twisted off the stool and flung off her three-pointed apron. The matching headpiece followed as she whipped out her compact. A dash of fresh blaze orange on her lips, a check of the seams in her silk stockings and she was out the door.

Gladys Beasley looked up as the door opened a second time that afternoon. Her mouth puckered and her chin tripled.

"Afternoon, Mizz Beasley," Lula chirped, her voice ringing off the twelve-foot ceiling.

"Shh! Read the sign!"

Lula glanced at the sign on the front of Miss Beasley's desk: SILENCE IS GOLDEN. "Oh, sorry," she whispered, covering her mouth and giggling. She glanced around—ceiling, walls, windows—as if she'd never seen the place before, which wasn't far from the truth. Lula was the kind of woman who read *True Confessions,* and Gladys didn't stoop to using the taxpayers' money for smut like that. Lula stepped farther inside.

Cleats!

"Shh!"

"Oh, sorry. I'll tiptoe."

Will Parker glanced up, scanned Lula disinterestedly and resumed his reading.

The library was U-shaped, wrapped around the entry steps. Miss Beasley's desk, backed by her private workroom, separated the huge room into two distinct parts. To the right was fiction. To the left nonfiction. Lula had never been on the left where Parker sat now. Remembering about finesse, she moved to the right first, drifting along the shelves, glancing up, then down, as if examining the titles for something interesting. She removed a book bound in emerald green—the exact shade of a dress she'd been eyeing over at Cartersville in the Federated Store. Classy color that'd look swell with her new Tropical Flame nail polish—she spread her hands on the book cover and tipped her head approvingly. She'd have to think up something good to entice Harley to buy that little number for her. She stuck the book back in its slot and moved to another. Melville. Hey, she'd heard of this guy! Must've done something swell. But the spine was too wide and the printing too small, so she rammed it back on the shelf and looked further.

Lula *finessed* her way through a full ten minutes of fiction before finally tiptoeing past Miss Beasley to the other side. She twiddled two fingers as she passed, then clamped her hands at the base of her spine, thrusting her breasts into bold relief.

Gladys tightened her buttocks and followed where Lula had been, pushing in a total of eleven books she'd left beetling over the edges of the shelves.

Lula found the left side arranged much as the right, a spacious room with fanlight windows facing the street. Bookshelves filled the space between the windows and the floor, and covered the remaining three walls. The entire center of the room was taken up by sturdy oak tables and chairs. Lula sidled around the perimeter of the room without so much as peeking at Will. She grazed one fingertip along the edge of a shelf, then sucked it with studied provocativeness. She turned a corner, eased on to where a bank of shelves ran perpendicular to the wall and moved between them, putting herself in profile to Will, should he care to turn his head and see. She clasped her hands at the base of her spine, creating her best silhouette, watching askance to see if he'd glance over. After several minutes, when he hadn't, she grabbed a biography of Beethoven and, while turning its pages, eyed Will discreetly.

God, was he good looking. And that cowboy hat did things to her insides, the way he wore it low, shadowing his eyes in the glare of the afternoon sun. *Still waters*, she thought, taken by the way he sat with one finger under a page, so unmoving she wished she were a fly so she could land on his nose. What a nose. Long instead of pug like *some* she knew. Nice mouth, too. Ooo, would she like to get into that.

He leaned forward to write something and she ran her eyes all over him, down his tapered chest and slim hips to the cowboy boots beneath the table, back up to his crotch. He dropped his pencil and sat back, giving her a clearer profile shot of it.

Lula felt the old itch begin.

He sat there reading his book the way all the "brains" used to read in school while Lula thought about bettering herself. When she could stand it no longer she took Beethoven over and dropped it on the table across from him.

"This seat taken?" she drawled, inverting her wrists, leaning on the tabletop so that her breast buttons strained. His chin rose slowly. As the brim of the cowboy hat lifted, she got a load of deep brown eyes with lashes as long as spaghetti, and a mouth that old Lula had plenty of plans for.

"No, ma'am," he answered quietly. Without moving more than his head, he returned to his reading.

"Mind if I sit here?"

"Go ahead." His attention remained on the book.

"Watcha studyin'?"

"Bees."

"Hey, how about that! I'm studyin' *B*'s, too." She held up her book. "Beethoven." In school she'd liked music, so she pronounced it correctly. "He wrote music, back when guys wore wigs and stuff, you know?"

Again Will refused to glance up. "Yeah, I know."

"Well . . ." The chair screeched as Lula pulled it out. She flounced down, crossed her legs, opened the book and flapped its pages in rhythm with her wagging calf. "So. Haven't seen y' around. Where y' been keepin' yourself?"

He perused her noncommittally, wondering if he should bother to answer. Mercy, she was one hard-looking woman. She had so much hair piled onto her forehead it looked as if she could use a neck brace. Her mouth was painted the color of a chili pepper and she wore too much rouge, too high on her cheeks, in too precise a pattern. She overlapped her wrists on the table edge and rested her breasts on them. They jutted, giving him a clearer shot of cleavage. It pleased Will to let her know he didn't want any.

"Up at Mrs. Dinsmore's place."

"Crazy Elly's? My, my. How is she?" When Will declined to answer, she leaned closer and inquired, "You know why they call her crazy, don't you? Did she tell you?" Against his will, he became curious, but it would seem like an offense against Mrs. Dinsmore to encourage Lula, so he remained silent. Lula, however, needed no encouragement. "They locked her in that house when she was a baby and pulled all the shades down and didn't let her out until the law forced 'em to—to go to school—and then they only turned her loose six hours a day and locked her up again, nights." She sat back smugly. "Ah, so you didn't know." Lula smiled knowingly. "Well, ask her about it sometime. Ask her if she didn't live in that deserted house down by school. You know—the one with the picket fence around it and the bats flyin' in the attic window?" Lula leaned closer and added conspiratorially, "If I were you, I wouldn't hang around up there at her place any longer than I had to. Give you a bad reputation, if you know what I mean. I mean, that woman ain't wrapped too tight." Lula sat back as if in a chaise, letting her eyelids droop, toying absently with the cover of Beethoven, lifting it, letting it drop with soft repeated *plops*. "I know it's tough being new around town. I mean, you must be bored as hell if you have to spend your time in a place like this." Lula's eyes made a quick swerve around the bookshelves, then came back to him. "But if you need somebody to show y' around, I'd be happy to." Beneath the table her toe stroked Will's calf. "I got me a little bungalow just four houses off the town square on Pecan Street—"

"Excuse me, ma'am," Will interrupted, rising. "Got some eggs out in the sun that need selling. I'd better see to 'em."

Lula smirked, watching him move to the bookshelves. He'd got the message. Oh, he'd got it all right—loud and clear. She'd seen him jump when her foot touched his leg. She watched him slip one book into place, then squat down to replace the other. Before he could escape, she sidled into the aisle behind him, trapping him between the two tiers of shelves. When he rose to his feet and turned, she was gratified by his quick blush. "If you're interested in my offer, I work most days at Vickery's. I'm off at eight, though." She slipped one finger between his shirt buttons and ran it up and down, across hair and hard skin. Putting on her best kewpie doll face, Lula whispered, "See y' round, Parker."

As she swung away, exaggeratedly waggling her hips, Will glanced across the sunlit room to find the librarian's censoring eyes taking in the whole scene. Her attention immediately snapped elsewhere, but even from this distance Will saw how tightly her lips pursed. He felt shaky inside, almost violated. Women like Lula were a clear path to trouble. There was a time when he'd have taken her up on the offer and enjoyed every minute of it. But not anymore. Now all he wanted was to be left to live his life in peace, and that peace meant Eleanor Dinsmore's place. He suddenly felt a deep need to get back there.

Lula was gone, cleats clicking, by the time Will reached the main desk.

"Much obliged for the use of the paper and pencil, ma'am."

Gladys Beasley's head snapped up. The distaste was ripe on her face. "You're welcome."

Will was cut to the quick by her silent rebuff. A man didn't have to make a move on a hot-blooded woman like that, all he had to do was be in the same pigeonhole with her. Especially—Will supposed—if he'd done time for killing a whore in a Texas whorehouse and people around town knew it.

He rolled his notes into a cylinder and stood his ground. "I was wonderin', ma'am—"

"Yes?" she snapped, lifting her head sharply, her mouth no larger than a keyhole.

"I got a job. I'm workin' as a hired hand for Mrs. Glendon Dinsmore. If she'd come in here and tell you I work for her, would that be enough to get me a library card?"

"She won't come in."

"She won't?"

"I don't believe so. Since she married she's chosen to live as a recluse. I'm sorry, I can't bend the rules." She picked up her pen, made a check on a list, then relented. "However, depending upon how long you've been working for her, and how long you intend to stay, if she would verify your employment in writing, I should think that would be enough proof of residency."

Will Parker flashed a relieved smile, hooked one thumb in his hind pocket and backed off boyishly, melting the ice from Gladys Beasley's heart. "I'll make sure she writes it. Much obliged, ma'am." He headed for the door, then stopped and swung back. "Oh. How late you open?"

"Until eight o'clock weekdays, five Saturdays, and of course, we're closed Sundays."

He tipped his hat again and promised, "I'll be back."

As he turned the doorknob she called, "Oh, Mr. Parker?"

"Ma'am?"

"How is Eleanor?"

Will sensed that this inquiry was wholly different from Lula's. He stood at the door, adjusting his impression of Gladys Beasley. "She's fine, ma'am. Five months pregnant for the third time, but healthy and happy, I think."

"For the third time. My. I remember her as a child, coming in with Miss Buttry's fifth grade class—or was it Miss Natwick's sixth? She always seemed a bright child. Bright and inquisitive. Greet her for me, if you will."

It was the first truly friendly gesture Will had experienced since coming to Whitney. It erased all the sour taste left by Lula and made him feel suddenly warm inside.

"I'll do that. Thanks, Mrs. Beasley."

"Miss Beasley."

"Miss Beasley. Oh, by the way. I got a few dozen eggs I'd like to sell. Where should I try?"

Exactly what it was, Gladys didn't know—perhaps the way he'd assumed she had a husband, or the way he'd rejected the advances of that bleached whore, Lula, or perhaps nothing more than the way his smile had transformed his face at the news that he could have a library card after all. For whatever reason, Gladys found herself answering, "I could use a dozen myself, Mr. Parker."

"You could? Well . . . well, fine!" Again he flashed a smile.

"The rest you might take to Purdy's General, right across the square."

"Purdy's. Good. Well, let me go out and— Oh—" His thumb came out of the pocket, his hand hung loosely at his hip. "I just remembered. They're all in one crate."

"Put them in this." She handed him a small cardboard filing box.

He accepted it, nodded silently and went out. When he returned, she asked, "How much will that be?" She rummaged through a black coin purse and didn't look up until realizing he hadn't answered. "How much, Mr. Parker?"

"Well, I don't rightly know."

"You don't?"

"No, ma'am. They're Mrs. Dinsmore's eggs and these're the first I've sold for her."

"I believe the current price is twenty-four cents a dozen. I'll give you twenty-five, since I'm sure they're fresher than those at Calvin Purdy's store, and since they're hand delivered." She handed him a quarter, which he was reluctant to accept, knowing it was higher than the market value. "Well, here, take it! And next week, if you have more, I'll take another dozen."

He took the coin and nodded. "Thank you, ma'am. 'Preciate it and I know Mrs. Dinsmore will, too. I'll be sure to tell her you said hello."

When he was gone Gladys Beasley snapped her black coin purse shut, but held it a moment, studying the door. Now *that* was a nice young man. She didn't know why, but she liked him. Well, yes, she did know why. She fancied herself an astute judge of character, particularly when it came to inquiring minds. His was apparent by his familiarity with the card catalogue, his ability to locate what he wanted without her assistance and his total absorption in his study, to say nothing of his eagerness to own a borrower's card.

And, too, he was willing to go back out to Rock Creek Road and work for Eleanor Dinsmore even after the pernicious twaddle spewed by Lula Peak. Gladys had heard enough to know what that harlot was trying to do—how could anyone have missed it in this echoing vault of a building? And more power to Will Parker for turning his back on that hussy. Gladys had never been able to understand what

people got out of spreading destructive gossip. Poor Eleanor
had never been given a fair shake by the people of this town,
to say nothing of her own family. Her grandmother, Lottie
McCallaster, had always been eccentric, a religious fanatic
who attended every tent revival within fifty miles of Whitney.
She was said to have fallen to her knees and rolled in the
throes of her religious conviction, and it was well known she
got baptized every time a traveling salvation man called for
sinners to become washed in the Blood. She'd finally nabbed
herself a self-proclaimed man of God, a fire-and-brimstone
preacher named Albert See who'd married her, gotten her in
a family way, installed her in a house at the edge of town and
gone on circuit, leaving her to raise her daughter, Chloe,
chiefly alone.

Chloe had been a silent wraith of a girl, with eyes as large
as horse chestnuts, dominated by Lottie, subjected to her fa-
naticism. How a girl like that, who was scarcely ever out of
her mother's scrutiny, had managed to get pregnant remained
a mystery. Yet she had. And afterward, Lottie had never
shown her face again, nor allowed Chloe to, or the child,
Eleanor, until the truant officer had forced them to let her out
to attend school, threatening to have the child legally removed to a foster home unless they complied.

What the town librarian remembered best about Eleanor as
a child was her awe of the spacious library, and of her freedom to move through it without reprimand, and how she
would stand in the generous fanlight windows with the sun
pouring in, absorbing it as if she could never get enough. And
who could blame her—poor thing?

Gladys Beasley wasn't an overly imaginative woman, but
even so, she shuddered at the thought of what life must have
been like for the poor bastard child, Eleanor, living in that
house behind the green shades, like one buried alive.

She'd almost be willing to give Will Parker a borrower's
card on the strength of his befriending Eleanor alone, now
that she knew of it. And when she marched back to nonfiction and found a biography of Beethoven lying on a table, but
"Bees" and "Apples" tucked flush in their slots, she knew
she'd judged Will Parker correctly.

CHAPTER

7

Calvin Purdy bought the eggs at twenty-four cents a dozen. The money belonged to Mrs. Dinsmore, but Will had nine dollars of his own buttoned safely into his breast pocket. He touched it—hard and reassuring behind the blue chambray— and thought of taking something to her. Just because people called her crazy and she wasn't. Just because she'd been locked inside some house most of her life. And because they'd had words before he left. But what should he take? She wasn't the perfume type. And anyway, perfume seemed too personal. He'd heard that men bought ribbons for ladies, but he'd feel silly walking up to Purdy and asking him to cut a length of yellow silk ribbon to match her yellow maternity dress. Candy? Food made Eleanor sick. She pecked like a sparrow, hardly ate a thing.

In the end he chose a small figurine of a bluebird, gaily painted. She liked birds, and there wasn't much around her house in the way of decorations. The bluebird cost him twenty-nine cents, and he spent an additional dime on two chocolate bars for the boys. Pocketing his change, he felt a keen exhilaration to get home.

On his way out of town he passed the house with the tilting picket fence surrounding it like the decaying ribs of a dead animal. He stopped to stare, involuntarily fascinated by the derelict appearance of the place, the grass choking the front steps, the rangy morning glories tangling around the doorknob and up a rickety trellis on the front stoop. Tattered green shades covered the windows, their bottoms shredded into ribbons. Gazing at them, he shivered, yet was tempted to investigate closer, to peek inside. But the shades seemed to warn him away.

They'd locked her in? And pulled down the shades? A woman like Eleanor, who loved birds and katydids and the sky and the orchard? Again Will shivered and hurried on with his cargo of two chocolate bars and a glass bluebird, wishing he could have bought her more. It was a curious feeling for a man to whom gift-giving was foreign. The exchange of gifts implied that a person had both friends and money, but Will had seldom known both at once. Though he'd often imagined how exciting it would be to get gifts, he'd never expected this exhilaration at giving them. But now that he knew about Eleanor Dinsmore's past, he felt provoked by a great impatience to make reparation for the kindness she'd been robbed of as a child.

Would she still be peeved at him? An unexpected ripple of disquiet swept through him at the thought. He stalked along, studying the ground. The wagon rattled behind him. How do a man and woman learn to make up their differences? At thirty years old, Will didn't know, but it suddenly became vital that he learn. Always before, if a woman harassed him, he moved on. This was different, Eleanor Dinsmore was different. She was a good mother, a fine woman who'd been locked in a house and called crazy, and if he didn't tell her she wasn't, who would?

Eleanor had been miserable ever since Will left. She'd been churlish and snappy with him and he'd been gone nearly three hours on a trip that should have taken only half that time and she was sure he wasn't coming back. *It's your own fault, Elly. You can't treat a free man that way and expect him to come back for more.*

She put supper on to cook and looked out the back door every three minutes. No Will. She put on a clean dress and combed her hair, twisting it tight and neat on her head. She studied her wide, disturbed eyes in the small mirror on the kitchen shelf, thinking of his face trimmed with shaving lather. *He ain't comin' back, fool. He's ten miles in the other direction by now and how you gonna like choppin' that wood in the morning? And how you gonna like mealtimes lookin' at his empty chair? And talkin' to nobody but the boys?* Closing her eyes, she wrapped her fists around one another and pressed them to her mouth. *I need you, Parker. Please come back.*

As Will hurried up the rutted driveway he heard his own heart drumming in his ears. Reaching the edge of the clearing, his footsteps faltered: she was waiting on the porch. Waiting for him, Will Parker. Dressed in her yellow outfit with her hair freshly combed, the boys romping at her ankles and the smell of supper drifting clear across the yard. She raised a hand and waved. "What took you so long? I was worried."

Not only waiting, but worried. A burst of elation ricocheted through his body as he smiled and stretched his stride.

"Studying takes time."

"Will!" Donald Wade came running. "Hey, Will!" He collided with Will's knees and clung, head back and hair hanging, making the welcome complete. Will roughed the boy's silky hair.

"Hi, short stuff. How's things around here?"

"Everything's peachy." He fell into step beside Will, helping to pull the wagon.

"What'd you do while I was gone?"

"Mama made me take a nap." Donald Wade made a distasteful face.

"A nap, huh?" Reaching the bottom of the porch steps, Will dropped the wagon handle and lifted his eyes to the woman above him. "Did she take one with you?"

"No. She took a bath in the washtub."

"Donald Wade, you hush now, you hear?" Eleanor chided, her cheeks turning suspiciously bright. Then, to Will, "How'd you do?"

"Did good." He handed her the money. "Miss Beasley at the library took one dozen eggs for twenty-five cents, and I sold the rest to Calvin Purdy for twenty-four cents a dozen. It's all there, a dollar twenty-one. Miss Beasley said to tell you hello."

"She did?" Eleanor's palm hung in midair, the money forgotten.

"Said she remembers you comin' in with Miss Buttry's fifth grade class or Miss Natwick's sixth."

"Well, imagine that." Her smile was all amazement and wide eyes. "Who'd have thought she'd remember me?"

"She did, though."

"I never even thought she knew my name."

Will grinned. "Don't think there's much that woman doesn't know."

Eleanor laughed, remembering the librarian.

"I'll bet it was pretty in the library, wasn't it?"

"Sure was. Bright." Will gestured in the air. "With big windows, rounded at the top. Smelled good, too."

"Did you get your card?"

"Couldn't. Not without you. Miss Beasley says you'll have to verify that I work for you."

"You mean go in there?" The animation left Elly's face and her voice quieted. "Oh, I don't think I could do that."

Yesterday he'd have asked why. Today he only replied, "You can write a note. She said that'd be okay and I can bring it next time I go in. Have to go in next week again. Miss Beasley said she'll want another dozen eggs."

"She did?" Eleanor's elation returned as quickly as it had fled.

"That's right. And, you know, I was thinking." Will tipped his hat brim back, hooked one boot on the bottom step and braced a hand on the knee. "If you were to pack the extra cream in pint jars I think I could sell it, too. Make a little extra."

She couldn't resist teasing, "You gonna turn into one of those men who loves money, Mr. Parker?"

He knew full well there was more than teasing behind the remark—there was her very real aversion to town. A recluse,

Miss Beasley had called her. Was she really? To the point of avoiding contact with people even if it meant making money? She hadn't even bothered to count what he'd handed her. He supposed this was something they'd have to work out eventually. "No, ma'am." He withdrew his boot from the step. "It's just that I don't see any sense in losing the opportunity to make it."

Donald Wade spotted the brown paper bag and tugged Will's sleeve. "Hey, Will, what you got in there?"

Will reluctantly pulled his attention from Eleanor and went down on one knee beside the wagon, an arm around the boy's waist. "Well, what do you think?" Donald Wade shrugged, his eyes fixed on the sack. "Maybe you better look inside and see." Donald Wade's hazel eyes gleamed with excitement as he peeked into the bag, reached and withdrew the two candy bars.

"Candy," he breathed, awed.

"Chocolate." Will crossed his elbows on his knee, smiling. "One for you, one for your little brother."

"Chocolate," Donald Wade repeated, then to his mother, "Lookit, Mama, Will brung us chocolate!"

Her appreciative eyes sought Will's and he felt as if someone had just tied a half-hitch around his heart. "Now wasn't that thoughtful. Say thank you to Mr. Parker, Donald Wade."

"Thanks, Will!"

With an effort, Will dropped his attention to the boy. "You peel one for Thomas now, all right?"

Grinning, he watched the boys settle side by side on the step and begin to make brown rings around their mouths.

"I appreciate your thinkin' of them, Mr. Parker."

He slowly stretched to his feet and looked into her face. Her lips were tipped up softly. Her hair was drawn back in a thick tied-down braid the color of autumn grain. Her eyes were green as jade. How could anybody lock her in a house?

"Boys got to have a little candy now and then. Brought something for you, too."

"For me?" She spread a hand on her chest.

He extended an arm with the sack caught between two fingers. "It isn't much."

"Why, whatever—" Elly excitedly plunged her hand inside, wasting not a second on foolish dissembling. Withdrawing the figurine, she held it at shoulder level. "Oh myyy . . . oh, Mr. Parker." She covered her mouth and blinked hard. "Oh, myyyy." She held the bluebird at arm's length and caught her breath. "Why, it's beautiful."

"I had a little money of my own," he clarified, since she hadn't bothered to count the egg money and he didn't want her thinking he'd spent any of hers. He could tell by her expression the thought hadn't entered her mind. She smiled into the bluebird's painted eye, her own shining with delight. "A bluebird . . . imagine that." She pressed it to her heart and beamed at Will. "How did you know I like birds?"

He knew. He knew.

He stood watching her, feeling ready to burst with gratification as she examined the bird from every angle. "I just love it." She flashed him another warm smile. "It's the nicest present I ever got. Thank you."

He nodded.

"See, boys?" She squatted to show them. "Mr. Parker brought me a bluebird. Isn't it about the prettiest thing you ever saw? Now where should we put it? I was thinkin' on the kitchen table. No, maybe on my nightstand—why, it would look good just about anyplace, wouldn't it? Come in and help me decide. You too, Mr. Parker."

She bustled inside, so excited she forgot to hold the screen door open for Thomas to scramble inside. Will plucked him off the step and got chocolate on his shirt, but what was a little chocolate to a man so happy? He stood just inside the kitchen doorway with the baby on his arm, watching Eleanor try the bird everywhere—on the table, on the cupboard, beside the cookie jar. "Where should we put it, Donald Wade?" Always, she made the boy feel important. And now Will, too.

"On the windowsill, so all the other birds will see it and come close."

"Mmm . . . on the windowsill." She pinched her lower lip and considered the sills—east, south and west. The kitchen jutted off the main body of the building, a room with ample brightness. "Why of course. Now why didn't I think of that?"

She placed the bluebird on a west sill, overlooking the back-yard, where the clothespoles had been repaired and now stood straight and sturdy. She leaned back, clapped once and pressed her folded hands against her chin. "Oh, yes, it's exactly what this place needed!"

It needed a lot more than a cheap glass figurine, but as Eleanor danced across the room and squeezed Will's arm, he felt as if he'd just bought her a collector's piece.

If Will had been eager to make improvements around the place before his trip to town, afterward he worked even harder, fired by the zeal to atone for a past which was none of his making. He spent hours wondering about the people who'd locked her in that house behind the green shades. And how long she'd been there, and why. And about the man who'd taken her away from it, the one she said she still loved. And how long it might take for that love to begin fading.

It was during those days that Will became aware of things he'd never noticed before: how she hadn't hung a curtain on a window; how she paused to worship the sun whenever she stepped outside; how she never failed to find praise for the day—be it rain or shine—something to marvel over; and at night, when Will stepped out of the barn to relieve himself, no matter what the hour . . . her bedroom light was always burning. It wasn't until he'd seen it several times that he realized she wasn't up checking on the boys, but sleeping with it on.

Why had her family done it to her?

But if anyone respected a person's right to privacy it was Will. He needn't know the answers to accept the fact that he was no longer laboring only to have a roof over his head, but to please her.

He mended the road—oiled the harness and hitched Madam to a heavy steel road scraper shaped like a giant grain shovel, with handles like a wheelbarrow, an ungainly thing to work with. But with Madam pulling and Will pushing, directing the straight steel cutting edge into the earth, they tackled the arduous task. They shaved off the high spots, filled in the washouts, rolled boulders off to the sides and grubbed out erupted roots.

Donald Wade became Will's constant companion. He'd take a seat on a bank or a branch, watching, listening, learning. Sometimes Will gave him a shovel and let him root around throwing small rocks off to the side, then praised him for his fledgling efforts as he'd heard Eleanor do.

One day Donald Wade observed, "My daddy, he didn't work much. Not like you."

"What did he do, then?"

"He puttered. That's what Mama called it."

"Puttered, huh?" Will mulled this over a moment and asked, "He treated your mama nice though, didn't he?"

"I guess so. She liked him." After a moment's pause, Donald Wade added, "But he din't buy her bluebirds."

While Will considered this, Donald Wade voiced another surprising question.

"Are you my daddy now?"

"No, Donald Wade, I'm sorry to say I'm not."

"You gonna be?"

Will had no answer. The answer depended on Eleanor Dinsmore.

She came twice a day—morning and afternoon—pulling Baby Thomas and a jug of cool raspberry nectar in the wagon. And they'd all sit together beneath the shade of her favorite sourwood tree and relish the treat while she pointed out the birds she knew. She seemed to know them all—doves and hawks and warblers and finches. And trees, too—the sourwood itself, the tulip poplar, redbud, basswood and willow, so many more varieties than Will had realized were there. She knew the small plants, too—the gallberry and snow vine, the sumac and crownbeard and one with a lovely name, summer farewell, which brought a winsome tilt to her lips and made him study those lips more closely than the summer farewell.

Those minutes spent resting beneath the sourwood tree were some of the finest of Will's life.

"My," she would say, "this is gonna be some road." And

it would be all the charge Will needed to return to the scraper and push harder than before.

The day the road was done Will whispered his thanks into Madam's ear, fed her a gold carrot from the garden and gave her a bath as a treat. After supper, he and Eleanor took the boys for a wagon ride down the freshly bladed earth that rose firm into the trees before dipping to link their house with the county road below.

"It's a beautiful road, Will," she praised, and he smiled in quiet satisfaction.

The next day he tightened up a wagon, replaced two boards on its bed, hitched up Madam and took his first load of junk to the Whitney dump. He took, too, a note from Eleanor, and Miss Beasley's eggs, plus several dozen more and five pints of cream, one which never made it farther than the library.

"Cream!" Miss Beasley exclaimed. "Why, I've had the worst craving for strawberry shortcake lately and what's strawberry shortcake without whipped cream?" She chuckled and got out her black snap-top coin purse.

And though Will checked out his first books with his own library card, just before he left she remembered, "Oh, I *did* find some pamphlets on beekeeping while I was sorting in the back room. You need not return these." She produced a mustard-yellow envelope bearing his name and laid it on the desk. "They're put out by the county extension office . . . *every five years*, mind you, when the bee is the only creature on God's green earth that hasn't changed its habits or its habitat since before man walked upright! But when the new pamphlets come in, the old ones get thrown—useful or not!" She blustered on, busying her hands, carefully avoiding Will's eyes. "Why, I've got a good mind to write to my county commissioner about such outright waste of the taxpayers' money!"

Will was charmed.

"Thank you, Miss Beasley."

Still she wouldn't look at him. "No need to thank me for something that would've gone to waste anyway."

But he saw beyond her smokescreen to the woman who had difficulty befriending men and his heart warmed more.

"I'll see you next week."

She looked up only when his hand gripped the brass knob, but even from a distance he noted the two spots of color in her cheeks.

Smiling to himself, Will loped down the library steps with his stack of books on one hip and the yellow envelope slapping his thigh.

"Myyy, myyy . . . if it isn't Mr. Parker."

Will came up short at the sight of Lula Peak, two steps below, smiling at him with come-hither eyes. She wore her usual Betty Grable foreknot, lipstick the color of a blood clot, and stood with one hip permanently jutted to hold her hand.

"Afternoon, ma'am." He tried to move around her but she sidestepped adroitly.

"What's your hurry?" She chewed gum as gracefully as an alligator gnawing raw meat.

"Got cream in the wagon that shouldn't be sitting in the sun."

She smoothed the hair up the back of her head, then, raising her chin, skimmed three fingertips down the V of her uniform. "Lawzy . . . it's a hot one all right." Standing one step below Will, Lula was nearly nose to navel with him. Her eyes roved lazily down his shirt and jeans to the envelope on which Miss Beasley had written his name. "So it's Will, is it?" she drawled. Her eyes took their time climbing back up, lingering where they would. "Will Parker," she drawled, and touched his belt buckle with the tip of one scarlet nail. "Nice name . . . Will." It took control for him to resist leaping back from her touch, but he stood his ground politely while she tipped her head and waggled her shoulders. "So, Will Parker, why don't you stop in at the cafe and I'll fix you a ni-i-ice glass of iced tea. Taste good on a hot one like this, mmm?"

For one horrified moment he thought she might run that nail straight down his crotch. He jumped before she could. "Don't think I'll have time, ma'am." This time she let him pass. "Got things to do." He felt her eyes following as he climbed the wagon wheel, took the reins and drove around the town square to Purdy's.

That woman was trouble with a capital T, and he didn't

want any. Not of it or of her. He made sure he avoided glancing across the square while he entered the store.

Purdy bought the cream and the eggs and said, "Fine, anytime you got fresh, just bring 'em in. I got no trouble getting rid of fresh."

Lula was gone when Will came out of the store, but her kewpie doll act left him feeling dirty and anxious to get back home.

Eleanor and the boys were waiting under their favorite sourwood tree this time. Will gravitated toward them like a compass needle toward the North Pole. Here was where he belonged, here with this unadorned woman whose simplicity made Lula look brassy, whose wholesomeness made Lula look brazen. He found it hard to believe that in his younger days he'd have chosen a woman like *that* over one like this.

She stood, brushing off the back of her skirt as he drew up and reined in Madam.

"You're back."

"Yup."

They smiled at each other and a moment of subtle appreciation fluttered between them. She boosted the boys up onto the wagon seat and he transferred them into the back, swinging them high and making them giggle. "You sit down back there now so you don't tumble off." They scrambled to follow orders and Will leaned to extend a helping hand to their mother. He clasped her palm and for the space of two heartbeats neither of them moved. She poised with one foot on a wagon cleat, her green eyes caught in his brown. Abruptly she clambered up and sat down, as if the moment had not happened.

He thought about it during the days that followed, while he continued improving the place, scrubbing walls and ceilings, finishing the plastering and painting walls that appeared to never have seen paint before. He put doors on the bottom kitchen cabinets and built new ones for above. He bartered a used kitchen sink for a piece of linoleum (both at a premium and growing scarcer) with which he covered the new cabinet top. The linoleum was yellow, streaked, like sun leaching through daisy petals: yellow, which seemed to suit Eleanor best and set off her green eyes.

She grew rounder and moved more slowly. Day after day he watched her hauling dishpans and slop buckets out to slew in the yard. She washed diapers for only one now, but soon there'd be two. He dug a cesspool and ran a drainpipe from underneath the sink, eliminating the need for carrying out dishpans.

She was radiant with thanks and rushed to dump a first basin of water down the drain and rejoice when it magically disappeared by itself. She said it didn't matter that he hadn't been able to find enough linoleum for the floor, too. The room was brighter and cleaner than it had ever been before.

He was disappointed about the linoleum for the floor. He wanted the room perfect for her, but linoleum and bathtubs and so many other commodities were getting harder and harder to come by with factories of all kinds converting to the production of war supplies. In prison Will had read the newspaper daily but now he caught up with world events only when he went to the library. Still, he was aware of the rumblings in Europe and wondered how long America could supply England and France with planes and tanks without getting into the fighting herself. He shuddered at the thought, even as he took his first load of scrap metal to town and got a dollar per hundredweight for Glendon Dinsmore's "junk."

There was talk of America actively joining the war, though America Firsters—among them the Lone Eagle, Charles Lindbergh—spoke out against the U.S. drift toward it. But Roosevelt was beefing up America's defenses. The draft was already in force, and Will was of age, healthy and single. Eleanor remained blissfully ignorant of the state of the world beyond the end of their driveway.

Then one day Will unearthed a radio in one of the sheds. It took some doing to find a battery for it—batteries, too, were being gobbled up by England to keep walkie-talkies operable. But again he bartered with a spare can of paint, only to find that even when the battery was installed, the radio still refused to work. Miss Beasley found a book that told him how to fix it.

The particular hour he coaxed it back to life, "Ma Perkins" was on the air on the blue network. The boys were having their afternoon nap and Eleanor was ironing. As the staticky program filled the kitchen, her eyes lit up like the amber tube behind the RCA Victor grille.

"How 'bout that—it works!" Will said, amazed.

"Shh!" She pulled up a chair while Will knelt on the floor and together they listened to the latest adventure of the widow who managed a lumberyard in Rushville Center, U.S.A., where she lived, by the golden rule, with her three kids, John, Evey and Fay. Anybody who loved their kids as much as Ma Perkins was all right with Eleanor, and Will could see Ma had gained a faithful listener.

That evening they all hovered close to the magical box while Will and Eleanor watched the boys' eyes alight at the sound of "The Lone Ranger" and Tonto, his faithful Indian friend, who called him *kemo sabe*.

After that, Donald Wade never walked; he galloped. He whinnied, shied, made hoof sounds with his tongue and hobbled "Silver" at the door each time he came in. Will playfully called him *kemo sabe* one day, and after that Donald Wade tried their patience by calling everybody else *kemo sabe* a hundred times a day.

The radio brought more than fantasy. It brought reality in the form of Edward R. Murrow and the news. Each evening during supper Will tuned it in. Murrow's grave voice with its distinctive pause would fill the kitchen: "This . . . is London." In the background could be heard the scream of German bombers, the wail of air raid sirens and the thunder of antiair-craft fire. But Will thought he was the only one in the kitchen who truly believed they were real.

Though Elly refused to discuss it, the war was coming, and when it did his number might be called. He pushed himself harder.

He put up next year's wood, scraped the old linoleum off the kitchen floor, sanded and varnished it, and began fantasizing about installing a bathroom—if he could come up with the fixtures.

And in secret, he read about bees.

They held, for him, an undeniable fascination. He spent hours observing the hives from a distance, those hives he'd at first believed abandoned by the insects but were not. He knew better now. The appearance of only a few bees at the hive opening meant nothing, because most of them were either inside waiting on the queen or out in the fields gathering pollen, nectar and water.

He read more, learned more—that the worker bees carried pollen in their back legs; that they needed saltwater daily to drink; that the honey was made in stackable frames called supers which the beekeeper added to the tops of the hives as the lower ones filled; that the bees ate their own honey to survive the winter; that during summer, the heaviest production time, if the laden supers weren't removed the honey grew so heavy it sometimes crowded the bees out and they swarmed.

Experimentally, he filled a single pan with saltwater one day. The next day it was empty, so he knew the hives were active. He watched the workers leaving with their back legs thin and returning with their pollen sacs filled. Will knew he was right without even opening the hives to see inside. Glendon Dinsmore had died in April. If no supers had been added since then, the bees could swarm anytime. If none had been taken since then, they were laden with honey. A lot of honey, and Will Parker wanted to sell it.

The subject hadn't come up again between himself and Eleanor. Neither had she produced any veiled hat or smoker, so he decided to go it without them. Every book and pamphlet advised that the first step toward becoming a beekeeper was to find out if you are bee-immune.

So Will did. One warm day in late October he followed instructions minutely: took a fresh bath to wash any scent of Madam from his body, raided Eleanor's mint patch, rubbed his skin and trousers with crushed leaves, folded his collar up, his sleeves down, tied string around his trouser cuffs and went out to the derelict Whippet to find out what the bees thought of Will Parker.

Reaching the car, he felt his palms begin to sweat. He dried them on his thighs and eased closer, reciting silently, Move slow ... bees don't like abrupt movement.

He inched toward the car . . . into the front seat . . . gripped the wheel . . . and sat with his heart in his throat.

It didn't take long. They came from behind him, first one, then another, and in no time at all what seemed like the whole damn colony! He forced himself to sit motionless while one landed in his hair and walked through it, buzzing, the rest still in flight about his face. Another lighted on his hand. He waited for it to drill him, but instead the old boy investigated the brown hair on Will's wrist, strolled to his knuckles and buzzed away, disinterested.

Well, I'll be damned.

When he told Eleanor about it, she made up for the stings the bees had forgone.

"You did what!"

She spun from the cupboard with her hands on her hips, her eyes fiery with anger.

"I went out and sat in the Whippet to see if I was bee-immune."

"Without even a veiled hat!"

"I figured you never found one."

"Because I didn't want you out there!"

"But I told you, I rubbed mint on myself first and washed the smell of Madam off me."

"Madam! What in the sam hell has she got to do with it?"

"Bees hate the smell of animals, especially horses and dogs. It gets 'em mad."

"But you could have been stung. Bad!" She was livid.

"The book says a beekeeper's got to expect to get stung now and then. It comes with the job. But after a while you get so you hardly notice it."

"Oh, swell!" She flung up a hand disparagingly. "And that's supposed to make me feel good?"

"Well, I figured since I read it in the pamphlet it must be the right way to start. And the book—"

"The book!" She scoffed. "Don't tell me about books. Did you wear gloves?"

"No. I wanted to find out—"

"And you didn't take the smoker either!"

"I would have if you'd have given it to me."

"Don't you blame me for your own stupidity, Will Parker! That was a damn-fool thing to do and you know it!"

She was so upset she couldn't countenance him any longer. She spun back to the cake she'd been making, grabbed an egg and cracked it against the lip of the bowl with enough force to annihilate the shell.

"Damn! Now see what you've done!"

"Well, if I'd have known you were gonna get mad—"

"I'm not mad!" She fished out a smashed shell and flung it aside vehemently.

"You're not mad," he repeated dryly.

"No, I'm not!"

"Then what are you hollering about?"

"I'm not hollering!" she hollered and rounded on him again. "I just don't know what gets into men's heads sometimes, that's all! Why, Donald Wade would've had more sense than to go out there into a beehive with no more protection than a smear of *mint*!"

"I didn't get bit though, did I?" he inquired smugly.

She glared at him, cheeks mottled, mouth pursed, and finally swung away, too frustrated to confront him any longer. "Go on." The order came out low and sizzling. "Git out of my kitchen." She slammed another egg against the bowl, smashing it to smithereens.

He stood five feet away, arms crossed, one shoulder braced indolently against the front room doorway, admiring her angry pink face, the spunky chin, the bounce of her breasts as she whipped the batter. "You know, for someone who's not mad, you're sure makin' a hell of a mess out of those eggshells."

The next thing he knew, an egg came flying through the air and hit him smack in the middle of the forehead.

"Wh—what the hell—"

He bent forward while yolk ran down his nose and white dangled from his chin, dripping onto his boots.

"You think it's so funny, go stick your head in a beehive and let them clean it off for you!" She stabbed a finger at the door. "Well, git, I said! Git out of my kitchen!"

He turned to follow orders but even before he reached the

door, he was laughing. The first bubble rippled up as he reached the screen door, the second as he jogged down the steps, scraping the slime from his face. By the time he hit the yard he was hooting full-bore.

"Git!"

He shook his head like a dog after a swim and cackled merrily. Behind him the screen door opened and he spun just in time to form a mitt for the next egg she let fly. It burst in his palms, against his hip.

He jigged backward, chortling. "Whooo—ee! Look out, Joe DiMaggio!"

"Damn you, Parker!"

"Ha! Ha! Ha!"

All the way to the well he laughed, and kept it up while he inspected his shirt, stripped it off and rinsed it and himself beneath the pump. He was still chuckling as he hung it on a fencepost to dry.

Then the truth struck him and he became silent as if plunged underwater.

She cares!

It caught him like an uppercut on the chin, snapped him erect to stare at the house.

She cares about you, Parker! And you care about her!

His heart began pounding as he stood motionless in the sun with water streaming down his face and chest. *Care about her? Admit it, Parker, you love her.* He scraped a hand down his face, shook it off and continued staring, coming to grips with the fact that he was in love with a woman who had just fired an egg at him, a woman seven months pregnant with another man's baby, a woman he had scarcely touched, never kissed and never desired carnally.

Until now.

He began moving toward the house in long, unhurried strides, feeling the awesome thump of his pulse in his breast and temples, wondering what to say when he reached her.

She was already on her knees with a bucket and rag when he opened the screen door and let it thud quietly behind him. She went on scrubbing, riveting her attention on the floor.

The boys were napping, the radio silent. He stood across the room, watching, wondering, waiting.

Go on, then. Lift her to her feet and see if you were right, Parker.

He moved to stand over her, but she toiled stubbornly, her entire body rocking as she scrubbed with triple the energy required for a simple egg.

"Eleanor?"

He'd never called her by her first name before and it doubled his awareness of her as a woman, and hers of him as a man.

"Go away."

"Eleanor"—spoken softer this time while he gripped her arm as if to tug her up. Her head snapped back, revealing green eyes glimmering with unshed tears.

She was angry, so angry. And the tender tone of his voice added to it, though she didn't completely understand why. She dashed away the infuriating tears and looked up the considerable length of him, to his bare, wet chest, his attractive face still moist with well water, his hair standing in rills. His eyes appeared troubled, the lashes spiky with moisture. His skin was brown from a long summer's shirtless labor, and he had filled out until he looked like a lean, fit animal. The sight of him sent a thrill through her vitals. He was all the things that Glendon hadn't been—honed, hard and handsome. But what man who looked like that would welcome the affections of a plain, crazy woman seven months pregnant, shaped like a watermelon?

Eleanor dropped her chin. He tipped it up with one finger and gave her face a disarming perusal before letting a grin tip the corner of his mouth. "You got one hell of an arm, you know that?"

She jerked her chin away and felt his charm seep through her limbs, but nothing in her life had led her to believe she could attract a man like him so she assumed he was only having fun with her. "It's not funny, Will."

Standing above her, he felt disappointment spear him deeply. He dropped to a squat, his gaze falling on her hands, which rested idly over the edge of a white enamel bucket.

"No, it's not," he replied quietly. "I think we'd better talk about this."

"There's nothing to talk about."

"Isn't there?"

She suddenly made an L of her arms and dropped her face against her knuckles.

"Don't cry."

"I'm n—not." Whatever was wrong with her? She never cried, and it was embarrassing to do so before Will Parker for absolutely no good reason at all.

He waited, but she continued sobbing softly, her stomach bobbing. "Don't . . ." he whispered, pained.

She threw back her head, rubbed the tears aside and sniffed. "Pregnant women cry sometimes, that's all."

"I'm sorry I laughed."

"I know, and I'm sorry I threw that egg." She dried her face roughly with her apron. "But, Will, you got to understand about the bees."

"No, *you've* got to understand about the bees."

"But, Will—"

He held up both palms. "Now wait a minute before you say anything. I'm not going to lie to you. I *have* been in the orchard . . . a lot. But I'm not him, Eleanor, I'm not Glendon. I'm a careful man and I'm not going to get hurt."

"How do you know that?"

"All right, I don't. But you just can't go through life shying away from things you're scared are going to happen. Chances are they never will anyway." He suddenly dropped both knees to the floor and rested his hands on his thighs, leaning forward earnestly. "Elly, there are bees all over the place. And honey out there, too, a lot of it. I want to gather it and sell it."

"But—"

"Now wait a minute, let me finish. You haven't heard it all." He drew a deep breath and plunged on. "I'll need your help. Not with the hives—I'll take care of that part so you don't have to go near them. But with the extracting and bottling."

She glanced away. "For money, I suppose."

"Well, why not?"

She snapped her gaze back to him, spreading her palms. "But I don't care about money."

"Well, maybe I do. If not for myself, for this place, for you and the kids. I mean, there are things I'd like to do around here. I've thought about putting in electricity . . . and a bathroom maybe. With the new baby coming, I thought you'd want those things, too. And what about the baby—where you gonna get the money to pay the doctor?"

"I told you before, I don't need any doctors."

"Maybe you didn't the day the boys got stung—we were lucky that day—but you'll need one when the baby is born."

"I'm not having any doctor," she declared stubbornly.

"But that's ridiculous! Who's going to help you when the time comes?"

She squared her chin and looked him dead in the eye. "I was hopin' you would."

"Me?" Will's eyebrows shot up and his head jutted forward. "But I don't know the first damn thing about it."

"There's nothing to it," she hurried on. "I'll tell you everything you need to know beforehand. About all you'd have to do is tie the—"

"Now, wait a minute!" He leaped to his feet, holding up both palms like a traffic cop.

Riveting her eyes on him, she got clumsily to her feet. "You're scared, aren't you?"

He stuffed his hands into his back pockets, gripping his buttocks. A pair of creases appeared between his eyebrows. "Damn right I'm scared. And it doesn't make a bit of sense, not when there's a qualified doctor down there in town who can do it."

"I told you once, the town's got no use for me, I got no use for it."

"But that's cr—" He stopped himself short.

"Crazy?" She finished for him.

"I didn't mean to say that." Damn his thoughtless tongue. "It's risky. All kinds of things could happen. Why, it could be born with the cord wrapped around its neck, or breech—what if that happened?"

"It won't. I had two that come out with no trouble at all. All you'd have to do—"

"No!" He put six feet of space between them before facing her again, scowling. "I'm no midwife, goddammit!"

It was the first time Elly had seen him truly angry and she wasn't sure how to handle him. They faced off, as motionless as chess pieces, their color high and their mouths set while Eleanor felt uncertainty creeping in. She needed him, but he didn't seem to understand that. She was afraid, but couldn't let it show. And if what she was about to say backfired, she'd be the sorriest woman in Gordon County.

"Well, then, maybe you'd better collect your things and move on."

A shaft of dread speared through him. So much for love. How many times in his life had he been through this? *Sorry, boy, but we won't be needin' you anymore. Wish we could keep you on, boy, but—* No matter how hard he worked to prove himself, the end was always inevitable. He should have grown used to it by now. But it hurt, goddammit. It hurt! And she was being unreasonable to expect this of him.

He pulled in a deep, shaky breath and felt his stomach quiver. "Can't we talk about this, Elly?"

She loved the sound of her name rolling off his tongue. But she wasn't keeping him around as an ornament. If he was going to stay he had to understand why. Obstinately she knelt and returned to her scrubbing. "I can do it alone. I don't need you."

No, nobody ever had. He'd thought this once maybe it'd turn out different. But he was as dispensable to Eleanor Dinsmore as he'd been to everyone from his mother on down to the state of Texas. He could give up and simply walk away from this place, away from her, but whether she loved him or not, he was happy here, happier than he ever remembered being, happy and comfortable and busy and achieving. And that was worth fighting for.

He swallowed his pride, crossed the half-scrubbed floor and squatted beside her, resting both elbows on his knees. "I don't want to go . . . but I didn't hire on here to deliver babies," he argued quietly, reasonably. "I mean, it's"—he swallowed—"it's a little personal, wouldn't you say?"

"I guess that would bother you," she returned tightly, continuing to scrub, moving to a new patch of floor to avoid his eyes.

He considered long and hard, fixing his attention on the top of her head. "Yes . . . yes it would."

"Glendon did it . . . twice."

"That was different. He was your husband."

Still scrubbing, she said, "You could be, too."

A shaft of hot surprise sizzled through his veins. But what if he'd misunderstood? Weighing her words, he balanced on the balls of his feet, watching her rock above the scrub rag as the wet spot spread. Her cheeks grew flushed as she clarified, "I mean, I've been thinking, and it's okay with me if we went ahead and got married now. I think we'd get along all right, and the boys like you a lot and you're real good with them, and . . . and I really don't throw eggs very often." Still she wouldn't look up.

He contained a smile while his heartbeat clattered. "Is that what you want?"

"I guess."

Then look at me. Let me see it in your eyes.

But when she finally glanced up he saw only embarrassment at having asked. So . . . she was not in love, only in a bind . . . and he was convenient. But, after all, he'd known that from the first time he'd walked in here, hadn't he?

The silence remained tense. He stretched to his feet and crossed to a window, looked out at the backyard he'd cleaned, the clothespoles he'd sturdied, thinking of how much more he wanted to do for her. "You know, Eleanor, it's silly for us to do this just because you put up some ad in the sawmill and just because I answered it. That isn't reason enough for two people to tie up for life, is it?"

"Don't you want to?"

He glanced over his shoulder to find her watching him with face ablaze.

"Do you?"

I'm pregnant and unbright and unpretty, she thought.

I'm an ex-con woman-killer, he thought.

And neither of them spoke what was in their hearts.

At length, he glanced out at the yard again. "It seems to me there should be some . . . some feeling between people or something." It was his turn to flush, but he kept it hidden from her.

"I like you fine, Will. Don't you like me?"

She might have been discussing which new rake to select, so emotionless was her tone.

"Yeah," he said throatily, after a moment. "I like you fine."

"Then I think we ought to do it."

Just like that—no harp music swelling out of the heavens, no kissing beneath the stars. Only Elly, seven months pregnant, struggling to her feet and drying her hands on her apron. And Will standing six feet clear of her, staring in the opposite direction. The way they'd laid it out made it sound as exciting as President Roosevelt's Lend-Lease Program. Well, enough was enough. Before Will agreed, he was going to know exactly what he was getting into here. Resolutely he turned to face her.

"You mind my asking something?"

"Ask."

"Where would I sleep?"

"Where would you want to sleep?"

He really wasn't sure. Sleeping with her would be tough, lying beside her pregnant body and not touching it. But sleeping in the barn was mighty lonely. He decided to give away no more or less than necessary. "The nights are getting pretty cool out in that barn."

"The only place in here is where Glendon slept, you know."

"I know." After an extended silence, "So?"

"You'd be my husband."

"Yeah," he said expressionlessly, realizing she wasn't too thrilled at the prospect.

"I . . . I sleep with the light on."

"I know."

Her eyebrows lifted. "You do?"

"I've been up at night and seen it."

"It'd probably keep you awake."

What was she doing arguing against it when the idea made her have to fight for breath?

He thought long and hard before trusting her enough to reveal a crack in his defenses. "In prison it was never completely dark either."

He noted a softening in her expression and wondered if someday he could trust her with the rest of his vulnerabilities.

"Well, in that case . . ." The silence welled around them while they tried to think of what to say or do next. Had this been a regular proposal with the expected emotions on both sides, the moment would undoubtedly have been intimate. Because it wasn't, the strain multiplied.

"Well . . ." He rubbed his nose and chuckled nervously.

"Yes . . . well." She spread her hands, then linked them beneath her swollen belly.

"I don't know how a person goes about getting married."

"We do it at the courthouse in Calhoun. We can get the license right there, too."

"You want to drive in tomorrow, then?"

"Tomorrow'd be fine."

"What time?"

"We'd better start early. We'll have to take a wagon, 'cause the boys'll be with us. And as you know, Madam's pretty slow."

"Nine o'clock then?"

"Nine should be fine."

For a moment they studied each other, realizing to what they'd just agreed. How awkward. How incredible. Self-consciousness struck them simultaneously. He reached up to pull his hat brim down, only to discover he'd left his hat hanging on the fencepost. So he hooked a thumb in his hind pocket and backed up a step.

"Well . . . I got work to finish." His thumb jabbed the air above his shoulder.

"So do I."

He backed up two more steps, wondering what she'd do if he switched directions and kissed her. But in the end he followed his own advice and left without trying.

CHAPTER
8

Falling into bed that night, Eleanor lay wide-awake, thinking of the day past, the day to come, the years ahead. Would she and Will live peaceably or fight often? Fighting was something new to her. In the years she'd been married to Glendon, they'd never fought—perhaps because Glendon was just too lazy.

In the place where she'd grown up there was no fighting either. And no laughter. Instead, there had been tension, never-ending tension. From her earliest memories it was there, always hovering like a monster threatening to swoop down and scoop her up with its black wings. It was there in the way Grandmother carried herself, as if to let her shoulders wilt would displease the Lord. It was there in her mother's careful attempts to walk quietly, carry out orders without complaint, and never meet Grandmother's eyes. But it was greatest when Grandfather came home. Then the praying would intensify. Then the "purifying" would begin.

Eleanor would kneel on the hard parlor floor, as ordered, while Grandfather raised his hands toward the ceiling and, with his scraggly gray beard trembling and his eyes rolled back in his head, would call down forgiveness from God. Beside her, Grandmother would moan and carry on like a dog having fits, then start talking gibberish as her body trembled.

And Mother—the sinner—would squeeze her eyes shut and interlace her fingers so tightly the knuckles turned white, and rock pitifully on her knees while her lips moved silently. And she, Eleanor—the child of shame—would lower her forehead to her folded hands and peek out with one eye at the spectacle, wondering what it was she and her mother had done.

It seemed impossible that Mother could have done anything bad. Mother was meek as a violet, hardly ever spoke at all, except when Grandfather demanded that she pray aloud and ask forgiveness for her depravity. What was depravity? the child, Eleanor, wondered. And why was she a child of shame?

While Eleanor was small Mother sometimes talked to her, quietly, in the privacy of the bedroom they shared. But as time went on, Mother grew more tacit and withdrawn. She worked hard— Grandmother saw to that. She did all the gardening, while Grandmother pulled back the edge of the shade and stood sentinel. If anyone passed on the road, Grandmother would hasten to the back door and hiss through a crack, "Ssst! Get in here, Chloe!" until in time, Chloe no longer waited for the order, but scuttled inside at the first glimpse of anyone approaching.

Three were allowed near, only three, and these out of necessity: the milkman, who left his bottles on the back step; the Raleigh man from whom they bought their pantry stock; and an old man named Dinsmore who delivered ice for their icebox until his son, Glendon, took over. If anyone else knocked on their door—the school principal, an occasional tramp looking for a free meal, the census taker—they saw no more than a front shade being bent stealthily from inside.

Eventually the truant officer began coming, pounding on the door authoritatively, demanding that it be opened. Did they have a child in there? If so, she had to attend school: it was the law.

Grandmother would stand well away from the drawn shades, her face a deadly mask, and whisper, "Silence, Eleanor, don't say a word!"

Then one time the truant officer came when Grandfather

was home. This time he shouted, "Albert See? We know you have a child in there who's school age. If you don't open this door I'll get a court order that'll give me the right to break it down and take her! You want me to do that, See?"

And so Eleanor's schooldays began. But they were painful for the colorless child already a year older and a head taller than the others in her first grade class. The other children treated her like the oddity she was—a gawky, silent eccentric who was ignorant of the most basic games, didn't know how to function in a group, and stared at everything and everybody with big green eyes. She was hesitant at everything and when she occasionally showed moments of glee, jumping and clapping at some amusement, she did so with disquieting abruptness, then fell still as if someone had turned off her switch. When teachers tried to be kind, she backed away as if threatened. When children snickered, she stuck out her tongue at them. And the children snickered with cruel regularity.

School, to Eleanor, seemed like exchanging one prison for another. So she began playing hooky. The first time she did it she feared God would find out and tell Grandmother. But when He didn't, she tried it again, spending the day in the woods and fields, discovering the wonder of true freedom at last. She knew well how to sit still and silent—in that house behind the green shades she did a lot of that—and for the first time, it reaped rewards. The creatures learned to trust her, to go about their daily routine as if she were one of them— snakes and spiders and squirrels and birds. Most of all the birds. To Eleanor, those wonderful creatures, the only ones not restrained to earth, had the greatest freedom of all.

She began studying them. When Miss Buttry's fifth grade class went to the library Eleanor found an Audubon book with colored plates and descriptions of birds' habitats, nests, eggs and voices. In the wilds, she began identifying them: the ruby-crowned kinglet, a spirited bundle of elfin music; the cedar waxwings, who appeared in flocks, seemed always affectionate and sometimes got drunk on overripe fruit; the blue jay, pompous and arrogant, but even more beautiful than the meek cardinals and tanagers.

She brought crumbs in her pockets and laid them in a circle around her, then sat as still as her friend, the barred owl, until a purple finch came and perched in a nearby pine bough, serenading with its mellifluous warble. In time it descended to a lower branch where it cocked its head to study her. She outwaited the finch until eventually he advanced and ate her bread. She found the finch a second day—she was convinced it was the same bird—and yet a third, and when she'd learned to imitate its call, summoned it as effortlessly as other children whistled up their dog. Then one day she stood like the Statue of Liberty, the crumbs in her palm, and the finch perched on her hand to eat.

At school shortly thereafter, a group of children were exchanging boasts. A little girl with black pigtails and an overbite said, "I can do thirty-seven cartwheels without getting dizzy." Another, with the fattest belly in class, boasted, "I can eat fourteen pancakes at one time!" A third, the most notorious liar in class, claimed, "My daddy is going on a safari hunt to Africa next year and he's taking me with him."

Eleanor edged close to their exclusive circle and offered timidly, "I can call the birds and make them eat off my hand."

They gaped at her as if she were a lunatic, then tittered and closed their ranks once again. After that the taunts were whispered loudly enough so they wouldn't fail to reach her ears— Crazy Elly See, talks to birds and lives in that house with the shades pulled down, she and her batty mother and her battier grandma and grandpa.

It was during one of her truancies from school that she first spoke to Glendon Dinsmore. She was late heading home and came bursting from the woods, clattering down a steep embankment, sending rocks tumbling to the road below, startling a mule that brayed and sidestepped, nearly overturning Dinsmore's wagon.

"Whoa!" he barked, while the animal nearly splintered the singletree with a powerful kick. When he'd gotten the beast under control, he took off his dusty felt hat and whacked it on the wagon seat in agitation. "Lord a-mighty, girl, what you mean by stormin' outa the woods that way!"

"I'm in a hurry. Gotta get home before the schoolkids walk by."

"Well, you scared poor Madam out of her last-year's hair! You ought to be more careful around animals."

"Sorry," she replied, mollified.

"Aww ..." He thumped his hat back on and seemed to mellow. "Guess you didn't stop to think. But you be more careful next time, you hear?" He glanced speculatively at the woods, then back at her. "So you're playin' hooky, huh?" When she didn't answer, his look grew shrewder and he thrust his head forward. "Hey, don't I know you?"

She crossed her arms behind her back, rocked left to right twice. "You used to deliver ice to our house when I was little."

"I did?" She nodded while he scratched his temple, pushing the hat askew. "What's your name again?"

"Elly See."

"Elly See ..." He paused to recall. "Why, of course. I remember now. And mine's Glendon Dinsmore."

"I know."

"You know?" He gave a crooked smile of surprise. "Well, how about that? Don't come to your house no more, though."

Elly scuffed the dirt with her toe. "I know. Grampa bought an electric refrigerator so we wouldn't have to have ice delivered no more. They don't like people comin' in."

"Oh ... so ... I wondered." He motioned along the road with a thumb and offered, "I'm goin' your way. Can I give you a lift?"

She shook her head, clasping her hands more tightly behind her back, making her dress front appear as if she'd tucked two acorns inside. He was a grown-up man by now, a good seventeen, eighteen years old, she figured. If Grandma saw her coming home in his wagon she'd end up doing hours on her knees.

"Well, why not? Madam don't mind pullin' two."

"I'd get in trouble. I'm s'posed to come straight home from school and I ain't supposed to talk to strangers."

"Well, I wouldn't want to get you in trouble. You come up this way often?"

She studied him warily. "Just . . . sometimes."

"What you do up there in the woods?"

"I study birds." As an afterthought, she added, "For school, you know?"

He raised his chin and nodded wisely, as if to say, Ah, I see.

"Birds is nice," he offered, then picked up the reins. "Well, maybe I'll run into you again someday, but I better not keep you now. So long, Elly."

She watched him drive away, mystified. He was the first person in her twelve-year experience who'd ever treated her as if she weren't either crazy or a child of shame. She thought about him during prayers after that, to take her mind off her aching knees. He was a rather scruffy-looking fellow, dressed in overalls and thick boots, with only enough beard to make him look prickly. But she didn't care about his looks, only that he treated her as if she weren't some oddity.

The next time she escaped to the woods she found a spot high above the rocky bank behind a juniper bush where she could watch the road and remain hidden. From her secret perch she waited for him to reappear. When he didn't, she was surprised to find herself disappointed. She watched for three days before giving up, never fully understanding what she'd expected had he come along the road as before. Talk, she supposed. It had felt good to simply talk to someone.

Nearly a full year passed before she ran into him again. It was autumn but warm, a day of bright leaves and dusky sky. Elly was stalking bobwhites, the little lords of the fencerows whose voices she loved. Unable to flush any along the fenceline, she headed into the woods to search in heavier cover where they roosted in bevies on the ground, facing outward. She was calling in a clear whistle: *quoi-lee, quoi-lee,* when she flushed not a quail from the sumac bushes, but Glendon Dinsmore from over the next hill. She stopped in her tracks and watched him approach, cradling a gun in one arm. He raised the other, waved, and called, "Hey, Elly!"

She stood sober, awaiting his arrival. Stopping in front of her, he repeated, "Hey, Elly."

"Hey, Glendon," she returned.

"How you doin'?"

"Doin' all right, I reckon."

They stood for a moment in a void. She appraised him smilelessly, while he appeared pleased at having run into her. He looked exactly as he had last time: same overalls, same scruffy beard, same dusty hat. Finally he shifted his stance, rubbed his nose and inquired, "So, how's them birds of yours?"

"What birds?" Her birds were her business, nobody else's.

"You said you was studyin' birds. What you learnin'?"

He'd remembered for a whole year that she studied birds? Elly softened. "I'm tryin' to call the bobwhites outa hiding."

"You can *call* 'em? Golly." He sounded impressed, unlike the girls at school.

"Sometimes. Sometimes it don't work. What you doin' with that there gun?"

"Huntin'."

"Huntin'! You mean you shoot critters?"

"Deer, I do."

"I couldn't never shoot no critter."

"My daddy and me, we eat the deer."

"Well, I hope you don't get one."

He reared back and laughed, one brief hoot, then said, "Girlie, you're somethin'. I 'membered, you was somethin'. So, did you see any bobwhites?"

"Nope. Not yet. You see any deer?"

"Nope, not yet."

"I seen one, but I won't tell you where. I see him almost every day."

"You come out here every day?"

"Pret' near."

"Me too, during huntin' season."

She pondered that momentarily, but any suggestion of meeting again seemed ludicrous. After all, she was only thirteen and he was five years older.

Frightened by the mere thought, she spun away abruptly. "I gotta go." She trotted off.

"Hey, Elly, wait!"

"What?"

She halted twenty feet away, facing him.

"Maybe I'll see y' out here sometime. I mean, well, huntin' season's on a couple more weeks."

"Maybe." She studied him in silence, then repeated, "I gotta go. If I ain't home by five after four they make me pray an extra half hour."

Again she spun and ran as fast as her legs would carry her, amazed by his friendliness and the fact that he seemed to care not a whit about her craziness. After all, he'd been inside that house; he knew where she came from, knew her people. Yet he wanted to be her friend.

She went back to the same spot the next day but hid where he couldn't see her. She watched him approach over the same hill, the gun again on one arm, a fat cloth sack in his other. He sat down beneath a tree, laid the gun across his lap and the sack at his hip. He pushed back his dusty hat, fished a corncob pipe from his bib, filled it from a drawstring sack and lit it with a wooden match. She thought she had never in her life seen anyone so content.

He smoked the entire pipe, his lumpy boots crossed, one arm resting over his stomach. When he knocked the dottle from his pipe and ground it dead with his boot, she grew panicky. In a minute he would leave!

She stepped out of hiding and stood still, waiting for him to spot her. When he did, his face lit in a smile.

"Well, howdy!"

"Howdy yourself."

"Fine day, id'n't it?"

One day was pretty much like the next to her. She squinted at the sky and remained silent.

"Brought you somethin'," he said, getting to his feet.

"For me?" Her eyes grew suspicious. Where she came from nobody did anything nice for anybody.

"For your birds." He leaned down and picked up the fat sack tied with twine.

She stared at it, speechless.

"How's your bird studyin' comin'?"

"Oh . . . fine. Just fine."

"Last year you was studyin' them for school. What you doin' it for this year?"

"Just for fun. I like birds."

"Me too." He set the sack near her toes. "What grade you in?"

"Seventh."

"You like it?"

"Not as much as last year. Last year I had Miss Natwick."

"I had her, too. Didn't care much for school, though. I dropped out after eighth. Took the ice route then and help my daddy around the place." He gestured with his head. "Me and him, we live back there, up on Rock Creek Road."

She glanced in that direction but her eyes dropped quickly to the sack lying on the forest floor.

"What's in it?"

"Corn."

The shy blue grosbeaks might like corn. Maybe with it she could get closer to them. She should thank him, but she'd never learned how. Instead she gave him the second-best thing, a tidbit of her precious knowledge of birds.

"The orioles are my favorite. They don't eat corn, though. Only bugs and grapes. The grosbeaks, though, they'll prob'ly love it."

He nodded, and she saw that her reply was all the thanks he needed. He asked more questions about school and she told him she studied the birds sometimes in library books. Sometimes she brought those books to the woods. Other times she came with only a tablet and crayons and drew pictures which she took back to the library to identify the birds.

Out at his place, he told her, he'd put up gourds for birdhouses.

"Gourds?"

"The birds love 'em. Just drill 'em a hole and they move right in."

"How big of a hole?"

"Depends on the size o' the bird. And the gourd."

In time he pulled out a watch and said, "It's goin' on four. You best be gittin'."

She got only as far as the deadfall beyond the nearby hill

before dropping to her knees and untying the twine with trembling fingers. She stared into the sack and her heart raced. She plunged her hands into the dry golden kernels and ran them through her fingers. Excitement was something new for Elly. She'd never before had something to look forward to.

The next day he didn't show up. But near the sumac bushes where they'd met twice before he left three lumpy green and yellow striped gourds, each drilled with a different-sized hole and equipped with a wire by which to hang it.

A gift. He had given her another gift!

All of the hunting season passed before she saw him again on the last day. He sauntered over the hill with his shotgun and she stood waiting in plain sight, straight as a needle, a flat, unattractive girl whose eyes appeared darker than they really were in her pale, freckled face. She neither smiled nor quavered, but invited him straight-out, "Wanna see where I hung the gourds?" Never in her life had Elly placed that much trust in anyone.

They met often after that. He was easy to be with, for he understood the woods and its creatures as she did, and whenever they walked through it he kept a respectable distance, walking with his thumbs in his rear overall pockets, slightly bent.

She showed him the orioles, and the blue grosbeaks, and the indigo buntings. And together they watched the birds who came to take up residence in the three striped gourds—two families of sparrows and, in the spring, a lone bluebird. Only after they'd been meeting for many months did she lift a palmful of corn and show him how she could call the birds and entice them to eat from her hand.

The following year, when she was fourteen, she met him one day with a glum expression on her face. They sat on a fallen log, watching the cavity in a nearby tree where an opossum was nesting.

"I can't see you no more, Glendon."

"Why's that?"

"Because I'm sick. I'm prob'ly gonna die."

Alarmed, he turned toward her. "Die? What's wrong?"

"I don't know, but it's bad."

"Well . . . did they take you to the doctor?"

"Don't have to. I'm already bleedin'—what could he do?"

"Bleeding?"

She nodded, tight-lipped, resigned, eyes fixed on the opossum hole.

His eyes made one furtive sweep down her dress front, where the acorns had grown to the size of plums.

"You tell your mother about it?"

She shook her head. "Wouldn't do any good. She's tetched. It's like she don't even know I'm there anymore."

"How 'bout your grandma?"

"I'm scared to tell her."

"Why?"

Elly's eyes dropped. "Because."

"Because why?"

She shrugged abjectly, sensing vaguely that this had something to do with being a child of shame.

"You bleedin' from your girl-place?" he asked. She nodded silently and blushed. "They didn't tell you, did they?"

"Tell me what?" She flicked him one glance that quickly shied away.

"All females do that. If they don't, they can't have babies."

Her head snapped around and he shifted his attention to the sun peeking around the trunk of an old live-oak tree. "They shoulda told you so you'da known to expect it. Now you go on home and tell your grandma about it and she'll tell you what to do."

But Eleanor didn't. She accepted Glendon's word that it was something natural. When it happened at regular intervals, she began keeping track of the length of time between the spells, in order to be prepared.

When she was fifteen she asked him what a child of shame meant.

"Why?"

"Because that's what I am. They tell me all the time."

"They tell you!" His face grew taut and he picked up a stick, snapped it into four pieces and flung them away. "It's nothin'," he said fiercely.

"It's somethin' wicked, isn't it?"

"Now how could that be? You ain't wicked, are you?"

"I disobey them and run away from school."

"That don't make you a child of shame."

"Then what does?" When he remained silent, she appealed, "You're my friend, Glendon. If you won't tell me, who will?"

He sat on the forest floor with both elbows hooked over his knees, staring at the broken stick.

"All right, I'll tell you. Remember when we saw the quails mating? Remember what happened when the male got on top of the female?" He gave her a quick glance and she nodded. "That's how humans mate, too, but they're only supposed to do it if they're married. If they do it when they're not, and they get a baby, people like your grandma call it a child of shame."

"Then I am one."

"No, you ain't."

"But if—"

"No, you ain't! Now that's the last I wanna hear of it!"

"But I ain't got no daddy."

"And it ain't your fault neither, is it? So whose shame is it?"

She suddenly understood the cleansings, and why her mother was called the sinner. But who was her daddy? Would she ever know?

"Glendon?"

"What?"

"Am I a bastard?" She'd heard the word whispered behind her back at school.

"Elly, you got to learn not to worry about things that ain't important. What's important is you're a good person inside."

They sat silently for a long time, listening to a flock of sparrows twittering in the buckthorn bushes where the gourds hung. Eleanor raised her eyes to the swatches of blue sky visible between the branches overhead.

"You ever wish somebody would die, Glendon?"

He considered soberly before answering. "No, guess I haven't."

"Sometimes I wish my grandparents would die so my

mother and me wouldn't have to pray no more and I could pull up the shades in the house and let Mother outside. A person who's good inside wouldn't wish such a thing, I don't think."

He reached out and laid a consoling hand on her shoulder. It was the first time he'd ever touched her deliberately.

Eleanor got her wish the year she turned sixteen. Albert See died while on circuit ... in the bed of a woman named Mathilde King. Mathilde King, it turned out, was black and gave her favors only for money.

Elly reported his death to Glendon with no show of grief. When he touched her cheek she said, "It's all right, Glendon. He was the real sinner."

The shock and shame of the circumstances surrounding her husband's death rendered Lottie See incapable of facing even her daughter and granddaughter thereafter. She lived less than a year, most of that year spent sitting in a hard, spindle-backed chair facing one corner of the front parlor where the green shades had been sealed to the edges of the window casings with tape. She no longer spoke except to pray, or forced Chloe to repent, but simply sat staring at the wall until one day her head slumped over and her hands dropped to her sides.

When Elly reported her grandmother's death to Glendon there were again no tears or mourning. He took her hand and held it while they sat silently on a log, listening to the woodlife around them.

"People like them ... they're probably happier dead," he said. "They had no notion of what happiness is."

Elly stared straight ahead. "I can see you whenever I want from now on. Mother won't stop me, and I'll be quittin' school to stay home and take care of her."

Eleanor removed the tape from the shades, but when she pulled them up Chloe screeched and huddled, protecting her head as if from a blow. Her manic fright no longer held any connection to reality. The death of her parents, instead of freeing Chloe, cast her deeper into her world of madness. She could do nothing for herself, so her care was left to Eleanor, who fed and clothed her and saw to her daily needs.

When Elly was eighteen Glendon's father died. His grief was a sharp contrast to Elly's own lack of emotions upon the deaths of her grandparents. They met in the woods and he cried pitifully. She opened her arms and held him for the first time. "Aw, Glendon, don't cry . . . don't cry." But secretly she thought it beautiful that anyone could cry for the death of a parent. She cradled him against her breast, and when his weeping stopped, he expunged his residual grief within her virgin body. For Elly it was an act not of carnal, but of spiritual love. She no longer prayed, nor would she, ever again. But to comfort one so bereaved in such a manner was a prayer more meaningful than any she'd ever been forced to say on her knees in that house of shadow.

When it was over, she lay on her back, studying the pale gold sky through the tender new shoots of spring buds, and said, "I don't want no children of shame, Glendon."

He held her hand tightly. "You won't have. You'll marry me, won't you, Elly?"

"I can't. I have to take care of my mother."

"You could take care of her just as good at my house, couldn't you? And it's gonna be awful lonely there. Why, we could take care of her together. I wouldn't mind having her live with us—and she remembers me, doesn't she? From when I used to deliver ice to your house?"

"I never told her about you, Glendon. She wouldn't understand anyway. She's crazy, don't you see? Scared of the daylight. She never goes out of our house anymore, and I'm afraid if I tried to take her out she'd just plain die of fright."

But Chloe died anyway, within a year of her parents, peacefully, in her sleep. The day she was buried, Elly packed her few meager possessions, closed the door on all those drawn shades, boarded Glendon's wagon and never looked back. They drove to Calhoun, picked up a wedding license at the courthouse and were married within the hour. Their wedding was not so much the consummation of a courtship as a natural extension of two lonely lives that were less lonely when combined. Their married life was much the same: companionship, but no great passion.

And now Elly was marrying again, in a similar way, for similar reasons. She lay in her bed, thinking about tomorrow, a lump in her throat. How was it crazy Elly See never ended up making a marriage that was more than a commonsense agreement? She had feelings too—hurts, wishes, wants like anybody else. Had they been sealed inside her so long that they'd become dried up by all the years she'd been forced into submission and silence in that darkened house? Nobody had taught her a woman's ways with a man. Loving the boys was easy, but letting a man know how you felt about him was another thing.

Why couldn't she have said, Will, I'm scared you'll get hurt out there with the bees? Instead she'd thrown an egg. An egg, for mercy sake, when he'd done so much for her and only wanted to do more. Tears of mortification stung her eyes and she covered them with an arm, remembering. Something strange had happened when he went away laughing instead of angry. Something strange in the pit of her stomach. It was still there when he returned to the house for supper, a feeling she hadn't had before, not even with Glendon. A highness, sort of. A pushing against the bottom of her heart, a tightness in the throat.

It came again, strong and insistent as she pictured Will, all lank and lean and so different from Glendon. Shaved every morning, washed three times a day and put on clean britches each sunrise. Made her more dirty laundry in one week than Glendon had made in a month. But she didn't mind. Not at all. Sometimes, ironing his clothes, she'd think of him in them, and the feeling would come again. A tumble in her stomach, a rise in her blood.

When he had come into the kitchen earlier, and had taken her arm, naked-chested, dark-skinned and still wet from washing at the well, she'd felt almost lightheaded from it. Crazy Elly, wishing Will Parker would kiss her. For a minute she'd thought he might, but he hadn't after all, and common sense told her why. 'Cause she was pregnant, plain and dumb.

She curled into a ball on the bed, miserable, because to-morrow was her wedding and she'd been the one who'd had to do the asking.

CHAPTER
9

On his wedding day Will awakened excited. He had a secret. Something he'd been working on for two weeks and had finished by lanternlight last night at two A.M. Stepping from the barn, he checked the sky—dull as tarnished silver, promising a gloomy, damp day. Women, he supposed, liked sun on their wedding days, but his surprise should cheer her up. He knew exactly when and how he'd present it to her, not until it was time to leave.

They met in the kitchen, feeling uncomfortable and anxious with each other. An odd start to a wedding day with the bride dressed in a blue chenille house robe and the groom in yesterday's overalls. Their first glances were quick and guarded.

"Mornin'."

"Mornin'."

He brought in two pails of bathwater, set them on the stove and began building a fire.

"I suppose you were hopin' for sun," he said with his back to her.

"It would've been nice."

Smiling to himself, thinking again of his secret, he offered, "Maybe it'll break up by the time we leave."

"It don't hardly look like it, and I don't know what I'll do

142

with the boys if it rains. If it does, should we wait till tomorrow?"

He glanced back over his shoulder. "You want to?"

Their eyes met briefly. "No."

Her answer made him smile inside as he headed for the chores. But at breakfast time the tension escalated. It was, after all, their wedding day, and at its end they'd be sharing a bed. But something more was bothering Will. He put off approaching the subject until the meal ended and Elly pushed back her chair as if to begin clearing the table.

"Elly . . . I . . ." He stammered to a stop, drying his palms on his thighs.

"What is it?" She paused, holding two plates.

He wasn't a money-hungry man, but he suddenly understood greed with disarming clarity. He pressed his hands hard against his thighs and blurted out, "I don't know if I got enough money for a license."

"There's the egg money and what you got for selling the scrap metal."

"That's yours."

"Don't be silly. What will it matter after today?"

"A man should buy the license," he insisted, "and a ring."

"Oh . . . a ring." Her hands were in plain sight as she stood beside the table, holding the dirty dishes. He glanced at her left hand and she felt stupid for not having thought to take off her wedding band and leave it in her bureau drawer. "Well . . ." The word dwindled into silence while she pondered and came up with one possible solution. "I . . . I could use the same one."

His face set stubbornly as he rose, pulled his hat on low and lunged across the room toward the sink. "That wouldn't be right."

She watched him gather soap, towels and bathwater and head for the door, pride stiffening his shoulders and adding force to his footsteps.

"What does it matter, Will?"

"It wouldn't be right," he repeated, opening the back door. Half out, he turned back. "What time you wanna leave?"

"I have to get me and the boys ready to go and the dishes washed. And I suppose I should pack some sandwiches."

"An hour?"

"Well . . ."

"An hour and a half?"

"That should be fine."

"I'll pick you up here. You wait in the house for me."

He felt like a fool. Some courtship. Some wedding morning. But he had exactly eight dollars and sixty-one cents to his name, and gold rings cost a damn sight more than that. It wasn't only the ring. It was everything missing in the morning. Touches, smiles, yearning.

Kisses. Shouldn't a bride and groom have trouble restraining themselves at a time like this? That's how he always imagined it would be. Instead they'd scarcely glanced at each other, had discussed the weather and Will Parker's financially embarrassed state.

In the barn he scrubbed his hide with a vengeance, combed his hair and donned freshly laundered clothes: jeans, white shirt, jean jacket, freshly oiled boots and his deformed cowboy hat, brushed for the occasion. Hardly suitable wedding apparel, but the best he could do. Outside thunder rumbled in the distance. Well, at least she didn't have to worry about rain. He had that much to offer his bride this morning, though much of his earlier elation over the surprise had vanished.

In the house Eleanor was on her knees, searching for Donald Wade's shoe under the bed while upon it he and Thomas imitated Madam, kicking and braying.

"Now settle down, boys. We don't want to keep Will waitin'."

"Are we really goin' for a ride in the big wagon?"

"I said so, didn't I?" She caught a foot and started forcing the brown high-top shoe on. "Clear into Calhoun. But when we get to the courthouse you got to be good. Little boys got to be like mice in the corner during weddings, y' understand?"

"But what's weddings, Mama?"

"Why, I told you, honey, me and Will are gettin' married."

"But what's married?"

"Married is—" She paused thoughtfully, wondering exactly what this marriage would be. "Married is when two people say they want to live with each other for the rest of their lives. That's what me and Will are gonna do."

"Oh."

"That's all right with you, ain't it?"

Donald Wade flashed a smile and nodded vigorously. "I like Will."

"And Will likes you, too. And you too, punkin." She touched Thomas's nose. "Nothin's gonna change after we're married, 'cept . . ." The boys waited with their eyes on their mother. " 'Cept y' know how sometimes I let you come in with me at night—well, from now on there won't be no room 'cause Will's gonna be sleepin' with me."

"He is?"

"Aha."

"Can't we even come in when it thunders and lightnin's?"

She pictured them four abreast beneath the quilts and wondered how Will would adjust to the demands of fatherhood. "Well, maybe when it thunders and lightnin's." Thunder rumbled at that moment and Eleanor frowned at the window. "Come on. Will should be comin' any minute." Distractedly she added, "Lord, I got a feelin' we're gonna be soaked before we get to any courthouse."

She helped the boys into jackets, donned her own coat and had just picked up the red sandwich tin from the kitchen cupboard when the thunder growled again, long and steady. She turned, glanced toward the door and cocked her head. Or was it thunder? Too unbroken, too high-pitched and drawing closer. She moved toward the back door just as Donald Wade opened it and a rusty Model A Ford rolled into the clearing with Will at the wheel.

"Glory be," Eleanor breathed.

"It's Will! He gots a car!" Donald Wade tore off at a dead run, slamming the screen, yelling, "Where'd you get it, Will? We gonna ride in it?"

Will pulled up at the foot of the path and stepped out in his coarse wedding attire. Standing with a hand draped over the

top of the car door, he ignored Donald Wade in favor of
Eleanor, who came onto the porch in his favorite yellow dress
covered by a short brown coat that wouldn't close over her
stomach. Her hair was pulled back in a neat tail and her face
glowed with surprise.

"Well, you ain't got a ring," he called, "but you got a jit-
ney to ride to your wedding in. Come on."

With the sandwich tin in one hand and Baby Thomas on
her free arm, she left the porch. "Where did you get it?" she
asked, moving toward Will like a sleepwalker, picking up
speed as she neared.

He let a grin quirk one corner of his mouth. "Out in the
field. Been working on it whenever I could sneak in an hour
here and there."

"You mean it's one of the old junkers?"

"Well . . . not exactly one." With a touch at the back of his
hat brim he tilted it well forward, his eyes following as she
reached the Ford and circled it with a look of admiration on
her face. "More like eight or ten of the junkers, a little bit of
this one and a little bit of that one, held together with baling
twine and Bazooka, but I think it'll get us there and back all
right."

She came full circle and smiled up into his face. "Will
Parker, is there anything you can't do?"

He relieved her of the red sandwich tin and handed it to
Donald Wade, then plucked Thomas from her arms. "I know
a little about engines," he replied modestly, though inside he
glowed. With so few words she'd restored his exhilaration.
"Get in."

"It's actually running!" She laughed and clambered under
the wheel to the far side while the idling engine shimmied the
car seat.

"Of course it's running. And we won't have to worry about
any rain. Here, take the young 'un." He handed Thomas inside, then swung Donald Wade onto the seat and followed,
folding himself behind the wheel. Donald Wade stood on the
seat, wedging himself as tightly against Will as possible. He
laid a proprietary hand on Will's wide shoulder. "We ridin' to
town in *this*?"

"That's right, *kemo sabe*." Will put the car in gear. "Hang on." As they rolled away, the children giggled and Eleanor clutched the seat. Pleased, Will observed their expressions from the corner of his eye.

"But where did you get gasoline?"

"Only got enough to get us to town. Found it in the tanks out there and strained the rust out of it with a rag."

"And you fixed this all by yourself?"

"There were plenty of junkers to take parts from."

"But where'd you learn how?"

"Worked in a filling station in El Paso one time. Fellow there taught me a little about mechanics."

They turned around in a farmyard which was far neater than it had been two months ago. They motored down a driveway which two months ago had been unusable. They traveled in a car that two weeks ago had been a collection of scrap metal. Will couldn't help feeling proud. The boys were entranced. Eleanor's smile was as broad as a melon slice as she steadied Thomas on her knees.

"Like it?"

She turned shining eyes toward Will. "Oh, it's a grand surprise. And my first time, too."

"You mean you never rode in a car before?" he asked, disbelievingly.

"Never. Glendon never got around to fixing any of 'em up. But I rode on his steel mule one time, down the orchard track and back." She shot him a sportive grin. "The noise like to shake m' teeth outa my skull, though."

They laughed and the day lost its bleakness. Their smiles brought a gladness missing till now. While their gazes lingered longer than intended, the fact struck: they were chugging off to the courthouse to get married. Married. Husband and wife forever. Had they been alone, Will might have said something appropriate to the occasion, but Donald Wade moved, cutting off his view of Eleanor.

"We done good on the driveway, huh, Will?" The boy cupped Will's jaw, forcing his direct attention.

"We sure did, short stuff." He ruffled Donald Wade's hair. "But I got to watch the road."

Yes, they'd done good. Guiding the wheel of the Model A, Will felt as he had the day he'd bought the candy bars and bluebird—heated and good inside, expansive and optimistic. In a few hours they would be his "family." Putting pleasure on their faces put pleasure on his own. And it suddenly didn't matter so much that he had no gold ring to offer Eleanor.

Her elation dimmed, however, as they approached Whitney. When they passed the house with the drawn shades she stared straight ahead, refusing to glance at the place. Her lips formed a grim line and her hands tightened on Thomas's hips.

Will wanted to say, I know about that house, Eleanor. It don't matter to me. But a glance at her stiff pose made him bite back the words.

"Got to stop at the filling station," he mentioned, to distract her. "It'll only take a minute."

The man at the station cast overt, speculative glances at Eleanor, but she stared straight ahead like one walking through a graveyard at midnight. The attendant gave Will the twice-over, too, and said, "Nasty weather brewin', looks like."

Will only glanced at the sky.

"Feller'd be happy to have a car on a day like this," the attendant tried again while his eyes darted to Eleanor.

"Yup," Will replied.

"Goin' far?" the man inquired, obviously less interested in pumping gas than in gawking at Eleanor and trying to puzzle out who Will might be and why they were together.

"Nope," Will answered.

"Goin' up Calhoun way?"

Will gave the man a protracted stare, then let his eyes wander to the gas pump. "Five gallons comin' up."

"Oh!" The pump clicked off, Will paid 83 cents and returned to the car, leaving the attendant unenlightened.

When they were on their way again and had left Whitney behind, Eleanor relaxed.

"Someone you know?" Will inquired.

"I know 'em all and they all know me. I seen him gawkin'."

"Prob'ly 'cause you're lookin' right pretty this mornin'."

His words did the trick. She turned a wide-eyed look his way and her ears turned pink. Cheeks, too, before she transferred her attention to the view ahead.

"You don't need to make up pretty words just 'cause it's my weddin' day."

"Wasn't makin' 'em up."

And somehow he felt better, having spoken his mind and given her a touch of what a bride deserves on her wedding day. Better yet, he'd made her forget the house with the picket fence and the gawking gas station attendant.

The ride took them through some of the prettiest country Will had ever seen—rolling hills and gurgling creeks, thick stands of pine and oaks just beginning to turn a faint yellow. Outside, the mist put a sheen on each leaf and rock and turned the roads a vibrant, glistening orange. Wet tree trunks appeared coal black against the pearl-gray sky. The road curved and looped, the elevation constantly dropping until they rounded a bend and saw Calhoun nestled below.

Situated in a long narrow valley, the lowest spot between Chattanooga and Atlanta, the town stretched out along the tracks of the L & N Railroad, which had spawned its growth. U.S. 41 became Wall Street, the main street of town. It paralleled the tracks and carried travelers into a business section that had taken on the same rangy shape as the steel rails themselves. The streets were old, wide, built in the days when mule and wagon had been the chief mode of transportation. Now there were more Chevrolets than mules, more Fords than wagons, and, as in Whitney, blacksmith shops doubling as filling stations.

"You know Calhoun?" Will inquired as they passed a row of neat brick houses on the outskirts.

"Know where the courthouse is. Straight ahead on Wall Street."

"Is there a five-and-dime somewhere?"

"A five-and-dime?" Eleanor flashed him a puzzled look but he watched the road beyond the radiator cap. "What do you want with a five-and-dime?"

"I'm gonna buy you a ring." He'd decided it somewhere between the compliment and Calhoun.

"What's a five-and-dime, Mommy?" Donald Wade interrupted.

Eleanor ignored him. "Oh, Will, you don't have—"

"I'm gonna buy you a ring, I said, then you can take his off."

His insistence sent a flare to her cheeks and she stared at his stubborn jaw until the warmth spread down to her heart. She turned away and said meekly, "I already did."

Will shot a glance at her left hand, still resting on the baby's hip. It was true—the ring was gone. On the steering wheel his grip relaxed.

Donald Wade patted his mother's arm, demanding, "What's a five-and-dime, Mommy?"

"It's a store that sells trinkets and things."

"Trinkets? Can we go there?"

"I reckon that's where Will's takin' us first." Her eyes wandered to the driver and found him watching her. Their gazes locked, fascinated.

"Oh-boy!" Donald Wade knelt on the seat, balancing himself against the dashboard, staring at the town with unbridled fascination. "What's that, Mommy?" He pointed. She didn't hear and he whapped her arm four times. "Mommy, what's that?"

"Better answer the boy," Will advised quietly, and turned his attention back to the street, releasing her to do the same.

"A water tower."

Baby Thomas repeated, *"Wa-doo tow-woo."*

"What's that?" Donald Wade asked.

"A popcorn wagon."

"Pop-cone," the baby echoed.

"They sell it?"

"Yes, son."

"Goll-eee! Can we git some?"

"Not today, dear. We got to hurry."

He watched the wagon until it disappeared behind them and Will mentally tallied up the remainder of his money. Only seven bucks, seventy-eight cents, and he had to buy a ring and a license yet.

"What's that?"

"A theater."

"What's a theater?"

"A place where they show movies."

"What's a movie?"

"Well, it's sort of a picture story that moves on a big screen."

"Can we see it?"

"No, honey. It costs money."

The marquee said *Border Vigilantes*, and Will noted how both Donald Wade's and Eleanor's eyes lingered on it as they passed. Seven measly bucks and seventy-eight measly cents. What he wouldn't do for full pockets right now.

Just then he spotted what he was looking for, a brick-fronted building with a sign announcing, WISTER'S VARIETY—HOUSEWARES, TOYS & SUNDRIES.

He parked the car and reached for Donald Wade. "Come on, *kemo sabe*, I'll show you a five-and-dime."

Inside, they walked the aisles on creaking wood floors between six rows of pure enchantment. Donald Wade and Thomas pointed at everything and squirmed to get down and touch—toy cars and trucks and tractors made of brightly painted metal; rubber balls of gay reds and yellows; marbles in woven sacks; bubble gum and candy; six-shooters and holsters and cowboy hats like Will's.

"I want one!" Donald Wade demanded. "I want a hat like Will's!"

"Hat," parroted Thomas.

"Maybe next time," Will replied, his heart breaking. At that moment the only thing he wanted worse than a ring for Eleanor was enough cash to buy two black cardboard cowboy hats.

They came to the costume jewelry and stopped. The display was dusty, spread on rose taffeta between glass dividers. There were identification bracelets; baby necklaces shaped like tiny gold crosses; little girls' birthday sets—rings, bracelets and necklaces—all dipped in gold paint, set with brightly colored glass gems; women's earrings of assorted shapes and colors; and beside them, on a blue velvet card, a sign that said, "Friendship Rings—19¢."

Will studied the cheap things, stung at having to offer his bride a wedding band that would surely turn her finger green before a week was up. But he had little choice. He set Donald Wade down. "You take Thomas's hand and don't let him touch anything, all right?"

The boys headed back toward the toys, leaving Will and Eleanor standing self-consciously side by side. He slipped his hands into his hind pockets and stared at the fake-silver rings with their machine-stamped lattice designs covered with crudely formed roses. He reached for one, plucked it from the card and studied it glumly.

"I never cared much before whether I had money or not, but today I wish my name was Rockerfeller."

"I'm glad it ain't, 'cause then I wouldn't be marrying you."

He looked down into her eyes—eyes as green as the fake peridots in the August birth rings—and it struck Will that she was one of the kindest persons he'd ever met. How like her to try to make him feel good at a moment like this. "It'll probably turn your finger green."

"It don't matter, Will," she said softly. "I shouldn't have offered to use my old one again. It was thoughtless of me."

"I'd give you gold if I could, Eleanor. I want you to know that."

"Oh, Will . . ." She reached out and covered his hand consolingly as he went on.

"And I'd take them two to the movies, and afterwards maybe buy 'em an ice cream cone at the drugstore, or popcorn at that popcorn wagon like they begged for."

"I brought the egg and cream money, Will. We could still do that."

His gaze shifted to the ring. "I'm the one that should be payin', don't you see?"

She released his hand and took the ring to try it on. "You got to learn not to be so proud, Will. Let's see if it fits." The ring was too big, so she chose another. The second one fit and she spread her fingers in the air before them, as proud as if she wore a glittering diamond.

"Looks fine, doesn't it?" She wiggled the ring finger. "And I *do* like roses."

"It looks cheap."

"Don't you dare say that about my weddin' ring, Will Parker," she scolded him with mock haughtiness, slipping it off and depositing it in his palm. "The sooner you pay for it the sooner we can get on down to the courthouse and speak our words."

She turned away blithely, but he caught her arm and spun her around.

"Eleanor, I . . ." He looked into her eyes and didn't know what to say. A lump of appreciation clotted his throat. The value of the ring honestly made no difference to her.

She cocked her head. "What?"

"You never complain about anything, do you?"

It was subtle praise, but no poetry could have pleased her more.

"We got a lot to be thankful for, Will Parker. Come on." Her smile flashed as she grabbed his hand. "Let's go get married."

They found the Gordon County courthouse with no trouble, a red brick Victorian edifice on a crest of land framed by sidewalks, green grass and azalea bushes. Will carried Donald Wade; Eleanor, Thomas, as they ascended a bank of steps and crossed the lawn, gazing up at the rounded turret on the right, and on the left, a square cenotaph to General Charles Haney Nelson. It sat sturdily on thick brick arches culminating in a pointed clock tower that overlooked the chimneyed roof. The mist was cold on their uplifted faces, then disappeared as they mounted the second set of steps beneath the arches and entered a marble-floored hall that smelled of cigar smoke.

"This way." Eleanor's voice rang through the empty hall, though she spoke quietly. Turning right, she led Will to the office of the Ordinary of the Court.

Inside, at an oak desk beyond a spindled rail, a thin, middle-aged woman—her nameplate read Reatha Stickner—stopped typing and tipped her head down to peer over rimless octagonal spectacles.

"May I help you?" She had a cheerless, authoritarian voice. It echoed in the barren, curtainless room.

"Yes, ma'am," Will replied, stopping just inside the door. "We'd like to get a marriage license."

The woman's sharp gaze brushed from Donald Wade to Baby Thomas to Eleanor's stomach, then back to Will. He firmly grasped Eleanor's elbow and ushered her toward the breast-high counter. The woman pushed away from her desk and shuffled toward them with an extreme limp that dipped one shoulder and left one foot dragging. They met on opposite sides of the barrier and Reatha Stickner fished inside the neck of her dress to pull up an underwear strap that had slipped down while she walked.

"Are you residents of Georgia?" From beneath the counter she drew a black-bound book the size of a tea tray and clapped it down between them without glancing up again.

"I am," Eleanor spoke up. "I live in Whitney."

"Whitney. And how long have you lived there?" The black cover slapped open, revealing forms separated by carbons.

"All my life."

"I'll need proof of residency."

Will thought, *Oh no, not again.* But Eleanor surprised him by depositing Thomas on the high counter and producing a folded paper from her coat pocket. "Got my first wedding license here. You gave it to me, so it should be okay."

The woman examined Eleanor minutely, without a change of expression—pursed lips, haughty eyebrows—then turned her attention to the license while Thomas reached for a stamp pad. Eleanor grabbed his hand and held it while he objected vocally and struggled to pull it free.

"Don't touch," she whispered, but of course, he grew stubborn and insisted, louder than before. Will set Donald Wade on the floor and plucked the baby off the counter to hold him. Donald Wade immediately tried to climb Will's leg, complaining, "I can't see. Lift me up." The boy's fingertips curled over the countertop and he tried to climb it with his feet. Will gave him a yank to straighten him up. "Be good," he ordered, bending momentarily. Donald Wade wilted against the counter, pouting.

Reatha Stickner cast a disapproving glance at the faces visible above her counter, then moved away to fetch a pen and inkholder. She had to adjust her strap again before writing in the wide book.

"Eleanor Dinsmore—middle name?"

"I ain't got one."

Though the clerk refused to lift her eyes, the pen twitched in her fingers. "Same address?"

"Yes ..." Imitating Will, Eleanor added belatedly, "... ma'am."

"And are there any encumbrances against you getting married?"

Eleanor fixed a blank look on the woman's spectacles. Reatha Stickner glanced up impatiently and said, "Well?"

Eleanor turned to Will for help.

Will felt his hackles rise and spoke sharply. "She's not married and she's not a Nazi. What other encumbrances are there?"

Everything was silent for three seconds while the stern-faced clerk fixed Will with a disapproving glare. Finally, she cleared her throat, dipped her pen and loftily returned her attention to the application blank. "And how about you? Are *you* a Nazi?" It was asked without a hint of humor while she gave the impression that she might have looked up but for the fact that the person she was serving wasn't worthy.

"No, ma'am. Just an ex-convict." Will felt a deep thrill of satisfaction as her head snapped up and a white line appeared around her lips. He reached casually into his shirt pocket for his release papers. "Think you have to see these."

Her strap fell down and had to be hitched up again as she accepted Will's papers. She examined them at length, gave him another sour glance and wrote on the application.

"Parker, William Lee. Address?"

"Same as hers."

The clerk's eyes, magnified by her glasses, rolled up for another lengthy visual castigation. In the silence Donald Wade's footsteps could be heard climbing the desk wall as he hung on it and gazed at the door, upside-down.

Will thought, *Go to it, Donald Wade!*

Primly, the woman wrote on, taking the information from

Will's papers. "How long have you been at this address?" she
asked, while her pen scratched loudly.

"Two months."

Her eyes flickered to Eleanor's bulbous stomach, the thin
band of yellow showing behind the brown coat. Her chin
drew in, creating two folds beneath it. She applied her official
signature, and ordered coldly, "That'll be two dollars."

Will stifled a sigh of relief and dug the money from his
breast pocket. The clerk dipped below the counter, came up
with an official rubber stamp and with curt motions stamped
the license, tore it out, slapped the book closed—fap! sktch!
whp!—and brandished the paper across the counter.

Stone-faced, but seething, Will accepted it and tipped his
hat. "Much obliged, ma'am. Now, who marries us?"

Her eyes drifted over his blue denim work clothes, then
dropped to the rubber stamp. "Judge Murdoch."

"Murdoch." When she looked up, Will gave her a cool
nod. "We'll find him."

Acidly she hurried to inform them, "He has a full docket
this morning. You should have made arrangements in advance."

Will settled Baby Thomas more comfortably on his arm,
peeled Donald Wade off the counter, headed him toward the
door, then clasped Eleanor's elbow and guided her from the
office without acknowledging Reatha Stickner's high-handed
order. His grip was biting and his footsteps unnaturally
lengthy. In the corridor, he grated, "Goddamn old biddy. I
wanted to slap her when she looked at you like that. What
right's she got to look down her nose at you!"

"It don't matter, Will. I'm used to it. But what about the
judge? What if he's too busy?"

"We'll wait."

"But she said he—"

"We'll wait, I said!" His footsteps pounded harder. "How
long can it take him to mutter a few words and sign a paper?"
Coming up short, he stopped Eleanor. "Just a minute." He
stuck his head inside an open doorway and asked, "Where do
we find Judge Murdoch?"

"Second floor, halfway down the hall, the double doors on your left."

With the same stubborn determination, Will herded them to the second floor, through the double doors, where they found themselves in a courtroom presently in session. They stood uncertainly in the aisle between two flanks of benches while voices from up front reverberated beneath the vaulted ceiling. An officer in a tan uniform left his station beside the doors. "You'll have to be seated if you want to stay," he whispered.

Will turned, ready to do mortal injury to anyone who got uppity with them again. But the man was no more than twenty-five, had a pleasant face and polite manner. "We want the judge to marry us but we don't have an appointment."

"Step outside," the deputy invited, opening one of the doors and holding it while they filed into the hall. Joining them, he checked his watch. "He's got a pretty full day, but you can wait outside his chambers if you want. See if he can squeeze you in."

"We'll do that. Appreciate it if you'd head us in the right direction," Will returned tightly.

"Right this way." He led them to the end of the hall and pointed to a narrower corridor leading off at a right angle. "I have to stay in the courtroom, but you'll find it easily. His name is above the door. Just have a seat on the bench across from it."

Neither Will nor Eleanor owned a watch. They sat on an eight-foot wooden bench, staring at a maple door for what seemed hours. They read and reread the brass plaque above it: ALDON P. MURDOCH, DISTRICT COURT JUDGE. The boys tired of climbing over the curved arms of the bench and grew fractious. Donald Wade badgered, "Mommy, let's *go-o-o*." Thomas started whining and flailing his feet against the seat. Finally he fell asleep, sprawled on the bench with his head in Eleanor's lap, leaving Will to keep Donald Wade occupied.

The door opened and two men bustled out, talking animatedly. Will jumped to his feet and raised a finger, but the pair marched away, deep in discussion, without sparing a glance for the four on the bench.

The wait continued; Eleanor got a backache and had to

find the bathroom. Thomas woke up with an ugly disposition and Donald Wade whined that he was hungry. When Eleanor returned, Will ran to the car for their sandwiches. They were sitting on the bench eating them, trying to convince Baby Thomas to give up crying and try a bite, when one of the two men returned.

This time he stopped voluntarily. "Got a cranky one there, huh?" He smiled indulgently at Thomas.

"Judge Murdoch?" Will leaped to his feet, whipping his hat from his head.

"That's right." He was gray-haired, rotund and had jowls like a bloodhound. But though he wore the air of a busy man, he seemed approachable. "I'm Will Parker. And this is Eleanor Dinsmore. We were wondering if you'd have time to marry us today."

Murdoch extended a hand. "Parker." He nodded to Eleanor. "Miss Dinsmore." He gave each of the boys a grandfatherly glance, then assessed Eleanor thoughtfully. "You were here when I left for lunch, weren't you?"

"Yessir," she answered.

"How long before that?"

"I don't know, sir, we ain't got no watch."

The judge shot a cuff and checked his own. "Court reconvenes in ten minutes."

Eleanor rushed on. "We ain't got no phone either, or we'd've called to make an appointment. We just drove up from Whitney, thinkin' it'd be all right."

Again the judge smiled at the boys, then at the sandwich in Eleanor's hand. "Looks like you brought your witnesses with you."

"Yessir . . . I mean, no sir. These are my boys. That's Donald Wade . . . and this here is Baby Thomas."

The judge leaned down and extended a hand. "How do you do, Donald Wade." The youngster glanced up uncertainly at Will and waited for his nod before hesitantly giving his hand to the judge. Murdoch performed the handshake with gravity and a half-smile. Next he offered Thomas a wink and a chuckle. "You boys have had a long enough morning. How would you like a jelly bean?"

Donald Wade inquired, "What's a jelly bean?"

"Well, come into my office and I'll show you."

Again Donald Wade looked to Will for guidance.

"Go ahead."

To the adults, Judge Murdoch advised, "I think I can squeeze you in. It won't be fancy, but it'll be legal. Step inside."

It was a crowded room with a single north window and more books than Will had ever seen anywhere except in the Whitney library. He glanced around, his hat forgotten against his thigh, while the judge gave his attention first to the boys. "Come around here." He moved behind a cluttered desk and from a lower drawer extracted a cigar box labeled "Havana Jewels." The boys peered inside as he opened it and announced, "Jelly beans." Without objection they allowed the district court judge to set them side-by-side on his chair and roll it close to the desk, where he placed the cigar box on an open law book. "I keep them hidden because I don't want my wife to catch me eating them." He patted his portly stomach. "She says I eat too many of them." As the boys reached for the candy, he warned with a twinkle in his eye, "Now be sure you save some for me."

From a coat tree he took a black robe, inquiring of Will, "Do you have a license?"

"Yessir."

A door opened on his left and the same young deputy who'd directed Will and Eleanor to the judge's chambers stuck his head inside. "One o'clock, your honor."

"Come in here, Darwin, and close the door."

"Pardon me, sir, but we're runnin' a little late."

"So we are. They won't go anyplace, not until I say they can."

As the young man followed orders, the judge buttoned his robe and performed introductions. "Darwin Ewell, this is Eleanor Dinsmore and Will Parker. They're going to be married and we'll need you to act as witness."

The deputy shook their hands, wearing a pleasant smile. "Pleasure, sir . . . ma'am."

The judge indicated the boys. "And the two with the jelly beans are Donald Wade and Baby Thomas."

Darwin laughed as he observed the pair selecting another color from the cigar box, paying no attention to the others in the room. In moments the judge stood before Will and Eleanor, examining their license, then placing it on the desk behind him and crossing his hands over his mounded stomach.

"I've got books I could read from," he informed them with a benevolent expression on his face, "but they always sound a little stilted and formal to me so I prefer to do this my own way. The books always manage to miss some of the most important things. Like do you know each other well enough to believe what you're doing is the right thing?"

Taken by surprise at the unorthodox beginning, Will was a little slow to reply. He glanced at Eleanor first, then back at the judge.

"Yessir."

"Yessir," Eleanor repeated.

"How long have you known each other?"

Each waited for the other to answer. Finally Will did. "Two months."

"Two months . . ." The judge seemed to ponder, then added, "I knew my wife exactly three and a half weeks before I proposed to her. We've been married thirty-two years—happily, I might add. Do you love each other?"

This time they stared straight at the judge. Both of them turned slightly pink.

"Yessir," came Will's answer.

"Yessir," Eleanor's echoed, more softly. Will's heart thundered, while he wondered if it was true.

"Good . . . good. Now the times when I want you to remember that are the times when you'll be at cross purposes—and nobody who remains married for thirty-two, or fifty-two or even *two* years can avoid them. But disagreements can become arguments, then battles, then wars, unless you learn to compromise. It's the wars you'll have to avoid, and you do that by remembering what you've just told me. That you love each other. All right?" He waited.

"Yessir," they replied in unison.

"Compromise is the cornerstone of marriage. Can you work things out and reach compromises instead of giving way to anger?"

"Yessir."

"Yessir." Eleanor's eyes couldn't quite meet the judge's as she remembered the egg running down Will's face. Then honesty got the best of her and she added, "I'll try real hard."

The judge smiled, then nodded approvingly. "And you'll work hard for Eleanor, Will?"

"Yessir, I already do."

"And will you provide a good home for Will, Eleanor?"

"Yessir, I already do."

To the judge's credit, he didn't bat an eye.

"I take it the children are yours by a former marriage, is that right?"

She nodded.

"And the one you're expecting—that makes three." He turned his attention to Will. "Three children is a grave responsibility to take on, and in the future there may be more. Do you accept responsibility for them, along with that of being a husband and provider for Eleanor?"

"Yessir."

"You're both young yet. In your lives you may meet others who attract you. When that happens, I exhort you to recall this day and what your feelings were for each other as you stood before me, to remember your vows of fidelity and remain true to one another. Would that be hard for you?"

Will thought of Lula. "No, it wouldn't."

Eleanor thought of the jeers she'd received from boys in school and how Will was the only one since Glendon who'd treated her kindly. "No, not at all."

"Then, let's seal it with a promise—to love each other, to remain true to each other, to provide love and material care for each other and for all the children entrusted to you, to work hard for one another, practice patience, forgiveness and understanding, and treat each other with respect and dignity for the rest of your lives. Do you so promise, William Lee Parker?"

"I do."

"And do you so promise, Eleanor Dinsmore?"

"I do."

"Are there rings?"

"Yessir." Will found the dime-store ring in his breast pocket. "Just one."

The judge seemed unsurprised by its obvious cheapness. "Put it on her finger now and join right hands."

Will reached for Eleanor's hand and slid the ring partially over her knuckle. Their eyes met briefly, then skittered downward as he held her hand loosely. Judge Murdoch continued, "Let this ring be a symbol of your constancy and devotion. Let it remind you, William, who gives it, and you, Eleanor, who wears it, that from this day until you're parted by death you will remain forever one, inseparable. Now, by the power invested in me by the sovereign state of Georgia, I pronounce you husband and wife."

It had been so quick, so undramatic. It didn't feel done. And if done, not real. Will and Eleanor stood before the judge like a pair of tree stumps.

"Is that it?" Will inquired.

Judge Murdoch smiled. "All but the kiss." Then he twisted around to sign the marriage certificate on the desk behind him.

The pair stared at Murdoch's shoulders but didn't move. On the chair the boys munched jelly beans. From the courtroom came the murmur of voices. On the stiff paper the pen scratched while Deputy Ewell watched expectantly.

The judge dropped his pen and turned back to find the newlyweds standing stiffly, shoulder to shoulder.

"Well . . ." he prompted.

Their faces bright with color, Will and Eleanor turned toward each other. She lifted her face self-consciously and he looked down likewise.

"My court is waiting," Judge Murdoch admonished softly.

With his heart racing, Will placed his hands lightly on Eleanor's arms and bent to touch her lips briefly. They were warm and open, as if in surprise. He got a glimpse of her eyes at close range—also open, as his own were. Then he straightened, ending the uncomfortable moment as they faced the judge self-consciously.

"Congratulations, Mr. Parker." Judge Murdoch pumped Will's hand. "Mrs. Parker." And Eleanor's. As he pronounced her new name Eleanor's discomfort intensified. Heat climbed her body and her cheeks burned hotter.

Judge Murdoch handed the marriage certificate to Will. "I wish you many years of happiness, and now I'd better get back to my courtroom before they start beating on my door." He turned toward it in a flurry of black robes and paused with a hand on the knob. "You have a fine pair of boys there—so long, boys!" With one last wave, he disappeared. Darwin Ewell, also due back in court, wished them luck and hastily ushered them out.

It had taken less than five minutes from the time they'd entered the judge's chambers until they found themselves in the hall again, united for life. The judge's whirlwind pace left them both feeling disoriented but scarcely married. It had been startlingly unceremonious; they hadn't even been aware that the first questions were part of the judge's unorthodox rite. It had ended much the same—no pomp, no pageantry, only a simple pronunciation beneath clasped hands, and— bango!—back in the hall. If it hadn't been for the kiss, they might not believe a marriage had taken place at all.

"Well," Will said breathlessly with a mystified laugh. "That was that."

Eleanor's perplexed gaze remained on the closed door. "I guess it was. But . . . so quick."

"Quick, but legal."

"Yes . . . but . . ." She lifted dubious eyes to Will and thrust her head forward. "But do you *feel* married?"

Unexpectedly, he laughed. "Not exactly. But we must be. He called you Mrs. Parker."

She lifted her left hand and gazed at it disbelievingly. "So I am. Mrs. Will Parker."

The belated impact struck them full force. *Mr. and Mrs. Will Parker.* They absorbed the fact with all its attendant implications while their eyes were drawn to one another as if by polaric force. He thought about kissing her again, the way he wanted to. And she wondered what it would be like. But neither of them dared. In time they realized how long they'd been staring. Eleanor grew flustered and let her gaze drop. Will chuckled and scratched his nose.

"I think we should celebrate," he announced.

"How?" she asked, reaching down for Baby Thomas. Will nudged her aside and hoisted Thomas onto his arm.

"Well, if my arithmetic is right, I still have four dollars and fifty-nine cents. I think we should take the boys to the movie."

Excitement splashed across Eleanor's face. "Really?"

Donald Wade began jumping up and down, clapping. "Yeah! Yeah! The movie! Take us to the movie, Mommy, pleeeease!" He clutched Eleanor's hand.

Will took Eleanor's free elbow, guiding her down the hall. "I don't know, Donald Wade," he teased, turning a crooked grin on his wife's eager face. "It looks to me like we might have some trouble convincing your mama."

Then Mr. and Mrs. William Lee Parker—and family—left the courthouse smiling.

CHAPTER

10

The smell of popcorn greeted them in the theater lobby. With eyes wide and fascinated, the boys stared up at the red and white popcorn machine, then appealed to their mother. "Mama, can we have some?" Will's heart melted. He was reaching into his shirt pocket before Eleanor could frame a refusal. Inside the dimly lit auditorium, Donald Wade and Thomas sat on their knees, munching, until the screen lit up with *Previews of Coming Attractions.* When scenes from *Gone With the Wind* radiated overhead, their hands and jaws seemed to stop functioning. So did Eleanor's. Will eyed her askance as myriad reactions flashed across her face—amazement, awe, rapture.

"Oh, Will," she breathed. "Oh, Will, look!"

Sometimes he did. But he found the study of their faces—especially hers—far more fascinating as they were transported for the first time into the world of celluloid make-believe.

"Oh, Will, look at that dress!"

His attention wavered briefly to the billowing, hoop-skirted garment, then returned to his wife's face, realizing something new about her: she was a woman whose head could be turned by finery. He would not have guessed so from the ordinary way she dressed. But her eyes shone and her lips looked as if they were about to speak to the images on the screen.

The color film disappeared and a newsreel came on in black and white: goose-stepping German soldiers, bombs, mortar shells, the battlefront in Russia, wounded soldiers—an abrupt plunge from fantasy to reality.

Will watched the screen with rapt interest, wondering how long America could possibly stay out of the war, wondering how long he himself could stay out of it if the inevitable happened. He had a family now; his welfare suddenly mattered fiercely, whereas it never had before. It was a shock to him to realize this.

As the newsreel ended he turned and caught Eleanor watching him above the boys' heads. The gaiety had disappeared from her eyes, replaced by a troubled frown. Obviously the grim reality of war had finally imposed itself upon her. He felt a stab of remorse for having been the one to expose her to it, the one who'd brought her here to have her sunny illusions shattered. He wanted to reach above the pair of blond heads and touch her eyelids, say to her, close your eyes for a moment and go back to pretending it isn't happening. Be the happy recluse you were.

But just as he could not ignore the battles in Europe, and America's ever-increasing support for England and France, neither must she. She couldn't remain an ostrich forever, not when she was married to a man of prime age for induction, one with a prison record who was sure to be one of the first called up.

The newsreel ended and the main feature began.

Border Vigilantes turned out to be a Hopalong Cassidy movie, and the boys' reaction made it well worth the six bits Will had laid out. He himself enjoyed the show, and Eleanor's elation returned. But the boys—oh, those two little boys. What a sight they made with their entranced faces lifted to the silver screen while the hero fought for law and justice on his white steed, Topper. Donald Wade's mouth hung open when Topper galloped into view for the first time and reared up majestically, his rider flourishing a black hat like Will's own. Baby Thomas pointed and stared with owl eyes, his mouth forming a tight O. Then he squealed and clapped and had to be shushed. Eleanor's expression shifted from one of rapt wonder to childlike delight as the scenes rolled on.

Hopalong got the lady in the end, and when he kissed her Will glanced over at his new wife. As if she felt his survey, she turned again. Their profiles, illuminated by fluttering light, appeared as half-moons in the dark theater while their own first kiss came back afresh, and they were reminded of the night ahead. In that brief moment feelings of anxiety somersaulted through them. Then the finale music swelled, Hopalong rode off into the sunset and the boys set up an excited babbling.

"Is it all done? Where did Hopalong go? Can we come again, Will, can we, huh?"

In the car there was no talk between Will and Eleanor as there'd been that morning. Baby Thomas slept curled on her lap. Donald Wade—wearing Will's hat—pressed himself against Will's shoulder and exuberated over the wonders of Hopalong and Topper. Though Will answered, his thoughts projected to the night ahead. Bedtime. He cast occasional covert glances at Eleanor but she stared straight ahead and he wondered if she was thinking about the same thing as he.

At home, Will tended the evening chores automatically, his mind on the bedroom he'd never seen, their first kiss today, how guarded they'd been with each other, the night ahead, a real bed and a woman to share it. But a pregnant woman, pregnant enough to eliminate the possibilities of any conjugal commerce. He wondered what a woman as pregnant as Elly looked like naked and his body felt taut with a combination of chagrin at the thought of possibly seeing her that way, and the idea of lying beside her all night long without touching her.

Had he imagined a wedding day, ever, it wouldn't have been like this—himself in blue jeans, the bride seven months pregnant, a dime-store ring, five minutes in a judge's chamber and a Hopalong Cassidy movie with two rambunctious boys. But the unlikely events of the day weren't over yet.

Supper—due to their late return—was scarcely a wedding feast. Scrambled eggs, green beans and side pork. Donald

Wade bawled when Eleanor refused to let him wear Will's hat at the table. Baby Thomas spit out his green beans on Eleanor's yellow dress, and when she scolded him he swatted his tumbler of milk across the room. Eleanor, her skirt soaked, leaped up and slapped his hand. Thomas howled like a fire siren while Will sat by helplessly, realizing that family life had some surprises in store for him. Eleanor went off to fetch a basin and a rag, leaving him to ponder the probability that if this wedding day seemed a letdown to an unsentimental fool like him, it must seem a sore disappointment to her. She returned to the fiasco at the table but he wouldn't let her get down on her hands and knees in her pretty yellow dress, especially when she had to struggle these days to get up and down.

"Here, I'll do that." He took the pail from her hand, trying to imagine what it must be like to carry a bride across the threshold of a honeymoon suite on the twentieth floor of the Ritz Hotel. He wished he could do that for her. Instead he could only offer, "You go take care of your dress."

She lifted her face and he saw in her green eyes the same misgivings he had, the same strain, intensified by the boys' uncharacteristic naughtiness on this night when it was the last thing they needed. He was touched more deeply by the fact that she was near tears.

"Thank you, Will."

"Go." He turned her toward the bedroom and gave her a gentle shove.

Funny how one bit of cooperation led to another. A half hour later he found himself beside her, drying dishes, and a half hour after that, helping her get the boys ready for bed.

The pair had had a tiring day and they surrendered to their pillows with remarkable docility. While she tucked them in he wandered the room collecting their discarded clothes, small items that smelled of spilled milk and first trips to town, popcorn and broomstick cowboys. From beside a scarred chest of drawers Will watched Eleanor kiss them goodnight, smiling at the scene. Two pajama-clad boys with faces scrubbed shiny being reassured by their mother that they were loved in spite of their recent misbehavior. She had

changed into a worn smock of faded brown that bellied out
as she leaned over Donald Wade, kissed his mouth, his cheek,
touched his nose with her own and murmured something for
his ears only. And next, Baby Thomas, over the side of the
crib, kissing him, toppling him into a tired heap, then brushing his hair back while he clasped a favorite blanket and
stuck a thumb in his mouth.

Resting an elbow on the dresser top, Will smiled softly.
Again came the yearning for things missed, but watching was
almost as good as taking part. In those moments, his love for
Eleanor swelled, became something more than the love of a
husband for a wife. She became the mother he'd never
known, the boys became himself—safe, secure, cared for.

With a pang of awe he realized he would be part of this
tableau every night. He could wash freckled faces, stuff arms
into pajama sleeves, collect dirty clothes and hover over their
affectionate goodnights. Vicariously he might recapture a por-
tion of what he'd missed.

The ritual ended. Eleanor lifted the side of the crib and
waggled two fingers at Donald Wade. Abruptly he sat up and
demanded, "I wanna kiss Will goodnight."

Will's elbow came off the dresser and his face registered
surprise. Eleanor turned and met his gaze across the lamplit
room.

She noted his hesitation but saw beyond it to the stronger
tug of anticipation. "Donald Wade wants to kiss you," she reiterated.

"Me?" He felt like an interloper though his chest tightened
expectantly. Donald Wade lifted his arms. Will glanced again
at Eleanor, chuckled, scratched his chin and crossed the room,
feeling awkward and out of place. He sat on the edge of the
bed and the boy's arms clasped his neck without restraint.
The small mouth—moist and smelling faintly of milk—
pressed Will's briefly. It was so unexpected, so . . . so . . .
genuine. He'd never kissed a child goodnight before, had
never guessed how it got to your insides and warmed you
from there, out.

" 'Night, Will."

" 'Night, *kemo sabe*."

"I'm Hopalong."

Will laughed. "Oh, my mistake. I shoulda checked to see which horse was tied at the hitchin' rail outside."

When Will rose from Donald Wade's bed, Baby Thomas was no longer lying down. He was standing at the rail of his crib with his mouth plump and his eyes unblinking, watching. Baby Thomas . . . who'd taken longer to warm to Will. Baby Thomas . . . who still intimidated the grown man at times. Baby Thomas . . . who imitated everything his older brother did. His kiss was hugless, but his tiny mouth warm and moist when Will bent to touch it.

Lord a-mighty, he'd never have guessed how a pair of goodnight kisses could make a man feel. Wanted. Loved.

" 'Night, Thomas."

Thomas stared at him with big hazel eyes.

"Say goodnight to Will," his mother prompted softly.

"G'night, Wiw."

Never before had Thomas spoken Will's name. The distorted pronunciation went straight to the thin man's heart as he watched Eleanor settle him down a second time before joining Will in the doorway.

They stood a moment, shoulder to shoulder, studying the children. A closeness stole over them, binding them with an accord that washed away the many shortcomings of this day, leaving them with a faith in better things to come.

Leaving the boys' door ajar, they stepped into the front room. It was dark but for the trailing light from the boys' lantern and another on the kitchen table.

Will ran a hand through his hair, draped it around his neck and smiled at the floor. After a moment his chest lifted with a pleasured chuckle.

"I never did that before."

"I know."

He searched for a way to express the fullness in his heart. But there was no way. To an orphan turned drifter, a drifter turned prisoner, a prisoner turned hired hand, a hired hand turned stand-in daddy, there was no way to express what the last five minutes had meant to him. Will could only waggle his head in wonder. "That's somethin', isn't it?"

She understood. His surprise and wonder said it all. He had never expected the right to her children to come along with the right to her house. Yet she recognized his growing affection for them, saw clearly what kind of father he could be— gentle, patient, the kind who'd take none of the small pleasures for granted.

"Yes, it is."

He dropped his hand and lifted his head. A soft smile curved his lips. "I really like those two, you know?"

"Even after the way they acted at supper?"

"Oh, that—that was nothin'. They'd had a big day. I reckon their springs were still twangin'."

She smiled.

He did, too, briefly before sobering. "I want you to know I'll do right by them."

Her voice softened. "Oh, Will . . . I know that."

"Well," he went on almost sheepishly, "they're pretty special."

"I think so, too."

Their gazes met momentarily. They searched for something to say, something to do. But it was bedtime; there was only one thing to do. Yet both of them were reluctant to suggest it. In the kitchen the radio was playing "Chattanooga Choo Choo." The strains came through the lighted doorway into the shadows where they paused uncertainly. Across from the boys' room, their own bedroom door stood open, an oblique shadow waiting to take them in. Beyond it waited uncertainty and self-consciousness.

Eleanor fiddled with her hands, searching for a subject to put off bedtime. "Thank you for the movie, Will. The boys will never forget it and neither will I."

"I enjoyed it, too."

End of subject.

"I liked the popcorn, too," she added hurriedly.

"So did I."

End of subject, again.

This time Will found a diversion—the boys' clothes, still balled in his hands. "Oh, here!" He thrust them into hers.

"Forgot I still had 'em." He rammed his hands into his pockets.

Looking down at Thomas's milk-streaked shirt, she said, "Thanks for helping me get them ready for bed."

"Thanks for letting me."

A quick exchanged glance, two nervous smiles, then silence again, immense and overpowering, while they stood close and studied the collection of clothes in her hands. It was her house, her bedroom— Will felt like a guest waiting to be invited to stay the night, but still she made no mention of retiring. He heard his own pulse drumming in his ears and felt as if he were wearing somebody else's collar, one size too small. Somebody had to break the ice.

"Are you tired?" he asked.

"No!" she replied, too quickly, too wide-eyed. Then, dropping her head, "Well . . . yes, I am a little."

"I guess I'll step out back then."

When he was gone, her shoulders wilted, she closed her eyes and pressed her burning cheeks into the stale-smelling clothes. *Silly woman. What's there to be skittish about? He's going to share your mattress and your quilts—so what?*

She freed her hair, washed her face and got ready for bed in record time. By the time she heard him reenter the kitchen she was safely dressed in a white muslin nightgown with the quilts tucked to her armpits. She lay stiffly, listening to the sounds of him washing up for bed. He turned off the radio, checked the fire, replaced a stovelid. Then all remained quiet but for the beat of her own pulse in her ears and the tick of the windup alarm clock beside the bed. Minutes passed before she heard his footsteps cross the front room and pause. She stared at the doorway, imagining him gathering courage while her own heart throbbed like the engine of Glendon's old Steel Mule the time she'd ridden it.

Will paused outside the bedroom doorway, fortifying himself with a deep breath. He crossed the threshold to find Eleanor lying on her back in a proper, white, long-sleeved nightie. Her brown hair lay free against the white pillow and her hands were crossed over the high mound formed by her stomach beneath the quilts. Though her expression was carefully bland, her cheeks wore two blots of pink, as if some seraph had winged in and placed a rose petal upon each. "Come in, Will."

He swept a slow glance across the room—curtainless window, homemade rag rug, hand-tied quilt, iron bedstead painted white, a closet door ajar, a bedside table and kerosene lamp, a tall bureau with a dresser scarf and a picture of a man with large ears and a receding hairline.

"I've never seen this room before."

"It's not much."

"It's warm and clean." He advanced two steps only, forcing his eyes to range further until they were drawn, against his will, back to the picture.

"Is that Glendon?"

"Yes."

He crossed to the bureau, picked up the framed photo and held it, surprised at the man's age and lack of physical attractiveness. A rather beaked nose and a bony, hollow-eyed face with narrow lips. "He was some older than you."

"Five years."

Will studied the picture in silence, thinking the man looked much older.

"He wasn't much of a looker. But he was a good man."

"I'm sure he was." A good man. Unlike himself, who had broken the laws of both God and man. Could a woman forget such transgressions? Will set the picture down.

Eleanor asked, "Would it bother you if I left the picture there—so the boys don't forget him?"

"No, not at all." Was it a reminder that Glendon Dinsmore still held a special place in her heart? That though Will Parker might share her sheets tonight, he had no right to expect to share anything else—ever? He faced the wall while pulling his shirttails out, wanting to impose nothing upon her, not even glimpses of his bare skin.

She watched him unbutton his shirt, shrug it off, hang it on the closet doorknob. Her fascination came as a surprise. There were moles on his back, and firm, tan skin. He was tapered as a turnip from shoulder to waist, and his arms had filled out considerably in the two months he'd been here.

Though she felt like a window-peeper, she continued gaping. He unbuckled his belt and her eyes dropped to his hips—thin, probably even bony inside his jeans. When he sat down the mattress sagged, sending her heart aflutter—even so slight a sharing of the bed felt intimate, after having it to herself for over half a year. He hoisted a foot, removed a cowboy boot and set it aside, followed by its mate. Standing, he dropped his jeans to the floor, then stretched into bed with one fluid motion, giving no more than a flash of thighs textured with dark hair and an old pair of Glendon's shorts before the quilt covered him and he stretched out beside her with his arms behind his head.

They stared at the ceiling, lying like matched bookends, making sure not so much as the hair on their arms brushed, listening to the tick of the clock, which seemed to report like rifle shots.

"You can turn down the lantern some. It doesn't need to be that bright."

He rolled and reached, tugging the bedclothes. "How's that?" He peered back over his outstretched arm while the light dimmed to pale umber, enhancing the shadows.

"Fine."

Again he stretched flat. The silence beat about their ears. Neither of them risked any of the settling motions usually accompanying the first minutes in bed. Instead they lay with hands folded primly over quilts, trying to adjust to the idea of sharing a sleeping space, dredging up subjects of conversation, discarding them, tensing instead of relaxing.

Presently, he chuckled.

"What?" She peeked at him askance. When his face turned her way she fastened her gaze on the ceiling.

"This is weird."

"I know."

"We gonna lay in this bed every night and pretend the other one isn't there?"

She blew out a long breath and let her eyes shift over to him. He was right. It was a relief, simply acknowledging that there was another person in the bed. "I wasn't looking forward to this. I thought it'd be awkward, you know?"

"It was. It is," he admitted for both of them.

"I been jumpy as a flea since suppertime."

"Since morning, you mean. Hardest thing I ever did was to open that door and walk into the kitchen this morning."

"You mean you were nervous, too?"

"Didn't it show?"

"Some, but I thought I was worse that way than you."

They mulled silently for some time before Will remarked, "A pretty strange wedding day, huh?"

"Well, I guess that was to be expected."

"Sorry about the judge and the kiss—you know."

"It wasn't so bad. We lived through it, didn't we?"

"Yeah, we lived through it." He crossed his hands behind his head and contemplated the ceiling, presenting her with a hairy armpit that smelled of Ivory soap.

"I'm sorry about the lantern. It'll keep you awake, won't it?"

"Maybe for a while, but it doesn't matter. If you hadn't slept in a real bed for as long as me, you wouldn't complain about a lantern either." He lowered one hand and ran it across the coarse, clean sheet which smelled of lye soap and fresh air. "This is a real treat, you know. Real sheets. Pillow cases. Everything."

No reply entered Eleanor's mind, so she lay in silence, adjusting to the feeling of his nearness and scent. Outside a whippoorwill sang and from the boys' room came the sound of the crib rattling as Thomas turned over.

"Eleanor?"

"Hm?"

"Could I ask you something?"

"Course."

"You afraid of the dark?"

She took her time answering. "Not afraid exactly . . . well, I don't know. Maybe." She thought a moment. "Yeah, maybe. I been sleepin' with the lantern on so long I don't know anymore."

Will turned his head to study her profile. "Why?"

Her eyes met his, and she thought about her fanatic grandparents, her mother, all those years behind the green shades.

But to talk about it would make her seem eccentric in his
eyes, and she didn't want to be. Neither did she want to ruin
her wedding day with painful memories. "Does it matter?"

He studied her green eyes minutely, wishing she'd confide
in him, tell him the facts behind Lula's gossip. But whatever
secrets she held, he wouldn't hear them tonight. "Then tell
me about Glendon."

"Glendon? You want to talk about him . . . tonight?"

"If you do."

She considered for some time before asking, "What do you
want to know?"

"Anything you want to tell. Where did you meet him?"

Studying the dim circle of light on the ceiling, she
launched into her recollection. "Glendon delivered ice to our
house when I was a little girl. We lived in town then, my
mother and my grandparents and me. Grandpa was a preacher
man, used to go out on circuit for weeks at a time." She
peered at Will from the corner of her eye, gave a quirk of a
smile. "Fire and brimstone, you know. Voice like a cyclone
throwing dirt against the house." She told him what she
chose, winnowing out any hints of her painfully lonely youth,
the truth about her family, the bad memories from school. Of
Glendon she spoke more frankly, telling about their meetings
in the woods when she was still a girl, and of their shared respect for wild creatures. "The first present he ever brought
me was a sack of corn for the birds, and from then on we
were friends. I married him when I was nineteen and I been
livin' here ever since," she finished.

At the end of her recital, Will felt disappointed. He'd
learned nothing of the house in town nor why she had been
locked in it, none of the secrets of Eleanor Dinsmore Parker.
The truth seemed strange: she was his wife, yet he knew less
about her than he knew of some of the whores he'd fre-
quented in his day. Above all, he wanted to know about that
house so that he could assure her it made no difference to
him. Given time, she might tell him more, but for now he respected her right to privacy. He, too, had secret hurts too
painful to reveal yet.

"Now your turn," she said.

"My turn?"

"Tell me about you. Where you lived when you were a boy, how you ended up here."

He began with sterile facts. "I lived mostly in Texas but there were so many towns I couldn't name 'em all. Sometimes in orphanages, sometimes people would take me in. I was born down around Austin, they tell me, but I don't remember it till I grew up and went back there one time when I was doing some rodeoing."

"What *do* you remember?"

"First memories, you mean?"

"Yes."

Will thought carefully. It came back slowly, painfully. "Spilling a bowl of food, breakfast cereal, I think, and getting whupped so hard I forgot about being hungry."

"Oh, Will . . ."

"I got whupped a lot. All except for one place. I lived there for a half a year, maybe . . . it's hard to remember exactly. And I've never been able to remember their names, but the woman used to read me books. She had this one with a real sad story I just loved called *A Dog of Flanders*, and there were drawings of a boy and this dog of his, and I used to think, Wow, it must be something to have a dog of your own. A dog would always be there, you know?" Will mused a moment, then cleared his throat and went on. "Well, anyway, this woman, the thing I remember about her most is she had green eyes, the prettiest green eyes this side of the Pecos, and you know what?"

"What?" Elly turned her face up to him.

Smiling down, he told her, "The first time I walked into this house that was what I liked best about you. Your green eyes. They reminded me of hers, and she was always kind. And she was the only one who made me think books were okay."

For a moment they gazed at each other until their feelings came close to surfacing, then Elly said, "Tell me more."

"The last place I lived was with a family named Tryce on a ranch down near a dump called Cistern. The old man's watch came up missing and I figured soon as I heard what

was up that they'd pin the blame on me, so I lit out before
he could whup me. I was fourteen and I made up my mind
as long as I stayed on the move they couldn't stick me in any
more schools where all the kids with ma's and pa's looked at
me like I was a four-day-old pork chop left in somebody's
pocket. I caught a freight and headed for Arizona and I been
on the road ever since. Except for prison and here."

"Fourteen. But that's so young."

"Not when you start out like I did."

She studied his profile, the dark eyes riveted on the ceiling, the crisp, straight nose, the unsmiling lips. Softly, she
asked, "Were you lonely?" His Adam's apple slid up, then
down. For a moment he didn't answer, but when he did, he
turned to face her.

"Yeah. Were you?"

Nobody had ever asked her before. Had he been anyone
from town, she could not have admitted it, but it felt remarkably good to answer, "Yeah."

Their gazes held as both recognized a first fallen barrier.

"But you had a family."

"A family, but no friends. I'll bet you had friends."

"Friends? Naww." Then, after thoughtful consideration,
"Well, one maybe."

"Who?"

He tipped an eyebrow her way. "You sure you wanna hear
this?"

"I'm sure. Who?"

He never talked about Josh. Not to anyone. And the story
would lead to a conclusion that might make Eleanor Parker
rethink her decision to invite him into her bed. But for the
first time, Will found he wanted it off his chest.

"His name was Josh," he began. "Josh Sanderson. We
worked together on a ranch down near a place called Dime
Box, Texas. Near Austin." Will chuckled. "Dime Box was
somethin'. It was like . . . well, maybe like watchin' the black
and white movie after seeing the previews in color. A sorry
little dump. Everything kind of dead, or waitin' to die. The
people, the cattle, the sagebrush. And nothing to do there on

your night off. Nothing." Will paused, his brow smooth while
his thoughts ranged back in time.

"So what'd you do?"

He shot her one quick glance. "This ain't much of a subject for a wedding night, Eleanor."

"Most wives already know this kind of stuff about their
husbands by their wedding night. Tell me—what'd you do?"

As if settling in for a long talk, he rolled his pillow into a
ball, crooked his head against it, lifted one knee and linked
his fingers over his belly. "All right, you asked, I'll tell you.
We used to go down to La Grange to the whorehouse there.
Saturday nights. Take a bath and get all duded up and take
our money into town and blow damn near all of it on booze
and floozies. Me, I wasn't fussy. Take anyone that was free.
But Josh got to liking this one named Honey Rossiter." He
shook his head disbelievingly. "Honey—can you believe
that? She swore it was her given name but I never believed
her. Josh did, though. Hell, Josh'd believe anything that
woman told him. And he wouldn't hear anything bad about
Honey. Got real pissed off if I said a word against her. He
had it bad for her, that's a fact.

"She was tall—eighteen hands, we used to joke—and had
this head full of hair the color of a palomino, hung clear
down to her rump. It was some hair all right, curly but coarse
as a horse's mane, the kind a man could really sink his hands
into. Josh used to talk about it, laying in his bunk at night—
Honey and her honey hair. Then pretty soon he started talking
about marrying her. Josh, I says, she's a whore. Why would
you want to marry a whore? Josh, he got real upset when I
said that. He was so crazy over her he couldn't tell truth from
lies.

"She was like . . ." He rested a wrist on the updrawn knee,
absently toying with a piece of green yarn on the quilt.
". . . well, like an actress in a picture show—played at being
whatever a man needed. She'd change herself to suit the man,
and when she was with Josh she acted like he was the only
man for her. Trouble is, Josh started believing it.

"Then one night we came there and when Josh asked for

Honey the old harlot who ran the place says Honey's been spoken for for the next two hours. Who else would he like?

"Well, Josh never wanted anybody else, not after Honey. He waited. But by the time she come back down he was so steamed his lid was rattlin' and he was ready to blow. She comes saunterin' into the Leisure Room—that's what they called the bar where the men waited on the women—and Lord a-mighty, you never heard such a squall as when Josh jumped her about who she was spendin' *two hours* with while he was left downstairs coolin' his heels.

"She says to him, You don't own me, Josh Sanderson, and he says, Yeah, well, I'd like to. Then he pulls a ring out of his pocket and says he'd come there that night intendin' to ask her to marry him."

Will shook his head. "She laughed in his face. Said she'd have to be crazy to marry a no-count saddle bum who'd probably keep her pregnant nine months out of twelve and expect her to take care of a houseful of his squallin' brats. Said she had a life of luxury, spendin' a few hours on her back each night and wearing silk and feathers and eatin' oysters and steak anytime she wanted 'em.

"Well, Josh went wild. Told her he loved her and she wasn't gonna screw anybody else—never. She was gonna leave with him—*now*! He made a grab for her and out of nowhere she pulls this little gun—Christ, I never knew the girls there even carried 'em. But there it was, pointed right at Josh's eye and I reached for a bottle of Old Star whiskey and let her have it. Hell, I didn't think. I just ... well, I just beaned her. She went down like a tree, toppled sideways and cracked her head on a chair and laid there in a puddle of broken glass and blended whiskey and hardly even bled, she died so fast. I don't know if it was the bottle or the chair that killed her, but it didn't matter to the law. They had me behind bars in less than half an hour.

"I figured things'd come out all right—after all, I was defending Josh. If I hadn't clunked her, she'd have shot Josh smack through his left eye. But what I didn't figure was how serious he was about marrying her, how broke up he was when she died.

"He . . ." Will closed his eyes against the painful memory. Eleanor sat up, watching his face closely.

"He what?" she encouraged softly.

Will opened his eyes and fixed them on the ceiling. "He testified against me. Told this sob story about how he was gonna make an honest woman out of Honey Rossiter, take her away from her lousy life in that whorehouse and give her a home and respectability. And the jury fell for it. I did five years for savin' my *friend's* life." Will ran a hand through his hair and sighed. For seconds he stared at the ceiling, then rolled to a sitting position with arms loosely linked around his knees. "Some friend."

Eleanor studied the moles on his back, wanting to reach out and touch, comfort. Like him, she'd had only one friend. But hers had turned out loyal. She could imagine how deep her own hurt would have gone had Glendon betrayed her.

"I'm sorry, Will."

He threw his head aside as if to look back at her, but didn't. Instead his gaze dropped to his loosely linked wrists. "Aw, what the hell. It was a long time ago."

"But it still hurts, I can tell."

He flopped back, ran both hands through his hair and clasped them behind his head.

"How'd we get on a subject like that anyway. Let's talk about something else."

The mood had grown somber, and as they lay side by side Eleanor could think of little except Will's sad, friendless youth. She had always thought herself the loneliest soul on earth, but . . . poor Will. Poor, poor Will. Now he had her at least, and the boys. But how long would it last if the war came?

"Is the war really like that, Will . . . like they showed in the movies?"

"I guess so."

"You think we're gonna be in it, don't you?"

"I don't know. But if not, why is the President drafting men for the military?"

"If we were, would you have to go?"

"If I got drafted, yes."

Her mouth formed an oh, but the word never made it past her lips. The possibility pressed upon her, bringing with it a startling dread. Startling because she hadn't guessed she'd feel so possessive about this man once he was her husband. The fact that he was made a tremendous difference. The black and white pictures from the newsreel flashed through her memory, followed by the colored ones of the War Between the States. What an awful thing, war. She supposed, in the days when Grandpa had been alive, they would have prayed that America stay out of it. Instead, she closed her eyes and forced the grim pictures aside to make way for those of the beautiful ladies in their enormous silk skirts, and the men in their top hats, and Hopalong waving his hat . . . and Donald Wade in Will's black one . . . and eventually when she rode the thin line between sleep and wakefulness, Will himself riding Topper, waving his hat at her from the end of the driveway . . .

Minutes later, Will turned to say, Let's not worry about it until the time comes. But he found she had fallen asleep, flat on her back, lips parted, hands crossed demurely beneath her breasts. He watched her breathe, a strand of hair on her shoulder catching the light with each beat. His gaze drifted down to her stomach, back up to her breasts, soft and unsculptured beneath her nightgown. He thought about how good it would feel to roll her onto her side, curl up behind her with his arms where hers were now and fall asleep with his face against her back. But what would she think if she awakened and found him that way? He would have to be on guard, even asleep.

His eyes wandered once more to her stomach.

It moved!

The quilts shifted as if a sleeping cat had changed positions underneath. But she slept soundly, as still as a mummy. The baby? Babies moved . . . *that much*? Cautiously, he braced up on one elbow until he sat over her, studying the movements at close range. Boy or girl? It shifted again and he smiled. Whatever it was, it was rambunctious; he couldn't believe all that commotion didn't wake her up. He resisted the urge to turn the quilts back for a better look, the even greater one to rest a hand on her and feel what he was watching. Either—of course—was out of the question.

He lay back down to worry that he'd agreed to deliver that baby. God, what had he been thinking? He'd kill it for sure with his big, clumsy hands.

Don't think about it, Will.

He closed his eyes and concentrated instead on the goodnight kisses of Donald Wade and Baby Thomas. He recalled their childish voices wishing him goodnight, especially Thomas—" 'Night, Wiw . . ." He tried to wipe his mind clean of all thought so sleep would come. But the light shone through his eyelids, urging them open once again.

Eleanor flipped onto her side, facing him. He studied her eyelashes lying like fans against her cheeks, the palm of her left hand resting near his chin with the friendship ring peeking through her relaxed fingers. He let his eyes roam over the button placket of her nightgown, the quilt that had slipped down to her waist, the white cloth covering her breasts. He reached out carefully—very carefully—and took the fabric of her sleeve in his fingers, rubbing it as a greedy man rubs two coins together. Then he withdrew his hand, flipped over in the opposite direction and tried to forget the light was on.

CHAPTER

11

In the morning Eleanor opened her eyes to the back of Will Parker's head. His hair was flattened into a pinwheel, giving a clear view of his white skull underneath. She smiled. The intimacies of marriage. She watched each breath lift his shoulder blades, studied his back with its distinctive triangle of moles, the hindside of one ear, the pattern of the hairline at his nape, the ridges of his vertebrae disappearing beneath the covers just above his waist. His skin was so much darker than Glendon's, so much barer; Glendon always slept in an undershirt. Will's skin looked seasoned, whereas Glendon's had been doughy.

The object of her study snuffled and rolled onto his back. His eyeballs moved behind closed lids, but he slept on, his face exposed to the sun. It turned him all gold and brown and put glints of color in his pale hair like those in a finch's wing. His beard grew fast, much faster than Glendon's, and there was more hair on his arms and chest. Studying it gave her an unexpected jolt of reaction, down low.

She slammed her eyes closed only to realize that he smelled different from Glendon. No smell she could name, only the distinctive one given him by Nature—warm male hide and hair and breath—as different from Glendon's as that of an apple from an orange. Her eyes opened stealthily, halfway, as if such caution would prevent him from waking. Through nearly closed eyelids she admired him? letting the sunlight shatter on her lash tips and diffuse over his image as if he were sprinkled with sequins. A handsome, well-built man. The whores in La Grange probably fought over him.

Again the queer radiant disturbance intensified low in her belly as she lay with her knees only inches from his hip, his unfamiliar man-smell permeating her bedclothes, his warmth and bulk taking up half the sleeping space. It was a shock to find herself susceptible to fleshly thoughts when she'd thought pregnancy made her immune.

Another disturbing consideration struck. Suppose he had studied her as intimately as she now studied him? She tried to recall falling asleep but couldn't. They'd been talking—that was the last she remembered. Had she been lying on her back? Facing him? She glanced at the table; the lantern still hissed. He had left it on, could have lain awake for hours after she'd dropped off, taking an up-close tally of her short-comings. Studying his becoming face, she became all too aware of how she suffered by comparison. Her hair was dirt brown, plain, her eyelashes thin and stubby, her fingers wide-knuckled, her stomach popping, her breasts mammoth. Some-times she snored. Had she snored last night while he watched and listened?

She rolled toward her edge of the bed, thinking, just forget he's back there and go about dressing as if it were any other day.

At her first movement Will came awake as if she'd set off a firecracker. He glanced at her back, the alarm clock, then sat up and reached for his pants, all in one motion.

They dressed facing opposite walls, and only when the fi-nal buttons were closed did they peer over their shoulders at each other.

"Mornin'," she offered self-consciously.

"Mornin'."

"Sleep okay?"

"Fine. Did I crowd you?"

"Not that I remember. Did I crowd you?"

"No."

"You always wake up that quick?"

"It's nearly eight. Herbert's gonna bust." He sat down on the edge of the bed and yanked his boots on. A moment later he was stalking out the door, stuffing in his shirttails.

When he was gone, she dropped onto the bed and sighed with relief. They'd done it! Gone to bed, slept together, gotten up and dressed without once making physical contact, and without him seeing her ugly, bloated body.

She sat moments longer staring despondently at the mopboard.

Well, that's what you wanted, wasn't it?

Yes!

Then why are you sitting here moping?

I'm not moping!

Oh?

Well, I'm not!

But you're thinking about when the judge ordered him to kiss you.

Well, what's wrong with that?

Nothing. Nothing at all.

Leave me alone.

Silence. For minutes and minutes only obedient silence hummed inside her head.

If you wanted him to kiss you goodnight, you should've just leaned over and done it yourself.

I didn't *want* him to kiss me goodnight.

Oh, sorry. I thought that's why you were moping.

I wasn't moping.

But she was, and she knew it.

At midmorning that day, with breakfast eaten and his routine chores done, Will returned to the house to find the veiled hat, hive tool and smoker on the back-porch steps. He grinned. So ... no more egg grenades. Going inside to thank her, he almost regretted the loss.

The house was empty, on the table, a note: *Gone to pick pecans with the boys.* He took the stub of a pencil, scrawled across the bottom, "Thanks for the wedding gift!" and hit for the mint patch.

Their first twenty-four hours as husband and wife seemed
to set the tone for the days that followed. They lived together
amicably if not intimately, helping one another in small ways,
adapting, sharing a mutual enjoyment of the children and
their uncomplicated family life. From the first they accommodated each other—as with the beekeeping gear—so there
were no more bursts of anger. Life was peaceful.

Though the sudden appearance of the hive tool, hat and
smoker was never mentioned between them, it signaled the
true beginning of Will's work with the bees. He sensed that
Eleanor would rather not know when he was out in the orchard, so he kept the equipment in an outbuilding when it
was not in use, and retrieved it without telling her. Only when
he returned to the house with the honeycomb frames did she
know he'd been among the bees.

He learned to respect them. There was a calm about the orchard that seeped into him each time he passed there, a seren-
ity not only among the insects, but within himself for the
necessity of having to move slowly while among them. But
as slowly as he moved, it was inevitable that he should eventually get stung. The first time it happened he jumped, swatted and yowled, "Ouch!" For his efforts he received three
additional stings. He learned, in time, not to jump and most
certainly not to swat, forcing the stinger farther into his skin.
But more importantly, he learned to recognize the variations
in the sounds of the bees—from the squeaky piping of the
contented workers as they moved about their business on
humming gauze wings to the altogether different "quacking"
occasionally set up by a single provoked bee, warning him to
anticipate the sting and be ready to fend it off. He came to
recognize the feel of bee feet digging into his body hair for
a good grip, and to pluck the insect away gently before the
grip became a sting. He learned that bees are soothed by the
sound of human whistling, that their least favorite color is red
and their most favorite, blue.

So it was a happy man who walked among the peach trees,
whistling, dressed all in blue, a veiled hat protecting his face.
He could never get used to the clumsiness of gloves, so
worked barehanded, scraping at the hard, varnishlike propolis

with which the bees sealed every minute crack between the supers. Inside the smoker, which was little more than a spouted tin can with an attached bellows, he lit a smudge of oiled burlap. Several puffs into the open hive subdued the bees, enabling him to remove the comb cases without danger. These he transported back to the house, where he carefully scraped the wax caps off the comb with a knife heated above a kerosene lantern. The first time Eleanor saw him doing so she opened the porch door and stepped outside, shrugging into a sweater, carrying a knife. "You'll need a little help with that," she said flatly, without casting him a glance. But she sat down on the opposite side of the lantern and showed him that it wasn't the first time she'd scraped wax. Nor was it the first time she'd extracted, nor rendered, when it came time to do those jobs.

The extracting—pulling the honey from the combs—was done in a fifty-gallon drum equipped with a crank that spun the combs and forced the honey out by centrifugal force. From a spigot at the bottom the honey was drained—littered with fragments of comb and wax—then heated and strained before the wax was allowed to separate to the top and be skimmed off. The two products were then packed separately for sale.

There was much Will didn't know, particularly about the rendering process, knowledge that could be learned only by experience. Eleanor taught him—albeit grudgingly most of the time, but she taught him just the same.

"How do we clean up this mess?" Will inquired of the sticky drum with its honey-coated paddles and spigot.

"We don't. The bees do," she replied.

"The bees?"

"Bees eat honey. Just leave it outside in the sun and they'll find it."

Sure enough, any honey-coated tool left outside soon became cleaner than if it had been steamed.

Will knew perfectly well she saw the occasional welts on his skin, but she made no comments about them and soon his body built up a natural immunity until the bee stings scarcely reacted. When he came in with a load of comb, she tacitly went into the cellar for fruit jars, washed and scalded them, then lent a hand processing and bottling the honey.

Those honey days were a time of acquaintance for Will and Eleanor. As with their first night in bed when they'd lain so still, growing accustomed to lying side by side, working with the honey lent them proximity and time to adjust to the fact that they were bound for life. Sometimes, while scraping wax or holding a funnel, Will would look up and find himself being studied. The same was true for Eleanor. There would follow quick mutual smiles and a sense of growing acceptance, each for the other.

At night in bed, they talked. He, of the bees. She of the birds. Never of the birds and bees.

"Did you know a male worker bee has thirteen thousand eyes?"

"Did you know the flycatcher makes his nest out of discarded snakeskin?"

"There are nurses in a bee colony and all they do is take care of the nymphs."

"Most birds sing, but the titmouse is the only one who can actually whisper."

"Did you know the bees' favorite color is blue?"

"And the hummingbird is the only bird that can fly backwards?"

These discussions sometimes led to insights into each other. One night Will spoke of the worker bees. "Did you know they work so hard during their lifetime that they actually work themselves to death?"

"No . . ." she replied disbelievingly.

"It's true. They wear down their wings till they're so frayed they can't fly anymore. Then they just die." His expression turned troubled. "That's sad, isn't it?"

Eleanor studied her husband in a new light and found she liked what she saw. He lay in the dim lanternlight, contemplating the ceiling, saddened by the plight of the worker bees. How could a woman remain aloof to a man who cared about such things? Moved, she reached out to console, grazing the underside of his upraised arm.

His glance shot down to her and their gazes caught for several interminable seconds, then her fingers withdrew.

On a night shortly thereafter Will came up with another amazing apian phenomenon. "Did you know the workers practice something called flower fidelity? It means each bee gathers nectar and pollen from only one species of flower."

"Oh, you're making that up!" Her head twisted to face his profile.

"I am not. I read about it in one of the books Miss Beasley gave me. Flower fidelity."

"Really?"

"Really."

He lay as he did every night during their talks—on his back with his hands behind his head. Silent, she regarded him, digesting this new snippet of information. At length she squared her head on the pillow and fixed her attention on the pale glow overhead. "I guess that's not so unusual. Some birds practice fidelity, too. To each other. The eagles, the Canadian geese—they mate for life."

"Interesting."

"Mm-hmm."

"I've never seen an eagle," Will mused.

"Eagles are ..." Eleanor gestured ceilingward—"Majestic."—then let her hands settle to her stomach again. A smile tipped her lips. "When I was a girl I used to see a golden eagle in a huge dead tree down in the swamp near Cotton Creek. If I were a bird, I'd want to be an eagle."

"Why?" Will turned to study her.

"Because of something I read once."

"What?"

"Oh ... nothing." She twined her fingers and looked down her chest at them.

"Tell me." He sensed her reluctance but kept his gaze steady, unrelenting. After some time she sent Will a quick peek.

"Promise you won't laugh?"

"I promise."

For several seconds she concentrated on aligning her thumbnails precisely, then finally quoted shyly.

"He clasps the crag with crooked hands;
Close to the sun in lonely lands,
Ring'd with the azure world, he stands.

"The wrinkled sea beneath him crawls;
He watches from his mountain walls,
And like a thunderbolt he falls."

She paused before adding, "Somebody named Tennyson wrote that."

In that moment Will saw a new facet of his wife. Fragile. Impressionable. Touched by poets' words, articulate combinations of words such as she herself never used.

"It's beautiful," he said softly.

Her thumbnails clicked together as she vacillated between the wish to hide her feelings and reveal more. The latter won as she swallowed and added softly, "Nobody laughs at eagles."

Oh, Elly, Elly, who hurt you so bad? And what would it take to make you forget it? Will rolled to face her and braced his jaw on a fist. But she wouldn't turn, and her cheeks burned brightly.

"Did somebody laugh at you?" His voice was deep with caring. A tear plumped in the corner of her eye. Understanding her chagrin at its arrival, Will pretended not to notice. He waited motionlessly for her answer, studying the ridge of her nose, the outline of her compressed lips. When she spoke it was an evasion.

"For a long time I didn't know what azure meant."

He watched as her throat contracted and the florid spots in her cheeks stood out like pennies on an open palm. His hand burned to touch her—her chin maybe, turn it to face him so she would see that he cared and would never ridicule her. He wanted to take her close, cradle her head and rub her shoulder and say, "Tell me . . . tell me what it is that hurts so bad, then we'll work at getting you over it." But every time he considered touching her his insecurities reared up to confront and confine him. Woman killer, jailbird, she'll jump and yelp if you touch her. On the first day you were warned to keep your distance.

So he stayed on his own side of the bed with one wrist riveted to his hip, the other folded beneath an ear. But what he couldn't relay by touch he put into his expressive voice.

"Elly?" It came out softly, the abbreviated name falling from his lips as an endearment. Their gazes collided, her green eyes still luminous with unshed tears, his brown ones filled with understanding. "Nobody's laughing now."

Suddenly everything in her yearned toward him.

Touch me, she thought, *like nobody ever did before, like I touch the boys when they feel bad. Make it not important that I'm plain and unpretty and more pregnant than I wish I was right now. You're the man, Will—don't you see? A man's got to reach first.*

But he couldn't. Not first.

Touch me, he thought, *my arm, my hand, a finger. Let me know it's all right for me to have these feelings for you. Nobody's cared enough to touch me for years and years. But you've got to reach first, don't you see? Because of how you felt about him, and what I am, what I did, what we agreed to the first day I came here.*

In the end, neither of them moved. She lay with her hands atop her swollen stomach, her heart hammering frantically, afraid of rejection, ridicule, the things she had been seasoned by life to expect.

He lay feeling unlovable due to his spotty past and the fact that no woman including his own mother had found him worth the effort, so why should Elly?

And so they talked and gazed during those lanternlit nights of acquaintance—crazy Eleanor and her ex-con husband—learning respect for each other, wondering when and if that first seeking might happen, each hesitant to reach out for what they both needed.

The honey was all bottled. The hives received fresh coats of white paint, their bases—as suggested in print—a variety of colors to guide the workers back from their forays. When

Will left the orchard for the last time, the hives held enough honey to feed the bees through the winter.

He packed away the extractor in an outbuilding until the spring honey run began and announced that night at supper, "I'll be going to town tomorrow to sell the honey. If there's anything you need, make a list."

She asked for only two things: white flannel to make diapers and a roll of cotton batting.

The following day when Will stepped through the library doors, Gladys Beasley was immersed in lecturing a cluster of schoolchildren on the why and wherefore of the card catalogue. With her back to Will, she looked like a dirigible on legs. Packed into a bile-green jersey dress, wearing club-heeled shoes and the same cap of precise blue ringlets against a skull of baby pink, she gestured with her head and spoke in her inimitable pedantic voice.

"The Dewey Decimal System was named after an American librarian named Melvil Dewey over seventy years ago. James," she digressed, "quit picking your nose. If it needs attention, please ask to be dismissed to the lavatory. And in the future please see to it that you bring your handkerchief with you to school. Under the Dewey Decimal System books are divided into ten groups . . ." The lecture continued as if the remonstration had not interrupted.

Meanwhile, Will stood with an elbow braced on the checkout desk, waiting, enjoying. A little girl pirouetted on her heels—left, right—gazing at the overhead lights as if they were comets. A red-headed boy scratched his private rear quarters. Another girl balanced on one foot, holding the opposite ankle as high against her buttock as she could force it. Since coming to live with Elly and the boys Will had grown to appreciate children for their naturalness.

". . . any subject at all. If you'll follow me, children, we'll begin with the one hundreds." As Miss Beasley turned to herd stragglers, she caught sight of Will lounging against the desk. Involuntarily her face brightened and she touched her heart. Realizing what she'd done, she dropped and clasped her hand and recovered her customary prim expression. But it was too late—she was already blushing.

Will straightened and tipped his hat, pleasantly shocked by her telling reaction, warmed more than he'd have thought possible by the idea of such an unlikely woman getting flustered over him. He'd been doing everything in his power to get his wife to react that way but he'd certainly never expected it here.

"Excuse me, children." Miss Beasley touched two heads in passing. "You may explore through the one hundreds and the two hundreds." As she approached Will the tinge of pink on her cheeks became unmistakable and he grew more amazed.

"Mornin', Miss Beasley."

"Good morning, Mr. Parker."

"Busy today," he observed, glancing at the children.

"Yes. Mrs. Gardner's second grade."

"Brought you something." He held out a pint jar of honey.

"Why, Mr. Parker!" she exclaimed, touching her chest again.

"From our own hives, rendered this week."

She accepted the jar, lifting it to the light. "My, how clear and pale."

"Lots of sourwood out our way. Sourwood honey's light like that. Takes on a little color from the tupelo, though."

She drew in her chin and gave him a pleased pout. "You *did* do your homework, didn't you?"

He crossed his arms and planted his feet firmly apart, smiling down at her from the shadow of his hat brim. "I wanted to thank you for the pamphlets and books. I couldn't've done it without them."

She held the jar in both hands and blinked up at him. "Thank *you*, Mr. Parker. And please thank Mrs. Dinsmore for me, too."

"Ah . . ." Will rubbed the underside of his nose. "She's not Mrs. Dinsmore anymore, ma'am. She's Mrs. Parker now."

"Oh." Surprise and deflation colored the single word.

"We got married up at Calhoun the end of October."

"Oh." Miss Beasley quickly collected herself. "Then congratulations are in order, aren't they?"

"Well, thank you, Miss Beasley." He shifted his feet uneasily. "Ma'am, I don't want to keep you from the kids, but I got honey to sell and not much time. I mean, there's a lot to do out at the place before—" Again he shifted uneasily. "Well, you see, I'm wantin' to put in an electric generator and a bathroom for Eleanor. I was wondering if you'd see what you got for books on electricity and plumbing. If you could pick 'em out, I'll stop back for 'em in an hour or so when I get rid of the honey."

"Electricity and plumbing. Certainly."

"Much obliged." He smiled, doffed his hat and moved toward the door. But he swung back with designed offhandedness. "Oh, and while you're at it, if you could find any books about birthing, you could add them to the stack."

"Birthing?"

"Yes, ma'am."

"Birthing what?"

Will felt himself color and shrugged, feigning nonchalance. "Oh . . . ah . . . horses, cows . . ." He gestured vaguely. "You know." His glance wandered nervously before flicking back to her. "Humans, too, if you run across anything. Never read anything about that. Might be interesting."

He felt transparent beneath her acute scrutiny. But she set the jar in the place of honor beside her nameplate and advised in her usual caustic voice, "Your books will be ready in one hour, Mr. Parker. And thank you again for the honey."

Calvin Purdy bought half the honey and, after some dickering, took four more jars in exchange for ten yards of white flannel and a bat of cotton. At the filling station Will bartered two more pints of honey for a tankful of gasoline—it had been on his mind to keep the tank full from now until the baby came, just in case. While the gas was being pumped he lowered his brows and ruminated on Vickery's Cafe, down at the corner. Biscuits and gravy in the morning; biscuits and *honey* in the evening, he'd guess. But to make a sale he'd probably have to face Lula Peak again, and there was no telling where she might decide to run her scarlet claw this time. He scratched his chest and glanced away in distaste. The honey wouldn't spoil.

With a full tank of gas, he motored around the square to the library again. Mrs. Gardner's second grade was gone, leaving silence and an empty library.

"Hello?" he called.

Miss Beasley came out of the back room, dabbing her mouth with a flowered handkerchief.

"Am I interrupting your lunch?"

"Actually, yes. You've caught me sampling your honey on my muffin. Delicious. Absolutely delicious."

He smiled and nodded. "The bees did most of the work." She chuckled tightly, as if laughter were illegal. But he could see how pleased she was over his gift. On the surface she wasn't a very likable woman—militant, uncompromising— probably hadn't many friends. Perhaps that was why he was drawn to her, because he'd never had many either. Her lips were surrounded by more than their fair share of baby-fine, colorless hair. A tiny droplet of honey clung to one on her top lip. Had he liked her less, he might have let it go unmentioned. As it was, he pointed briefly—"You missed something"—then hooked his thumb on his back pocket.

"Oh! . . . Oh, thank you." Fussily she mopped her mouth but managed to miss what she was after.

"Here." He reached. "May I?" Taking her hand, hanky and all, he guided it to the proper spot.

It was one of the most decidedly personal touches Miss Beasley had ever experienced. Men were put off by her, always had been, especially in college, where she'd proved herself vastly more intelligent than any who might have taken an interest. The men in Whitney were either married or too stupid to suit her. Though she had accepted her spinsterhood long ago, it startled Gladys to find a man who—given other circumstances, other times—might have suited nicely in both temperament and intellect. When Will Parker touched her, Gladys Beasley forgot she was shaped like a herring barrel and old enough to be his grandmother. Her old maid's heart flopped like a fresh-caught bream.

The touch was brief and not untoward. Quickly, almost shyly, he backed off and let his thumb find his rear pocket again. When Gladys lowered the handkerchief she was decidedly rattled, but he graciously pretended not to notice.

"So. Did you find anything for me?" he inquired.

She produced a stack of five books, some with slips of paper marking selected spots. Curious, he tried to read the titles upside down as she stamped each card. But she was very efficient with her *Open, stamp, slap! Open, stamp, slap!* He hadn't made out one title before she pushed the pile his way with his card placed neatly on top.

"Much obliged, Miss Beasley."

"That's my job, Mr. Parker."

His smile spread slowly, formed only halfway before he touched his hat brim and slipped the books to his hip. "Much obliged anyway. See you next week."

Next week, she thought, and her heart raced. Fussily she tamped the tops of the recessed cards to cover her uncharacteristic flutteriness.

She had chosen for him *The Plumber's Handbook, The ABC's of Electricity, Edison's Invention, Animal Husbandry for the Common Farmer,* and another entitled *New Era Domestic Science.*

That night after supper while Eleanor shelled pecans at the kitchen table, Will sat at a right angle to her, turning pages. He spent an informative half hour spot-reading in three of the books, then picked up the fourth—*New Era Domestic Science.* It covered a range of subjects, some vital, others—to Will—silly. He smiled in amusement at such subjects as "How to Choose a House Boy," "How to Clean a Flatiron by Rubbing on Salt." There was a recipe for "Meat Jelly," another for fried tomatoes, then dozens of others; a discourse on insomnia, entitled, "The Science of Sleep"; a tip about cleansing the interior of your teakettle by boiling an oyster shell in it. His finger stopped shuffling when he arrived at "A Chapter for Young Women." His eyes scanned ahead, then retreated to an essay on "Choosing a Husband." As he began reading, he slumped lower and lower in his chair until his spine was bowed, the book rested against the edge of the table and an index finger covered his grin.

You now need the advice of your parents more than ever before, the essay advised, *for the young man will be attracted by you and you will be attracted by him. This is natural. If you make a mistake it may wreck your whole life. Take your mother into your confidence. There are some rules that are safe to follow in this matter. Never have anything to do with a young man who is "sowing his wild oats," or who has sown them.*

Will absently rubbed his lip and peeked at Eleanor, but she was busy with the nutcracker.

Never marry a man to reform him. Leave those who need reforming severely alone. There are men who do not drink and yet who are more dangerous to you than drunkards. A man who sows his wild oats or is morally lax may be afflicted with diseases that can be given to an innocent and pure wife and thus entail upon her life-long suffering. Marriage is a lottery. You may draw a prize, or your life may be made miserable. Tell your parents if you are attracted toward a young man so that they may find out if he is a man of good character and pure in heart and life. It is so much better to remain single than to make an unfortunate marriage.

He wondered how many ignorant virgins had read this stuff and ended up more confused than ever about the facts of life.

His speculative gaze wandered to Elly. She dropped a pecan into the bowl and his eyes followed. Her stomach had grown so full it barely left room for the bowl on her knees. Her breasts seemed to have doubled in size in the last three months. Had she been a virgin when she married Glendon Dinsmore? Had Glendon "sowed wild oats" like Will Parker had? Had Elly consulted her parents and had they checked out Dinsmore's character and found him pure in heart and life—unlike her second husband?

She picked another pecan clean and raised the last morsel to her mouth. Will's eyes again followed and he absently stroked his lips. One thing about Elly—she sure hadn't married to reform him. If he had reformed it was because of her acceptance, rather than the lack of it.

He turned a page to a section in which Miss Beasley had

left a marker. "How to Conceive and Bear Healthy Children."
All right, he thought, secretly amused, tell me how.

*The one main reason for the establishment of marriage was
for the bearing and rearing of children. Nature has provided
for man and woman the organs for this purpose and they are
wonderfully constructed.*

End of enlightenment. Will swallowed another chortle and
his finger continued hiding the grin. He couldn't help picturing Miss Beasley reading this, wondering what her reaction
had been.

From his delight over the construction of human organs the
author had skipped directly to a passel of ludicrous advice on
conception: *If the parents are drunk at the time the child is
conceived they cannot expect healthy offspring, either physically or mentally. If the parents dislike each other they will
transmit something of that disposition to their offspring. If either one or both of the parents are much worried at the time
of conception the child will be the sufferer.*

Without warning Will burst out laughing.

Eleanor looked up. "What's so funny?"

"Listen to this . . ." He straightened in his chair, laid the
book flat on the table and read the last passage aloud.

Eleanor gazed at him unblinkingly, her hands poised
around a pecan in the jaws of the nutcracker. "I thought you
were reading about electricity."

He sobered instantly. "Oh, I am. I mean, I . . . I was."

She reached across the table and, with the nose of the nutcracker, tipped the book up.

"New Era Domestic Science?"

"Well, I . . . it . . ." He felt his cheeks warming and ran-
domly flipped the pages. They fell open to a diagram of a
homemade telephone. "I was thinking about making one of
these." He turned the book and showed her.

She glanced at the diagram, then skeptically at him before
the pecan shell cracked and fell into her palm. "And just who
did you think we'd call on it?"

"Oh, I don't know. You never can tell."

He hid his discomposure by delving into the book again.

After you become pregnant you owe it to yourself, your

*husband and especially your unborn young one to see that it
comes into the world endowed with everything that a true,
good, and devoted mother can possibly give it, both physically and mentally. To this end, keep yourself well and happy.
Eat only such foods as are easily digested and that will keep
your bowels regular. Read only such books as will tend to
make you happier and better. Choose the company of those
whom you feel will lift you up. Gossips will not do this so do
not listen to croakers who are so ready to converse with you
at this time.*

Such capricious advice went on and on, but Will's amusement died when he found what he'd been looking for: "Prep-
arations for Labor." It began with a list of recommended
articles to have on hand:

            5 basins
            1 two-quart fountain syringe
            15 yards unsterilized gauze
            6 sanitary bed pads; or,
            2 pounds cotton batting for making same
            1 piece rubber sheeting, size 1 by 2 yards
            4 ounces permanganate of potash
            8 ounces oxalic acid
            4 ounces boric acid
            1 tube green soap
            1 tube Vaseline
            100 Bernay's bichloride tablets
            8 ounces alcohol
            2 drams ergotol
            1 nail brush
            2 pounds absorbent cotton

My God, they'd need all that? Will began to panic.

The opening instructions read, *The nurse should prepare
enough bed and perineal pads, sterilizing them a week before,
along with towels, diapers, 1/2 pound absorbent cotton and
some cotton pledgets.*

Nurse? Who had a nurse? And enough? What was enough?
And what did perineal mean? And what were pledgets? He

couldn't even understand this, much less afford it! Pale now, he turned the page only to have his disillusionment doubled. Phrases jumped out and grabbed him by the nerve-endings.

Cramp-like pains in the lower abdomen . . . rupturing membranes . . . watery discharge . . . a marked desire to go to stool . . . bulging of the pelvic floor . . . tearing of the perineal flesh . . . temple bones engaged in the vulva . . . proper manipulation to expel the afterbirth . . . stout clean thread . . . sever immediately . . . exception being when child is nearly dead or does not breathe properly . . .

He slammed the book shut and leaped to his feet, pale as seafoam.

"Will?"

He stared out a window, knees locked, cracking his knuckles, feeling his pulse thud hard in his gut.

"I can't do it."

"Do what?"

Fear lodged in his throat like a hunk of dry bread. He gulped, but it stayed. "I wasn't reading about electricity. I was reading about delivering babies."

"Oh . . . that."

"Yes, that." He swung to face her. "Elly, we've never talked about it since the night we agreed to get married. But I know you expect me to help you, and I just plain don't know if I can."

She rested her hands in the bowl and looked up at him expressionlessly. "Then I'll do it alone, Will. I'm pretty sure I can."

"Alone!" he barked, lurching for the book, agitatedly flapping pages until he found the right one. "Listen to this—'The cord is usually tied before being cut, the exception being when the child is nearly dead and does not breathe properly. In such a case it is best to leave the cord untied so that it may bleed a little and aid in establishing respiration.' " He dropped the book and scowled at her. "Suppose the baby died. How do you think I'd feel? And how am I supposed to know what's proper breathing and what isn't? And there's more—all this stuff we're supposed to have on hand. Why, hell, some of it I don't even know what it is! And it talks about you tearing, and maybe hemorrhaging. Elly, *please* let me get a doctor when the time comes. I got the car filled with gas so I can run into town quick and get him."

Calmly she set the bowl aside, rose and closed the book. "*I* know what we'll need, Will." Unflinchingly she met his worried brown eyes. "And I'll have it all ready. You shouldn't be reading that stuff, 'cause it just scares you, is all."

"But it says—"

"I know what it says. But having a baby is a natural act. Why, the Indian women squatted in the woods and did it all alone, then walked back into the fields and started hoeing corn as soon as it was over."

"You're no Indian," he argued intensely.

"But I'm strong. And healthy. And if it comes down to it, happy, too. Seems to me that's as important as anything else, isn't it? Happy people got something to fight for."

Her calm reasoning punctured his anger with surprising suddenness. When it had disappeared, one fact had impressed him: she'd said she was happy. They stood near, so near he could have touched her by merely lifting a hand, could have curled his fingers around her neck, rested his palms on her cheeks and asked, Are you, Elly? Are you really? For he wanted to hear it again, the evidence that for the first time in his life, he seemed to be doing something right.

But she dropped her chin and turned to retrieve the bowl of nuts and carry them to the cupboard. "Not everyone can stand the sight of blood, and I'll grant you there's blood when a baby comes."

"It's not that. I told you, it's the risks."

She turned to face him and said realistically, "We got no money for a doctor, Will."

"We could get up enough. I could take another load of scrap metal in. And there's the cream money, and the eggs, and now the honey. Even pecans. Purdy'll buy the pecans. I know he will."

She began shaking her head before he finished. "You just rest easy. Let me do the worrying about the baby. It'll turn out fine."

But how could he not worry?

In the days that followed he watched her moving about the place with increasing slowness. Her burden began to ride lower, her ankles swelled, her breasts widened. And each day brought him closer to the day of delivery.

November tenth brought a temporary distraction from his worries. It was Eleanor's birthday—Will hadn't forgotten. He awakened to find her still asleep, facing him. He rolled onto his stomach and curled the pillow beneath his neck to indulge himself in a close study of her. Pale brows and gold-tipped lashes, parted lips and pleasing nose. One ear peeking through a coil of loose hair and one knee updrawn beneath the covers. He watched her breathe, watched her hand twitch once, twice. She came awake by degrees, unconsciously smacking her lips, rubbing her nose and finally opening sleepy eyes.

"Mornin', lazybones," he teased.

"Mmm . . ." She closed her eyes and nestled, half on her belly. "Mornin'."

"Happy birthday."

Her eyes opened but she lay unmoving, absorbing the words while a lazy smile dawned across her face.

"You remembered."

"Absolutely. Twenty-five."

"Twenty-five. A quarter of a century."

"Makes you sound older than you look."

"Oh, Will, the things you say."

"I was watching you wake up. Looked pretty good to me."

She covered her face with the sheet and he smiled against his pillow.

"You got time to bake a cake today?"

She lowered the sheet to her nose. "I guess, but why?"

"Then bake one. I'd do it, but I don't know how."

"Why?"

Instead of answering, he threw back the covers and sprang up. Standing beside the bed with his elbows lifted, he executed a mighty, twisting stretch. She watched with unconcealed interest—the flexing muscles, the taut skin, the moles, the long legs dusted with black hair. Legs planted wide, he shivered and bent acutely to the left, the right, then snapped over to pick up his clothes and begin dressing. It was engrossing, watching a man donning his clothes. Men did it so much less fussily than women.

"You gonna answer me?" she insisted.

Facing away from her, he smiled. "For your birthday party."

"My birthday party!" She sat up. "Hey, come back here!"

But he was gone, buttoning his shirt, grinning.

It was a toss-up who had to work harder to conceal his impatience that day—Will, who'd had the plan in his head for weeks, Eleanor, whose eyes shone all the while she baked her own cake but who refused to ask when this party was supposed to happen, or Donald Wade, who asked at least a dozen times that morning, "How long now, Will?"

Will had planned to wait until after supper, but the cake was ready at noon, and by late afternoon Donald Wade's patience had been stretched to the limit. When Will went to the house for a cup of coffee, Donald Wade tapped his knee and whispered for the hundredth time, "Now, Will . . . pleeeease?"

Will relented. "All right, *kemo sabe*. You and Thomas go get the stuff."

The stuff turned out to be two objects crudely wrapped in wrinkled white butcher's paper, drawn together with twine. The boys each carried one, brought them proudly and deposited them beside Eleanor's coffee cup.

"Presents?" She crossed her hands on her chest. "For me?"

Donald Wade nodded hard enough to loosen the wax in his ears.

"Me 'n' Will and Thomas made 'em."

"You *made* them!"

"One of 'em," Will corrected, pulling Thomas onto his lap while Donald Wade pressed against his mother's chair.

"This one." Donald Wade pushed the weightier package into her hands. "Open it first." His eyes fixed on her hands while she fumbled with the twine, pretending difficulty in getting it untied. "This dang ole thing is givin' me fits!" she exclaimed. "Lord, Donald Wade, help me." Donald Wade reached eagerly and helped her yank the bow and push the paper down, revealing a ball of suet, meshed by twine and rolled in wheat.

"It's for your birds!" he announced excitedly.

"For my birds. Oh, myyy . . ." Eyes shining, she held it aloft by a loop of twine. "Won't they love it?"

"You can hang it up and everything!"

"I see that."

"Will, he got the stuff and we put the fat through the grinder and I helped him turn the crank and me 'n' Thomas stuck the seeds on. See?"

"I see. Why, I s'pect it's the prettiest suet ball I ever seen. Oh, thank you so much, darlin' . . ." She gave Donald Wade a tight hug, then leaned over to hold the baby's chin and smack him soundly on the lips. "You too, Thomas. I didn't know you were so clever."

"Open the other one," Donald Wade demanded, stuffing it into her hands.

"Two presents—my goodness gracious."

"This one's from Will."

"From Will . . ." Her delighted eyes met her husband's while her fingers sought the ties on the scroll-shaped package. Though his insides were jumping with impatience, Will forced himself to sit easy in the kitchen chair, an arm propped on the table edge with a finger hooked in a coffee cup.

Opening the gift, Eleanor gazed at him. With an ankle braced on a knee his leg formed a triangle. Thomas was draped through it. It suddenly occurred to Eleanor that she wouldn't trade Will for ten Hopalong Cassidys. "He's somethin', isn't he? Always givin' me presents."

"Hurry, Mama!"

"Oh . . . o' course." She turned her attention to opening the gift. Inside was a three-piece doily set—an oval and two crescents—of fine linen, all hemstitched and border stamped, ready for crochet hook and embroidery needle.

Eleanor's heart swelled and words failed her. "Oh, Will . . ." She hid her trembling lips behind the fine, crisp linen. Her eyes stung.

"The sign called it a Madeira dresser set. I knew you liked to crochet."

"Oh, Will . . ." Gazing at him, her eyes shimmered. "You do the nicest things." She stretched a hand across the table, palm-up.

Placing his hand in hers, Will felt his pulse leap.

"Thank you, dear."

He had never thought of himself as dear. The word sent a shaft of elation from his heart clear down to the seat of his chair. Their fingers tightened and for a moment they forgot about gifts and cakes and pregnancies and pasts and the two little boys who looked on impatiently.

"We got to have the cake now, Mama," Donald Wade interrupted, and the moment of closeness receded. But everything was intensified after that, tingly, electric. As Eleanor moved about the kitchen, whipping cream, slicing chocolate cake, serving it, she felt Will's eyes moving with her, following, questing. And she found herself hesitant to look at him.

Back at the table, she handed him his plate and he took it without touching so much as her fingertips. She sensed his distance as a cautious thing, an almost unwillingness to believe. And she understood, for in her craziest moments she'd never have believed anything as crazy as this could happen. Her heart thundered at merely being in the same room with him. And a sharp pain had settled between her shoulder blades. And she found it hard to draw a full breath.

"I'll take Baby Thomas." She tried to sound casual.

"He can stay on my lap. You enjoy your cake."

They ate, afraid to look at each other, afraid they had somehow misread, afraid they wouldn't know what to do when the plates were empty.

Before they were, Donald Wade looked out the window and pointed with his fork. "Who's that?"

Will looked and leaped to his feet. "Lord a-mighty!"

Eleanor dropped her fork and said, "What's she doing here?"

Before Will could conjure a guess, Gladys Beasley mounted the porch steps and knocked on the door.

Will opened it for her. "Miss Beasley, what a surprise."

"Good afternoon, Mr. Parker."

"Come in."

He had the feeling she would have, whether invited or not. He poked his head outside. "Did you *walk* clear out here from town?"

"I don't own an automobile. I didn't see any other way."

Surprised, Will ushered her inside and turned to perform introductions. But Gladys took the matter out of his hands.

"Hello, Eleanor. My, haven't you grown up."

"Hello, Miss Beasley." Eleanor stood behind a chair, nervously fingered her apron edge as if preparing to curtsy.

"And these are your sons, I suppose."

"Yes, ma'am. Donald Wade and Baby Thomas."

"And another one on the way. My, aren't you a lucky child."

"Yes'm," Eleanor answered dutifully, her eyes flashing to Will's. *What does she want?*

He hadn't an inkling and could only shrug. But he understood Eleanor's panic. How long had it been since she'd engaged in polite conversation with anyone from town? In all likelihood Miss Beasley was the first outsider Eleanor had ever allowed in this house.

"I understand congratulations are in order, too, on your marriage to Mr. Parker."

Again Eleanor's eyes flashed to Will, then she colored and dropped her gaze to the chair, running a thumbnail along its backrest.

Miss Beasley glanced at the table. "It appears I've interrupted your meal. I'm—"

"No, no," Will interjected. "We were just having cake."

Donald Wade, who never spoke to strangers, inexplicably chose to speak to this one. "It's Mama's birthday. Will and me and Baby Thomas was givin' her a party."

"Won't you sit down and have some?" Eleanor invited.

Will could scarcely believe his ears, but the next moment Miss Beasley settled her hard-packed bulk in one of the chairs and was served a piece of chocolate cake and whipped cream. Though Will hadn't actually missed having outsiders around, he found their absence unhealthy. If there was ever the perfect person to draw Eleanor out of her reclusiveness, it was Miss Beasley. Not exactly the gayest person, but fair-minded to a fault, and not at all the sort to dredge up painful past history.

Miss Beasley accepted a cup of coffee, laced it heavily with cream and sugar, sampled the cake and pursed her hairy lips. "Mmmm . . . quite delectable," she proclaimed. "Quite as delectable as the honey you sent, Eleanor. I must say I'm not accustomed to receiving gifts from my library patrons. Thank you."

Donald Wade piped up. "Wanna see the ones we give Mama today?"

Miss Beasley deferentially set down her fork and focused full attention on the child. "By all means."

Donald Wade scrambled around the table, found the suet ball and brought it, couched in his hand, to the librarian. "This here's for her birds. Me'n Will and Baby Thomas made it all ourselfs."

"You made it . . . mmm." She examined it minutely. "Now aren't you clever. And a homemade gift is certainly one from the heart—the best kind, just like the honey your mother and Mr. Parker gave me. You're a lucky child." She patted him on the head in the way of an adult unused to palavering socially with children. "They're teaching you the things that matter most."

"And this here . . ." Donald Wade, excited at having someone new on whom to shower his enthusiasm, reached next for the doilies. "These're from Will. He bought 'em with the honey money and Mama she can embroidry on 'em."

Again Miss Beasley gave the items due attention. "Ah, your mother is lucky, too, isn't she?"

It suddenly struck Donald Wade that the broad-beamed woman was a stranger, yet she seemed to know his mother. He looked up at Miss Beasley with wide, unblinking eyes. "How do you know 'er?"

"She used to come into my library when she was a girl not much bigger than you. Occasionally I was her teacher, you might say."

Donald Wade blinked. "Oh." Then he inquired, "What's a lie-bree?"

"A library? Why, one of the most wonderful places in the

world. Filled with books of all kinds. Picture books, story-
books, books for everyone. You must come and visit it sometime, too. Ask Mr. Parker to bring you. I'll show you a book
about a boy who looks quite a bit like you, actually, named
Timothy Totter's Tatters. Mmmm . . ." Leaning back, she
tapped an index finger on her lips and examined Donald
Wade as if a decision hung in the balance. "Yes, I should say
Timothy Totter is just the book for a boy . . . what? Five
years old?"

Donald Wade made his hair bounce, nodding.

"Do you have a dog, Donald Wade?"

Mystified, he wagged his head slowly.

"You don't? Well, Timothy Totter does. And his name is
Tatters. When you come, I'll introduce you to both Timothy
and Tatters. And now, if you'll excuse me, I must speak to
Mr. Parker a moment."

Miss Beasley could not have chosen a gentler method of
bringing Eleanor around to the idea of bumping up against
the outside world again. If there was an ideal way to reach
Eleanor it was through her children. By the time Miss
Beasley's interchange with Donald Wade ended, Eleanor was
sitting, looking less as if she was preparing to bolt. Miss
Beasley told her, "That's the best chocolate cake I've ever
had. I wouldn't mind having the recipe," then turned to Will
without pause. "I've come bearing some sad news. Levander
Sprague, who has cleaned my library for the past twenty-six
years, dropped dead of a heart attack night before last."

"Oh . . . I'm sorry." He'd never heard of Levander
Sprague. Why in the world had she brought the news clear
out here?

"Mr. Sprague shall be sorely missed. However, he lived a
long and fruitful life, and he leaves behind nine strapping
boys to see their mother through her last years. I, however,
am left without a custodian. The job pays twenty-five dollars
a week. Would you like it, Mr. Parker?"

Will's face flattened with surprise. His glance shot to Elly,
then back to the librarian, as she hastened on. "Six nights a
week, after the library closes. Caring for the floors, dusting
the furniture, burning the trash, stoking the furnace in the

winters, occasionally carrying boxes of books to the base-
ment, building additional shelves when we need them."

"Well ..." Will's amazement modified into a crooked
smile as he chuckled and ran a hand down the back of his
head. "That's quite an offer, Miss Beasley."

"I thought about offering it to one of Mr. Sprague's sons,
but quite frankly, I'd rather have you. You have a certain respect for the library that I like. And I heard that you were
summarily dismissed from the sawmill, which irritated my
sense of fair play."

Will was too surprised to be offended. His mind raced.
What would Elly say? And should he be gone evenings when
she was so close to due? But twenty-five dollars a week—
every week—and his days still free!

"When would you want me to start?"

"Immediately. Tomorrow. Today if possible."

"Today ... well, I ... I'd have to think it over," he replied,
realizing Elly ought to have a say.

"Very well. I'll wait outside."

Wait outside? But he needed time to feel Elly out. He
should have guessed that Miss Beasley would tolerate no
shilly-shallying. He was already scratching his jaw in conster-
nation as the door closed. At the same moment Eleanor arose
stiffly from her chair and began clearing away the cake
plates.

"Elly?" he asked.

She wouldn't look at him. "You take it, Will. I can see you
want to."

"But you don't want me to, right?"

"Don't be silly."

"I could buy fixtures for a bathroom and I'd still have days
free to put it in for you."

"I said, take it."

"But you don't like me hangin' around town, do you?"

She set the dishes in the dishpan and did an about-face.
"My feelings for town are mine. I got no right to keep you
from it, if that's what you want."

"But Miss Beasley's fair. She never put you down for anything, did she?"

"Take it."

"And what about when the baby starts coming?"

"A woman has plenty of warning."

"You're sure?"

She nodded, though he could see that it cost her dearly to let him go.

He crossed the room in four strides, grasped her jaw and planted a quick, hard kiss on her cheek. "Thank you, honey." Then he slammed out the door.

Honey? When he was gone she placed her palms where his had been. She was probably the most unhoney female within fifty miles, but the word had warmed her cheeks and tightened her chest. Before the thrill subsided, Will came slamming back inside.

"Elly? I'm giving Miss Beasley a ride back to town and she'll show me around the library, then I'll probably sweep up for her before I come back. Don't wait supper for me."

"All right."

He was half out the door before he changed his mind and returned to her side. "Will you be all right?"

"Fine."

Looking up into his eager face, she bit back all her misgivings. He'd never know from her how badly she wanted him here from now until the baby came. Or how she feared having him working in town where everyone called her crazy, where prettier and brighter women were bound to make him take a second look at what he'd married and regret it.

But how could she hold him back when he could scarcely stand still for excitement?

"I'll be fine," she repeated.

He squeezed her arm and was gone.

CHAPTER
12

Will took the car, in deference to Miss Beasley. On the way into town they spoke of the boys, the birthday, and finally of Elly.

"She's a stubborn woman, Miss Beasley. You might as well know, the reason I asked for that book on human birthing was because she refuses to have a doctor. She wants me to deliver the baby."

"And will you?"

"Reckon I'll have to. If I don't she'll do it alone. That's how stubborn she is."

"And you're scared."

"Damn right, I'm scared!" Will suddenly remembered himself. "Oh, sorry, ma'am—I mean, well, who wouldn't be?"

"I'm not blaming you, Mr. Parker. But apparently her other two were born at home, weren't they?"

"Yes."

"Without complications."

"Now you sound like her."

He told her about the book and how it had scared him. She told him about going off to college and how it had scared her, but how the experience had made her a stronger person. He told her about the boys and how awkward he'd felt around them at first. She told him she too had felt awk-

212

ward around them today. He told her how scared Elly was of the bees and how he himself loved working with them. She told him how she loved working among the books and that in time Elly would come to see he was cautious and industrious, but he must be patient with her. He asked her what kind of man Glendon Dinsmore had been and she answered, as different from you as air is from earth. He asked which he was, air or earth? She laughed and said, "That's what I like about you—you really don't know."

They talked all the way to town—argued some—and neither of them considered what a queer combination they made—Will, with his prison record and slapdash education, Miss Beasley with her estimable position and college degree. Will with his long history of drifting, Miss Beasley with her long one of permanence. He with his family of near-three, she an old maid. Both had been lonely in their own way. Will, because of his orphaned past, Gladys because of her superior intellect. He was a man who rarely confided, she a woman in whom people rarely confided. He felt lucky to have her as a sounding board and she felt flattered to be chosen as such.

Diametric opposites, they found in each other the perfect conversational complement, and by the time they reached town their mutual respect was cemented.

The library was closed that afternoon in memory of Levander Sprague, who'd worked there nearly a third of his life. It was a cloudy day, but inside the building was warm and bright. Entering, Will looked at the place through new eyes—gleaming wood, towering windows and flawless order. How incredible that he could work in such a place.

Miss Beasley walked him through, explained his duties, showed him the janitor's supplies, the furnace, asked that he arrive each day five minutes before closing so she could give him any special instructions, then extended a key.

"For me?" He stared as if it were her great-grandfather's gold watch.

"You'll be locking up when you leave each night."

The key. My God, she was willing to trust him with the key. In all his life he'd had no place. Now he had a house *and* a library he could walk into anytime he chose.

Staring at the cool metal in his palm, he told her quietly, "Miss Beasley, this library is public property. Some folks around here might object to your giving the key to an ex-con."

She puffed out her chest until her bosom jutted, and locked her wrists beneath it. "Just let them try, Mr. Parker. I'd welcome the war." She reached down and closed his fingers over the key. "And I'd win it."

Without a doubt, she was right. In his palm the brass warmed while a smile lifted one corner of his lips and spread to the other. Some poor damn fool could have had her behind him all his life and had passed up the opportunity, he thought. This town had to be filled with some mighty stupid men.

She left him, then, went home to spend the remainder of her rare day off. He walked through the silent rooms in wonder, realizing there'd be no supervisor, foreman or guard; he could do things his way, at his own pace. He liked the silence, the smell, the spaciousness and purpose of the place. It seemed to represent a facet of life he'd missed. Stationary people came here, secure ones. From now on he'd be one of them—leaving his comfortable home and coming here to work each day, picking up a paycheck each week, knowing he'd do the same next week and the next and the next. Brimming with feelings he could find no other way to express, he pressed both hands flat on one of the study tables—solid, functional, necessary, as he'd be now. Good wood, good hard oak in a table built to last. He'd last, too, at this job because he'd found in Miss Beasley a person who judged a man for what he was, not what he had been. He stood at one of the enormous fanlight windows and looked out on the street below. *Levander Sprague, wherever you are, thank you.*

The janitor's room smelled of lemon oil and sweeping compound. Will loved it and the idea that it was his own domain. Gathering supplies, he went eagerly into the public area and upended chairs and swept the hardwood floors with an oiled rag-tail mop. He dusted the windowsills, the furniture, the top of Miss Beasley's neat desk, emptied the wastebasket, burned the papers in the incinerator and felt as if he'd just been elected governor.

At six-thirty, he headed home.

Home.

The word had never held such promise. She was waiting there, the woman who'd called him dear. The one whose cheek he'd kissed. The one whose bed he shared. At the thought of returning to her, visions filled his head—of walking into her arms, feeling her hands close over his shoulders, burying his face in her neck. Of being held as if he mattered.

He felt different now that he had a job. Bolder, worthier. Perhaps tonight he'd kiss her and to hell with the consequences.

The kitchen was empty when he arrived, but his supper waited in a pie tin on the reservoir lid. The birthday cake sat in the middle of the cleared table. From the boys' room came a spill of light and the murmur of voices. He carried his plate and fork to the doorway and found Elly sitting beneath the covers in Donald Wade's bed, an arm around each of the boys.

". . . took a scamper 'round that hen house a-yowlin' at that fox fit to kill, and when he—" She glanced up. "Oh . . . . Will . . . . hi." Her face registered pleasure. "I was tellin' the boys a bedtime story."

"Don't stop."

Their eyes held for several electric beats while her color heightened and she tucked a stray hair behind one ear. Finally, she continued her tale. He lounged against the doorframe, eating his leftover hash and black-eyed peas, listening and chuckling while she entertained the boys with a sprightly story peopled with furry critters. When the tale ended she gave each of her sons a kiss, then edged off the bed and held out her hands for Thomas.

Will pushed off the doorway. "You shouldn't be lifting him. Here, hold this." He handed her his plate and swung Thomas up, transferring him to the crib. There followed the ritual goodnight kisses, then they left the boys' door ajar and ambled toward the kitchen.

"So, how was it at the library?"

"Do you know what she did?" he asked, amazed.

"What?"

"She gave me the key. Feature that. Me with a key to anything."

Eleanor was touched, not only by his astonishment, but by Miss Beasley's trust in him. He rinsed his dish and described his duties while she settled into a rocker and pressed one of the Madeira doilies into an embroidery hoop. He dragged a kitchen chair near, sipped a cup of coffee and watched her fingers create colored flowers where only blue ink had been. They talked quietly, calm on the surface but with an underlying tension simmering as the clock inched closer to bedtime.

When it arrived, Will arched and stretched while Eleanor tucked her handiwork away. They made their trips outside, battened down the house for the night and retired to their room to undress, back to back, as had become their habit. When he had stripped to his underwear, Will turned to glance over his shoulder and caught a glimpse of her naked back and the side of one breast as she threw a white nightgown over her head.

Dear. The memory of the simple word gripped him with all its attendant possibilities. Had she meant it? Was he really dear to someone for the first time in his life?

He sat on the edge of the bed and wound the alarm clock, waiting for the feel of her weight dipping the mattress before he settled back and lowered the lantern wick.

They lay memorizing the ceiling while memories of the day returned—a birthday gift, an endearment, a handclasp, a parting kiss—none very remarkable on the surface. The remarkable was happening within.

They lay flat, quivering inside, disciplining themselves into motionlessness. From the corner of her eye she glimpsed his bare chest, the looming elbows, the hands folded behind his head. From the corner of his eye he saw her pregnant girth and her high-buttoned nightie with the quilts covering her to the ribs. Beneath her hands she felt her own heartbeat driving up through the quilt. On the back of his skull he felt the accelerated rhythm of his pulse.

The minutes dragged on. Neither moved. Neither spoke. Both worried.

One kiss—is that so hard?

Just a kiss—please.

But what if she pushes you away?

What is there for him in a woman so pregnant she can scarcely waddle?

What woman wants a man with so many tramps under his bridge?

What man wants to roll up against someone else's baby?

But most of them were paid, Elly, all of them meaningless.

Yes, it's Glendon's baby, but he never made me feel like this.

I'm unworthy.

I'm undesirable.

I'm unlovable.

I'm lonely.

Turn to her, he thought.

Turn to him, she thought.

The lantern wick sputtered. The flame twisted, distorting the impression of the chimney rim on the ceiling. The mattress seemed to tremble with their uncertainties. And when it seemed the very air would sizzle with heat lightning, they spoke simultaneously.

"Will?"

"Elly?"

Their heads turned and their eyes met.

"What?"

A pause. Then, "I . . . I forgot what I was going to say."

Ten seconds of beating silence before she said softly, "Me too."

They stared at each other, feeling as if they were choking, each afraid . . . each desperate . . .

Then all of his past, all of her shortcomings, billowed up in a conflagration and exploded as might some distant star.

Her lips parted in unconscious invitation. His shoulder came off the bed and he rolled toward her, slowly enough to give her time to skitter if she would.

Instead her lips shaped his name. "Will . . ." But it escaped without a sound as he bent above her and touched her mouth with his own.

No passionate kiss, this, but a touch fraught with insecurities. Tentative. Uncertain. A mingling of breath more than of skin. A thousand questions encapsulated in the tremulous brushing of two timid mouths while their hearts thundered, their souls sought.

He lifted ... looked ... into eyes the color of acceptance, deep-sea green in the shadow of his head. She, too, studied his eyes at close range ... brown, vulnerable eyes which he'd hidden so often beneath the brim of a battered hat. She saw the doubts that had accompanied him to this brink and marveled that someone so good, so inwardly and outwardly beautiful, should have harbored them when she was the one ... she. Plain and pregnant Elly See, the brunt of laughter and pointed fingers. But in his eyes she saw no laughter, only a deep mystification to match her own.

He kissed her again ... lightly ... lightly ... the brush of a jaconet wing upon a petal while her fingertips brushed his chest.

And at long, long last the loneliness of Will Parker's life stopped hurting. He thought her name over and over—Elly ... Elly—a benediction, as the kiss deepened, firmer, fuller, but still with a certain reserve—two people schooled to reject the possibility of miracles now forced to change their beliefs.

His hand closed over her arm and hers flattened on the silken hairs of his chest, but he remained a space apart as he urged her lips open with his own, bringing the first touch of tongues—warm, wet and still atremble. Hearts that had hammered with uncertainty did so now in exultation. They searched for and found a more intimate fit, enhanced by the sway and nod of heads that built the kiss into something more than either had expected. Sweet sweet commingling, bringing more than the rush of blood and the thrust of hearts, bringing too, the assurance that Will and Eleanor were to one another beings of great moment.

He hovered above her, bearing his weight on both elbows, afraid of hurting her. But she bade him come. Nearer ... heavier ... to the spot where her heart lifted toward his. And he rested upon her breasts, gingerly at first, until her acquiescence seemed unmistakable.

For long wondrous minutes they sated themselves with

what both had known too little of before Will broke away, looked down into her face to find the same expression of wonder he himself was feeling. They stared—renewed—then wrapped each other tight and rocked because kissing hardly seemed an adequate expression of all they felt.

In time he hauled them safely to their sides, pressing his face to her throat, folding himself like a jackknife around her protruding stomach.

"Elly . . . Elly . . . I was so scared."

"So was I."

"I thought you'd turn me away."

"But that's what I thought you'd do."

He pulled back to see her face. "Why would I do that?"

"Because I'm not very pretty. And I'm pregnant and awkward."

He cradled her cheek tenderly. "No . . . no. You're a beautiful person. I saw that the first morning I was here."

She held the back of his hand and hid her eyes in its palm. These things were easier to admit behind closed eyes. "And I'm not very bright, and maybe I'm crazy. You knew all that."

He made her lift her chin and look at him. "But I killed a woman. And I've been in prison and in whorehouses. You knew that."

"That was a long time ago."

"Most people never forget."

"I thought because it was Glendon's baby inside me you wouldn't want to touch me."

"What does that have to do with anything?"

Her heart seemed too small to contain such joy. "Oh, Will."

He asked, "Could I touch it once? Your stomach? I never touched a woman who was pregnant."

She felt warm and shy but nodded.

His hands molded the sides of her stomach as if it were a bouquet of crushable flowers. "It's hard . . . you're hard. I thought it'd be soft. Oh God, Elly, you feel so good."

"So do you." She touched his hair, thick and springy and

smelling of his unmistakable individual scent. "I've missed this."

He closed his eyes and gave her license. If he lived to be a thousand he'd never get enough of the feeling of her hands in his hair.

In time he let his eyes drift open and they lay for minutes, gazing, taking their fill. She of his incredible eyes and jumbled hair. He of her softly swollen lips and green, green eyes. He found himself unreasonably jealous of her early years with Glendon Dinsmore. "Do you still think of him?"

"I haven't for weeks."

"I thought you still loved him."

She drew courage and repeated his words. "What does that have to do with anything? Do you think I'll love this baby any less, just because two others came before it?"

He braced up on an elbow, stared at her and swallowed. He felt as if a great fist had closed around his chest. When he spoke the words sounded pinched. "Elly, nobody ever—" Abashed, he couldn't go on.

"Nobody ever loved you before?" She tenderly cupped his cheek. "Well, I do."

His eyes slid closed and he turned his mouth hard into her palm, clasping it to his face. "Nobody. Ever," he reiterated. "Not in my whole life. No mother, no woman, no man."

"Well, your life ain't even half over yet, Will Parker. The second half's gonna be much better'n the first, I promise."

"Oh, Elly . . ." Above all the things he'd missed, this had left the greatest void. Just once in his life he wanted to hear it, the way he'd dreamed of hearing it during five long years in a cell, and all the lonely years he had drifted, and all through childhood while he watched other children—the lucky ones—pass the orphanage and gawk from the security of their parents' carriages and cars. "Could you say it once," he entreated, "like they say people do?"

Her heart beat like the wings of an eagle, taking her soaring as she spoke the words. "I love you, Will Parker."

The sting hit his eyelids and he hung his head because nobody had prepared him for this, nobody had said, When it happens you'll be resurrected. All that you were you will not be. All that you weren't, you are. He lunged against her, burying his face above her breasts, holding fast. "Oh, God, . . ." he groaned. "Oh, God."

She held his head as if he were a child awakening from a bad dream.

"I love you," she whispered against his hair, feeling her own tears build.

"Oh, Elly, I love you, too," he uttered in a broken voice, "but I was so afraid nobody could love me. I thought maybe I was unlovable."

"Oh no, Will . . . no . . . not you." His bittersweet words filled her with the deep wish to heal, left her throat aching as she curled around him, held his head protectively and felt him breathe against her breasts. She threaded her hands through his hair and felt him grow still with pleasure. She raked her nails over his skull in long, slow sweeps . . . time . . . and time . . . and time again, lifting his scent, memorizing it, impressing it forever in her senses. His hair was thick, coarse, the color of dry grass. It had grown since she'd cut it, become shaggy at the neck where she brushed it up from his nape, then smoothed it before beginning another long, sensuous stroke at the crown of his head. He shivered and made a sound of gratification, deep in his throat.

His whole life he'd longed for someone to touch him this way, to touch the boy in him as well as the man, to soothe, reassure. The feel of her fingers in his hair brought back a measure of all he'd missed. He was parched earth, she fresh rain. He a waiting vessel, she rich wine. And in those moments of closeness she filled him, filled all the lacks endowed him by his shiftless, loner's life, becoming at once all the things he'd needed—mother, father, friend, wife, and lover.

When he felt sated he lifted his head as if drunk with pleasure.

"I used to watch you touch the boys that way. I wanted to say, Touch me, too, like you touch them. Nobody ever did that to me before, Elly."

"I'll do it anytime you like. Wash your hair, comb it, rub your back, hold your hand—"

His mouth stopped her words. It seemed risky to accept too

much in this first, grand rush. He kissed her with gratitude changing swiftly to the lushness of fresh-sprung love. He braced higher and pushed her softly into the pillow, letting his hand rove over her neck and shoulder, suckling her mouth, spreading his fingers on her face, resting a thumb so near it almost became part of the kiss. His body beckoned to join more fully in this union. Realizing this was impossible, he broke the kiss but spanned her throat with his hand. Her pulsebeat matched the quickness of his own.

"You know how long I've loved you?"

"How long?"

"Since the day you threw the egg at me."

"All that time and you never said anything. Oh, Will . . ."

A swift slew of possessiveness hit him. He claimed her mouth again, washing its interior with his tongue, holding her arms locked hard around his neck. He bit her lips. She bit back. He lifted a knee and pressed it high and hard between her legs. She opened them and squeezed his thigh. He circled her immense waist and held her as if forever.

"Tell me again," he demanded insatiably.

"What?" she teased.

"You know. Tell me."

"I love you."

"Once more. I got to hear it more."

"I love you."

"Will you get tired of me asking you to say it?"

"You won't have to ask."

"Neither will you. I love you." Another kiss—a hard, short stamp of possession, then a question filled with boyish impatience. "When did you know?"

"I don't know. It just came upon me."

"When we got married?"

"No."

"When we bottled the honey?"

"Maybe."

"Well, sure's heck not when you threw that egg."

She chuckled. "But I noticed your bare chest for the first time that day and I liked it."

"My chest?"

"Aha."

"You liked my chest before you liked me?"

"When you were washing, down by the well."

"Touch it." Jubilantly he flattened her hand against it. "Touch me anyplace. God, do you know how long it's been since a woman touched me?"

"Will . . ." she chided timidly.

"Are you shy? Don't be shy. I thought I was, too, but all of a sudden it seems like we got so much time to make up for. Touch me. No, wait. Get up. First I gotta see you." He piled onto his knees and pulled her up to kneel before him, holding her hands out from her sides. "Mercy, are you a pretty sight. Let me look at you." Her chin dropped shyly and he lifted it, pressed the tousled hair back from her temples, then fluffed it with his fingertips and arranged it on her collarbones. "You mean I don't have to sneak anymore when I want to look at you? You got the greenest eyes. Green is my favorite color, but you knew that."

She folded her hands between her knees, quite overcome by this exuberant, demonstrative Will.

"I used to think if I was ever lucky enough to have a woman of my own, she'd have to have green eyes. Now here you are. You and your green eyes . . . and your pink cheeks . . . and your pretty little mouth . . ." With his thumbs he touched its corners and let his hands trail down to her shoulders, to her upper arms where they stopped. "Elly," he whispered, "don't move." He slipped his palms to the sides of her breasts and held them lightly while the blood rushed to her cheeks and she searched for a safe place to rest her gaze. The dim light shifted on the folds of her nightgown as he cupped a breast in each hand, his palms too narrow to contain their prenatal fullness. Gently, he reshaped and lifted, then released them to glide one hand down the fullest part of her belly. There it rested, fingers splayed. He watched the hand, soon joined by the other to smooth the cloth toward her hips where he held it taut, disclosing the impression of her distended navel. Bending, he kissed her. There. On the stomach she'd thought ugly enough to put him off.

"Will." She found his chin and attempted to lift it. "I'm fat as a pumpkin. How can you kiss me there?"

He straightened. "You're not fat, you're only pregnant. And if I'm going to deliver that baby I'd better get to know him."

"I thought I married a shy, quiet man."

"I thought so too."

He smiled for the length of three glad heartbeats, then laughed. And wondered if life would ever again be this good. And decided surely tomorrow and tomorrow and tomorrow it could only get better.

He was right. He'd never imagined happiness such as he knew in the days and nights that followed. To roll over in sleep and draw her back against him and drift off again in a cocoon of bliss. Or better yet, to roll the other way and feel her follow, then press close behind him. To feel her hand circle his waist, her feet beneath his, her breath on his back. To awaken and find her lying with an elbow beneath her cheek, studying him. To kiss her then in the buttery light of early morning and know that he could do so anytime. To leave her with a goodbye kiss and return anxious. To step into the kitchen and find her working at the sink, glancing shyly over her shoulder then down at her hands until he crossed the room and slipped both hands into her apron pockets and rested his chin on her shoulder. To kiss—over her shoulder—awaiting the exquisite moment when she'd turn and loop her arms up in a welcoming embrace. To eat cake from her fork, braid her hair, refill her coffee cup, watch her embroider. To lean over the sink and shiver while she washed his hair, then wilt on a kitchen chair while she dried, combed and cut it, and sometimes kissed his ear, and sometimes teased him when he dropped off and she had to awaken him with a kiss on the mouth. To walk down the driveway holding hands, pulling the boys in the wagon.

Only one thing disturbed him during those serene days. Lula Peak. It hadn't taken her long to get the news that Will was the custodian at the library. One evening within a week of his starting she walked in the back door and found Will in the storeroom gluing a loose chair rung. "Hey, sugar, where y' been keepin' yourself?"

Will jumped and swung around, startled by her voice.

"Library's closed, ma'am."

"Well now, I know that. So's the cafe, 'cause I just shut off the light. Thought I'd sashay on over and congratulate you on your new job." She leaned against the doorframe, one arm crossing her waist, the other hand dangling near the white V of her uniform collar. "That's the neighborly thing to do, i'nt it?"

" 'Preciate it, ma'am. Now if you'll excuse me, I got work to do."

He squatted again, turning his back, minding the chair. She moved into the windowless room and stood behind him with her knee against his back. "You thought any more about what I said, sugar?" She kneaded the side of his neck. "Man like you makes a girl lay awake nights. Figured maybe you lay awake, too, what with that wife o' yours bein' pregnant. No sense in both of us losin' sleep now, is there?"

He spun to his feet, took her by the shoulders and pushed her back.

"I ain't lookin' for trouble, I told you once before." He stuffed his hands in his pockets, feeling soiled from touching her. "I'm a happily married man, Miss Peak. Now I'm afraid I'll have to ask you to leave, 'cause I got work to do."

She let her eyes meander over him, from forehead to hips and back up. "You're blushin', sugar, you know that? Must mean you're hot . . . let's see." She reached to touch his face but he grabbed her wrist and held it away, squeezing hard.

"Dammit, Lula, I said leave off!"

Her eyes took fire, radiating excitement. "Well, that's an improvement. At least we're on a first-name basis."

"I don't want you comin' here again."

"Some men don't know what they want." Like a cobra she struck, biting his knuckles and retreating in one flashing movement.

"Ouch, goddammit!" He nursed the hand and already saw blood.

"What's it take, Parker, huh?" she challenged from the

doorway, shoulders thrown back, hands on hips, eyes glinting with demonic glee. "I know things that crazy wife of yours never dreamed of. You think about it." She turned and ran.

He felt violated. And angry. And guilty. And powerless because she was a woman and he couldn't level her with his fists as he had the men who'd tried to seduce him in prison. That night, returning to Elly, he held his feelings inside, afraid to tell her about Lula, afraid to jeopardize their new burgeoning closeness.

At the library he had always locked the front door. After Lula's intrusion he locked the back, too. But she cornered him one night when he took the trash out to burn in the incinerator behind the building, slipping up behind him in the dark and touching him before he was aware of her presence. He shoved her harder this time, knocking her against the incinerator, cursing, raising his fist but halting himself just in time.

"Do it," she goaded. "Do it, Parker," and he realized she was sick, driven by some twisted need that scared him.

"Keep outa my way, Lula," he growled, picked up his trash can and ran.

He tried to put the incident from his mind, but found himself looking over his shoulder every time he stepped out the library door, every time he locked it at the end of the night. He grew closer to Elly, appreciated her more, soothed himself with her goodness.

Nights, when he'd return home, she'd awaken and stretch and watch him shuck off his outerwear and slip in beside her. And her arms would open and they'd lie kissing and murmuring until the hour grew wee and the moon began its descent. Though they were husband and wife, their embraces remained chaste. Sometimes he caressed her breast, but as her time grew closer she'd flinch and he was smitten by a wave of guilt.

"Elly, honey, I'm sorry. Did I hurt you?"

"They're always a little tender, late like this."

After that he kissed and held her, but no more. She always wore her long white nightie and he knew she was shy about exposing her distorted body. Though he was tempted to do more, he never pushed, but settled for kissing and lying with their limbs entwined, their hands safely removed from intimate territory.

Until one night in early December when he'd found a note from Lula on the back door as he left work. It was graphic, obscene, suggesting how she might thrill him when he finally broke down and accepted her invitation. That night he had a dream. He was walking through a dry wash in Texas. It was high noon and so hot the earth burned through the soles of his boots. His mouth felt parched and a dull ache bowed his shoulders. He labored up a rocky ridge, panting and tired, then halted in surprise at the sight beyond the crest. A layer of sky might have dropped from overhead, so brilliant was the valley below. Filled with Texas bluebonnets, it seemed to reflect the hard cobalt blue of the bowl overhead. A ribbon of sparkling water bisected the field as he wallowed through it in flowers as deep as a man's boot tops. He knelt to drink, swashing his face and neck, dampening his collar and leather vest. He cupped his hand again, and as he knelt, sipping, a pair of feet waded into view beneath his nose. A gauzy yellow skirt floated on top of the water. He looked up into eyes as black as Apache tears, and hair to match.

"Hola, Weel—jew been lookin' for me?" It was Carmelita, one of the women from the whorehouse in La Grange. She had Mexican blood, enough to make her skin dusky and her lips a ripe plum red.

He pushed himself onto his haunches and backhanded his mouth slowly, eyeing her as she caught her hands on both hips and rocked seductively. Her feet were widespread, thighs silhouetted through the yellow gauze skirt. She reached down and lazily wet her arms, bending forward until her breasts hung pendulously within the peasant-style blouse.

" 'Ey, Weell Parker, wot jew lookin' at, eh?" She straightened, still with legs spraddled, and wrung out her skirt, enticing him with a glimpse of bare skin and black pubic hair underneath. She laughed throatily and wallowed to the bank. Standing ankle-deep, she began washing his face with the wet skirt. He reached beneath it and gripped her bare hips. Immediately she shoved him away, scuttled backward into the swifter water, laughing throatily. "Jew want Carmelita . . . come and get hur." He was stripping off his vest before the words cleared her lips. Down to bare skin, he shucked, then plunged into the cold, rippling creek. She shrieked and ran, but he caught and spun her, took her down and himself, too, into the purling water that turned her clothes transparent. He bit her nipple through the wet gauze and she shrieked again, laughing, then squiggled away, fighting against the current while stripping off her dress and flinging it back in his face. He plunged after her, scraping the clinging gauze off his head, and tackled her as she scrambled up the bank, kissing her voluptuously while her wet black hair got between their tongues. His finger was inside her before their ripples disappeared downstream, and she bucked up lustily, chuckling in a rich contralto. They rolled wildly, collecting sand on their backs. When they stopped, breathless, she was on top, urging him with practiced hips.

"Jew like, eh, hombre?" She growled low in her throat and took him in hand with little gentleness and less pause. Firmly stroking him, she let her eyes flash wickedly. "Jew will like this even more." She dove down without invitation, opened her mouth and narrowed his world to a thin corridor where carnality was all that mattered.

"Will . . . wake up, Will!"

Disoriented, he opened his eyes to find himself not in a field of Texas bluebonnets but in an iron bed; with a face dampened not by creekwater but by his own sweat; not with Carmelita, but with Elly. His body was swelled like a cactus in a March rain and his hand was inside Elly's cotton underwear, in her pregnant body.

Startled, she looked back over her shoulder. He held himself rigid, too near climax to risk even the faintest movement.

"I was dreaming," he managed in a raspy voice.

"You awake now?"

"Yes." He withdrew his hand and rolled onto his back, covering his eyes with a wrist. "Sorry," he mumbled.

"What were you dreaming?"

"Nothin'."

"Of me?"

Afraid of hurting her feelings, he remained silent, damning
Lula, and the dream, and his own body for needing release.
"Elly, you scared to let me touch you?"

"You touch me all the time."

"Not there."

Silence ... then, "I don't want you to see me. Pregnant
women aren't so pretty to look at."

"Who told you that?"

"They just aren't."

"I'll see you when the baby is born."

"Not for long. And afterwards I won't look like this."

He moved his wrist and stared at the ceiling, thinking, *It
isn't natural, two people lying beside each other, married all
this time and never touching deliberately.* "I'm gonna turn off
the lamp, Elly."

No reply, so he reached over and lowered the wick. In the
unaccustomed darkness they lay in the strong scent of kerosene smoke.

"Come here." He reached, closed his hand over her arm
and pulled gently. "It's time for this, don't you think?"

"Will, I like it when you kiss me and hold me, but I can't
do any more."

"I know." He found her hips and rolled her to face him.
"But I'm dying every night, wondering. Aren't you? I'll be
gentle as anything you ever felt." He pulled her nightgown up
and laid both hands on her. "I want you to know somethin',
Elly." He kissed her mouth, breathed on her, felt his heart
drumming everywhere, everywhere. "I wish this baby was
mine."

He explored her skin as if it were braille, leaving no further secrets. "Ah, Elly ... Elly ..." he murmured throatily.
Then he found her hand and placed it upon himself and his
breathing became a battle for air. He shuddered and ejacu-
lated in her hand. Swiftly. Afterward he felt healed and renewed and reached for her again, to repay her in kind. But
she pushed his hand away, sighed and curled close against
him.

He lay holding her while emotions came to cleanse him.
He thought of thanking her, but considered himself inarticu-

late in a moment too precious to jade with words. So he enfolded her, rubbed her back, her spine, her hair, pressing her even closer at intervals when his sense of fulfillment cried for expression.

Outside a solitary woodcock called, rising on whistling wings. The wind rested, stilling the tree tips. Off in the distance a barred owl called, like the bark of a dog at first, then, as if questioning, *Who-looks-for-you? Who looks for you?*

Inside, entwined, Will and Elly drifted to sleep.

And neither of them thought to turn the light back on.

CHAPTER
13

Elly went into labor near noon of December fourth. She'd had a low backache all morning, then a bloody show, and by dinnertime her first two distinguishable contractions had come, fifteen minutes apart. The second hit hard enough to perch her on the edge of a chair, trying to catch her breath for the better part of a minute. When it ended she braced her back and rose awkwardly, then waddled into the front room.

Will was working on the bathroom, sitting crosslegged on the floor, whistling. He had cut a doorway through the front-room wall and sectioned off an end of the porch, which already had a window installed and the pipes jutting up from the crawl space underneath. With his first check he had proudly purchased bathroom fixtures—used, though neither Will nor Elly cared in their excitement over the prospect of having such a room. The sink and stool were stored else-where, but the tub was in place, standing inside the skeletal walls which, too, awaited finishing after the pipework was done.

Elly paused in the bathroom doorway, watching Will, listening to him whistle "In My Adobe Hacienda," which they'd been hearing on the radio lately. Wielding a pipe wrench, he faced the far wall. His cowboy hat sat at a jaunty angle on the back of his head. Sawdust coated its brim, and the back of his blue shirt was smudged with dirt from lying on his back in the crawl space. She smiled as he hit several sour notes.

He gave the wrench a last mighty tug that interrupted his song, then set it down with a clatter and tested the pipe junction with his fingers, picking up the tune again, softly, through his teeth. He got to one knee and picked up a copper elbow joint, bending forward while figuring the height at which it should adjoin the pipe connections on the tub.

"Hey, you," she greeted amiably, wearing an appreciative smile.

He twisted at the waist and sent her an answering grin. "Hiya, doll."

She laughed and leaned against the doorframe. "Some doll, shaped like a bloated horse."

"C'm'ere." He fell to his seat, legs outstretched, leaning against a wall stud and reaching out one dirty hand. They grinned at each other silently for a long moment. "Over here." He patted his lap.

She boosted off the doorframe and picked her way through tools and pipes scattered upon the floor to stand above him.

"Right here." He patted his lap again as she turned sideways.

"No, not that way—this way." He grabbed her ankle and planted it beyond his far hip, grinning suggestively. "Come on down here."

"Will . . . the boys," she whispered, throwing a cautious glance over her shoulder at the doorway.

"So what?" Gripping her hands he forced her to straddle him with her skirt bunched up to midthigh.

"But they might come in."

"So they find me kissing their mother. Be good for 'em." He linked his wrists behind her waist and settled her paunch against his belly while she crossed her arms behind his neck.

"Will Parker . . ." She smiled into his upraised face. "You're the crazy one, not me."

"Damn right, woman. Crazy for you." He lifted his mouth for a long, involved kiss—lips, tongues, and plenty of head motion. It was something new for Eleanor, necking in the middle of the day. With Glendon there had been restraint dur-

ing daylight hours, perhaps even less than restraint, for the
idea of an interlude like this never entered their heads. But
with Will ... oh, her Will. He was insatiable. She couldn't
carry a stack of clean laundry through his vicinity without being waylaid, and pleasantly so. He was a devilishly good
kisser. She'd never before given much consideration to the
quality of kisses. But straddling Will's lap, with his mouth
wide, sucking gently on hers, with his silky tongue stroking
everything reachable within her mouth, she appreciated his
skill. He didn't simply kiss. He lavished, then lingered, then
drew away by slow degrees, as if he would never tire of her.
Sometimes he murmured wordlessly, often nuzzled, making
parting as sweet as joining had been.

The kiss ended with all due reluctance, and with Will's
nose buried in her collar, his hat fallen to the floor.

"My hands are dirty or you know where they'd be, don't
you?"

Eyes closed, face tilted up, she held his head and lightly
raked his skull the way he loved. "Where?"

He closed his teeth on her collarbone, chuckled and teased,
"In the kitchen, building a sandwich. I'm starved."

She laughed and pushed away in mock rebuff. "You're always starved. What do you think I came in here for?"

"To call me for dinner?" He leaned back and grinned into
her happy green eyes.

"What else?"

"And instead you pinned me to the floor and wasted all
this time when I could've been eating?"

"Who wants to eat when you can neck?"

He feigned disgust and reached for his hat, plunking it on
his head. "Here I am, minding my own business, puttin' in a
bathroom, when out of nowhere this woman jumps me. I
mean, I got my wrench out and I'm connectin' pipe and not
botherin' a livin' soul when—"

"Hey, Will?" she interrupted teasingly. "Guess what."

"What?"

"Dinner's ready."

"Well, it's about time." He tried to rise, but she remained
on his lap.

"Guess what else."

"I dunno."

"My labor's started."

His face flattened as if she'd struck him across the Adam's apple with the pipe wrench.

"Elly. Oh, my God, you shouldn't be sitting here. Lord, did I hurt you, pulling you down? Can you get up?"

She chuckled at his overzealous reaction. "It's all right. I'm between pains. And sitting here took my mind off 'em."

"Elly, are you sure? I mean, is it really time?"

"I'm sure."

"But how can it be? It's only December fourth."

"I said December, didn't I?"

"Yeah, but—well, December's a long month!" His brow furrowed as he carefully boosted her up and followed. "I mean, I thought it'd be later. I thought I'd have time to finish the bathroom so it'd be ready when the baby came."

"It's a funny thing about babies." She held his dirty hands and lifted a reassuring smile. "They don't wait for things to get done. They just come whenever they feel like it. Now listen, I got some things to get ready, so if you'd fix the boys' plates and your own it'd sure be a help."

Will became a bundle of nerves. She shouldn't have found it amusing, but couldn't help smiling covertly. He balked at being out of her sight, even for the short time it took him to settle the kids at the table with their plates. Instead of filling a plate for himself he followed her to the bedroom, where he found her stripping the bed.

"What're you doing?"

"Getting the bed ready."

"Well, *I can do that!*" he reprimanded sharply, clumping inside.

"So can I. Will, please . . . listen." She dropped the corner of the quilt and clasped his wrist. "It's best if I move around, all right? It could be hours yet."

He elbowed her aside and began jerking the soiled bedclothes off the mattress. "I don't see how you could've just sat there on the bathroom floor letting me make jokes while it was already started."

"So what else should I do?"

"Well, I don't know, but Jesus, Elly, there I was, pulling at your ankles, making you sit on me." She moved as if to resume her chore, and he erupted. "I said I'll fix the bed! Just tell me what you want on it."

She told him: old newspapers against the mattress, covered by absorbent cotton flannel sheets folded into thick pads, and finally the muslin sheet. No blankets at all. It looked so stark and foreboding, the sight of it scared him worse than ever. But while he stood staring she had a new surprise in store for him.

"I want you to go down to the barn and get a pair of tugs."

"Tugs?" His unblinking eyes grew round.

"Tug straps. From Madam's harness."

"What for?"

"And you might as well start carrying water. Fill the boiler and the reservoir and the teakettle. We need to have both warm and cold on hand. Now go."

"What for? What d'you need those tug straps for?"

"Will . . . please," she said with forced patience.

He raced down to the barn, cursing himself for not getting the running water in before this, for not hooking the water heater up to the wind generator, for not realizing babies sometimes come early. He tore the spare harness from the wall and fumbled with the leather, removing the tugs. Less than three minutes later he panted to a halt at the bedroom door to find her poised on the edge of a hard wooden chair, back arched, eyes closed, her hands gripping the edge of the seat.

"Elly!" He dropped the tugs and fell to one knee before her.

"It's all right," she managed, breathless, her eyelids still closed. "It's going away now."

He touched her kneecaps, quaking with fear. "Elly, I'm sorry I shouted before. I didn't mean to. I was just scared."

"It's all right, Will." The pain eased as she opened her eyes and slowly sank back in the chair. "Now listen to me. I want you to take that harness and lay it out flat on the porch floor and scrub it hard with a brush and that yellow soap. On both sides. Scrub good around the buckles and even in the buckle holes. And scrub your hands and fingernails at the same time. Then bring the tugs inside and boil them in the dishpan. While they're boiling in one pan, I want you to boil the scissors and two lengths of hard string in a separate one. You'll find them in the kitchen in a cup next to the sugar bowl. Then as soon as the water is hot, bring some in here, and the yellow soap so I can take a bath."

"All right, Elly," he answered meekly, rising, backing away doubtfully.

"And put the boys down for a nap as soon as they're finished eating."

He followed her instructions minutely, rushing from task to task, afraid something would happen while he wasn't at her side. When he brought the empty washtub into the bedroom he found her drawing fresh white baby clothing from the bureau drawer—a tiny flannel kimono, a receiving blanket, an undershirt, a diaper. He stood and watched as she lovingly catalogued each item and placed it on a stack. Next came the pink shawl she'd crocheted herself, and a pair of incredibly small booties to match. She turned and found him watching.

Her smile was so peaceful, so unafraid, it brought a measure of ease to him. "I just know it's going to be a girl," she said.

"I'd like that, too."

He watched as Elly got the laundry basket from behind the bedroom door, emptied it of dirty clothes and prepared it with a white pad, followed by rubber and cotton sheets. Then came the pink shell-designed shawl and lastly a white flannel receiving blanket. "There." She smiled down at the basket with the same pride a queen might have exhibited over a golden cradle lined with swansdown.

He set the washtub down without dropping his eyes from her, stepped around it and touched her tenderly, below the jaw. "Rest now while I bring the water."

She looked into his eyes and told him, "I'm awful glad you're here, Will."

"So am I."

It wasn't strictly true. He'd rather be in the car on his way to fetch the doctor, but it was too late for discussing that. He filled her washtub and went to the kitchen to clean up the lunch dishes. Returning to the bedroom minutes later, he found Elly standing in the washtub, covered with soap. She stood at half-profile to him, presenting a view of her back and the side of one breast. He'd never seen her naked before. Not out of bed. The sight stirred him deeply. She was misproportioned, bulky, but the reason for it lent her a different feminine beauty from any he'd ever witnessed. She passed the cloth down her stomach, between her thighs, cleansing the route for the awaited one, and he stood watch, unabashed, without a thought of turning away. Suddenly she was seized by a new pain and dropped into a half-crouch. Her fist closed around the washcloth, sending lather plopping into the water. Will moved as if propelled by black powder, across the room to slide an arm around her slick body, supporting her through the brunt of it. When it began ebbing, he eased her lower until she rested on the edge of the tub, panting.

He felt helpless and distraught, wanting to do more, *needing* to do more than simply comfort. He wished he could bear the next pain himself.

When it was over, she wilted. "That was a strong one. They're comin' faster this time than when Thomas was born."

"Here. Kneel down."

She knelt and he rinsed her back, arms, breasts, relieved to be doing something concrete. He held her hand as she stepped over the rim of the tub, then dried her back.

"Thank you, Will. I can finish." While he carried the tub away she dressed in a clean white nightgown and beneath the bed found a white cloth sack from which she drew several large folded dried leaves. Taking them, she followed Will to the kitchen. She stood a moment, watching him spill her bathwater at the sink. With the dipper he rinsed the tub, then mopped it with a rag. Only then did he turn and find her standing behind him, watching.

"Should you be out here?"

"You mustn't worry so, Will. Please. For me?"

"That's not an easy order."

"I know." She could see on his face how difficult it was for him to remain stalwart, and loved him for his valiant effort. "But now I need to talk to you about what to expect, what to do."

"I know it all." He set the tub down. "I read it in the book so many times that it might as well be branded on my arm. But reading it and doing it are two different things."

She moved close to him and touched his hand. "You'll do fine, Will." Calmly she found a kettle into which she put the leaves, covering them with water from the teakettle. She set them to simmer on the rear of the range.

Will watched, feeling his stomach tensing more each minute. "What's that?"

"Comfrey."

He was almost afraid to ask. It took two tries before his throat released the sound. "What for?"

"Afterwards, if I tear, you got to make a poultice of it and put it on me. It'll draw the skin back together and help it heal. But you got to remember—don't waste no time on me till you seen to the baby, understand?"

If she tears. The words shook him afresh. It took an effort for Will to concentrate on the remainder of her instructions.

"Only use the sterilized rags I laid on the dresser. Everything else you need is there too. Scissors, strings, pledgets, alcohol and gauze for the baby's cord, and Vaseline for under the cotton when you bandage her. You'll do that after you give her a bath. Make sure you keep enough warm water for that, and a tubful of cold for the sheets, 'cause you'll have to change them when it's over. When you give her a bath don't use the yellow soap, but the glycerine. Make sure you hold her head all the time—soon as it comes out of me, and while you're waiting for the rest of her body to be born, and when you give her a bath, too. But, Will, you got to remember, through it all, the baby comes first. The most important thing is to get her breathing, then bathed and dressed and warm so she doesn't get chilled."

"I know, I know!" he replied impatiently, wishing she wouldn't talk about it. He'd read the birth attendant's instructions until he could recite them verbatim. It was the very images they conjured that rattled him.

Quietly she said, "Now walk with me."

"Walk?"

"It'll bring it on faster."

If he could choose, he'd postpone it indefinitely. The thought brought a spear of guilt for her plight, and he did as bid. He had never felt as protective as during the following two hours while they strolled the length of the small rooms, back and forth, stopping only for each new contraction. She was intrepid; to be less himself would have made him a burden rather than a support. So he held her hand in the crook of his arm and accompanied her as if they were out for a sojourn on the town green at the height of the season. He teased when she needed brightening. And soothed when she needed support. And talked when she needed talking. And learned what a pledget was when he saw a stack of carefully formed rectangular cotton pads bound in gauze.

At half past two the boys woke up and he dressed them in their warm jackets and sent them out to play, hoping fervently they'd stay out till sunset.

Shortly past three Elly announced quietly, "I think I'd like to lay down now. Bring the tug straps, dear." In the bedroom, with a sigh she rolled onto the clean white sheet and ordered, "Tie them to the footrail as far apart as my knees."

His stomach lurched, his salivary glands seemed to kick into overtime and his hands felt clumsy. When the leather straps were knotted, leaving ample leads and loops for her legs, they appeared like trappings in a medieval torture chamber. He found them hideous as he waited for her next contraction. When it hit, it seemed to hit them both. With acute shock, Will felt the sympathetic pain rip through his groin and down his thighs just as it did down Elly's. It was a hard one, and long, lasting nearly a minute, markedly advanced from those before.

When it ended, she rested, panting, then whispered, "Wash your hands again, Will, and trim your nails. It won't be long now."

Trim his nails? This time he didn't ask why. He feared he

knew. In case trouble developed and he had to help from the inside.

He scrubbed his knuckles until they stung, and snipped his nails to the quick with the sterilized scissor, fighting down panic. Oh God, why hadn't he gone against her wishes and driven into town for the doctor the minute she'd had her first pain? What if the cord was wrapped around the baby's neck? What if Elly hemorrhaged? What if the boys came in in the middle of it?

As if his very thought conjured them, the pair clattered into the kitchen, calling for their mother.

Will went out to waylay them, soiling his sterilized hands as he stopped Donald Wade and Thomas with a hand on each chest as they charged for the closed bedroom door.

"Hold up there, buckaroos!" He went down on one knee and gathered them close.

"We got to show Mama somethin'!" Donald Wade held a bird's nest.

"Your mama's resting."

"But, look what we found!" Donald Wade strained toward the door but Will tightened his arm.

"You remember when your mama told you about how that baby was gonna come out someday in the basket?" They stopped struggling and gazed at Will with innocent curiosity. "Well, the baby's gonna be born pretty soon, and your mother's not gonna feel so good while it's happening, but the same was true when you guys were born, so don't be scared, okay?" He gently squeezed their necks. "Now, I want you to be good boys. Donald Wade, you get some cookies and take your brother outside, and don't come back in till I call you, all right?"

"But—"

"Now listen, I ain't got time to argue, 'cause your mama needs me. But if you do like I say I'll take you to the movie house one day soon. Deal?" Donald Wade vacillated, glancing from Will toward the bedroom door.

"To Hopalong Cassidy?"

"You bet. Go on now," Will gave them each a little shove toward the kitchen and the cookie jar. As soon as they were

safely outside, he rescrubbed his hands, jogged back to the
bedroom, closed the door with his boot and pushed it tight
with a shoulder.

"The boys—I bribed them with a trip to the movie house
and sent them outside with a handful of cookies. How're
you?" He moved to the side of the bed and sat on the hard
wooden chair.

"I hurt." She chuckled and cradled her stomach.

He reached as if to brush Elly's brow.

"Don't touch me, Will. You mustn't."

Reluctantly he withdrew his cleansed hand to sit in misery,
waiting, feeling useless.

The next pain lifted her midsection off the mattress and
brought Will from his chair to lean over her, watching her
face contort as her knees parted and she reached up to grip
the iron rails above her head. When she held her breath, he
held his. When she grimaced, he grimaced. When she bared
her teeth, he bared his. The sixty seconds during her contraction felt longer than his stint in prison.

At its end, she opened her dazed eyes and rolled her head
to look at him. "It's t–time, W–Will," she managed. "Wash
me with alcohol n–now, and h–help me find the t–tugs."

His hands trembled as he moved to the foot of the bed,
folded back her nightgown and stared. Oh, Lord. Lord o'
mercy, how she must hurt. She was swollen, distended, distorted beyond anything he'd imagined. He could actually see
the bulge caused by the baby's head just above the apex of
her legs. Her genitals appeared inflamed, as if bee-stung, and
they were seeping, staining the bedclothes a dim pink. He
gulped, but came from his stupor when she reared up and a
great gush of transparent fluid flowed from her body, wetting
a wide circle on the sheet. The sight of it galvanized him into
action. He knew what it was, knew it meant the baby was
pressing low, preparing for its arrival into the world.

Suddenly his purpose here became crystal clear, and as it
dawned all Will's fears disappeared. His stomach grew calm.
His hands grew steady. The jitters fled, chased away by the
realization that he was needed by both the baby and its
mother. But they needed him competent.

With a pad of cotton he generously swabbed her stomach, thighs and genitals with alcohol. It stung his own fingers where he'd broken the cuticles with the scrub brush, but he scarcely noticed. For good measure, he swabbed the tug straps before gently lifting her heels and slipping the leather loops snug behind her knees. Then he placed an additional clean folded flannel sheet beneath her.

"W–W–Will," she panted as another contraction began.

"Yes, love," he answered quietly, but stood at his post, eyes riveted on her constricting belly, watching it slowly begin to arch, watching her dilation grow with the pain.

"W–W–*Wiiiiill!*" It tore from her as a rasping cry while the contraction built and peaked. He placed his palms beneath her thighs and helped her through it, feeling her muscles tighten as she lifted. Only when she relaxed did he raise his eyes to her face. Beads of sweat stood on her brow. The fine strands of hair at her hairline were damp and darkened to the color of aged cornsilk. Her lips looked dry and cracked. She wet them with her tongue while he thought of the jar of Vaseline he dared not touch. Before her lips had dried, another pain arrived and with it the sight of the baby's dark scalp.

"I see her!" Will cried. "Come on, darlin', once more and she'll be here!"

He waited with his hands spread in welcome, chancing not so much as a glance away from the dark hair now clearly visible. Elly's womb arched, her legs tightened on the straps, her hands on the iron rails. A ragged scream rent the air and Will learned what perineum meant as he watched Elly's tear. But he had no time to dwell on it, for at the same moment the baby's head slipped through—facing backward, as promised, facedown and slippery in his waiting hands. Then, as if by some miracle, it turned to the side, following the normal course of events, and he cradled it on his palm, tiny and sleek and red.

"Her head is out, darlin'. Oh, God, she has dark eyebrows." The distorted face was frighteningly dark and marked from the rigors of birth, but the warning in the book stood Will in good stead as he told himself it was to be expected; the child would not choke from the perineum drawn tightly about its neck. *Don't panic! Don't try to pull her out!* "Easy there, now, little one," he murmured to the baby. "I got to clean your mouth out." As if Nature knew exactly what she was doing, she allowed just enough time for Elly to rest and for Will to run his finger into the baby's mouth and clear it before Elly bore down and the baby's lower shoulder appeared, followed by the upper, then, in one grand release, the full birth happened. Into Will's waiting hands spilled a creature with a dark face, connected to its mother by a thin, crimped lifeline. Slippery and wet she came, filling his heart with a wild thrum of excitement, his face with a wide beam of wonder.

"She's here, Elly, she's born! And you were right. She's a girl. And . . . oh . . . lord, smaller than my hands." Even as he spoke, he rested his precious cargo on Elly's stomach while she panted in the brief natural respite following full birth. Releasing her grip on the headrail, Elly reached down to touch the baby's head, lifting her own with an effort and smiling wearily. As her head fell back she laughed and tears leaked down her temples.

"Is she pretty?"

"She's the sorriest mess I ever seen." He laughed in relief. Until Elly was hit by an aftershock and grunted, straining until her face shook and turned purple. He laid the baby down and tried to help Elly through the second wave of pushing pains. But the afterbirth refused to come. She fell back, panting, near exhaustion, her eyelids quivering. Another pushing pain produced the same results, and Will swallowed the lump of fear in his throat, doing what he knew he must do. He rested one hand in the soft hollow of her stomach, fitting its heel at the top of her womb and manipulating it to create a man-made contraction. She moaned and mindlessly tried to push his hand away. He forced from his mind the fact that he must hurt her to help her. His eyes smarted. He cleared them on his shoulder and vowed he'd never make her pregnant. He reached inside her tender flesh, loosening the afterbirth while kneading her soft stomach. Suddenly he felt a change as her own body took over. Her abdomen contracted and beneath his ministration the afterbirth pulled loose inside, dropping low to create a slight swelling beneath her matted hair. "Come on, Elly-honey, one more push and you can rest." From some hidden source she found the strength for another mighty effort that brought a last gush as her body delivered the afterbirth, severing her completely from the life she'd supported for nine months.

Will's shoulders drooped. He closed his eyes, sucked in a great lungful of air, dried his brow on a sleeve and praised simply, "Good, honey. It's all done. Hang on now." His hands were remarkably calm as he tied the first string an inch and a half from the baby's body, leaving only enough space between it and the second stricture for the scissor to do its work. The silver blades met and the deed was done. The baby was on her own.

Breathe! Breathe! Breathe!

The word resounded through Will's mind as he picked up the baby and watched it fold into a fetal position within his hands. Through his memory skittered the various directions for shocking a newborn into drawing its first breath. A smart smack. Cold water. Artificial respiration. But to do any of them to a creature so tiny seemed sadistic. Come on, girl, *breathe*! ... *Breathe!* Fifteen seconds sped by, then thirty. *Don't make me use that cold water. And I'd rather cut off my own hand than slap you.* He heard the boys come in and call from the other side of the door. They scarcely registered. His heart raced. Desperation clawed at him. He gave the baby a shake. *Breathe, dammit, breathe!* Panicking now, he tossed her a foot in the air and caught her as she dropped. A second after she hit his hands her mouth opened, she hiccuped, started flailing with all fours and began bawling in the puniest voice imaginable. It came in undulations—wauu, wauu, wauu—accompanied by a comical face with pinched mouth, flattened nose and the beat of her tiny fists against the air. It was a soft cry, but healthy and wonderfully vexed at being treated so roughly during her first minute in the outside world.

Will looked down into the bloody face, heard the welcome complaint and laughed. In relief. In celebration. He kissed the miniature nose and said, "Way to go, girl. That's what we wanted to hear." Then, to his wife, "She's breathing, and beautiful and looks as normal as a one-dollar bill." Abruptly his mood sobered. "Elly, you're shivering." During the minute he'd concentrated on his duty, she'd been gripped by natural chills. She lay now shuddering, her exposed limbs damp, the bedding beneath her soaked. Lord, a man needed six hands at a time like this.

"I'll be all right," Elly assured him. "Take care of her first."

It was hard to do, but he had little choice, given the fact that Elly's directive agreed with those he'd memorized. So far things had gone in perfect, natural order. He'd proceed by the book and hope their luck held. But he paused long enough to lay the baby down and gently remove Elly's legs from the tug straps, lower them and cover her. He brushed a light kiss on her dry lips, and whispered, "I'll be back as soon as I get her bathed. You be okay?"

She nodded weakly and closed her eyes.

He crooked the baby in one arm, opened the door with the other and found Donald Wade and Thomas on the other side, holding hands and crying pitifully.

"We heard Mama scream."

"She's better now—look." Will knelt. The sight of the red, squawling baby stopped their crying with amusing suddenness. "You got a baby sister." Donald Wade's mouth dropped open. The tears hung on Baby Thomas's sooty lashes. Neither of them spoke a word. "She just got here."

As one, they resumed bawling.

"I wanna see Mamaaaa!"

"Maamaaa!"

"She's fine—see?" Will held the door open a crack and let them peek inside for reassurance. All they saw was their mother lying at rest with her eyes closed. Will closed the door. "Shh. She's restin' now, but we'll all go in later and see her, soon as we get the baby a bath. Come on now, you might have to help me."

They followed as if mesmerized. "In the real bathtub?"

"No, the real one ain't ready yet."

"In the sink?"

"Yep."

They screeched chairs across the kitchen floor and stood one on either side of Will as he lowered their sister into a dishpan of warm water. Her crying stopped immediately. Cradled in Will's long hands, she stretched, opened dark eyes and peered at the world for the first time. Thomas reached out a tentative finger as if to test her for realness.

"Uh-uh. Mustn't touch her yet." Thomas withdrew the finger and gazed up at Will respectfully.

"Where'd she come from?" asked Donald Wade.

"From inside your mother."

Donald Wade looked skeptical. "She din't neither."

Will laughed and gently swished the baby through the water.

"She sure did. Been curled up inside her like a little butterfly inside a cocoon. You seen a cocoon, haven't you?" Of course they had. With a mother like theirs, the boys had been watching cocoons since they were old enough to say the word. "If a butterfly can come out of a cocoon, why can't a little sister come out of a mother?"

Because neither could answer, they believed.

Then Donald Wade remarked, "She ain't got no wink!"

"She's a girl. Girls don't have winks."

Donald Wade stared at his sister's pink skin. He looked up at Will. "She gonna get one?"

"Nope."

Donald Wade scratched his head, then pointed. "What's that?"

"It's gonna be her belly button."

"Oh." And after some thought, "Don't look like mine."

"It will."

"What's her name?"

"You'll have to ask your mother that."

The baby hiccuped and the boys laughed, then stood by watchfully while Will washed her with glycerine soap. He spread it over the pulsing scalp, down the spindly legs, between tiny toes and miniature fingers that had to be forced open. So fragile, so perfect. He had never felt skin so soft, never handled anything so delicate. Within the length of time it took to bathe her for the first time the tiny being had worked her way so deeply into Will's heart she'd never lose her place there. No matter that she wasn't his own. In his heart she was. He'd delivered her! He'd forced her to breathe her first breath, given her her first bath! A man couldn't have a heart this full and care about whose seed had spawned the life that was bringing this bursting sense of fulfillment to him. This little girl would have a father in Will Parker, and she'd know the love of two parents.

He laid her on a soft towel, cleaned her face and ears and dried all the nooks and crannies, experiencing a growing ebullience that put a soft smile on his face. She grew chilled and began crying in chuffy, hiccuping spurts.

"Hey there, darlin', the worst is over," Will murmured. "Get y' warm in a minute." He surprised himself by delighting in this first monologue to the infant. A person couldn't *not* talk to somethin' sweet as this, he realized.

Will carefully tended her cord, applying alcohol, and a cotton bandage, then Vaseline against her stomach before tying the bandage down and diapering her for the first time. She recoiled like a spring every time he tried to maneuver his hand into position for pinning. The boys giggled. She retracted her arms while he tried to feed them into her tiny undershirt and kimono. The boys giggled some more. When Will reached for one pink bootee, Donald Wade was proudly waiting to hand it to him.

"Thanks, *kemo sabe*," Will said, and tied the bootee on a skinny ankle. Thomas was waiting to hand him the other.

"Thanks, Thomas," he said, roughing the boy's hair.

When the baby was ready to present to her mother, Will picked her up carefully. "Now your mother wants to see her, and in about fifteen minutes or so she'll want to see you, so you both wash your hands and comb your hair and wait in your room. I'll call you when she's ready, okay?"

Pausing before the closed bedroom door, Will studied the baby who stared at him with unfocused eyes. She lay still, silent, her fists closed like rosebuds, her hair fine as cobwebs. He shut his eyes and kissed her forehead. She smelled better than anything else in the world. Better than sizzling bacon. Better than baking bread. Better than fresh air.

"You're somethin' precious," he whispered, feeling his heart swell with love so unexpected it made his eyes sting. "I think you'n me are gonna git along just fine."

Then he nudged the bedroom door open, stepped inside and closed it with his back.

Elly lay slumbering. She looked haggard and exhausted.

"Elly-honey?"

She opened her eyes and saw him standing with the baby in his arms, his shirt damp in spots, the sleeves rolled to the elbow, his hair messy and a soft smile on his lips.

"Will," she breathed, smiling, holding out an arm.

"Here she is. And more presentable now." He placed the bundle in Elly's arm and watched her tuck the blanket away from the baby's chin for a better look. Within him sprang a wellspring of emotion. Love for the woman, welcome for the baby, and in a corner of his soul, the lonely plaint of a man who would always wonder if his own mother had ever held him that way, smiled at him with such sweetness, explored his face with a fingertip and kissed his forehead with the reverence that brought a choking sensation as he looked on.

Probably not. He knelt beside the bed and folded aside the opposite edge of the soft flannel receiving blanket. Probably not. But he'd make up for it by watching Elly lavish this precious one with the love he'd never known.

"Oh, Will, isn't she pretty?"

"She sure is. Just like you."

Elly lifted her gaze and let it drop as the baby's fist closed around her little finger. "Oh, I'm not pretty, Will."

"I always thought you were."

The baby's other hand took Will's finger. Linked by her, the man and wife shared an interlude of closeness. Reluctantly, Will ended it.

"I'd better tend to you now, don't you think? Get you washed, and in some clean clothes."

Elly regretfully relinquished the baby, and Will laid her in the basket. Kneeling beside it on one knee, he adjusted the pink shawl around her tiny form, touched her hair with a fingertip and murmured, "Sleep now, precious one."

He rose to find Elly's eyes on him and experienced a brief stab of self-consciousness. He was a man who'd had to learn how to talk to the boys, who'd taken weeks to feel comfortable with them. Yet here he was, after less than an hour, murmuring soft things to the baby girl who couldn't even understand. His thumbs went to his rear pockets in the unconscious gesture that said Will Parker was out of his depth.

"I put her on her stomach like you said." Deep love softened Elly's smile while he stood fidgeting. "I—I'll get your bathwater and—and be right back," he sputtered.

"I love you, Will," she said. She knew the look well, the pacified one that overcame him when things got too perfect for him to contain. She knew the stance, the thumbs-in-the-pocket, still-as-a-shadow suppression that said things were working inside him, good things he sometimes failed yet to believe. That was when she wanted him close enough to touch.

"Come here first." He approached but stood a safe distance, as if touching the bed would damage her. "Here, beside me."

He sat gingerly on the edge of the mattress and she had to reach up and pull him down before she could give the hug she knew he needed.

"You done good, Will. You done so good."

"I'll hurt you, Elly, layin' on you this way."

"Never."

Suddenly they were hugging fiercely. He turned his face against her ear. "Jesus, she's so beautiful."

"I know. It's a miracle, ain't it?"

"I never knew I'd feel that way when I held her the first time. It didn't matter that she wasn't mine. It was as if she really was."

"I know. You can love her all you want, Will, and we'll pretend that she is. A year from now she'll be callin' you Daddy."

He squeezed his eyes shut and pressed his mouth to Elly's temple, then forced himself to sit up. "I best get that warm water now, little mother. The boys are waitin' to come in and see you."

With a soft cloth and the baby's soap, he sponged Elly's tired limbs and sore flesh. Of the comfrey he fashioned a poultice, laid it on her torn skin and secured it with a cotton pledget and her plain cotton undergarments. He helped her don a clean white brassiere, clasping it for her before holding a fresh nightgown and watching her slip it on. He changed the bed and lifted Elly back into it before carrying out the soiled sheets to soak and finally going to fetch the boys, who'd waited in their rooms with the mysterious docility lent to children by solemn occasions.

"Ready?"

They nodded silently. Will hid a smile: Donald Wade had combed his own and Thomas's hair, slicking it down with water until both heads looked flat as wheat in a cyclone.

"Your mother's waiting."

They paused inside their mother's bedroom door, holding Will's hands, glancing up at him questioningly.

"Go on then, but don't bounce on the bed."

They perched one on each side of Elly, studying her as if she'd turned into a character from one of her own fables, someone magical and shining.

"Hi," she said, taking their hands.

They stared as if mute.

"Did you see your li'l sister?"

"We hepped Wiw give her a baff."

"And we helped him dress 'er."

"I know. Will told me. He said you both done good." They smiled, proud. "Would you like to see her again?"

They nodded like horses making a harness jingle. Elly told Will, "Bring her here, honey."

She was asleep. When he laid her in the crook of Elly's arm her fist went to her mouth and she sucked hard enough to make noise. The boys laughed and Will knelt beside the bed, leaning forward on his elbows. For minutes they all studied the baby while awe stole their voices.

At last Elly asked, "What should we name her?" She glanced up. "You know a pretty name, Will?" But his mind went blank. "How 'bout you, Donald Wade, what do you wanna call her?"

Donald Wade had no more notion than Will.

"You got a name, Thomas?"

Of course he didn't. She'd asked him out of courtesy, so he wouldn't feel left out. Touching the baby's hair with a knuckle, Elly said, "I been thinkin' about Lizzy. What you all think o' that?"

"Lizzy?" Donald Wade scrunched up his nose.

"Lizzy the lizard?" Thomas put in.

They all laughed. "Now, where'd you get that?"

Donald Wade reminded her, "From the story you told us about how the lizard got bumps."

"Oh . . ." She continued fondling the fine black hair on the baby's head. "No, this one'll just be Lizzy. Elizabeth Parker, I think."

Will's eyes shot to Elly's. "Parker?"

"Well, you delivered her, didn't you? Man deserves some credit for a thing like that."

Lord, in a minute he was gonna burst. This woman would give him everything. Everything, before she was through! He reached for the baby's head and stroked her temple with the back of a finger. *Lizzy,* he thought. *Lizzy P. You'n me gonna be buddies, darlin'.* He stretched one hand to Elly's hair, and circled Donald Wade's rump with his free arm and touched Thomas's leg, on the far side of Elly. And he smiled at Lizzy P. and thought, *Heaven's got nothin' on being the husband of Eleanor Dinsmore.*

CHAPTER

14

Will's smile announced the news to Miss Beasley even before his words. "She had a girl."

"And *you* delivered her."

He shrugged and quirked his head at an angle. "It wasn't so hard after all."

"Don't be so humble, Mr. Parker. *I* would collapse in fright if I had to deliver a baby. It went all right?"

"Perfect. Started yesterday around noon and ended around three-thirty. Her name's Lizzy."

"Lizzy. Very fetching."

"Lizzy P."

"Lizzy P." She cocked an eyebrow.

"Yes'm." He fairly twitched with excitement, a rare thing.

"And what is the P for?"

"Parker. Feature that—she named that little girl after me. After a no-count drifter who doesn't even know where he got that name. Wait'll you see her, Miss Beasley, she's got hair black as coal and fingernails so small you can hardly find 'em. I never saw a baby up close before! She's incredible."

Miss Beasley beamed, hiding a swift pang of regret for the child she'd never had, the husband who'd never rejoiced over it.

"You must congratulate Eleanor for me and tell her I'll expect Lizzy to begin visiting the library no later than her fifth

252

birthday. You cannot get a child interested in books too
early."

"I'll tell 'er, Miss Beasley."

Those were special days and nights, immediately after the
baby's birth—Will awakening to the sound of Lizzy tuning
up in the basket, rising with Elly to turn her over and talk soft
nonsense to her. The two of them together, laughing when the
cold air hit the baby's skin and her face puckered in prepara-
tion for the adorable soft sobbing that hadn't yet grown to be
an irritation. And each morning, Will cooking breakfast for
the boys, delivering Elly a tray and a kiss, then giving Lizzy
P. her bath before washing diapers and hanging them out to
dry. He changed Lizzy's diaper whenever Elly didn't beat
him to it. He dusted the house and put the bluebird on her
bedside table. He sterilized the rubber nipples and prepared
the watered-down milk and got the bottles ready during the
days before Elly's milk came in. He prepared supper and got
the boys all fed and changed into pajamas before kissing
them and Elly and Lizzy goodbye and heading into town.

But afterward was best. After the long day when he'd return and there'd be lazy minutes lying in bed with the baby
between Elly and him while they watched her sleep, or hic-
cup, or cross her eyes or suck her fist. And they'd dream
about her future and theirs, and look into each other's eyes
and wonder if there'd be another like her, one of their own.

They had three such glorious days before the bombs fell.

On Sunday "Ma Trent" wasn't on, but Elly was lying in
bed listening to the Columbia Broadcast System while the
New York Philharmonic tuned up for Symphony #1 by somebody called Shostakovich when John Daly's voice announced, "The Japanese have attacked Pearl Harbor!"

At first Elly didn't fully understand. Then the tension in
Daly's voice struck home and she sat up abruptly. "Will!
Come quick!"

Thinking something was amiss with her or the baby, he
came on the run.

"What's wrong?"

"They bombed us!"

"Who?"

"The Japanese—listen!"

They listened, like all the rest of America, for the remainder of the day and evening. They heard of the sinking of five U.S. battleships on a peaceful Hawaiian island, of the destruction of 140 American aircraft and the loss of over 2,000 American lives. They heard the voice of Kate Smith singing "God Bless America" and the national army band playing the "Star-Spangled Banner." They heard of blackout alerts along the western seaboard, where a Japanese invasion was feared and where thousands rushed to volunteer for the armed forces. There were amazing stories of men rising from restaurant tables, leaving unfinished plates, walking to the closest recruiting office to find the line of volunteers—within an hour of the first radio reports—already eight city blocks long.

In Whitney, Georgia—a short plane ride from another vulnerable shore—Will and Elly turned out the lights early and went to bed wondering what the next day would bring.

It brought the voice of President Roosevelt.

"Yesterday, December 7, 1941—a date which will live in infamy—the United States of America was suddenly and deliberately attacked by naval and air forces of the Empire of Japan. In addition, American ships have been reported torpedoed on the high seas between San Francisco and Honolulu.

"Yesterday the Japanese Government also launched an attack against Malaya.

"Last night Japanese forces attacked Hong Kong.

"Last night Japanese forces attacked Guam.

"Last night Japanese forces attacked the Philippine Islands.

"Last night the Japanese attacked Wake Island.

"This morning the Japanese attacked Midway Island. . . . Hostilities exist. There is no blinking at the fact that our people, our territory, and our interests are in grave danger.

"With confidence in our armed forces—with the unbounded determination of our people—we will gain the inevitable triumph—so help us God.

"I ask that the Congress declare that since the unprovoked and dastardly attack by Japan on Sunday, December seventh, a state of war has existed between the United States and the Japanese Empire."

Will and Elly stared at the radio. At each other.

Not now, she thought. *Not now, when everything just got right.*

So this is it, he thought. *I'll go just like hundreds of others are going.*

He was surprised to find himself fired with some of the same outrage as that conflagrating through the rest of America: for the first time Will felt the righteousness of President Roosevelt's "Four Freedoms" because for the first time he enjoyed them all. And being a family man made them the more dear.

In bed that night he lay awake and thoughtful. Elly lay tense. After a long silence she rolled to him and held him possessively.

"Will you have to go?"

"Shh."

"But you're a father now. How could they take a father with a brand-new baby and two others to see after?"

"I'm thirty. I'm registered. The draft law says twenty-one to thirty-five."

"Maybe they won't call you up."

"We'll worry about it when the time comes."

Minutes later, when they'd lain clutching hands in the silence, he told her, "I'm gonna get that generator goin' for you, and fix up a refrigerator and an electric washer and make sure everything's in perfect shape around the place."

She gripped his hand and rolled her face against his arm. "No, Will . . . no."

At one in the morning, when Lizzy woke up hungry, Will asked Elly to leave the lamp on. In the pale amber lantern glow he lay on his side and watched her nurse the baby, watched the small white fists push the blue-tinged breast, watched the pocket-gopher cheeks bulge and flatten as they drew sustenance, watched Elly's fingers shape a stand-up curl on Lizzy's delicate head.

He thought of all he had to live for. All he had to fight for.

It was only a matter of making Elly and the kids secure before he left.

The radio was never off after that. Day by day they heard of an unprepared America at war. In Washington, D.C., soldiers took up posts at key government centers, wearing World War I helmets and carrying ancient Springfield rifles, while on December eighth Japanese bombers struck two U.S. airfields in the Philippines and on the tenth Japanese forces began to land on Luzon.

At first it all seemed remote to Elly, but Will brought the newspapers home from the library and studied the Japanese movement on tiny maps which brought the war closer. He worked in the town hall where recruiters were already posted twelve hours a day. Billboards out front and in the vestibule entreated, DEFEND YOUR COUNTRY—ENLIST NOW—U.S. ARMY. Across America it continued. The outrage. The bristling. The growing American frenzy to "join up."

Will found himself in a frenzy of his own—to get things done.

He finished the wind generator and hooked it to the radio because their batteries were nearly worn out and new ones unobtainable. Since the wind generator wouldn't create enough electricity to power larger appliances, he installed a gasoline-driven motor on an old hand-operated agitator washing machine and fashioned a homemade water heater fueled by kerosene. It stood beside the tub like a gangly monster with a drooping snout. The day he filled the bathtub for the first time they celebrated. The boys took the first baths, followed by Elly and finally by Will himself. But there was no denying that the elation they'd expected upon using the tub for the first time was tempered by the unspoken realization of why Will was hurrying to get so much done around the place.

Miss Beasley came to call when Lizzy was ten days old, surprising everyone. She brought a sweater and bootee set for the baby and *Timothy Totter's Tatters* for the boys—not the library copy but a brand-new one they could keep. They were awed by a stranger bringing them a gift and by the book itself and the idea that it belonged to them. Miss Beasley got them

set up studying the pictures with a promise to read the book
aloud as soon as she'd visited with their mother.

"So you're up and about again," she said to Eleanor.

"Yes. Will spoils me silly, though."

"A woman deserves a little spoiling occasionally." Without
the slightest hint of warmth in her voice she dictated, "Now,
I should very much like to see that young one of yours."

"Oh ... of course. Come, she's in our bedroom."

Elly led the way and Will followed, standing back with his
hands in his rear pockets while Miss Beasley leaned over the
laundry basket and inspected the sleeping face. She crossed
her hands over her stomach, stepped back and declared, "You
have a beautiful child there, Eleanor."

"Thank you, Miss Beasley. She's a good sleeper, too."

"A blessing, I'm sure."

"Yes'm, she is."

To Will's surprise, Miss Beasley informed Elly, "Mr.
Parker was quite, quite pleased that you named the child after
him."

"He was?" Elly peeked over her shoulder at Will, who
smiled and shrugged.

"He most certainly was."

Silence fell, strained, before Elly thought to offer, "Got
some fresh gingerbread and hot coffee if you'd like."

"I'm quite partial to gingerbread, thank you."

They all trooped back to the kitchen and Will watched Elly
nervously serve the sweet and coffee and perch on the edge
of her chair like a bird ready to take wing. Given a choice,
she would probably have forgone this entire visit, but nobody
turned Miss Beasley out of the house, not even out of the
bedroom when she came to call. Will studied the librarian
covertly, but she rarely glanced his way. The entire get-
together was being carried out with the same pedantic formal-
ity with which Miss Beasley conducted a library tour for the
children. It struck him that she was no more comfortable being here than Elly was having her. So why had she come?
Duty only, because he worked for her?

Eventually the talk turned to the war and how it was
spawning the most fierce patriotism in memorable history.

"They're signing up as if it was a free-ice-cream line," Miss Beasley said. "Five more today from Whitney alone. James Burcham, Milford Dubois, Voncile Potts and two of the Sprague boys. Poor Esther Sprague—first a husband and now two sons. Rumor has it that Harley Overmire received a draft notice, too." Miss Beasley didn't gloat, but Will had the impression she wanted to.

"I've been worried about Will maybe having to go," Eleanor confided.

"So have I. But a man will do what he must, and so will a woman, when the time comes."

Was this, then, why she'd come, to prepare Elly because she already guessed his decision was made? To ease into Elly's confidence because she knew Elly would need a friend when he was gone? Will's heart warmed toward the plump woman who ate gingerbread with impeccable manners while a tiny dot of whipped cream rested on the fine hair of her upper lip.

In that moment he loved her and realized leaving her would make his going more difficult. Yet leave them he would, for it had already become understood that to be of military age and not join up was to be physically or mentally impaired, or the subject of suspicion and innuendo about one's condition and courage.

Right after Christmas, Will decided. He'd wait until then to talk to a recruiter and to tell Elly. They deserved *one* Christmas together anyway.

He threw himself into holiday plans, wanting all the traditional trappings—the food, the tree, the gifts, the celebration—in case he never had the chance again. He made a scooter for the boys and bought them Holloway suckers, Cracker Jacks, Bunte's Tango bars and Captain Marvel comic books. For Elly he bought something frivolous—the popular Chinese Checker game. It took two to play Chinese Checkers, but he bought it anyway as a portent of hope for his return.

December 22 brought news that a large Japanese landing had been staged just north of Manila. On Christmas Eve came news of another, just south of that city, which was in danger of falling to the enemy.

After that Elly and Will made a pact to leave the radio off for the remainder of the holiday and concentrate on the boys' enthusiasm.

But she knew. Somehow, she knew.

Filling the stockings, Elly looked up and watched Will drop in a handful of roasted peanuts, nearly as excited as if the stocking were his instead of Thomas's. She felt a stinging at the back of her nose and went to him before any telltale evidence formed in her eyes. She laid her cheek against his chest and said, "I love you, Will."

He toyed with her hair as she stood lightly against him. "I love you, too."

Don't go, she didn't say.

I have to, he didn't reply.

And in moments they returned to filling the stockings.

For Will, Christmas morning was bittersweet, watching the boys' eyes light up at the sight of the scooter, laughing while they dug into their stockings, holding them—still in their pajamas—on his lap while they sampled the candy and ogled the comic books. These were firsts for Will. He lived them vicariously with Donald Wade and Thomas as he himself never had as a boy.

Elly gave him a mail-order shirt which he wore while they played Chinese Checkers and the boys rode the scooter across the living room and kitchen floor.

For dinner they had no traditional turkey. Will had offered to take Glendon's old double-bore shotgun and try his hand at bagging one, but Elly would hear none of it.

"One of my birds? You want to shoot one of my wild turkeys, Will Parker? I should say not. We'll have pork." And they did.

Pork and cornbread stuffing and fried okra and quince pie with Miss Beasley as their guest.

Miss Beasley, who had celebrated so many wretched Christmases alone that she glowed like a neon light when Will came to pick her up in the auto. Miss Beasley, who had actually *excited* Elly about having an outsider at her table for a meal. Miss Beasley, who brought gifts: for Elly a beautiful seven-piece china tea set decorated with yellow birds and clo-

ver on a background of tan luster; for Will a pair of capeskin
gloves; for the boys a pair of glass and Pyralin automobiles
filled with colorful soft cream candies shaped like elephants,
horns, guns and turtles, and a new book, *'Twas the Night Before Christmas*, which she read to them after dinner.

Christmas, 1941 . . . over too soon.

When Will returned Miss Beasley to her brick bungalow
on Durbin Street, he wore his new gloves and walked her to
the door.

"I want to thank you for all the gifts you brought."

"Nonsense, Mr. Parker. It is I who should be thanking
you."

"These gloves're . . ." He smacked them together and
rubbed them appreciatively. "Why, they're just . . . heck, I
don't even know what to say. Nobody ever gave me anything
so fine before. I felt awful 'cause we didn't give you anything."

"Didn't *give* me anything? Mr. Parker, do you know how
many Christmases I've spent alone since my mother passed
away? Twenty-three. Perhaps an intelligent man like you can
figure out exactly what it is you and Eleanor gave me today."

She often said things like that, calling him an intelligent
man. Things no other person had ever said to Will, things that
made him feel good about himself. Looking into her fuzzy
face, he clearly understood what today had meant to her,
though her expression would never show it. She remained as
persimonny-mouthed as ever. He wondered what she'd do if
he leaned over and kissed her. Probably cuff him upside the
head.

"Elly, she didn't know what to make of that tea set. I never
saw her eyes grow so big."

"You know what to make of it though, don't you?"

He studied her eyes for a long moment. They both knew;
that when he was gone Elly would need a friend. Someone to
have tea with perhaps.

"Yes, ma'am, I reckon I do," Will answered softly. Then he
put his gloved hands on Miss Beasley's arms and did what
his heart dictated: he placed an affectionate kiss on her cheek.

She didn't cuff him.

She turned the color of a gooseberry and blinked rapidly three times, then scuttled into the house, forgetting to bid him goodbye.

Within five weeks after Pearl Harbor Bell Aircraft built a huge new bomber factory in Marietta. The last civilian auto rolled off the assembly lines in Detroit, and Japan had seized Malaya and the Dutch East Indies, cutting off ninety percent of America's rubber supply. National Price Administrator Leon Henderson was pictured in every newspaper in America pedaling his "Victory bicycle" as a stand-in for the automobile. The wealthy deserted their Saint Simons Island mansions as German submarines began patrolling the coast, and the people of Georgia organized the Georgia State Guard, a citizens' army composed of those too young, too old, or too unfit for the draft, who set about preparing coastal defenses for an anticipated German invasion. Georgia convicts were conscripted and put to work round the clock to improve seashore approaches and build bridges over which the homegrown army would defend their state.

And up at the mill one day Harley Overmire set his jaw, shut his eyes and ran his trigger finger through a buzz saw.

The news had a curious effect on Will. It galvanized his intentions. He decided suddenly that not only would he join up, but he'd join the toughest branch—the Marines—so that when he came back cowards like Overmire could never look down on him or his again. It seemed almost fated that the very day he made his decision the draft board made it irreversible. The letter began with the infamous word that had already taken thousands of men from their homes and families:

"GREETINGS . . ."

Will opened the draft notice alone, down by the mailbox, read the words and shut his eyes, breathing deep. He gazed at the Georgia sky, blue and sunny. He walked at a snail's pace up the red clay road and sat for five minutes beneath their favorite sourwood tree, listening to the redbirds, the winter quiet. He'd rather do anything than tell Elly. Rather *go* than tell her he had to.

She was nursing the baby when he returned to the house,

lying diagonally on the bed. He stopped in the doorway and studied her, impressing the image in his memory for bleaker days—a woman in a faded print dress with the buttons freed, her hair in a loose tan braid, one arm crooked beneath her ear, the infant at her breast. A lump formed in Will's throat as he knelt beside the bed and laid the backside of a finger on Lizzy's pumping cheek, then skimmed it over her delicate skin. He leaned on his elbows close to Elly's head, his gaze still resting on the nursing infant.

Don't tell her yet.

"She's growin', isn't she?" he murmured.

"Mm-hmm."

"How long will you nurse her?"

"Till she gets teeth."

"When will that be?"

"Oh, when she's about seven, eight months."

I wanted to be here to see every new tooth.

His knuckle moved from the baby's cheek to his wife's breast.

"This is my favorite way to find you when I come in. I could watch this till the grass grew right up over the porch step and into the house and never get tired of it."

She rolled her head to study him, but his eyes followed his finger, which glided over her full breast.

"And I reckon I'd never get tired of you watchin', Will," she told him softly.

Elly, Elly, I don't wanna go but I got to.

Contemplating mortality made a man say things he otherwise would hold inside. "I wondered so many times if my mother ever held me, if she nursed me, if she was sorry to give me up. I wonder every time I watch you with Lizzy."

"Oh, Will . . ." She touched his cheek tenderly.

At that moment his feelings for her were convoluted and he struggled to understand them. She was his wife, not his mother, yet he loved her as if she were both. For some ungraspable reason he thought she had a right to know that before he left. "Sometimes I think I halfway wanted to marry you 'cause you were such a good mother and I never had one.

I know that sounds strange, but I ... well, I just wanted to tell you."

"I know, Will."

His head lifted and their eyes met at last. "You know?"

Her thumb brushed his lower lip. "Reckon I knew all the time. I figured it out when I washed your hair the first time. But I knew it wasn't the only reason. I figured that out, too."

He stretched to kiss her, his shoulder pocketing Lizzy's head while the sound of her suckling and swallowing continued. He would never forget this moment, the smell of the baby and the woman, the warmth of the one against his shoulder, the other beneath his hand, which rested on her warm hair. When the kiss ended he stared into Elly's green eyes while his thumb idled on the part in her hair. Slowly he collapsed to rest facedown against the mattress, still embracing them both.

"Will, what's wrong?"

He swallowed, his face flattened into the bedding, which smelled of them and of baby powder.

"You picked up the mail, didn't you?"

His thumb wagged across her skull. Tears stung his eyes but he pinched them inside. No man cried, not these days. They marched off to war triumphant.

"I was thinkin'," she continued chokily, "maybe I'll make a quince pie for supper. I know how you like your quince pie."

He thought of prison mess halls and soldiers' rations and Elly's quince pie with a lattice crust, and worked hard to keep his breath steady. *How long? How long?* The baby stopped suckling and heaved a delicate, broken sigh. Will pictured her milky mouth falling gently from Elly's skin and turned his temple to the mattress. Opening his eyes, he saw Elly's nipple at close range, almost violet in hue, still puckered while Lizzy's moist lips occasionally sucked from an inch away.

"I promised the boys I'd take 'em to a movie one day. I got to be sure to do that."

"They'd like that."

Silence settled, growing oppressive. "Can I come along?" she asked.

"Movie wouldn't be no fun without you."

They both smiled sadly. When the smiles faded they listened to each other breathe, absorbing the nearness and dearness of each other, storing memories against lorn days.

"I have to teach you to drive the car," he said at length.

"And I got to give you that birthday party I promised."

They lay in silence a long time before Elly uttered a desolate throaty sound, reached up and gripped the back of Will's jacket. Burying her face in the bedding, she held him so and grieved.

Later he showed her the letter and, while she read it, told her, "I'm volunteering for the Marines, Elly."

"The Marines! But why?"

"Because I can be a good one. Because I already had the training my whole life long. Because bastards like Overmire are cuttin' off their trigger fingers and I want to make sure his kind can never make degrading remarks about me or you again."

"But I don't care what Harley Overmire says about us."

"I do."

Her expression soured as the hurt set in: he'd made such a decision without consulting her, to jeopardize the life she now valued more than her own. "And I don't have anything to say about it, whether you go to the Army or the Marines?"

His face closed over, much as it had beneath his cowboy hat during his first days here. "No, ma'am."

He had nine days, nine bittersweet days during which they never spoke the word war. Nine days during which Elly remained cool, hurt. He took the family to the movie, as promised—Bud Abbott and Lou Costello. The boys laughed while Will took Eleanor's unresponsive hand and held it as both of them tried to forget the newsreel which showed scenes of the Pearl Harbor attack and other actions in the Pacific that had occurred since America had entered the war.

He taught Elly to drive the car but couldn't get her to promise she'd use it to go into town in case of an emergency. Even while practicing, she refused to leave their own land. In other days, under other circumstances, the lessons might have been a source of amusement, but with both of them counting down the hours, laughter was at a premium.

He put up more cordwood, wondering how many months she'd be alone, how long the supply would last, what she'd do when it was gone.

She gave him a birthday party on January 29, three days before he was due to leave. Miss Beasley came, and they used the new china tea set, but the occasion held an undertone of gloom, this arbitrary day of celebration for a man who'd never celebrated his birth before, celebrating it now because it might be his last chance.

Then came his last night at the library. Miss Beasley was waiting when he arrived for work and gave Will his last paycheck with as much warmth as General MacArthur issuing an order. "Your job will be waiting when you get back, Mr. Parker." No matter what her feelings for Will, she'd never used his familiar name. It wouldn't have seemed right to either of them.

He stared at the check while his throat tightened. "Thank you, Miss Beasley."

"I thought, if it's all right with you, I'd come down to the train station to see you off tomorrow."

He forced a smile, meeting her eyes. "That'd be nice, ma'am. I'm not sure Elly will make it."

"She still refuses to come to town?"

"Yes, ma'am," he replied quietly.

"Oh, that child!" Miss Beasley grasped her hands and began pacing in agitation. "At times I'd like to sit her down for a stern lecture."

"It wouldn't do any good, ma'am."

"Does she think she can hide in that woods forever?"

"Looks that way." Will studied the floor. "Ma'am, there's somethin' I got to ask you. Somethin' I been wonderin' for a long time." He scratched the end of his nose and looked anywhere but at her. "That day when that woman Lula was in here, I know you heard what she said to me about Elly, about how her family locked her in that house on the edge of town and that's why everybody calls her crazy. Is it true?"

"You mean she's never told you?"

Lifting his gaze, Will slowly wagged his head.

Miss Beasley considered at length, then ordered, "Sit down, Mr. Parker."

They sat on opposite sides of a study table amid the smell of wax and oil and books. Outside, plodding hooves sounded on the street, merchants closed their shops and went home for supper, an auto rumbled past and faded while Miss Beasley considered Will's question.

"Why hasn't she told you?"

"I don't rightly know, ma'am. It must bother her to talk about it. She's got touchy feelin's."

"It should be her place to tell you."

"I know that, ma'am, but if she hasn't yet I doubt she will tonight, and I'd sure like to know before I leave."

Miss Beasley debated silently, staring Will full in the face. Her lips pursed, relaxed, then pursed again. "Very well, I'll tell you." She twined her fingers and rested them on the tabletop with the air of a judge resting a gavel.

"Her mother was a local girl who became pregnant out of wedlock and was sent away by her parents to have the child. Eleanor was the result of that pregnancy. When she was born, Chloe See—that was her mother—brought her back here to Whitney. On the train, the story goes. They were picked up at the depot by Eleanor's grandparents and whisked off in a carriage with the black shades securely drawn, and taken to their house—the same one that still stands on the outskirts of town. Lottie See, Eleanor's grandmother, pulled down the shades and never pulled them up again.

"Albert See and his wife were queer people, to say the least. He was a circuit preacher, so it was understandably difficult for them to accept Chloe's illegitimate child. But they went beyond the bounds of reason by keeping their daughter a virtual prisoner in that house until the day she died. People say she went crazy in there and Eleanor watched it happen. Naturally, they thought the same thing of poor Eleanor, living all those years with the rest of that eccentric bunch.

"They might have kept Eleanor locked up forever, but the law forced them to let her out to go to school. That's of course when I first met her, when she came here to the library with her classes.

"The children were merciless to Eleanor, you yourself know *how* cruel after what that—that painted hussy Lula Peak spewed out to you in this very building." Miss Beasley tucked her chin back severely, creating bifolds beneath it. "With little more provocation I would have slapped that woman's face that day. She's a—a—" Miss Beasley puffed up and turned red, then forcibly squelched her choler. "If I were to express my true feeling for Lula Peak it would make me a twattler no better than she, so I'll restrain myself. Now where was I?

"Oh, yes—Eleanor. She wasn't gregarious like the rest of the children. She didn't know how to blend, having come out of the home life she did. She was dreamy and stared a lot. So the children called her crazy. How she endured those days I don't know. But she was—underneath her dreaminess— intelligent and resilient, apparently. She made out all right.

"This is all heresay, mind you, but the story goes that Albert See had a mistress somewhere. A black mistress in whose bed he died. The shame of it finally tipped his wife over the edge, and she became as tetched as her own daughter, hiding in that house, speaking to no one, mumbling prayers. All of Eleanor's family died within three years, but it was their deaths that finally freed her.

"How she knew Glendon Dinsmore, I can only guess. He delivered ice, you know, so I suppose he was one of the few people ever allowed into that house. Albert See died in 1933, his wife in '34 and his daughter in '35. The women died right in that house that had become their prison. It wasn't a week after Chloe's death that Eleanor married Glendon and moved to the place where you live now. Her grandparents' house has sat vacant all these years. Unfortunately, it keeps people's memories alive. I sometimes think it would be better for Eleanor if it had been torn down."

So now he knew. He sat digesting it, damning people he'd never known, wondering at cruelties too bizarre to comprehend.

"Thank you for telling me, Miss Beasley."

"Understand, I would not have if it weren't for this . . . this damned war."

In all the time he'd known her she'd never spoken an unladylike word. Her doing so now created an intimacy of sorts, an unspoken understanding that his leaving would break not one but two hearts. He reached across the table and took her hands, squeezing hard.

"You've been good to us. I'll never forget that."

She allowed her hands to be held for several wrenching seconds, then withdrew them and rose staunchly, affecting a stern voice to cover her emotionalism.

"Now get out of here. Go home to your wife. A library's no place to be spending your last night at home."

"But, my check . . . I mean, you paid me for today and I didn't do my work."

"Haven't you learned after all this time that I don't like to be crossed, Mr. Parker? When I say get, I mean get."

He let a grin climb his cheek, tugged at the brim of his hat and replied, "Yes, ma'am."

He reached home in time to help Elly put the boys to bed. Last times. Last times. *I'm comin' home, boys, I'm by-God comin' back home 'cause you need me and I need you and I love doin' this too much to give it up forever.*

Without discussing it, Will and Elly closed the boys' bedroom door for the first time ever. They stood in the front room much as they had on their wedding night, tense and uncertain because she had been remote and cool toward him throughout their last precious days together and now their final night had come and they'd never made love.

Sand seemed to be falling through an hourglass.

He hooked his thumbs in his back pockets and stared at the back of Elly's head, at the nape of her neck bisected by one thick braid, fuzzy at the edges. He wanted so badly to do this right, the way this woman deserved.

"I like your hair in a braid," he began uncertainly, lifting it, feeling inept at this business of courting a wife. Had she been some harlot he'd have known the procedure, but he supposed it must be different when you cared this much.

Abruptly she spun and threw her arms around his neck. "Oh, Will, I'm sorry I've been so mean to you."

"You haven't been mean."

"Yes, I have, but I've been so scared."

"I know. So have I." He rocked her, arms doubled around her back, and dropped his nose to her neck. She smelled of homey things—supper and starched cotton and milk and babies. Ah, how he loved the smell of this woman. He straightened and held her cheeks, the drawn hair at her temples. "What do you say we take a bath together? I always wanted to do that."

"I have too."

"Why didn't you ever say so before?"

"I didn't know if people did that."

He catalogued her features, branding each in his memory, then replied softly, "I reckon they do, Elly."

"All right, Will." Her hands trailed down, catching one of his as she turned and led the way to the bathroom. Inside, he lit a lantern on a shoulder-high shelf while she knelt to place the plug in the tub and turn on the taps. He closed and locked the door, then leaned against it, watching her.

"Put in some Dreft," he said. "I never took a bath in bubbles."

Her head lifted sharply. He leaned against the door, freeing his cuff buttons, marveling that they could be shy after he had delivered her baby, washed her, cared for her. But sex was different.

She reached for the cardboard box which was wedged between the copper pipes and the end of the clawfoot tub. When the bubbles were rising, she stood, turned her back to Will and began unbuttoning her dress. He pushed away from the door and captured her shoulders, swinging her to face him.

"Let me, Elly. I never have before, but I'm gonna have the memory—just one time." Her dress was faded green, a housedress as ordinary as quack grass, with buttons running from throat to belly. He took over the task of freeing them, then pushed the garment off and let it fall to the floor. Without hesitation he lowered her half-slip, then held her hand and ordered, "Sit down." While she perched on the closed lid of the stool, he went down on his knee, removed her scuffed brown oxfords, her anklets, then stood and drew her to her feet, reached beneath her arms and unclasped her bra. Before it hit the floor he was skinning her last remaining garment down her legs.

He stood for a long moment, holding both her hands, letting his eyes drift over her—weighty breasts, enlarged nipples, rounded stomach and pale skin. Had he the power, he would not have changed one inch of her contour. It spoke of motherhood, the babies she'd had, the one she was nursing. He wished it had been his babies that had shaped her this way, but had it been so, he couldn't have loved her more. "I want to remember you this way."

"You're a sentimental fool, Will. I'm—"

"Shh. You're perfect, Elly . . . perfect."

She would never get used to his adoring her. Her eyes dropped shyly while beside them the water rumbled and the bubbles rose in a fragrant white cloud.

"Who's going to undress me?" he teased, wanting other memories to carry away. He tipped up her chin. "Elly?"

"Your wife," she answered quietly and did what she'd never done with Glendon, what Will had to teach her a man liked. Shirt, T-shirt, boots, socks and jeans. And the last piece of clothing, which hooked on something on its way down.

They stood a foot apart, heartbeats falling like hammer-blows in the steamy room, studying each other's eyes while anticipation painted their cheeks shining pink. His head dipped, her face lifted and they kissed lingeringly, letting their bodies brush, swaying left and right, experiencing a hint of textures. Straightening, he slid his hands to her armpits, ordering, "Hang on," as he boosted her up. With her legs and arms wrapped around him, Will stepped into the tub. When he sat, the water rose to their elbows. She reached beneath his arms to turn off the taps, and when she would have backed up he clamped and held her there.

"Where you goin'?" he whispered near her lips.

"No place . . ." she breathed, closing the distance.

The first was a soft kiss—suspended anticipation. Two mouths, two tongues, sampling before the glut. With

Eleanor's legs still looped about Will's waist, their intimacy below the water made mockery of their guardedness above. Still they played at the kiss, letting it laze as it would— crossed mouths, brushing lips, teasing tongues, then a lackadaisical repeat at a new angle. A nudge, a parting, a search of eyes, a sinking together once more.

She pressed her warm, wet palms to his back and he settled her breasts against his chest. She was smooth, he rough. She soft, he hard. The difference intensified the kiss. Eagerness fired it and he clasped her close, running hands and arms over her soapy skin above and below the water—sleek, warm wife's skin so different from his own. He acquainted himself with her flaring hips, narrowing waist, firm back and bulging breasts that ruched tightly at his touch.

The water lapped her breasts as she reached down to cup bubbles over his shoulders until his skin turned to satin beneath her hands. Her fingertips found the three moles on his back, three slick beads which she read as braille. Her palms skimmed his ribs, arms, shoulder blades, learning each dip and furl, each shift of muscle as his hands moved likewise over her.

With her legs she clung, compressing him, herself, so nearly joined that they could not tell her heat from his.

"It'll be all right tonight, won't it, Elly?"

"Yes . . . yes."

"Will it hurt you?"

"Shh . . ." She muffled his question with her kiss.

He pulled back. "I don't want to hurt you."

"Then come back to me alive."

Neither of them had voiced it before. Desperation now became part of their embrace while urgency moved their hands to fondle, explore, stroke. They drew deep breaths, holding momentarily still, the better to absorb the moment, the memory.

" . . . ohhh . . ." she breathed, and her head dropped back until her braid touched the water.

He uttered a throaty approval, licked the underside of her chin and kissed what he could reach of her breasts. She was limp with acquiescence and he bade his time, pleasuring her, being pleasured, watching her eyelids flicker open, then close, her lips grow lax, her tongue tip appear as she drifted in a mindless torpor. In time she began moving, stirring the water until it lapped against his chest. Her caresses kept rhythm and he set his teeth, then arched like a strung bow.

The water became quicksilver. Tomorrow became an illusion. Here and now became the imperative.

"Oh, Elly, I wanted to do this so long ago."

"Why didn't you?"

"I was waiting for you to say it was all right."

"It would've been all right two weeks ago."

"Why didn't you say something?"

"I don't know . . . I was scared. Shy."

"Maybe I was, too. Let's not be shy."

"I never did things like this with Glendon."

"I can show you more."

She hid her face against his neck.

"Can I wash you?" he asked.

"You want to?"

"I want to be in you. That's what I want."

"That's what I want, too, so hurry."

They shared the soap. They shared each other. They got to their knees and forsook washcloths in favor of hands. They lathered and kissed, sleek as seals, and twined together and murmured sweet sentiments and adored with hands and tongues. And when the compulsion was magnified to a welcome ache, he grasped her wet arms and pushed her back, freeing his lips. "Let's go to bed."

They stood in the steamy bathroom, impatiently wielding towels, caring little about dry or wet, watching each other, grabbing a quick kiss, laughing excitedly—tense, aroused, ready. He plucked his jeans from the floor and found in a pocket a prophylactic.

"What's that?"

He closed it in his palm and looked at her. "I don't want to get you pregnant again. You got all you'll be able to handle with no man around the place."

"You won't need that."

"I don't want to leave you with another one, Elly."

She stepped across his wet towel, took the packet from his hand and laid it on the high shelf.

"Women don't get pregnant when they're nursing, didn't you know that, Will?"

By an arm she tried to lead him from the room, but he balked. "Are you sure?"

"I'm sure. Come."

He took the lantern and they tiptoed into their own bedroom. In it she turned, placed a finger over her lips and mouthed, "Shh." Each one taking an end of the basket, they moved Lizzy out into the front room for the night.

When their door was closed they turned to each other. Their pulses seemed to do a stutter step, but neither of them moved. Alone . . . suddenly hesitant. Until she took the first step and they came together swiftly, kissing and clinging, reminded again of the hourglass shifting its sand. So little time . . . so much love . . .

Impatiently he hooked her beneath her knees and carried her to the bed, whispering, "Pull down the covers." Riding in his arms, she dragged the spread and blanket over the foot of the bed. On knee and elbows he took her down, dropping across her with their mouths already joined in a frenzied kiss, tongues reaching deep, arms and legs taking possession. It was untamed, that prelude, all lust and anticipation drawn to its maximum. Twist and roll, thrust and rut. Sexual greed such as neither had experienced until now.

When it stopped, it stopped abruptly, he above, she below, their breaths gusty, labored.

"Do you need anything . . . to make it easier?" The baby's Vaseline was on the bureau. He'd studied it dozens of times while imagining this moment.

"I need you, Will . . . nothing else."

Her kiss silenced him as she hooked his neck with an arm and brought him down.

"I want to make it good for you, Green Eyes."

He knew how. He'd been taught by the best in a place called La Grange, Texas. He touched her—deep, shallow—with hands and tongue until she bent like a willow in the wind.

As he eased into her body she closed her eyes and saw him as he'd looked that first night, standing on the edge of the clearing, lean and hungry, wary and secretive, hiding beneath his hat—hiding his feelings, his loneliness, his needs.

She closed her eyes and opened her body, offering solace and love to equal his own. It hurt after all, but she hid it well, grasping his head and pulling it down for a deep kiss within which she disguised a soft moan. But soon the moan was dictated by pleasure instead of pain. He took her to the tallest tip of a tree, where she poised—a graceful bird at last, trembled upon the brink of flight, then soared for the first time. Becoming one with the sky, she called his name, twisting, lifting, reborn.

And when her cataclysm had passed, she opened her eyes and watched him follow the way she'd come, watched his gold-beaten hair tapping his forehead, the muscles in his arms standing out like formations in stone, beads of sweat dotting his brow.

He quivered, groaned and pressed deep, arching. He uttered her name, but the sound was trapped by his clenched jaw. When he shuddered in release, she found it glorious to witness, a blessing to receive. She held his shoulders and felt his deep tremors and thought it more beautiful than the flight of an eagle.

When it was over he fell to his side, draping a limp arm on her ribs, waiting for his breathing to slow. Eyes closed, he laughed once, satisfied, replete, then rolled her close, held her in a powerless caress with their damp skins touching.

He rolled his head tiredly and let his eyes caress her. "You all right, Elly?"

She smiled and touched his chin. "Shh . . . I'm holdin' it in."

"What?"

"Everything. All the feelin's you give me."

"Aw, Elly . . ."

He kissed her forehead and she spoke against his chin. "I had three babies, Will—three of 'em—but I never had this. I didn't know nothin' about this." She clutched him close.

"Now I find out about it on our last night. Oh, Will, why did we waste two weeks?"

He had no answer, could only hold her and stroke her hair.

"Will, I felt like I always wished I could feel—like I was flying at last. How come that never happened with Glendon?" She braced up on an elbow to look him in the face.

She was such an unspoiled thing, innocent like no woman he'd ever known. "Maybe 'cause you were married to a good man who never visited a whorehouse."

"You're a good man, Will, don't you say different. And if that's what you learned there, I'm glad you went." She drew up the covers while he smiled at her unexpectedness: shy one minute, earthy the next. He gathered his wife close and found reason to be glad. It had been a circuitous route that had led him to her. Without La Grange, without Josh, without prison, he'd never have ended up in Georgia. He'd never have married Elly. But he didn't want to dwell on it tonight.

"Elly-honey, you mind if we don't talk about that for a while? I wanna talk about . . . about the flowers you're gonna plant for next summer, and how you're gonna pick the quince and how the boys're gonna help you shell pecans and—"

"You're gonna be back before that, Will. I just know you will."

"Maybe."

Through the hourglass the sand spilled faster. She rested her cheek and hand on his chest, against his strong, sure heartbeat, praying it would never be stopped by a bullet.

"I'll write to you." More sand . . . more heartbeats . . . and two throats tightening.

"And I'll write to you."

"I'll remember this night forever, and how wonderful it was."

"I'll remember . . ." He tipped her head back to look into her glistening eyes. "I'll remember a lot of things." Beneath the covers he found her breast and tenderly took it in hand. "I'll remember that day you threw the egg at me. That was the day I realized I was falling in love with you. I'll remember you slicing bacon in the morning, and leaning on the door of the Whippet while the boys pretended they were driving up to Atlanta. And that first morning, you tying your hair up in a tail with a yellow ribbon. And whippin' up a cake, holding the bowl against your belly. And the way you looked sitting in the boys' bed when I come home from work, telling 'em a bedtime story. And you-all waiting beneath the sourwood tree when I come driving back from town. Ah, that one's gonna be the best. Did I ever tell you how much I liked sittin' under that sourwood tree with you?" He kissed her forehead and made her eyes sting.

"Oh, Will . . ." She clasped him and blinked hard. "You got to come back so we can do it again. All those things. This summer . . . promise?"

He rolled against her and looked into her eyes. "If I make a promise, you got to make one, too."

"Wh–what?" She sniffled.

"That you'll go to town, take the boys out. You got to go, Elly, don't you see? Donald Wade, he'll be seven next year and he'll be starting school. But if you—"

"I can teach him what he—"

"You listen to me, now. They got to get out. Take 'em to the library and get books for 'em so when they're old enough for school they'll know what to expect. You want 'em to grow up less ignorant than me and you, don't you? Look how little we went to school and how hard we have to fight for everything. Give 'em a chance to be smarter and better than us. Take 'em in and get 'em used to town, and people— and—and surviving. 'Cause that's what life's all about, Elly, surviving. And you—you go in and keep selling the eggs and milk to Purdy. You buy Dreft instead of making that home-made soap. It's too hard on you, Elly, to do all that. The Marines'll be sending my checks to you, so you'll have the money. But you put half in War Bonds and spend the other half, you hear? Buy good shoes for the boys and whatever Lizzy needs. And you hire somebody to do whatever needs doin' around the place. And if I'm not back by the time the honey runs, you hire somebody to open the hives and sell the honey. It'll bring good money with sugar being scarce."

"But, Will—"

"You listen now, Elly, 'cause I haven't got a whole lot of

time to convince you. Miss Beasley, she'll be your friend. You're gonna need a friend, and she's fair and honest and smart. If you need help you go to her and she'll help you or find somebody else who will. Promise, Elly?"

He held her lightly by the throat. Beneath his palm he felt her swallow.

"I promise," she whispered.

He forced a grin, made it teasing, the way he knew she needed right now. "You got your fingers crossed under them covers, missus?"

"N–no," she choked, releasing a laugh that was half sob.

"All right. Now listen." He wiped her cheek dry and said what needed saying. "I got to tell you this before I go. It might not've been fair of me to ask Miss Beasley, but I did, and she told me about how your mama she never was married, and how your family locked you up in that house when you were a little girl, and all the rest of it. Elly, how come you never told me?"

Her gaze dropped to his chest.

He lifted her chin with a finger. "You're as good as any of them down there—better. And don't you forget it, Mrs. Parker. You're bright, and you got a pair of real bright boys, too, you hear me? You got to go down into that town and show 'em."

He could see she was on the verge of big tears. "Aw, Elly, honey . . ." He wrapped her close and rocked her. "This war is gonna change things. Women're gonna have to do for themselves a lot more. And for you, facing town might be part of it. Just remember what I said. You're good as any of them down there. Now I got to ask you something, all right?" Once more he pressed her away and studied her eyes. "Do you own that house?"

"The one in town?"

"Yes. Where you used to live."

"Yes. But I ain't goin' in it."

"You don't have to. Just remember, though, if an emergency comes up and you need big money for anything, you can sell that place. Miss Beasley'll be able to help you. Will you do that if something goes wrong and I don't come home?"

"You're comin' home, Will, you *are!*"

"I'm gonna try, darlin'. A man with this much waitin' for him's got plenty to fight for, don't you think?"

They held each other and willed that it should be so. That when Lizzy took her first step he'd be there with his arms outstretched, waiting to catch her. When summertime came and the honey was running he'd be there to see after the bees. And when autumn came and the sourwood tree changed to scarlet he'd be there to join them beneath it.

"I love you, Elly. More'n you'll ever know. Nobody ever was as good to me as you. You got to remember one thing always. How happy you made me. When I ain't here and you get low, you think about what I said, how happy you made me, feedin' me quince pies and giving me three little babies to love, and making me feel like I'm somebody special. And remember how much I loved you, only you, the only one in my whole entire life, Eleanor Parker."

"Will . . . Will . . . oh, God . . ."

They tried to kiss but couldn't; their tears got in the way, filling their throats and thickening their tongues. They clung, legs braided, arms pulling as if to protect each other from tomorrow's separation.

But it would come. And it would take him and leave her and nothing they could do or say would prevent the sand from running out.

CHAPTER

15

They said goodbye under the sourwood tree. Donald Wade coasted down with one knee in the wagon; Thomas rode the scooter. Will and Elly followed, he with his few possessions in a brown paper bag and she carrying Lizzy P.

When they stopped beneath the outspread branches, his wrist rested on her shoulder. Instead of looking at her, he squinted at the sky.

"Well ... got a good day for it. Can almost feel spring comin'."

"Not a cloud in that sky."

Why were they talking weather when there were a dozen more urgent feelings tumbling through their hearts?

"Donald Wade said just yesterday he seen a nest with some speckled eggs in it."

Will put his palm on Donald Wade's hair. "That right, *kemo sabe?*"

"Three of 'em, down by the Steel Mule."

"You didn't touch 'em, did you?"

Donald Wade wagged his head hard. "Uh-uhhh! Mama said."

Will went down on one knee and set his sack in the wagon. "Come here. You too, Thomas." Thomas dropped the scooter and both boys stood close while Will looped his arms around

279

their waists. "You always do what your mama says, all right? I'm countin' on you to be good boys."

They both nodded solemnly, aware that Will's leaving was of import but too young to understand why.

"How long'll you be gone, Will?"

"Oh, a while, I reckon."

"But how *long*?" Donald Wade insisted.

Will carefully kept his eyes from Elly.

"Till them Japs're killed, I reckon."

"You gonna get a real gun, Will?"

He drew Donald Wade against his thigh. "Tell you what— I'll tell you all about it when I get back. Now you be a good boy and help your mother with Lizzy P. and Thomas, okay?"

" 'Kay." His voice lacked its usual vibrancy as Will's leavetaking became real. They kissed. Hard and hearty while the back of Will's nose stung.

" 'Bye, *kemo sabe*."

" 'Bye, Will."

" 'Bye, sprout."

" 'Bye, Wiw." Another soft mouth, another hard hug and Will clasped them both, closing his eyes.

"I love you two little twerps—an awful lot."

"I love you, Will."

"I wuv you, Wiw."

He got quickly to his feet, afraid of what would happen if he didn't.

"I want to hold Lizzy P. one time, all right?" He reached for the baby, held her upright with her feet at his chest. She peeked out from beneath a home-knit cap and a warm flannel quilt. When he put his nose to her cheek she smelled of a fresh bath and powdering. "I'm comin' back, Lizzy P., you sweet, sweet thing. Got to see them teeth you'll be sproutin' and see you ride the schoolbus to town." He made it brief—a nuzzle and a kiss—because it was too painful. "Here, Donald Wade, you hold your sister in the wagon, son."

When Lizzy P. was settled in her brother's lap, Will turned to Elly and took her by both hands. She was crying quietly. No sobbing, only the tears rolling down her pale cheeks.

"You keep them quince ready, missus, 'cause you never

can tell when I'm gonna come traipsin' into this yard hungry as a spring bear."

Though the tears continued streaming, she lifted her chin high and affected a discommoded attitude. "Always were a peck o'trouble, Will Parker, you 'n' that sweet tooth of yours."

The tears he'd contained so well could be hidden no longer. They glimmered on his eyelids as he and Elly lunged together in a fierce, possessive hug. He dropped his head and she lifted on tiptoe, each seizing the other while their false gaiety dissolved.

"Oh, Elly . . . Jesus."

"You come back to me, Will Parker, you hear?"

"I will, I will, I promise I will. You're the first thing I ever had to come back *to*. How could I not come back to you?"

They kissed, feeling cheated out of so much they hadn't had time for.

"Send me your picture soon as it's taken, in them fancy soldiers' clothes."

"I will. And remember what I said . . ." He held her face in both hands, looking into her precious green eyes. "You're as good as anybody in town. Take the boys in, and go to Miss Beasley if you need anything."

She nodded, biting her lips, then pulled him close, grasping the back of his denim jacket in her fists.

"I love you s–so m–much," she choked.

"I love you, too."

They kissed again, tongues reaching, arms clasping, tears falling while somewhere a train rolled toward Whitney to bear Will away. He forced his wife from his arms and ordered shakily, "Now get Lizzy P. and the boys and y'all sit under the sourwood tree. I wanna see you there when I go 'round the bend. 'Bye, boys. Be good."

He picked up his brown paper bag and watched Elly reach for the baby, swinging away before she'd straightened, striking off down the driveway, blinking to clear his vision, dashing a hard denim cuff against his eyes. He didn't turn until the last possible moment, when he knew the bend would hide them from his sight. He drew a deep breath . . . pivoted . . . and the picture branded itself upon his heart.

They were clustered beneath the sourwood tree, the boys pressed close to their mother as they sat on the sere grass of late winter. Blue overalls, brown boots, curled toes, thick woolen jackets . . . a green and pink quilt, a tiny face pointed in his direction . . . a faded blue housedress, a short brown coat, bare legs, brown oxfords, anklets, a long sandy braid. The boys were waving. Donald Wade was crying. Thomas was calling " 'Bye, Wiw! 'Bye, Wiw!" Elly held the baby high against her cheek, manipulating Lizzy's tiny hand and her own in a final wave.

Oh, God . . . God . . .

Will raised his free hand and forced himself to turn, stalk away.

Think about coming back, he recited like a litany. *Think about how lucky you are you got them four waitin' under a sourwood tree. Think about how pretty that little place is you're leaving, and what it's gonna be like to see those boys come runnin' when you walk back up this road, and what it'll be like to hold Elly again and know you won't have to let her go, and how you're gonna smile when Lizzy P. calls you daddy for the first time, and how you're gonna have one of your own someday just like her, and you and Elly'll watch all four of 'em grow up and get married and get grandbabies and bring 'em back home on Sundays and you'll show 'em the old sourwood tree and tell 'em all how you marched off to war and left their grandmama and mama and daddies sittin' under it wavin' you goodbye.*

By the time he reached Tom Marsh's place, he was calmer. He stood at the edge of their property, looking up at the neat white house, the empty clothesline in the backyard, the stump where the kettle held only dirt, no petunias. A new white picket fence surrounded the yard; he opened the gate, clicked it shut behind him and approached the house with his eyes fixed on it. A shaggy yellow dog came off the porch, barking and sniffing his calves, a half-grown pup, more inquisitive than threatening.

"Hey, girl . . ." Will bent and scratched her neck. "Where's your folks, huh?"

When he straightened, a woman had opened the door and stepped onto the back stoop. The same young woman as before, dressed in a trim red dress with a white mandarin collar, shrugging into a white sweater.

"Hello!" she called.

Will approached slowly and removed his hat. "Mrs. Marsh?"

"That's right."

"My name's Will Parker. I live up on Rock Creek Road. Eleanor Dinsmore's my wife."

She came down two steps and extended her hand. She was a pretty woman, thin and leggy, with bouncing black curls, cheek rouge and lipstick that made her look sweet, not hard like Lula Peak. "I've seen you pass on the road several times."

"Yes, ma'am. I work at the library for Miss Beasley. I mean, I did. I'm . . ." He gestured toward town with his hat. "I'm on my way to Parris Island."

"The Marine camp?"

"Yes, ma'am."

"You got drafted?"

"Yes, ma'am."

"So did my husband. He'll be leavin' at the end of the week."

"I'm sorry, ma'am. I mean . . . well, it's a heck of a thing, this war."

"Yes, it is. I have a brother, seventeen. He quit school and enlisted in the Navy already. Mama and Daddy just couldn't keep him at home."

"Seventeen . . . that's young."

"Yes . . . I worry about him so." A brief silence passed before she inquired, "Is there something I can do for you, Mr. Parker?"

"No, ma'am. Somethin' I had to do for you before I leave." Holding the paper sack against his stomach, Will reached in, pulled out a quart jar of honey and handed it to her. "A few months back I stole a quart jar full of buttermilk from your well. This here is it. Buttermilk's gone, of course, but that's our own honey—we keep bees at our place." Next came the towel. "Stole this green towel off your clothesline, too, and a set of your husband's clothes, but I'm afraid they're about worn out—"

"Well, I declare," she breathed, accepting the honey.

"—or I'd've returned them, too. I was hard up then, but that's no excuse. I just wanted to apologize, Mrs. Marsh. It's been on my mind a long time, is all, and it bothered me, stealin' from good people—Elly, she says you're good people." He backed away, pointing at the jar. "So there. Honey's not much, but—well—it's—" He donned his hat and rolled the top of the sack down tightly, still backing away. "My apologies, ma'am, and I sure hope your husband makes it back from this war."

"Just a minute, Mr. Parker!" He paused near the gate and she hurried down the walk.

"Give me a minute to let this sink in—nobody's ever—well, if this isn't the darndest thing." She chuckled as if in surprise. "I always wondered where those clothes went."

Will turned red to the ears while she seemed pleasantly amused.

"I got no excuse, ma'am, but I'm sorry. I'll rest easier now that I got it off my chest."

"Thank you for the honey. It'll come in handy with sugar being so dear."

"It's nothin'."

"It'll more than pay for those old clothes of Tom's."

"I hope so, ma'am." He pushed the gate open and the pup tried to slip through. She leaned down and grabbed its collar as Will closed the gate between them.

"I'm impressed by your honesty, Mr. Parker," she offered, rising.

He chuckled self-consciously and dropped his gaze to the gate while absently fingering one of its pointed slats.

"I appreciated the buttermilk and jeans at the time."

They studied each other, strangers caught in the backlash of war, considering the possibilities of death and loss, amazed that those possibilities could so swiftly create a tie between them. She reached out her hand once more and he took it in a prolonged handclasp.

"I hope to see you passing on the road again—soon."

"Thank you, Mrs. Marsh. If I do I'll give a holler and a hello."

"You do that."

He dropped her hand. "Well, . . . goodbye."

"God bless you."

He tipped his hat and headed for the road. Several paces away he turned back. She was dipping her finger into the honey. As she stuck it in her mouth she looked up and found him watching, grinning.

"It's delicious." She smiled broadly.

"I was just thinkin', ma'am. You asked if there was anything you could do and maybe there is."

"Anything for a soldier."

"My wife, Elly—she's got a new baby just two months old plus two others, and she doesn't get out much. If you should get—well, I mean, if you needed a friend, or someplace to go visit, I know you got kids of your own and maybe y'all'd like to walk up to our place and say hey sometime. Kids could maybe play together, you two ladies could have tea. Seein' as how your husband'll be gone, too."

Her pretty face puckered in thought. "Eleanor . . . Elly—your wife was Elly See, wasn't she?"

"That's right, ma'am. But what they say about her ain't true. She's a fine person, and brighter than some who spread rumors about her."

Mrs. Marsh recapped the quart jar, held it as a bride holds a bouquet and replied, "Then I'll want to thank her for the excellent honey, won't I?"

He smiled, gladdened, and thought how Mrs. Marsh's prettiness went deeper than skin and hair and cheek rouge.

"Enjoy that honey," he said by way of farewell.

She raised a hand and waved. "Come back."

As he turned away they both hoped fervently they'd meet again, felt a vague sense of deprivation, as if they might have been friends had they met when there was more time to explore the possibility.

* * *

The railroad station seemed to be the busiest building in town these days. Two young recruits—one white, one black—already waited with their tickets in hand, surrounded by their families on separate sides of the depot. A troop of Girl Scouts in uniform broke into two factions—the black girls to present the black recruit with a small white box, the white girls to do the same for the white recruit. A contingent of local DAR ladies waited for the train with juice and cookies for any war-bound men who might need a snack. A thin young man in a baggy suit and felt hat interrupted the family goodbye of the white recruit to get a last-minute interview for the local paper. A black minister with springy white curls rushed in to add his farewell to those of the black family.

And Miss Beasley was there, too, dressed in her usual puce coat, club shoes and a hideous black straw hat shaped like a soup kettle with netting. In her left hand she held a black purse, in her right a book.

"So Eleanor didn't come," she began before Will even reached her.

"No, ma'am. I said goodbye to her and the kids on our own road, where I want to remember them."

Miss Beasley shook a finger beneath his nose. "Now you stop talking so fatalistically, do you hear? I'll have none of it, Mr. Parker!"

"Yes, ma'am," Will replied meekly, warmed immediately by her stern demeanor.

"I have decided to give your job to a high school student, Franklin Gilmore, with the express understanding that it is a temporary arrangement until you return. Is that understood?" She gave the impression that she'd *get* any Japanese soldier who dared fire a bullet at Will Parker.

"Yes, ma'am."

"Good. Then take this and put it with your things. It's a book of poems by the masters, and I want your assurance that you'll read and reread it."

"Poems . . . well . . ."

"A man, it is said, can live three days without water but not one without poetry."

He accepted the book, looked down at it with a full heart. "Thank you."

"No thanks are necessary. Only the promise that you'll read it."

"I promise."

"I can see your dubiousness. Undoubtedly you've never thought of yourself as a poetic man, but I've heard you talking about the bees and the boys and the boughs—they have been your poetry. This shall stand in lieu of them . . . until your return."

He gripped the book in both hands as if swearing upon it. "Until my return."

"So be it. Now . . ." She paused as if putting aside one subject before attacking another. "Do you have money for your fare?"

It was a question a mother might have asked, and it went straight to Will's heart. "The draft board sent me a ticket."

"Ah, of course. And decent meals while you travel?"

"Yes, ma'am. Besides, Elly packed me some sandwiches and a piece of quince pie." He hefted his bag.

"Why, of course. How silly of me to ask."

They paused, trying to think of something to fill the awful void which seemed impacted with hidden emotions.

"I told her to come to you if she needs help with anything. She don't have nobody else, so I hope that's okay."

"No sense in getting maudlin, Mr. Parker. I'd be insulted if she didn't. I shall write to you and keep you informed of the goings-on about the library and town."

" 'Preciate it, ma'am. And I'll write back, tell you 'bout all them Japs and Jerries I get."

The train steamed in on a billow of smoke and noise. They were at once relieved and sorry it had finally arrived. He touched her arm and moved toward the silver car with the black and white families and the Girl Scouts and the DAR ladies and the local reporter, all who politely nodded and called Miss Beasley by name.

The sun still shone in an azure sky pocked with bundles of clouds a shade darker than the smoke spouting from the locomotive. A flock of pigeons dropped down in a flurry of wings to settle on the baggage dray. The black family kissed their boy goodbye. The white family kissed theirs. The conductor said, *"Boooooard!"* but Will Parker and Gladys Beasley stood uncertainly before one another—a portly old woman in an ugly black hat and a rangy young man in a battered felt one. They looked at their feet, their hands, her purse handle, his brown paper bag. And finally at each other.

"I shall miss you," she said, and for once her sternness was gone, the dry-pudding lines relaxed about her mouth.

"In my whole life I never had anybody to miss—now I got so many. Elly, the kids and you. I'm a lucky man."

"If I were a sentimental woman I might say, if I had a son, and all that."

"Booooard!"

"I imagine conductors these days get hoarse calling that word," she ventured, and suddenly they pitched together, his book pressed against her back, her purse thumping his hindside. Immersed in her spicy scent, he closed his eyes a moment, thinking of how grateful he was that she'd come into his life.

"If you get yourself killed I shall never forgive you, Mr. Parker."

"I know. Neither will I. Take care of yourself and I'll see you when I get back."

They lurched apart, searched each other's faces—hers pruned to keep her from breaking down, his wearing a soft grin—then he kissed her swiftly on the mouth and spun for the steps of the waiting car.

CHAPTER
16

Feb. 26, 1942

Dear Elly,

I'm at Parris Island and the trip down wasnt bad. I had to change trains in Atlanta, and made it into Yemassee in late afternoon. Met there by marine corp recruit bus and rode it thirty mi. to the base, which is just outside Buford an ugly town I was glad I dint live in. Crossed a bridge and traveled thru a big marsh to get here. Yellow grass and birds by the hundruds you would love to see em. Met by our drill sergeant a big mean bull name of Twitchum and he right away starts laying it to us. He roars like a sonuvabee and says how we got to start and end everything we say with sir, like—sir request permission to speak sir—and he makes a couple recruits crinj and feel dumb and theres a few farm boys here from Iowa and Dakota who never saw anything but the back end of a horse, and they're pretty big-eyed I dont know why they came to the marines but some think the armys the worst and would rather take the sea instead thinking to keep away from the front maybe. Them farmboys looked ready to jump the fence but Ive seen all kinds in prison, so boot camp's nothing new. Twitchum he likes to make those farmboys scart. Kept em up till all hours making them learn how to make up a bed before they could sleep in it cause their mamas allways made theres up at home so they never lurnd how. Me I had five years of making up my own and plenty worse to pay if it wasn't done right than around here. Twitchum he comes by and gives everybody the old eagle eye and he sees my bed done up good and stops with his nose so close to mine I could smell his snot and he says to me (testing me, see)—what's your name boy and I says sir-Parker-William-Lee-sir, and he says to me—northerner or southerner? But Ive seen his kind before and Ive seen how he looks at those yankee farmboys and enjoys making them squirm and how he takes digs at the black boys and makes them squirm too so I says to him—sir-westerner-sir. He thinks about it a hen's blink and barks—Bunk patrol every morning at 0-500 hours, Parker. You dont teach them farmboys how to do womens work and its your ass! So I reckon I got me a duty already. How about that. Miss Beasley gave me a fare-well book of poems and I gave her a kiss she din't seem to mind They issued us our fatigues and blankets and toilet artikles and marched us in here to our barracks and half of em are laying here snivveling for home I reckon. Me I know theres worse places than this cause I been there. But I sure miss you green eyes and those babies and our bed. I ate the sandwiches and the pie on the train and they tasted real good and I probly never told you before but you make the best quince pie of anything. Lites out theyre saying so I have to end here and I'm sorry if this aint so clear my writing never was good cause I hated school and dint go much less they made me.

> Your loving husband
> Will

Feb. 26, 1942
Dear Will,
   I never wrote no letter before I don't know how but its time I lurn don't you think. We ate supper without you but the boys were frack fracshus (sorry I ain't got no eraser) and I had trouble looking at your chair I kep wonderin where you were and if you had got there yet and if they fed you and give you a warm bed and all them things. And did miss Beasley come to the stashion like she said she would I can't spell nor

think clear on paper but feelings are a diffurnt thing and them I got aplenty I miss you so already Will and you been gone only today

This took me near an hour and it dont seem like much for so long but tomorr I'll write more.

With love
Eleanor

Feb. 28, 1942
Dear Will,

Your letter came and Parris Island sounds just awful I cried because I felt so bad for you like you are being brave on my account when you say it aint so bad there. I did *not* cry for myself this time but I feel bad for you being there I hope you are okay that Twitchum sounds like a regular satan and I read plenty about him in my time . . .

Parris Is., So. Carolina
28 Feb. 1942
Dear Elly,

. . . I'm sending you my application for war bonds and in-surance. Be sure to keep them in a safe place . . .

March 1, 1942
Dear Will,

I thot sure I'd get another letter from you Are you okay? Everyday when the mail comes I run down there and see if theres a letter in the box but there was only that one. Are you sure you are okay? . . .

Parris Is., So. Carolina
2 March 1942
Dear Eleanor,

I sure miss you green eyes and I would of writen before but they dont give us time we're up at 0430 hours (that's 4:30 in civvy time) and Twitchum wakes us up by kicking a shit can (that's a trash can) down the squad bay and we hit the deck running. They give us each exactly three minuts in the latrine to shower and shave and you know what else if we got to and he's in there barking like a mad dog all the time and the rest of the day its go go go till 0900 hours and then we get one hour of free time but it aint free cuz Twitchum comes in and makes us do drill or polish his boondockers (that's boots here). So no time for writing till now.

I been what they called processed so I got no hair left kiddo and I look ugly as a coot with mange but it saves time in the morning and you don't want no picture of anything this ugly. Anyways, they have'nt offered for us to get any pictures taken yet so maybe later. Also they fixed my teeth and gave me 7 shots in different places, four you-know-where. Ouch! Those needles could be a little sharper. In bed at night I think of you and the kids and your good cooking but the chow here ain't as bad as I expected, better than in prison I can tell you. I don't . . .

Ran out of time—mailing this on the run

Love,

W

4 March 1942

Dear Elly,

Your letter came in yesterdays mail call after I already sent mine the day before and I told you why I had not written. Dont worry about me I'm doing fine Twitchum lays off me but I see him watching close in case I make a mistak don't worry I ain't gonna make any I'm gonna act like his trained monkey. I sure do miss you and the kids and I suppose Lizzy P is growing. I have read your letters til the edges are getting raggy but don't you worry about me I'm just a little lonesome is all. They feed me good here and when your bellys full you can put up with near anything. Don't worry about me tho I'm just fine. Things here are speeding up. Today we got issued our .30 caliber rifles and bayonets and we have to memorize the model numbers—1903 & 1905. Every day I go to physical training, bayonet training and a class on military history who ever would've thought I'd be back in school again at my age but I am and next week we start first aid classes and articles-of-war classes and of course there is always close-order drill for hours and hours every day. They say all that marching teaches discipline and thats important in a military organization but now I reckon I know why they call this *boot* camp cause these boots sure get a workout ever day. Theres sure all kinds here Elly—course I was with all kinds in Huntsville too but heres diffrent cause your closer to them all the time. Some of them stink so bad we all got to go to hygiene lessons and lots of them can't read so they go to reading classes The blacks got their own barracks and we got ours but everybodys got a buddy it seems. Mine's this lanky redhead from Kentucky named Otis Luttrell. We get along good cause neither one of us likes to talk much . . .

March 13, 1942,
Dear Mr. Parker,

By now you are becoming acclimated to Marine life while we at home slowly become acclimated to the idea of our country being at war. We here in town are being propagandized more and more now that America is actively in it. It seems there's a new sign each week encouraging us to do our part, the latest one a picture of Uncle Sam shushing us, saying, "A slip of the lip can sink a ship." It seems incredible to believe there could be spies working among us in a place as small as Whitney.

Every organization from the Boy Scouts to the Jane Austen Society is sponsoring a scrap drive these days. To my chagrin they have even taken the Civil War cannon from the Town Square to be melted down as scrap iron. I raised a formal objection with the Town Council—after all, posterity must also be served—but of course their attitude was one of righteous patriotism, thus I was overridden.

Norris and Nat MacReady have volunteered to organize a Civil Patrol and be air raid wardens. They patrol each night to make sure everyone is in off the streets by ten and all blackouts are observed. Frankly, after all the years they have spent whittling on that bench across the street I thought they had grown into it!

I am making it a Saturday ritual to go out to visit Eleanor immediately after closing, since the days are longer now. Also it helps that we get an extra hour since "War Time" has gone into effect to save on electricity. Your wife and I always have a pleasant visit and a game or two of Chinese checkers. I take the boys books which occupy them while I'm there. They are looking healthy and robust, and Elizabeth is content and growing weekly.

I have put in a little Victory Garden but I fear I am not blessed with a green thumb like Eleanor. But I shall struggle on with it and perhaps get a tomato or two. Eleanor has volunteered to teach me to put up vegetables. I didn't want to hurt the poor child's feelings, but I'm afraid I've been behind a desk too long to be handy with colanders and sieves. Still, I shall try.

The butcher shop is acting as a collection depot for wastefats. The billboard there claims one pound of fat contains enough glycerine to make a pound of black powder, so we are all saving our bacon drippings for that cause.

Yet another new billboard has been posted in the town square right beside the MacReadys' bench. On it is listed the names of all the local boys who have joined up. Your name is listed on the right column between Okon, Robert Merle, United States Navy, and Sprague, Neal J., United States Army. Thankfully none have a star behind them yet.

Franklin Gilmore is working out fine at the library although he occasionally shirks when it comes to dusting the top shelves which he thinks I never check.

I hope this finds you well and tolerating the rigors of military life with a minimum of discomforts. I shall look forward to hearing from you only if you may spare the time, which I'm given to understand is at a minimum during basic training.

> My best to you,
> Gladys Beasley

Mar. 15, 1942
Dear Will,

You'll never guess who come over here today That pretty young Lydia Marsh from down the town road. Come up the road while I was planting my *victory garden*—ha! I been planting garden since I was old enough to hoe and all of a sudden they call it by some name so the town people will plant one too but thats neither here nor there. Mrs. Marsh she come to buy honey said she heard we had it for sale but she brung her two kids a girl four name Sally and a boy two name Lonn and the boys got along with them just fine and they were playin in the yard so I offered Mrs. Marsh tea and she stayed a bit and what a nice woman . . .

20 March 1942
Dear Miss Beasley,

Thank you for your letter and it sure was full of news I didnt know all that was going on back home Elly must not go to town cause she don't tell me about it. I read some of the poems and they were intresting My favorite was When a Man Turns Homeward by Daniel Whitehead Hicky. I picture it would be like that when I can come back home to Elly and the kids and we will close the door and leave the world like a kitten outside . . .

25 March 1942
Dear Elly,

This has probly been the worst day since I left home. The whole company is pretty upset the whole base really. You probly heard about it on the radio how this lieut. Calvin Murphree had a platoon out on bivouac and sent them under the barbed wire on their bellies while he was strafing (that means shooting shells over their heads) and he went berzerk and started shooting to kill and he killed one private named Kenser or Kunzor or something like that and wounded two others before somebody stopped him. A man expects to get shot at when he reaches the front but not in boot camp by your own officers. Oh God Elly I miss you so much tonight green eyes. I got out my book of poems from Miss Beasley and read my favorite one to make me feel better. It's about a man coming home through the moonfall and a woman is waiting with a candle. Only four weeks and one day and basic will be over and I should get leave and be able to come home . . .

March 25, 1942
Dear Will,

Everything is good here except for how much I miss you.
Miss Beasley she comes every Saturday after work when the
library closes early. She brought me a spelling book and is
helping me work on my writing so my letters are better. We
play Chinese checkers and guess what else she has done. She
has started the milk truck coming out here to pick up our
milk and the price is up to 11¢ a quart and 30¢ for a pound
of butter and eggs up to 30¢ a dozen too and the driver takes
them all for me . . .

27 March 1942
Dear Elly,

I shouldn't have written that last letter when I was in such
a rotten mood. I dont want you worrying about me you got
enough to worry about with the boys and anyway I'm better
now and things are going along fine. Did good on my first
aid class test but I drew KP this week and I dont care for that
much. Rifle practice every day and you know its a funny
thing about some of those backwoods boys that cant read and
write they can take apart a rifle and put it together in the
dark. Me and Red (that's what I call my buddy Otis) do good
on that too . . .

March 29, 1942
Dear Will,

I wonder what your doing tonight. I been listening to the
radio and they been playing The White Cliffs of Dover and
I wonder if you'll be shipped to England . . .

11 April 1942
Dear Elly,

It's a good thing we get to send these letters for free I
never thought I'd write so many letters in my whole life as
I wrote since I been here. I got a one-day pass and Red and
me went with a bunch who caught the recruit bus in to
Buford and we went to a movie. It was Suspicion starring
Cary Grant and Joan Fontaine and afterwards just about ev-

erybody got drunk and tried to pick up local girls but me.
Only 19 days and I should be able to come home ...

April 14, 1942
Dear Will,
   I just don't know how the days could go any slower. I keep
thinking about when you get here and how it will be. How
long will you be able to stay? Will you take the train again?
I got a surprise for you but I won't tell you till you get here.
The boys got a calendar and they drew a big yellow star on
the day you get off, and they put a big x on every day just
before bedtime ...

19 April 1942
Only six more days, green eyes! ...

April 19, 1942
Dear Will,
   How many quince pies you want? ...

21 April 1942
Dear Elly,
   I don't know how to tell you this because I know it's gonna
break your heart. I'd rather do anything than tell you this sugar but we just got orders and it looks like we are not gonna
get our weeks leave like we expected. Instead we're being as-
signed to the New River Marine Base at New River, North
Carolina and we leave direcly from here next Thursday. They
won't tell us why we don't get leave but theres plenty of
grumbling and a few already went AWOL soon as they got
the news. Now honey I don't want you to worry about me,
I'm doing fine. I just hope you and the kids are too and that
you'll understand and keep your spirits up ...

April 23, 1942
Dearest Will,
   I tried real hard not to cry because I know your the one whos
doing the hard part and I held off till bedtime after your letter
came but then I just couldnt hold the tears in any more ...

3 May 1942
Dear Elly,

Well, I'm here at the new barracks and you can send my mail to PFC William Lee Parker, 1st Raider Bn., 1st Marines, New River Marine Base, New River, North Carolina. I got my gold stripe and had to pay Bilinski a buck to sew it on for me cause I'm so clumsy with a needle. Bilinski is this Polish butcher from Detroit who's in my outfit and always out to make a buck. So we call him Buck Bilinski. Me and Red got bunks side by side this time and I'm sure glad we din't get separated ...

May 6, 1942
Dear Will,

Miss Beasley and I looked at a map and found New River and now I imagine you up there where the map shows that river poking into the land beside the ocean ...

14 May 1942
Dear Elly,

I'm sorry I haven't written for so long but they've really been keeping us busy the whole outfit is wondering what they intend to do with us and when but it seems like soon and it seems like it'll be the real thing whenever we leave here because they got us in intensive combat training, even close hand-to-hand combat. I made up my combat pack so many times I could do it in the dark with my fingers glued together. Theres five kinds and we got to know what to put into each kind. The full field transport packs got everything in it down to the marching pack thats only got the bare essentials. They got us in the water a lot in little rubber rafts. Me and Red were talking the other day and supposing why they're drilling us so hard and whatever it is, we think its gonna be big ...

May 17, 1942
Dear Will,

I know I ought to be brave but I get scared when I think about you going to the front. Your the kind of man who belongs in a orchard keeping bees and I think back to how I worried about you doing that and now compared to what you might have to do how foolish it seems that I worried about the bees. Oh my darling Will how I wish you could be here cause the honey is running and I wish I could see you out there in the orchard beneath the trees filling the water pans and taking off your hat to wipe your forehead on your sleeve . . .

4 June 1942
Dear Elly,
   We're under orders now for sure but they arent saying for where. All they say is we got to be ready to ship out when word comes down . . .

CHAPTER

17

"Good morning. Carnegie Municipal Library."

"Hello, Miss Beasley?"

"Yes."

"It's Will."

"Oh, my goodness, Will—Mr. Parker, are you all right?"

"I'm just fine but I'm in kind of a hurry. Listen, I'm sorry to call you at work but I couldn't think of any other way to get word to Elly. And I have to ask you to do me the biggest favor of my life. Could you possibly go out there or pay somebody else to get word to her? We just found out we ship out Sunday and we got forty-eight hours' leave but if I take a train clear down there I'll have to turn around and come right back. Tell her I want her to take the train and meet me in Augusta. It's the only thing I can figure out is if we meet halfway. Tell her I'll be leaving here on the next train and I'll wait at the train depot—oh, Jesus, I don't even know how big it is. Well, just tell her I'll wait near the women's rest room, that way she'll know where to look for me. Could you do that for me, Miss Beasley?"

"She'll have the message within the hour, I promise. Would you like to call back for her answer?"

"I haven't got time. My train leaves in forty-five minutes."

300

"There's more than one way to skin a cat, isn't there, Mr. Parker?"

"What?"

"If this doesn't get her off that place, nothing will."

Will laughed appreciatively. "I hadn't thought of that. Just tell her I love her and I'll be waiting."

"She shall get the message succinctly."

"Thank you, Miss Beasley."

"Oh, don't be foolish, Mr. Parker."

"Hey, Miss Beasley?"

"Yes?"

"I love you, too."

There followed a pause, then, "Mr. Bell didn't invent this instrument so Marines could use it to flirt with women old enough to be their mothers! And in case you hadn't heard, there's a war on. Phone lines are to be kept free as much as possible."

Again Will laughed. " 'Bye, sweetheart."

"Oh, bosh!" At her end, a blushing Gladys Beasley hung up the telephone.

Elly had ridden on a train only once before but she'd been too young to remember. Had someone told her four months ago that she'd be buying a ticket and heading clear across Georgia by herself she'd have laughed and called them a fool. Had someone told her she'd be doing it with a nursing baby and changing trains in Atlanta, heading for a city she'd never seen, a railroad depot she didn't know, she'd have asked who the crazy one was supposed to be.

Before he'd left, Will had said women will have to do more for themselves, and here she was, sitting in a rocking, rumbling railroad car surrounded by uniforms and dresses with shoulder pads, and noise and too little space and what appeared to be a week's worth of squashed cigarette butts on the floor. Trains grossly overbooked passengers these days, so people were standing, sitting in aisles and crowded three and four into a bank of seats meant for only two. But because she was traveling with a baby, people had been kind. And because Lizzy P. had been fractious they'd been helpful. A

woman with bright-red lipstick, bright-red high-heeled shoes
and a red and white tropical print dress offered to hold Lizzy
for a while. The soldier accompanying the woman took off
his dog tags and twirled them in the air to entertain the baby.
In the foursome of seats across the aisle eight soldiers were
playing poker. Everyone smoked. The air in the car was the
color of washwater but not nearly as transparent. Lizzy grew
tired of the dog tags and began crying again, grinding her
fists into her eyes, then twisting and reaching for Elly. When
the woman in the tropical dress figured out that the baby was
hungry but Elly nursed, she whispered to her young lieutenant and in no time at all he'd rounded up a porter who
cleared out a pullman unit and ushered Elly to it, giving her
thirty minutes of privacy to feed Lizzy and change her diaper.

The Atlanta train depot was as crowded as steerage, a me-
lee of people, all rushing, shouldering, bumping, kissing, crying. The loudspeaker and rumbling trains scared Lizzy and
she bawled for the entire forty-minute layover until Elly herself was close to tears. Her arms ached from battling the
bucking child. Her head ached from the noise. Her shoulder
blades ached from tension. Frightening questions kept hammering the inside of her skull: what would she do if she got
to Augusta and Will wasn't there? And where would they
sleep? And what would they do with Lizzy?

The final leg of the trip was on an older train, so dirty Elly
was afraid Lizzy would catch something, so crowded she felt
like a hen being crated off to market, so noisy Lizzy couldn't
sleep, no matter how tired she was. In a single seat a woman
slept on a man's lap, their heads clunking together in rhythm
with the wheels rolling over the uneven seams in the rails. A
group of soldiers were singing "Paper Doll" while one of
them strummed a guitar discordantly. They had sung it so
many times Elly wanted to put a foot through the guitar. Men
with loud voices told stories about boot camp, interspersing
them with curse words and simulated sounds of machine-gun
fire. In another part of the car the inevitable poker game created sporadic cheers and bursts of howling. In the seat next
to Elly a fat woman with a mustache and an open mouth
slept, snoring. A female with a shrill laugh used it too often.

Periodically the conductor fought his way through and bellowed out the name of the next town. Somebody smelled like used garlic. The cigarette smoke was suffocating. Lizzy kept bawling. Elly kept wanting to. But, looking around, she realized she was no different from hundreds of others temporarily misplaced by the war, many of them hurrying to a brief, frantic, final meeting with someone they loved, as she was.

She wiped Lizzy's dripping nose and thought, *I'm coming, Will, I'm coming.*

The train terminal of Augusta, servicing the traffic to and from countless military bases, was worse than any so far. Debarking, Elly felt lost in a sea of humanity. With Grandfather See's suitcase in one hand and the baby in the other, she struggled up a set of steps, swept along like flotsam at high tide, not knowing if she was heading in the right direction but having little choice.

Somebody bumped her shoulder and the suitcase fell. As Elly bent to retrieve it, Lizzy slipped down and somebody bumped them from behind, nearly knocking them to the floor. "Oops, sorry!" The private in the army green helped Elly up, snapped the suitcase and handed it to her. She thanked him, gave Lizzy a bounce to get her balanced and moved on with the crush toward what she hoped was the main body of the terminal. Overhead, a nasal, monotone voice announced as if echoing down a culvert, "The five-ten to Columbia, Charlotte, Raleigh, Richmond and Washington, D.C., is now boarding at gate three." She had vague impressions of passing a newspaper stand, a restaurant, a cigarette stand, a shoeshine boy, queues of faceless people waiting to buy tickets, a pair of nuns who smiled at Lizzy, and so many military uniforms that she wondered who was out there fighting the war.

Then she saw a swinging door that said "men" and a moment later its twin, swinging shut, adding "Wo—"

Women.

She stopped and reread the entire word to make sure, spun around, and there he was, already hurrying toward her.

"Elly!" He smiled, waved. "Elly!"

"Will!" She dropped her suitcase and waved back, jumping twice, her heart drumming crazily, her eyes already filling.

He zigzagged closer, moving people aside. Another moment and he reached her.

"Elly-honey—oh, God, you came!" He lifted her clean off the floor, kissing her open-mouthed, with Lizzy squashed between them. Is-it-really-you-I-missed-you-so-I-love-you-oh-God-it's-been-so-long . . .

The floor shook as trains rumbled, the air was a cacophony of voices, the room a melange of motion, while Will and Elly shared a lusty kiss, timeless and prolonged, with tongues swirling and arms clinging and the salt of Elly's tears flavoring their reunion.

Then Lizzy started squirming and they broke apart, laughing, suddenly aware that they'd been crushing her.

"Lizzy P., oh, sugar, you're here too . . . let me look at you . . ." Will took her from Elly and held her aloft, smiling up at her apple cheeks and eyes whose lashes and irises were much darker than last time he'd seen them. With so many new distractions Lizzy didn't know whether to fret or laugh. "Lizzy P., you sweet thing, look at how fat you're getting." He kissed her soundly, set her on his arm and said, "Hello, sweet thing."

"I'm sorry, Will, I had to bring—"

Will's mouth stopped Elly's explanation. The second kiss began jubilant, became sensual, then commandeering with full complement of tongue and lips while Lizzy squirmed on his arm but went ignored. He grasped the back of Elly's head and told her without words what she could expect when they were alone. When the kiss ended, he pulled back while they studied each other's faces.

She found him stunning in his crisp uniform and garrison cap, so incredibly handsome she felt as if she'd stepped into a fantasy.

He found her thinner, prettier, her face trimmed with a pale touch of makeup, the first he'd ever seen her wear.

"God," he whispered, "I can't believe you're here. I was so scared you wouldn't come."

"I might not have if it wasn't for Miss Beasley. She made me."

He laughed and kissed her again briefly, then held her hand

and backed up a step, scanning her length. "Where'd you get the dress?" It, too, was stylish: yellow with black military-type trim and buttons, padded at the shoulder, trim at the hip and flaring to a short hem that revealed her legs from the knee down. And she was wearing sling-back high heels with a cutaway toe!

Elly's gaze dropped self-consciously. "I made it for when you were supposed to come home the last time. Remember, I said I had a surprise for you?"

He gave a slow whistle and stole a phrase from radio's Captain Marvel. "Shazaam!"

Elly colored becomingly, touched a button at her waist and glanced up shyly into Will's handsome face. It was odd—she was almost afraid to stare at him too much, as if doing so might jeopardize her right to someone so dignified-looking, so attractive. "Lydia Marsh lent me her pattern and I ordered the cloth and shoes from the catalogue."

He was so impressed he didn't know on what to comment first, the fact that she'd made a friend or the updated change in her looks. Her hair was twisted high and away from her face the way the women in the munitions factories often wore theirs beneath safety scarves. One soft wave dipped low over the side of her forehead; her eyebrows had been slightly plucked and her lips painted pale pink.

"And makeup, too," he said approvingly.

"Lydia thought I ought to try it. She showed me how."

"Honey, you look so pretty you take my breath away."

"So do you." She took a full draught of him in his dress greens: wool blouse and crisply creased trousers, gleaming shoes, khaki shirt and tie and the Sam Browne belt running from his right shoulder to his left waist; the shining Marine Corps emblem—eagle, globe and anchor—centered above the leather bill of his garrison cap, which gave him the look of some important stranger. He had put on weight, was thicker at the shoulders and chest, but it definitely became him. The sight of her husband in the hard, tailored suit made Elly's heart swell with pride.

In a soft, teasing voice she asked, "Where is my cowboy?"

"Gone, ma'am." Will replied with banked pride. "He's a soldier now."

"You look like somebody who'd guard a door at the White House."

He chuckled and she requested, "Let me see that hair they cut off."

"Aww, you don't wanna see that."

"Yes, I do, Private First Class Parker." She playfully flicked the single gold chevron on his sleeve.

"All right—you asked for it."

He removed the garrison cap and she couldn't withhold a gulp of regret at the sight of his skull showing through the mere sprinkling of hair remaining on his head. Gone was the thick pelt she'd often washed and cut and combed. *The Marines ought to hire a new barber,* she thought. Why, she could do better with her plain kitchen scissors. But she searched for something heartening to say.

"I don't think I ever saw your ears before, Will. You got fine ears, and even without no hair you're still pretty to me."

"And you're a pretty li'l liar, Mrs. Parker." Laughing, he replaced the hat, stole another kiss, picked up her suitcase and his duffel in a single hand. "Hang on," he ordered. "I don't want to lose you in this mob. Lizzy P. is a surprise. How you doin', Lizzy-girl? You tired, babe?" He kissed her forehead while she whimpered softly and rubbed her eyes. "How was she on the train?"

"Terrible."

"Sorry for the quick orders. But on a *forty-eight* I didn't have time to think about arrangements for the kids. To tell you the truth, I wouldn't have cared if you had to bring 'em all, as long as I got to see you. Where are the boys?"

"At Lydia Marsh's. They kicked up a fuss when they found out I was comin' to see you, but it was bad enough havin' to bring this one. I had to though, 'cause she's still nursing."

"I realized that after I'd hung up. I made it awful hard for you, didn't I? How long ago did she eat?"

"Around three."

"And how 'bout you—are you hungry?"

"No. Yes." She glanced at the neon light over the door of

the coffee shop as they passed it. "Well, sort of." She hugged his arm. "I mean, I don't want to waste time in any restaurant and I don't know how much longer Lizzy will hold out."

He led her outside into the humid summer late-afternoon. "I got us a room at the Oglethorpe. What do you say we pick up some hamburgers and take 'em back there?" They stood at the curb, their eyes exchanging mixed messages of hunger and impatience.

"Fine," she forced herself to answer.

"It's eight blocks or so. You think you can walk it in those shoes?"

"A real hotel?"

"That's right, Green Eyes. For tonight, a real hotel."

Privacy.

They stood gazing at each other while a taxi honked and car doors slammed. His heart leaped. Hers answered. They wanted to kiss but refrained, postponing any further intimacies until time and place allowed them full savor.

"On second thought," she murmured, "I wouldn't mind forgetting about the hamburgers."

"You should eat something, and drink some milk, too—for Lizzy."

"Do I have to?"

"It won't take long." He smiled and led the way along the sidewalk.

Twenty-five minutes later they entered their room behind a "bellgirl" instead of a "bellboy." The young woman was friendly, hospitable and wore a red pillbox hat. While Will set their brown paper sack of hamburgers on the dresser, Elly stood by the door, taking in her surroundings. The bellgirl laid their suitcases on the bed, opened a window and pointed out the adjoining bath with its black and white hexagonal marble tile, claw-foot tub and pedestal lavatory. The bedroom itself was small, done in deep green with touches of maroon and peach. The floor was lined with a bound rug, the windows decorated with frond-patterned drapes, fronted by two overstuffed chairs and a table. The focal point of the room was a wooden bed covered with a peach chenille spread and a bedside stand bearing a lamp shaped like a maroon ocean wave.

Will politely allowed the bellgirl to do her job and show it all, suppressing the urge to shove her out the door and lock it behind her.

Finally he tipped her and the moment the door closed he turned to Elly for a kiss. Scarcely had their lips touched when Lizzy complained, forcing them to consider her first.

"Will she settle down?"

"I hope so. She's dead tired."

Their gazes met. *How long? A half hour? An hour? I want you now.*

"What're we gonna do with her, Will? I mean, where will she sleep?"

He scanned the room and suggested, "How about the chairs?" In four long strides he reached the pair of over-stuffed armchairs and turned them seat-to-seat, creating a perfect crib, soft and safe with the arms and seats butted.

"This would work, wouldn't it?"

She was so relieved her smile broke easily. "It'll be perfect."

He flashed her a return smile and moved toward the suit-case. "You get her wet stuff off and I'll find her clean clothes."

While Will dug through the suitcase, Elly laid the baby on the bed and began changing her clothes for nighttime. Lizzy rubbed her eyes and whimpered.

"She's beat, poor thing," Will said, sitting down beside Lizzy, bracing on an elbow, watching, enjoying. In minutes she was changed into clean diapers and a lightweight kimono.

"Keep your eye on her a minute, okay?" Elly plunked Lizzy on Will's arm and turned away. Talking sweet nothings to the baby, he watched Elly remove her yellow dress, hang it in the closet, then turn, barefoot, dressed in a white half-slip and bra.

For a moment their gazes locked and all was still but for Lizzy's soft whimpering and the clamoring of their two hearts. Will's eyes dropped, lingered on the bare band of skin between the two white garments while Elly's traced the length of his dark, flattering uniform. When their eyes met again his breathing had accelerated and her cheeks had taken on an added glow.

"God, you look good," he breathed in a tight, reedy voice.

"So do you," she whispered.

She reached behind herself, released the hook on her bra and removed it, all the while holding him captive with her eyes. Her breasts were heavy, the nipples wide and florid, radiating faint blue lines. She stood unmoving, framed by the bathroom doorway, learning the exquisite pleasure of letting another study her body through the eyes of love. How different she felt about herself now than in the days after she'd first met him. Love, she had discovered, left her with no desire to hide.

She watched Will swallow. His nostrils dilated and his breathing grew noticeably rushed. Though Lizzy still fretted, Elly crossed the room slowly and rested a knee on the mattress, bending over Will for one lingering kiss. He reached up and brushed her pendulous breast with a knuckle, nudged her lips away and whispered, "Hurry."

She sat on one of the overstuffed chairs with Lizzy in the crook of her arm. Will rolled onto his belly, crossed his wrists beneath his chin and observed as his wife looked down, took a nipple between two fingers and guided it to the baby's open mouth. His eyes became dark as onyx, his body aroused as he imbibed the image, both maternal and sexual. When he could bear it no longer he rose to prowl the room, striving to keep his eyes off her. He laid his hat upside down on the dresser, removed his wool blouse and hung it in the closet, opened the bag of food, peered inside and took out one hamburger wrapped in waxed paper. "You want one while you feed her?"

She accepted the hamburger and began eating it while he found the glass bottle of milk, removed the cardboard stopper, searched out a glass in the bathroom, filled it and set it on the table beside her. When he neared, her head swiveled, following his every movement. Her eyes lifted and lingered on his face, allowing him to witness how her impatience had grown to the same gnawing insistence as his own.

But the baby had to come first. Reluctantly he turned away.

She watched minutely, becoming aroused by the nuances of motion peculiar to him and no other man. He removed his tie, folded it neatly beside his hat, freed his cuff buttons and rolled his sleeves back to midarm. Watching him move about the room, performing mundane tasks, she became awed that such simple movements could stir her, make her feel carnal in a way she never had before. She welcomed the feeling, eager for the moment when she could loose it upon him.

He stacked both bed pillows and sat against them, with one foot outstretched, the other on the floor. The pose accentuated the masculinity already underscored by the uniform—the brilliant shine on his brown dress shoes, the sharp crease along his trousers, the fine press on his collar. She remembered him in scuffed cowboy boots, faded jeans hanging from lean hips, a crinkled shirt with sweat-stained arms. It struck her that the change in his clothing made him appear not only masculine and clean, but important and intelligent, and that this aspect of his appearance affected her as much as any other. It caught her in the hollow between her breasts like a sharp blow, made her heart leap and her blood sing. He reached into his breast pocket, removed a pack of Lucky Strikes and methodically tapped one against his thumbnail. Next he produced a book of matches, lit up and sat idly smoking, studying Elly through the rising skein of gray. She became mesmerized by the sight of his well-kept hands with the cigarette held deep between his fingers while he closed and opened the matchbook between drags, all the time watching her with his eyelids at half-mast.

"When did you start smoking?"

"A while ago."

"You never told me in your letters."

"I didn't think you'd like it. Everybody does it. They even give us free cigarettes in our K-rations. Besides, it calms the nerves."

"It makes you seem like a stranger to me."

"If you don't like it I'll—"

"No. No, I didn't mean that. It's just . . . I haven't seen you for so long and when I do you're wearing clothes like you never had before, and a haircut that makes you look different, and you've got new habits."

He inhaled deeply, expelled the smoke through his nostrils. "Inside I haven't changed though."

"Yes, you have. You're prouder." When he made no reply, she added, "So am I. Me and Lydia we talked about it. At first I told her how I hated having you go, but she said that I oughta be proud you're wearing a uniform. And now that I've seen you in it, I am."

"You know something, Elly?" She waited while he twirled the cigarette coal against a glass ashtray, rubbing ashes off. At last he looked up. "These're the nicest clothes I ever owned."

His remark made her understand as she never had before the extent of his early deprivation, and that in the Marines he was like everybody else, no longer the odd man out.

"When I saw you at the station—well, it was a funny thing. All the while I was on the train I pictured you like you looked back home, and me too. But then I saw you and—well, something happened—here." She touched her heart. "This crazy knocking, you know? I mean, I wanted you to be the same, but I was glad you weren't. Those clothes . . ." Her eyes flicked over his length. "I can't believe how you look in those clothes."

He smiled crookedly and kept his eyes steady on hers, but somehow she knew they wanted to rove. "The same thing happened when I saw you. Just sitting there in that chair, you make it happen all over again."

They studied each other while Lizzy suckled. Will's eyes fell to Elly's naked breast and he drew deeply on the cigarette.

"Aren't you going to eat your hamburger?" she asked.

"I'm not very hungry right now. How's yours?"

"It's delicious." But she had laid the sandwich aside, half-eaten, and they both realized why. She took a drink of milk. A droplet of condensation fell from the cool glass onto Lizzy's cheek and she awakened with a start, releasing Elly's nipple with a snap, her face and fists rebelling against the sudden interruption.

"Shh . . ." Elly soothed, and transferred her to the right breast.

Will's eyes homed in on the abandoned one with its wet, distended tip. Abruptly he swung off the bed, crushed out his cigarette and disappeared inside the bathroom. Elly dropped her head back, closed her eyes, and felt herself growing ready for him.

Oh, Lizzy P., hurry and finish, darlin'.

Inside the bathroom the water ran, a glass clinked, then silence . . . tense silence before Will appeared once more in the doorway, staring at her, wiping his hands on a white towel. He tossed the towel aside, skinned off his outer shirt and stood in a T-shirt that rode his muscles as closely as a skiff rides the sea.

When he spoke his voice was low, on the edge of control. "I want you like I never wanted a woman before in my life. You know that, Elly?"

"Come here, Will," she whispered.

He flung his shirt aside and moved behind her chair, stretching a hand over her naked shoulder, his fingers trailing over her breast. He dropped his head and she tipped hers to give him access to the side of her throat. She lifted her free arm, looped it around his head, feeling the unfamiliar stiffness of his bristly hair. His skin smelled of unfamiliar soap as his hand slipped over the unoccupied breast.

Her eyes drifted closed. "How much time do we have?"

"I have to report back at 1800 hours tomorrow."

"What time is that?"

"Six P.M. I catch a train at two-thirty. Lizzy's done eating. Can't we put her down now?"

She smiled at Will upside down and asked, "Is it always like this for you?"

"Like what?" he asked, his voice soft and gruff.

"Like you're gonna die if you have to wait another minute?"

The hand on her breast closed . . . lifted . . . molded. A thumb ran across its hardened tip.

"Yes, since the day I stood at the well with egg on my face and fell in love with you. Get up."

She rose and watched Will hurriedly push the chairs back together, counting seconds as he spread them with a quilt. When she bent to lay Lizzy down, his hand rode her naked shoulder. She straightened and they stood on opposite sides of the chairs, staring at each other, anticipating, suffering one last self-imposed hiatus that only made their blood beat stronger. He reached out a hand and she laid hers in it, feelings pouring already between their linked fingers.

His grip tightened, drawing her along the length of the makeshift crib while their eyes clung, dark with intent.

When they met it was lush and impatient, two bodies starved for one another, two tongues parched by months apart. It was love and lust complementing each other to the fullest. It was impact and immediacy following one upon the other, a fast hard seeking to touch all, taste all, even before their clothing was removed.

"Oh, Elly . . . I missed you." His hands skimmed low, drew her in.

"Our bed was so lonesome without you, Will." She ran her hands over his trousers, reaching for his buckle.

Their clothing fell like furled sails. Murmuring, they fell to the bed.

"Let me see you." He pulled back, let his hands and eyes travel over her, kissing where he would.

She fell back with arms upthrown, becoming the chalice from which he sipped. Likewise, she tasted him, and their timidity fled, chased by the distant acknowledgment of last chances.

Joined at last, they fit exquisitely.

They spun a web of wonder and trembled upon it, suspended in the sweet awaited union of hearts and bodies. They locked out the specters of death and war, those unpretentious intruders, and steeped themselves in each other, accepting gratification as their mortal due.

"I love you," they reiterated again and again in hoarse whispers. "I love you."

It was the sustenance they would take with them when they left this room.

* * *

The sun was setting somewhere on a horizon they could not see. A bell buoy chimed in the distance. The smell of humid salt-air drifted in the window. An arm, wilted and weighty, lay across Elly's shoulder, a knee across her thigh.

She hooked his lower lip with a finger, let it flip back up. He grinned tiredly, but his eyes remained closed.

"Hey, Will?"

"Hm?"

"Am I ever glad I came clear across Georgia on them dirty trains."

His eyes opened. "So'm I."

Their grins faded and they gazed at each other, replete. "I missed you so much, Will."

"I missed you, too, Green Eyes."

"Sometimes I'd turn around and look at the woodpile and expect to see you chopping wood there."

"I will be again—soon."

The reminder took them too close to tomorrow, so they withdrew into now, touching, whispering, kissing, loving being lovers. They lay brow to brow and trailed fingers up and down, fit knees and feet in places that accommodated as if made for the purpose. When they had rested they ignited one another again, and savored their second lovemaking at a more sedate pace, watching each other's faces as pleasure once more leached their bodies.

In time, when they had spoken of home and necessary things—the temperamental wind generator, the fall butchering, the gold mine of used auto parts—he lit another cigarette and lay with his shoulder pillowing her cheek.

She stared at the sheet draped over his toes and took the plunge she'd been dreading. "Where they sendin' you, Will?"

He took a deep, slow drag before answering. "I don't know."

"You mean they haven't told you yet?"

"There's scuttlebutt about the South Pacific but nobody knows where, not even the base commander. The CO's keep using the word 'spearhead'—and you know what that means."

"No, what?"

He reached for an ashtray, laid it on his stomach and tapped it with the cigarette. "It means we'd lead an attack."

"Attack?"

"Invasion, Elly."

"Invasion?" She lifted her head to search his eyes. "Of what?"

He didn't want to talk about it and, in truth, knew nothing. "Who knows? The Japs are all over the Pacific, controlling most of it. If they're sending us there we could end up anyplace from Wake to Australia."

"But how can they send you someplace and not even tell you where you're going?"

"Surprise is part of military strategy. If that's how they plan it we follow orders, that's all."

She digested that for long minutes, while his heart beat steadily beneath her ear. At length she asked quietly, "Are you scared, Will?"

He touched her hair. "Course I'm scared." He considered and added, "At times. Other times I remind myself that I'm part of the best-trained military unit in the history of the world. If I got to fight, I'd rather do it with the Marines than anybody else. And I want you to remember that when you get worried about me after I'm gone. In the Marines it's everybody for the group. Nobody thinks of himself first. Instead, everybody thinks of the group, so you always got that reassurance behind you. And every Marine is trained to take over the next higher position if his CO is injured in battle, so the company's always got a leader, the squad's always got a leader. That's what I have to concentrate on when I start gettin' the willies about maybe being shipped to the Pacific, and that's what you got to concentrate on, too."

She tried, but images of bayonets and guns got in the way.

He saw the images, too, the ones from the movie theater in the black and white newsreel. "Hey, come on, sweetheart." He crushed out his cigarette and gathered her close, rubbed her naked spine. "Let's talk about something else."

They did. They talked about the boys. And Miss Beasley. And Lydia Marsh. And the way Will had filled out. And the way Elly had learned to apply makeup and fix her hair. When dark had fallen they took a bath together, touching and teasing, giggling behind the closed bathroom door. They made love against it and ate the cold hamburgers and he talked about the food at the base and taught her all the "leatherneck lingo" he'd learned in the galley. She laughed at canned milk called armored heifer; eggs, cackleberries; pancakes, collision mats; tapioca, fish eyes; and spinach, Popeye. Around midnight they made love on the maroon rug with its green leaf design. Sometimes they laughed—perhaps a little desperately as they felt the hours slipping away. He told her about his buddy, Otis Luttrell, the carrottop fellow from Kentucky, and how they were hoping they'd ship out together. He said Otis was engaged to a pretty young woman named Cleo who worked in a grenade factory in Lexington, and that he'd never had a friend he liked as much as Otis.

The night sped by and they sat on the windowsill, watching the distant darkness where they knew ships rested at anchor. But all was pitch black, blacked out lest some German submarine be slipping through the East Coast defenses.

The war was there . . . happening . . . no matter how they tried to block it out. It was there, coloring each thought, each touch, each fleeting heartbeat they shared.

Toward dawn they slept, against their wills, touching even in slumber, then roused again to hoard each wakeful moment like misers counting pennies.

When Lizzy awakened shortly before seven they brought her into bed with them and Will lay on his side, head braced on a hand, watching once more the sight he'd never grow tired of. After the feeding he said he wanted to give Lizzy her bath. Elly watched, wistful and yearny while Will knelt beside the deep tub and took joy in caring for the baby. He did it all, dried and diapered her and dressed her in clean rompers, then lay on the bed playing with her and laughing at her gurgling baby-talk and teddy-bear poses. But often his eyes would lift to Elly's, on the other side of the baby, and the unspoken sorrow would be rife between them.

They ate in their room and remained in it until a different bellgirl came to inquire if they were staying a second day. They packed their meager bags and stood in the doorway, looking back at the room that had provided a haven for the past eighteen hours. They turned to each other and tried to look brave, but their last kiss in private was one of trembling lips and despairing thoughts.

They took to the streets of Augusta, ambling along the hot pavement until they found a park with a deserted bandstand surrounded by iron benches. They sat on one and spread a blanket on the grass where they settled Lizzy to play with Will's dog tags. They looked at the trees, the clear blue Georgia sky, the child at their feet—but most often at each other. Occasionally they kissed, but lightly, with their eyes open, as if to close out the sight of the other for even a moment was unthinkable. More often they touched—his hand lightly grazing her shoulder blade or her palm resting on his thigh while he toyed with the friendship ring which had, indeed, turned her finger green.

"When I come back I'm gonna buy you a real gold wedding ring."

"I don't want a real gold wedding ring. I want the one I wore the day I married you."

Their eyes met—sad eyes no longer denying what lay ahead.

"I love you, Green Eyes. Don't forget that."

"I love you, too, soldier boy."

"I'll try to write often but . . . well, you know."

"I'll write every day, I promise."

"They're gonna censor everything, so you still might not know where I am, even if I tell you."

"It won't matter. Long as I know you're safe."

Another extended gaze ended when he rested his forehead upon hers. They sat thus, fingers loosely entwined, for minutes. Somewhere in the park a pair of herring gulls screeched. Out on the water a steam whistle sounded. From nearer came the clink-clink of Lizzy flailing the chain and dog tags. And over all rested the smell of purple petunias blossoming at the foot of a tiny fountain.

Will felt his throat fill, swallowed and told his wife, "It's time to go."

She suddenly radiated false brightness. "Oh . . . course it is

. . . why, we better get Daddy to that station, hadn't we, Lizzy?"

He carried the baby and she carried their bags until they stood again in the noisy, crowded depot where they faced each other and suddenly found themselves tongue-tied. Lizzy became fascinated with a button on his blouse, trying to pull it off with a chubby hand.

"The two-thirty for Columbia, Raleigh, Washington and Philadelphia now boarding at gate three!"

"That's me."

"You got your ticket?" Elly asked.

"Yes, ma'am."

Their eyes met and he circled the slope of her neck with his free hand, squeezing hard.

"Give the boys a kiss from me and give 'em those choco-late bars."

"I w—will. And send me your address as soon as th—they—" She couldn't go on, afraid of releasing the choking sobs that filled her chest.

He nodded, his face doleful.

"Last call for Columbia, Raleigh—"

Her eyes were streaming, his filled to glittering.

"Oh, Will . . ."

"Elly . . ."

They hugged awkwardly, with the baby between them. "Come back to me."

"You damn right I will."

Their kiss was a terrible thing—goodbye, keep low, keep safe—with tongues thickened by the need to cry.

A whistle wailed. *"Booooard!"* The train lumbered to life.

He tore his mouth away, thrust the baby into her hands and ran, leaped and boarded the rolling car, turning at the last possible moment to catch a blurry glimpse of Elly and Lizzy waving from amid a crowd of strangers in a dirty train depot in a hot Georgia town.

Eleanor Parker no longer prayed, so perhaps it was more imprecation than prayer when she choked against her fist, "Damn it, k—keep him safe, you hear?"

CHAPTER
18

18 June 1942

Dear Elly,

What a crazy life this is. Yesterday I was with you and to-day I'm on a train heading for San Francisco. Red is with me but he isn't as much company as you. Ive just been thinking over and over about how wunderfull it was being with you and how much I love you and how glad I am that we had that one day together it was like being in heaven green eyes ...

June 18, 1942

Dear Will,

I'm writing this cuz I just got to. My hearts so full and feels like its gonna spill over less I tell you how I feel about our night in Augusta. I don't know when this will get to you cause I don't know where to send it but feelings are feelings and mine will be just as true even if you read this a month from now. (I'll save it and send it when you send me your ad-dress.) You know Will when I first met you I said I still loved Glendon and I thought I did. Glendon was the first real nice person that ever come into my life. He treated me like I was put on this earth for something besides repenting and being

319

poked fun at. He was a real good man Glendon was and at
the time when I was married to him I was real happy for the
first time in my life so I thought that meant I loved him
somethin fearful. And I did love him don't get me wrong but
when Glendon and me did private things together it was
never like it is with me and you. I never told you before but
the first time Glendon and me ever did it was in the woods
and we did it cause his daddy died and he was greevin. I remember how I layed there on my back lookin up at the green
branches and thought about the sound of this one bird that
kept calling and calling off in the distance, and I wondered
what it was and much later I found out it was a common
snipe doing his flight call which is this mournful whistle that
lifts up & up & up with each beat. Its funny now to think
back on how my mind was always on other things when
Glendon and me got private. He and me begot three children
and that ought to mean we were as close in spirit as a man
and woman can get but Will I had two nights being close
with you and they are the two nights that showed me what
love really is. The flight call of the snipe was the farthest
thing from my mind when you and me were making love
Will. I can't quit thinking about it and how I got to feeling
just looking at you before you even got undressed. I watch
you move around taking off your tie and your jacket and I
feel like heat lightnin is going thru my insides Will. I says to
myself nobody moves like him. Nobody unbuttons his cuffs
like him. Nobody's got eyes as pretty as him. Nobody's luck-
ier than me.

   I went back and read what I wrote and it still don't seem
to say it like I feel but telling what love is like is a lot like
telling what the call of a bird is like. You hear it and you
reckoniz it and its in yourself so strong you think for sure
you can repeat it for someone else. But you can't. I just
wanted you to know though that I love you different from
what I loved Glendon. They say everybody goes through life
searching for the other half of hisself and I know now
you're the other half of me cause when I'm with you I feel
hoel . . .

July 16, 1942
Dear Mr. Parker,

Eleanor shared your last letter with me and together she and I have looked at the atlas and tried to imagine exactly where you are. I have taken her books about the Pacific Islands so that she can see what the flora and fauna are like there, also the weather and the ocean itself.

Things are changing here. The town seems quite deserted. Not only are our young men gone, the young women are leaving, too. The latest billboard pictures a woman and the slogan, "What job is mine on the Victory line?" So many are leaving to find jobs at Lockheed in Marietta, the shipyards in Mobile and at Packard and Chrysler up north, making engines and fuselages and landing gear. When I was young there were few choices given to a woman who did not marry. Teaching, becoming a domestic, or a librarian. Even female nurses were frowned upon then. Today the women are driving city buses, using acetylene torches and running cranes. I cannot help but wonder what will happen when the Allies are victorious and all you men come home. Rest assured, *your* job will be waiting.

Everything is getting scarce here. Canned fruit (thank heavens I live in Georgia where it will soon be fresh on the vine), tar (the roads are abysmal), sugar (which I miss most of all), bobby pins (the women are shearing their hair until they look like recruits in basic training), cloth (Washington has issued a directive that for the duration of the war men's suits shall be manufactured without cuffs, pleats and patch pockets), can openers (thank heavens I own one). Even meat and cars. One only chuckles at the mention of a new car nowadays. Yesterday's paper reported that Mr. Edsel Ford is unable to get a new car of his own until a Detroit rationing board can consider his application. Isn't that unbelievable when his family has manufactured *thirty million* automobiles!

If there is one thing this war does it is to equalize.

Things at the library are much as when you left except that since you joined up Lula Peak doesn't come around any more *to better herself.* Forgive me my facetiousness but Lula, as you know, is a sore spot. I fear I may lose Franklin Gilmore,

who is talking about not going back to high school for his
senior year but enlisting instead. Fewer books are being manufactured what with so many of the lumber companies supplying wood for packing crates instead of paper. But one title
is being printed in greater numbers than any other, The Red
Cross First Aid Manual, which is the bestselling book ever.

I still go to see Eleanor and the children each Saturday but
have been unable to convince her to come into town. However, she has developed a friendship with Mrs. Marsh and
speaks of her fondly. I am taking it upon myself to send the
grade school principal out to your place to see that Donald
Wade is enrolled in first grade, come September. I shall not
tell Eleanor I sent him and I would prefer if you did not tell
her either. Donald Wade is a bright lad and is already reading
at first grade level. He can recite verbatim the announcements
of many radio shows and is quite a little singer, which you
may not know. He and Thomas sang for me the last time I
was there, the Cream of Wheat song from "Let's Pretend." It
was amusing but I praised them heartily and told Donald
Wade that when he is in school he will be singing every day
and took it upon myself to teach him one which I remember
from when I was a child.

> October gave a party
> The leaves by hundreds came
> The ashes, oaks and maples
> And leaves of every name
> The sunshine spread a carpet
> And everything was grand
> Miss Weather led the dancing
> Professor Wind the band.

I believe, however, that Eleanor liked the song as much as
Donald Wade, she who takes time to explore and appreciate
the wonders of the woods and all its creatures. She sang it
along with Donald Wade and hummed it while clearing away
our tea things. She is well but misses you greatly.

And with this I must end. I shall not dwell on good luck
wishes which seem so paltry in light of where you are and the

service you are providing for those of us who keep lights in our windows. I shall simply say, you are in my prayers nightly.

Affectionately,
Gladys Beasley

23 June, 1942
Somewhere on the Pacific Ocean
Dear Elly,

Well I'm on a ship green eyes but that's about all I'm allowed to tell you not the name of it or our destination, which none of us have been told yet. We all got ideas though, judging from the direction we're traveling. We rode the train to San Francisco and embarked here 21 June and life aboard a troop transport ain't so bad. The navy is playing host so we got the soft life for a while and can cork off. Chow is good, all fresh meat and vegtubles and spuds and the navy does KP. About all we do is attend classes on Japanese intelligence and do calesthenics on the deck every day but tomorrow they say we're gonna have a field day which means we got to clean our bunk area top to bottom. Mine's in the forward hold, starboard, which is good. Not much engine noise and pretty smooth sailing. Red's got the sack just below mine they're like canvas cots. We play a lot of poker and a lot of the guys read comic books and trade them. Some of them read paper books and everybody talks about his sweetheart back home I don't talk about you tho except to Red cause he's my buddy and he dont go blabbin everything a man says. I didnt tell him the personal stuff about in Augusta but I told him about the time you threw the egg at me and he laughed hisself sick. He wants to meet you when this damn war is over. Well here's my address till I let you know different—Pfc. William Lee Parker, 1st Raider Bn., 1st Marines, So. Pacific. I'll probly write every day till we get to wherever they're sending us cuz there's plenty of time on this ship. I told you before how we call our rifles our sweethearts but when I write it now it means you. I love you sweetheart.

Your Will

June 28, 1942
Dearest Will,

   This waiting is awful because I don't know where you are
and there's no way to tell when I'll find out . . .

22 July, 1942
Somewhere in the South Pacific
Dear Elly,

   We're anchored offshore again and where we are is the last
Navy post office and we're on definite orders. Tomorrow we
sail for the last time and this is it. So tonight is our last night
for writing letters and when we give em to our unit postal
clerk for mailing we don't know when we'll get a chance to
write again. We been told now where we're goin' and why
but I can't tell you sweetheart. All I can tell you is I'll be riding on a sub tomorrow. I just want you to know that everybody's calm here. It's funny, it don't seem like we're going
into battle except everybodys talking quieter tonight and pol-
ishing their rifles even though they're already shining like the
north star. I can tell you this much and hope they don't cross
it off. Where we are there ain't no north star. Instead we see
the southern cross which we have all learned to find in the
night sky. I'm laying in my sack thinking of you and the kids
and smoking a Lucky Strike and trying to think of all the
things that are in my heart that ought to be said in this letter.
But all I do is get a lump in my throat and think to myself
god damn it Parker your goin back home, you hear? Elly
what you did for me in the last year is more than anybody did
for me in my whole life. I love you so much Elly that it hurts
inside way deep down in my gut when I even think about it.
You gave me a home and a family and love and a place to
come back to and when I say thank you it sounds so damn
small and not nearly as powerful as what I feel in my heart.
I looked in Miss Beasley's book of poems to try to find one
that says what I'm feeling but there ain't even words in there
that'll do it. You just gotta know green eyes that youre the
best thing that ever came along in my whole life and no
ocean and no war is ever gonna change that. Now I got to go
cause I'm getting to feel a little blue and lonesome but dont

you worry about me cuz like I said before I'm with the best outfit there is. Just remember how much I love you and that I'm coming home when this thing is over.

All my love,
Will

August 1, 1942
Dear Will,

I got what I think is your last letter you wrote from on the ship and I got to feeling so blue I had to take a walk with the kids in the orchard to keep from breaking down. It's so awful not knowing where you are or if you're safe ...

August 4, 1942
Dear Will,

It's a big day today cause Lizzy P is 8 months old and I'm weaning her. My breasts are so full of milk they feel like they're ready to bust ...

August 10, 1942
Dear Will,

Miss Beasley brought the newspapers and the headlines are big today. I always get scared when I see the letters two inches high ... this time about a big battle in the Solomons and all the damage to our ships and I'm so scared you were on one of them ...

August 11, 1942
Dear Will,

... They just don't tell us much here except to say the offensive continues with "considerable enemy resistance encountered." It is only Monday but Miss Beasley came out again cause she believes like I do that youre someplace out there in the middle of that awful mess in the Solomons where the Japs are claiming they sank 22 ships and damaged 6 more ...

August 18, 1942
Dear Will,

   ... you can't imagine how hard it is to read the war news
in the papers and still not know anything ...

20 Aug 1942
Somewhere in the Pacific
Dearest Elly,

   I'm alive and unhurt but I been in battle now so I know
how it feels to kill another human being. You just have to
keep telling yourself that he's the enemy and thinking about
when you get home how good things will be. I'm sitting here
in a foxhole thinking about the back porch steps and that day
I washed the boys at the well and we dried them off together.
I'd give anything for a bath. Where I am it never stops
raining. There's palm trees and a lot of yellowish grass
stretching from the beach to the jungle. I can't say I like the
jungle much but it does have things to eat. We were cut off
from supplies for quite awhile and I want to tell you it was
a sickening feeling when we looked out at the water and saw
our ships gone. I drank so much coconut milk its coming out
of my ears, which by the way got some kind of fungus growing in them. Between that and mosquito bites and rain it's a
pretty hellish place here but I don't want you to worry because today our fighter planes got in. I wish you could've
heard us cheer when they swung over and landed. It was the
most beautifull sight Ive ever seen. Not only did they bring
fresh supplies but they said the mail can go out. We never
know if it'll reach you though, but if this does kiss those babies for me and tell Miss Beasley I had to leave my book of
poems behind but I tore out the page with my favorite one
and I carry it in my field pack. Reading it and your letters is
about the only thing that keeps me going ...

September 4, 1942
Dear Will,

   ... well, Donald Wade went off on the schoolbus for the
first time today ...

Oct. 3, 1942
Dearest Will,
    . . . The boys taught Lizzy P. to say daddy today . . .

Oct. 4, 1942
Dearest Will,
    Your letter finally reached me, the first one from the battle
zone. Oh Will I'm so worried about your ears I wish I could
drop some warmed sweet oil in them for you and wash your
hair and comb it the way you used to like for me to do. Miss
Beasley and I think we figured out for sure where you are
and we think it's Guadalcanal and it scares me to death to
think of you there cause I know the fighting has been terrible
there and its Japanese territory . . .

WESTERN UNION

REGRET TO INFORM YOU YOUR HUSBAND WAS SERIOUSLY
WOUNDED IN ACTION 25 OCT IN SOLOMON ISLANDS.
UNTIL NEW ADDRESS IS RECEIVED MAIL FOR HIM
QUOTE CORPORAL WILLIAM L. PARKER 37 773 785
HOSPITALIZED CENTRAL POSTAL DIRECTORY APO0640 CARE
POSTMASTER NEW YORK NY UNQUOTE NEW ADDRESS
AND FURTHER INFORMATION FOLLOW DIRECT FROM
HOSPITAL J A ULIO THE ADJT GENERAL 7:10 A.M.

Nov. 1, 1942
Dear Will,
    I'm so worried. Oh Will I got a telegram and they said you
were seriously wounded but nothing else—not where you are
or how you are or anything . . .

Nov. 2, 1942
Dear Will,
    I didn't sleep a wink last night just laid awake crying and
wondering if you're still alive or if you have lost an arm or
a leg or your beautiful brown eyes . . .

Nov. 3, 1942
Dear Will,

... Sometimes I get so upset because all anybody will tell you is Somewhere In The South Pacific but Miss Beasley pointed out an article about Mrs. Roosevelt visiting the troops overseas and even it started "Somewhere In England," so I guess if it's good enough for the president's wife it'll have to be good enough for me but I'm worried sick about you ...

November 4, 1942
Dear Will,

It just struck me that the telegram said corporal so you got promoted! I shucked off my drears and turned my thoughts positive cause thats the only thing to do. You're alive I know it I won't give up hope and I'll write every single day whether I hear from you or not ...

4193 US Navy Hosp. Plant
APO 515
New York, NY
Dear <u>Mrs. Parker,</u>

I am pleased to inform you that on <u>1 Nov 1942</u> your <u>husband, Corp. William L. Parker, 37 773 785, was making normal improvement.</u> Diagnosis <u>wound left thigh.</u>

Thomas M. Simpson
1st Lieut. M.A.O. Registrar

4193 US Navy Hosp. Plant
APO 515
New York, NY
Dear <u>Mrs. Parker,</u>

I am pleased to inform you that on <u>6 Nov 1942</u> your <u>husband, Corp. William L. Parker, 37 773 785, was evacuated to zone of noncombat and underwent surgery on wound, left thigh. Is making normal improvement.</u>

Virgil A. Saylor, 1st Lt.,
MAC Registrar

U.S. War Department
Official Business
20 Nov 1942
Dear Mrs. Parker,

As commanding officer of your husband, Corporal William L. Parker who was injured in action 1 Nov 1942 on the Island of Guadalcanal, I felt it imperative to reassure you that his condition is no longer life threatening and that eventual recovery can be fully expected. On 6 November he was transferred by air to the Navy hospital at Melbourne, Australia, where he underwent successful surgery and awaits transfer to the United States.

Corporal Parker is a credit to his company and to the United States Marines. He fought well and without complaint. On 14 Sept 1942, while engaging the enemy in action on Guadalcanal, Corporal Parker displayed conspicuous gallantry in attempting to rescue Private Otis D. Luttrell by dragging him to a foxhole under heavy enemy fire. On 25 October Corporal Parker again proved himself a leader by singlehandedly knocking out a Japanese dugout emplacement which was holding up our advance. The enemy hole-up was situated in a cave made inaccessible by severe enemy fire from inside. Corporal Parker voluntarily crawled to the cave from its blind side, attempted to knock a hole in the roof and when unable to do so, attempted to kick the rocks away at the foot of the cave. Four times he threw hand grenades inside only to have them promptly returned by the Japanese. Next Corporal Parker tried holding the grenades for three seconds before delivering them. When these were also returned, Parker reportedly "got mad" and made a dynamite bomb which he thrust into the breach killing eight Japanese soldiers but receiving injuries to himself from an enemy fragmentation grenade which simultaneously detonated at the mouth of the cave.

Because of Corporal Parker's determination and bravery the 1st Raider Bn. won a decisive victory over the Japanese at the mouth of the Ilu River, rendering them a loss of 12 tanks and some 600 troops in the 1st Marine sector.

It is with pride and pleasure that for heroism above and be-

yond the call of duty I am recommending to the Commander
in Chief of the United States Armed Forces that Corporal
William L. Parker, USMC 1st Raider Battalion, be awarded
the medal of valor of the Order of the Purple Heart.

Yours truly,
Col. Merritt A. Edson
Commander, 1st Marine Raiders
USMC

Balboa Naval Hospital
San Diego, California
Dear Mrs. Parker,
   I am pleased to inform you that on 6 Dec 1942 your husband, Corp. William L. Parker, 37 773 785, was transferred to Balboa Naval Hospital, San Diego U.S.A. for
further medical treatment.

Balboa Naval Hospital
San Diego
7 Dec. 1942
Dear Elly,
   I'm home again and you don't need to worry any more. A
Red Cross nurse is writing this for me because the doc won't
let me sit up yet. I finally got all your letters. They caught up
with me in a hospital in Melbourne. Elly honey it was so
good to read all those words from you, all about Donald
Wade going to school and Lizzy P. saying her first words and
how they taught her to say Daddy. I wish I was there with
you all now but it looks like that'll be a while yet. My leg
isn't so good but at least I've still got it and it might be stiff
but I'll be able to walk, they say. The docs here say I'm still
carrying a piece of metal in my left leg and I may have to
have surgery again. But what the heck, at least I'm alive.
   I'm sorry they didn't tell you more right after I got hit so
you wouldn't have worried so much. I would have done so
myself but I guess I wasn't in much shape for writing. But
don't you worry now. I'm okay and I mean it.
   By now you know I got hit by a Jap grenade while I was

trying to flush eight of them out of a holeup near the airfield on the Canal which it's okay now to tell you where I was, on Guadalcanal. The Canal was rough and we lost a lot there but we set them back and the airstrip is ours now. If we hadn't the Pacific would still be theirs and I'm damn proud of what we did. I might as well tell you now my buddy Red didn't make it and thats all I can say about it at the moment because its hard for me to think about it. So as I was saying it doesn't seem much to put up with a few chunks of steel in your leg. But I have to confess I never was so glad to see anything as I was to see Old Glory waving over the Navy Hospital on good old American soil when I debarked here. Damn, Elly, I wish I could see you but this leg will have to mend first so I'll be here a while but I'll sure be looking for your letters. It seems like since I joined the Marines I've lived for mail call. Now that I'm in one place your letters will get to me so write often, okay green eyes? Please don't worry about me. Now that I'm back things'll be just fine. Kiss the kids for me and tell Miss Beasley to write, too.

All my love,
Will

Dec. 9, 1942
Dear Will,

Oh Will your home at last. Your letter just came and I cryed when I read it I was so happy. They won't send you back will they? Is your leg healing any better? I'm so worried about it and what you must be going through with the operations and the pain. If you weren't so far away I'd come to you again like I did in Augusta, but I just don't see how I can come clear to California. But wouldn't it be something if we could be together for Christmas? . . .

24 Dec. 1942
Dear Elly,

The nurses strung colored lights across the foot of our beds but looking at them gives me that choky feeling again. I'm layin here thinking of last Christmas eve when you and me filled the stockings for the boys. I want to be home so bad.

Jan 29, 1943
Dear Will,
  Happy birthday . . .

5 Feb. 1943
Dear Elly,
  They got me up on crutches today . . .

CHAPTER
19

Calvin Purdy dropped Will at the end of his driveway.

"Thanks a million, Mr. Purdy."

"No thanks necessary, Will, not from a GI. You sure you don't want me to take you the rest o' the way on up't the house?"

"No, sir, I was always partial to this little stretch of woods. Sounds good to walk through the quiet alone, if you know what I mean."

"Sure do, son. Ain't no place prettier'n Georgia in May. You need any help with them crutches?"

"No, sir. I can manage." Leading with both feet, Will worked his way out of Calvin Purdy's '31 Chevrolet while Purdy retrieved Will's duffel bag and brought it around, then laced it over Will's shoulder.

"Be more'n happy to take your duffel up," Purdy repeated accommodatingly.

" 'Preciate it, Mr. Purdy, but I kinda wanted to surprise Elly."

"You mean she doesn't know you're comin'?"

"Not yet."

"We-e-e-ll, then I understand why you want to go up alone . . . Corporal Parker." Grinning, Purdy extended his hand and gripped Will's tightly. "Anytime I can give you a lift or be of any he'p, just holler. And welcome home."

After Purdy pulled away, Will stood for a moment, listening to the silence. No cannonade in the distance, no bullets *thupping* into the earth beside him, no mosquitos buzzing, no men screaming. All was silence, blessed May silence. The woods were in deep leaf, heavy green weighting down the branches. Beside the road a patch of wild chicory created a cloud of blue stars. Nearby a clump of wild clover startled, livid in the heat of its summer blush. Some creature had feasted on a smilax vine, spreading a scent like root beer in the air. A yellow warbler did a flight dance, landed on a branch and sang its seven clear, sweet notes, eyeing Will with head atilt.

Home again.

He moved up the driveway beneath the arch of branches that allowed the azure sky entry. He tipped his head and admired it, marveling that he need not cock an ear for the sound of distant engines, nor squint an eye in an effort to identify a wing shape or a rising red sun painted on a fuselage.

Forget it, Parker, you're home now.

The driveway was soft, the air warm, his crutches poked holes in the red earth. They must've had rain recently. Rain. He'd never much cared for rain, not in his early life when he'd lived mostly in the open, certainly not on the Canal, where the damned rain was ceaseless, where it filled foxholes, turned tent camps to fetid quagmires, rotted the soles off sturdy leather boots and fostered mosquitos, malaria and a host of creeping fungi that grew between toes, inside ears and anyplace two skin surfaces touched.

I said, forget it, Parker!

The odd thing was, though he'd been Stateside for six months he still couldn't acclimate to it. He still scanned the skies. Still listened for stealthy movement behind him. Still expected the telltale clack of two bamboo stalks rubbing. Still flinched at sudden noises. He closed his eyes and breathed deep. The air here had no mildewy smell, instead it held a tang of wild tansy which seemed familiar and welcoming and very native. During his drifting years whenever he'd caught a cold he'd brewed himself a cup of tansy tea, and once when he'd gashed his hand on a piece of rusty barbed wire he'd made a compress of it that cured the infection.

Walking up his own road amid the smells of tansy and smilax, he let the fact sink in: he was home for good.

At the sourwood tree he stopped, let his canvas duffel bag slip down and lowered his left foot to the ground. Real, solid ground, a little moist maybe, but American. Safe. Ground he'd shaped himself with a mule named Madam while a little boy sat and watched, and the boy's mother brought red nectar and a baby brother down the lane in a faded red wagon.

He resisted the urge to drop his crutches and ease onto the bank where the grass was green-rich and wild columbine blossomed. Instead, he shouldered his bag and moved westward toward the opening in the trees where the clearing lay.

Reaching it, he paused in surprise. During his stretch in the South Pacific, when he'd pictured home, he often saw it as it had first been, a motley collection of scrap iron and chicken dung beside a teetering house patched with tin. What he saw today made him hold his breath and stand stone still in wonder.

Flowers! Everywhere, flowers ... and all of them blue! Gay, uncivilized blossoms, clambering unchecked without a hint of order or precision. How like his Elly to sow wildly and let rain and sun—Will smiled—and all those years of chicken manure do the rest. He scanned the clearing. Blue—Lord a-mercy, he'd never seen so much blue! Flowers of every shade and tint of blue that nature had ever produced. He knew them all from his study of the bees.

Nearest the house tall Persian blue phlox bordered the porch, thick and high and tufted, giving way to Canterbury bells that bled from deepest royal purple to a pale violet-pink. At their feet began a rich spread of heliotrope in coiled blue-violet sprays. Against the east wall of the chicken house a clematis climbed a trellis of strings. There, too, began a carpet of long-stemmed cornflowers, as deep and true as the sky, continuing along the adjacent chicken-yard fence in a wall of royal color. At the shady border beneath the trees, pale violets began, giving way to deep-hued forget-me-nots which ranged

in the open sun, meeting a spread of blue vervain. On the opposite side of the yard a wooden wagon wheel had been
painted white and stood as a backdrop for a stand of regal
larkspur which covered the blue spectrum from purple to indigo to palest Dresden. Before them, much shorter and more
delicate, a patch of flax-flowers waved in the breeze on fern-
like stems. Somewhere in the conglomeration purple petunias
bloomed. Will could smell them as he moved up the path,
which was bordered by fuzzy ageratum. Where that path led
around the back of the house a new pergola stood, laden with
morning glories, their bells lifted to heaven. Birds darted everywhere, a chirping cacophony. A ruby-throated hummingbird at the morning glories. Wrens lambasting him with
music from the low branch of a crabapple tree, and appropri-
ately enough, a pair of bluebirds near one of the gourds.
Spotting them, he smiled, recalling Donald Wade placing the
bluebird figurine on the windowsill for just this reason. Well,
they had their bluebirds now.

And bees . . . everywhere, bees, gathering nectar and pollen
from the sea of color they loved best, humming, lifting on
gauzy wings to move to the next blossom and join their wing-
music to that of the birds.

Only as he neared the house did Will find a ruddy splash.
Several feet off the last porch step stood a washtub, painted
white, bulging with cinnamon pinks so thick they cascaded
over the sides—crimson and heliotrope and coral and
rose—so fragrant they made his head light. On the porch
steps lay a cluster of them, crushed, wilted. He picked them
up, held them, smelled them, glanced around the clearing before depositing them where they'd been, carefully, as if they
were the trappings of a religious ceremony.

He raised his eyes to the screen door, mounted the steps
and opened the screen, expecting any moment to hear Elly or
the kids call, "Who's there?"

The kitchen was empty.

"Elly?" he called, letting his duffel bag slip from his shoulder.

In the answering silence wands of sunlight angled across
the scrubbed floor and climbed the mopboard. The room

smelled good, of bread and spice. On the table was a crocheted doily and a thick white crockery pitcher filled with a
sampling of flowers from the yard; on the windowsill, the
bluebird figurine. The room was neat, orderly, clean. His eyes
moved to the cupboard where a white enamel cake pan was
covered with a dishtowel. He lifted a corner of the cloth—
bars, unfrosted, half-gone. He tucked a pinch into his mouth,
then poked his head into the front room.

"Elly?"

Silence. Summer afternoon silence, stretching into Will's
very soul.

Their bedroom was empty. He stood in the doorway imbib-
ing familiarities—the Madeira lace dresser set, a slipper-
shaped dish holding bobby- and hair-pins, a stack of freshly
folded diapers . . . the bed. It was not, he discovered, disap-
pointing to arrive to an empty house. He'd had so little time
alone. These minutes, reacclimating, seeped within his bones
in a wholly healing way.

Neither was anyone in the boys' room. The crib, he noted,
had been moved in here.

Back in the kitchen he cut an enormous square of the moist
golden bars and took a bite—honey, pecans, cloves and cinnamon. Mmmm . . . delicious. He anchored the remaining
piece in his teeth and stumped to the door, then outside.

"Elly?" he bellowed from the top of the steps, pausing, listening. "Ellllleeeee?"

From beyond the barn a mule brayed as if objecting to being awakened. Madam. He headed that way, found the beast
but no Elly. He checked the chicken coop—it was clean; the
storage sheds—their doors were all closed; the vegetable garden, it was empty; and finally the backyard, passing under the
pergola with its bonnet of morning glories. Nobody at the
clothesline either.

With all these flowers and the warm temperatures, undoubtedly the honey would be running. He'd walk down the
orchard to see, to pass the time reacquainting himself with the
bees while waiting for Elly.

The earth wore a mantle of heavy grass but he made his
way easily with the crutches, following the overgrown

double-trail compacted long ago by Glendon Dinsmore's
Steel Mule. Everything was as he remembered, the hickories
and oaks as green as watermelon rind, the katydids fiddling
away in the tall redtop grass, the dead branch shaped like a
dog's paw, and, farther along, the magnolia with the oak
growing from its crotch. He topped a small rise and there lay
the orchard on the opposite hill, steeping in the warm May
sun, smelling faintly of other years' fermented fruit and the
flowering weeds and wildings that bordered the trees and surrounding woods. He let his eyes wander appreciatively over
the squat trees—peach, apple, pear and quince, marching
around the east-sloping hill as if in formation. And along the
south edge, the hives, rimmed in red and blue and yellow and
green, as he'd painted them. And halfway down . . . a . . . a
woman? Will's head jutted. Was it? In a veiled hat and trousers? Filling the saltwater pans? Naw, it couldn't be! But it
was! A woman, working in fat yellow farmer gloves that met
the cuffs of one of his old blue chambray shirts whose collar
was buttoned tightly and turned up around her jaws. Toting
two buckets in the boys' wagon. Bending to dip the water
with a tin dipper and pour it into the low, flat pans. A
woman—*his wife*—tending the bees!

He smiled and felt a surge of love strong enough to end the
war, could it have been harnessed and channeled. Jubilantly,
he raised a hand and waved. *"Elly?"*

She straightened, looked, looked harder, lifted the veil up,
shaded her eyes . . . and finally the shock hit.

"Will!" She dropped the dipper and ran. Flat-out, arms and
feet churning like steel drivers. "Will!" The hat bounced off
and fell but she ran on, waving a yellow glove. "Will, Will!"

He gripped his crutches and stumped toward her, fast, hard,
reaching, his body swinging like a Sunday morning steeple
bell. Smiling. Feeling his heart clubbing. His eyes stinging.
Watching Elly race toward him while the boys spilled out of
the woods and ran, too, taking up the call, "Will's home!
Will! Will!"

They met beside a rangy apple tree with a force great
enough to send one crutch to the ground and Will, too, had
she not been there to clasp him. Arms, mouths, souls com-

bined once again while bees droned a reunion song and the
sun poured down upon a soldier's hat lying on the verdant
ground. Tongues and tears, and two bodies yearning together
amid a rush of kisses—deep, hurried, unbelieving kisses.
They clung, choked with emotion, burying their faces, smelling one another—Velvo shaving cream and crushed cinnamon
pinks—joined mouths and tongues to taste each other once
more. And for them the war was over.

The boys came pelting—"Will! Will!"—and Lizzy P. tod-
dled out of the woods crying, left behind.

"*Kemo sabe!* Sprout!" Will bent stiffly to hug them against
his legs, circling them both in his arms, kissing their hot,
freckled faces, clasping them close, smelling them, too—
sweaty little boys who'd been playing in the sun long and
hard. Elly warned, "Careful for Will's leg," but the hugging
continued in quartet, with her arms around Will even as he
greeted the boys, everybody kissing, laughing, teetering,
while down the lane Lizzy stood in the sun, rubbing her eyes
and wailing.

"Why didn't you tell us you were comin'?"

"I wanted to surprise you."

Elly wiped her eyes on the thick gloves, then yanked them
off. "Oh, lorzy, what am I doin' with them still on?"

"Come here." He snagged her waist, kissed her again amid
the scrambling boys, who still had him shackled and were
peppering him with news and questions: "Are you stayin'
home? ... We got kittens ... Wow, is this your uniform? ...
I got vacation ... Did you kill any Japs? ... Hey, Will, Will
... guess what ..."

For the moment both Elly and Will were oblivious to the
pair. "Oh, Will ..." Her eyes shone with joy, straight into his.
"I can't believe you're back. How is your leg?" She suddenly
remembered. "Here, boys, back off and let Will sit. Can you
sit on the grass—is it okay?"

"It's okay." He lowered himself stiffly and breathed in a
great gulp of orchard air.

Down the lane Lizzy continued bawling. Donald Wade
tried on Will's garrison cap, which covered his eyebrows and
ears. "Wow!" he crowed. "Lookit me! I'm a Marine!"

"Lemme!" Thomas reached. "I wanna wear it!"

"No, it's mine!"

"Ain't neither—I get it, too!"

"Boys, go get your sister and bring her here."

They dashed off like puppies after a ball, Donald Wade in the lead, wearing the hat, Thomas in pursuit.

Elly sat on her knees beside Will, her arms locked around his neck. "You look so good, all tan and pretty."

"Pretty!" He laughed and rubbed her hip.

"Well, prettier'n me in these durn britches and your old shirt." They couldn't quit touching each other, looking at each other.

"You look good to me—good enough to eat."

He tasted her jaw, nipping playfully. She giggled and hunched a shoulder. The giggling subsided when their gazes met, leading to another kiss, this one soft, unhurried, unsexual. A solemnization. When it ended he breathed the scent of her with his eyes still closed.

"Elly . . ." he prayed, in thanksgiving.

She rested her hands on his chest and gave the moment its due.

At length they roused from their absorption with one another and he asked, "So, what're you doing out here?"

"Tendin' your bees."

"So I see. How long's this been goin' on?"

"Since you been gone."

"Why didn't you tell me in your letters?"

" 'Cause I wanted to surprise you, too!"

There were a thousand things he wanted to say, as a poet might say them. But he was an ordinary man, neither glib nor eloquent. He could only tell her, quietly, "You're some woman, you know that?"

She smiled and touched his hair—it was long again, streaky yellow, bending toward his face just enough to please her. She rested her elbows on his shoulders and wrapped both arms around his head and simply held him, bringing to him again the scent of crushed cinnamon pinks from her skin. He buried his nose in her neck.

"Mercy, you smell good. Like you been rollin' in flowers."

She laughed. "I have. I didn't like the mint, but your pamphlets said cinnamon pinks worked just as good so I smeared myself with them. Guess what, Will?" Exhilarated, she backed up to see his face, leaving her arms twined about his neck.

"What?"

"The honey is runnin'."

He let his eyelids droop, let his lips soften suggestively and closed both hands upon her breasts, hidden between them. "Y' damned right it is, darlin'. Wanna feel?"

Her blood rushed, her heart pounded and she felt a glorious spill deep within.

"More than anything," she whispered, nudging his lips, but the children were near so he sat back with his hands flattened against the hot grass while she angled her head, tasted him shallow and deep. He opened his mouth and remained unmoving as her tongue played upon his in a series of teasing plunders. He returned the favor, washing her sweet mouth with wet kisses, sucking her lower lip.

"What you guys doin'?" Donald Wade stood beside them, holding Lizzy P. on his hip while Thomas approached, wearing Will's hat.

Leaving her arms across Will's collarbones, Elly squinted over her shoulder. "Kissin'. Better get used to it, 'cause there's gonna be a lot of it goin' on around here." Unrattled, she dropped down beside her man on the grass, raising her hands for the baby. "C'm 'ere, sugar. Come see Daddy. Well, goodness gracious, all those tears—did you think we all run off and left you?" Chuckling, she brought the baby's cheek against her own, then set her down and began cleaning up Lizzy's tearful face while the little girl trained a watchful stare on Will. The boys plopped down, doing the things that big brothers do. Thomas took Lizzy's palm and bounced it. "Hi, Lizzy." Donald Wade brought his eyes down to the level of hers and talked brightly. "This's Will, Lizzy. Can you say, *Daddy?* Say, *Daddy,* Lizzy." Then, to Will, "She only talks when she wants to."

Lizzy didn't say Daddy, or Will. Instead, when he took her, she pushed against his chest, straining and twisting back for

Elly, beginning to cry again. In the end he was forced to re-
linquish her until she grew used to him again.

"The orchard looks good. Did you have the trees sprayed?"

"Didn't *have* 'em sprayed, I did it myself."

"And the yard, why that's the prettiest thing I've seen in
years. You do all that?"

"Yup. Me'n the boys."

"Mama let me put seeds in the holes!" piped up Thomas.

"Good boy. Who built the archway for the morning glories?"

"Mama."

Elly added, "Me'n Donald Wade, didn't we, honey?"

"Yeah! An' I pounded the nails and everything!"

Will put on a proper show of enthusiasm. "You did! Well,
good for you."

"Mama said you'd like it."

"And I do, too. Walked into the yard and figured I was in
the wrong place."

"Did you really?"

Will laughed and pressed Donald Wade's nose flat with the
tip of a finger.

They all fell quiet, listening to the drone of bees and the
wind's breath in the trees around them. "You can stay now,
can't you?" Elly asked quietly.

"Yes. Medical discharge."

Keeping one arm around Lizzy's hip, she found Will's fingers in the grass behind them and braided them with her own.
"That's good," she said simply, running a hand down Lizzy's
hot hair while her eyes remained on her husband's face,
tanned to a hickory brown, compellingly handsome above the
tight collar and tie of his uniform. "You're a hero, Will. I'm
so proud of you."

His lips twisted and he chuckled self-consciously. "Well, I
don't know about that."

"Where's your Purple Heart?"

"Back at the house in my duffel bag."

"It should be right here." She lay a hand flat against his lapel, then slipped it underneath because she found within herself the constant need to touch him. She felt his heartbeat,

strong and healthy against her fingertips, and recalled the hundreds of images she'd suffered, of bullets drilling him, spilling his blood on some distant jungle floor. Her precious, dear Will. "Miss Beasley told the newspaper about it and they put an article in. Now everybody knows Will Parker is a hero."

His look grew pensive, fixed on a distant hive. "Everybody in that war is a hero. They oughta give a Purple Heart to every GI out there."

"Did you shoot anybody, Will?" Donald Wade inquired.

"Now, Donald Wade, you mustn't—"

"Yes, I did, son, and it's a pretty awful thing."

"But they were bad guys, weren't they?"

Will's haunted gaze fixed on Elly, but instead of her he saw a foxhole and in it six inches of water and his buddy, Red, and a bomb whistling down out of the sky turning everything before him scarlet.

"Now, Donald Wade, Will just got back and you're pepperin' him with questions already."

"No, it's okay, Elly." To the child he said, "They were people, just like you and me."

"Oh."

Donald Wade grew solemn, contemplating the fact. Elly rose from her knees and said, "I have to finish filling the water pans. It won't take me long."

She kissed Will's left eyebrow, drew on her farmer gloves and left the children with Will while she headed back to work, turning once to study her husband again, trying to grasp the fact that he was back for good.

"I love you!" she called from beside a gnarled pear tree.

"I love you, too!"

She smiled and spun away.

The children examined Will's uniform—buttons, chevrons, pins. Lizzy grew less cautious, toddling around in the grass. The sun beat down and Will removed his blouse, laid it aside and stretched out supine, shutting his eyes against the brightness. But the sun on his closed eyelids became scarlet. Blood scarlet. And he saw it happen all over again—Red, scrambling on his belly across a stretch of kunai grass beside the

Matanikau River, suddenly freezing in the open while from
the opposite shore enemy .25 calibers cracked like oxwhips,
submachine guns thundered, and a ranging grenade launcher
sent its deadly missiles closer and closer. And there lay poor
Red, stretched flat with no cover, facedown, shaking, biting
the grass, halted by an unholy terror such as a lucky Marine
never knows. Will saw himself scrambling back out amid the
strafing, heard the bullets' deceptively soft sigh as they sailed
over his head, the dull thud as they struck behind him, left,
right. The earth rained dirt upward as a grenade hit fifteen
feet away. "Christ, man, you gotta get outta here!" Red lay
unmoving, unable. Will felt again his own panic, the surge of
adrenaline as he grabbed Red and hauled him backward
through mud and tufts of uprooted grass into a foxhole with
six inches of muddy water—"Stay here, buddy. I'm going to
get them sonsabitches!"—then going over the top again, teeth
clenched, crawling on his elbows while the tip of his bayonet
swung left and right. Then, overhead, the planes wheeling out
of nowhere, the warning whistle, dropping, and behind him,
Red, in the foxhole where the bomb fell.

Will shuddered, opened his eyes wide, sat up. Beside him
the children still played. At the hive openings bees landed
with their gatherings. Elly was returning with the wagon in
tow, the two empty metal buckets clanging like glockenspiels
as the wheels bumped over the rough turf. He blinked away
the memory and watched his wife come on in her masculine
apparel. *Don't think about Red, think about Elly.* He watched
until her shadow slipped across his lap, then raised a hand
and requested quietly, "Come here," and when she fell to her
knees, held her. Just held her. And hoped she'd be enough to
heal him.

Their lovemaking that night was golden.
But when it was over Elly sensed Will's withdrawal from
more than her body.
"What's wrong?"
"Hm?"
"What's wrong?"
"Nothing."

"Your leg hurt?"

"Not bad."

She didn't believe him, but he wasn't a complainer, never had been. He reached for his Lucky Strikes, lit one and lay smoking in the dark. She watched the red coal brighten, listened to him inhale.

"You want to talk about it?"

"About what?"

"Anything—your leg . . . the war. I think you purposely kept the bad stuff out of your letters for my sake. Maybe you wanna talk about it now."

The red arc of the cigarette going to his mouth created a barrier more palpable than barbed wire.

"What's the sense in talking about it? I went to war, not an ice cream social. I knew that when I joined up."

She felt shut out and hurt. She had to give him time to open up, but tonight wouldn't be the night, that was certain. So she searched for subjects to bring him close again.

"I'll bet Miss Beasley was surprised when she saw you."

He chuckled. "Yeah."

"Did she show you the scrapbook of newspaper clippings she kept about all the action in the South Pacific?"

"No, she didn't mention that."

"She clipped articles only about the areas where she thought you might be fighting."

He chuckled soundlessly.

"You know what?"

"Hm?"

"I think she's sweet on you."

"Oh, come on, she's old enough to be my grandma."

"Grandmas got feelings, too."

"Lord."

"And you know what else? I think you kind of feel the same."

He felt himself blush in the dark, recalling times when he'd purposely charmed the librarian. "Elly, you're crazy."

"Yeah, I know, but it's perfectly okay with me. After all, you never had a grandma, and if you wanna love her a little bit it don't take nothin' away from me."

He tamped out his cigarette, drew her against his side and kissed the top of her head. "You're some woman, Elly."

"Yeah, I know."

He pulled back and looked down into her face, forgetting momentarily the haunting visions that sprang into his mind uninvited. He laughed, then Elly snuggled her cheek against his chest once more, and went on distracting him. "Anyway, Miss Beasley was wonderful while you were gone, Will. I don't know what I would've done without her—and Lydia, too. Lydia and I got to be such good friends. And you know what? I never really had a friend before." She mused before continuing. "We could talk about anything ... " She ruffled the hair on his chest and added, "I'd like to have her and the kids out sometime so you can get to know her better. Would that be all right with you, Will?"

She waited, but he didn't answer.

"Will?"

Silence.

"Will?"

"What?"

"Haven't you been listening?"

He removed his arm and reached for another cigarette. She'd lost him again.

There was no doubt about it, Will was different. Not only the limp, but the lapses. They happened often in the days that followed, lengthy silences when he became preoccupied with thoughts he refused to share. An exchange would become a monologue and Elly would turn to find his eyes fixed on the middle distance, his thoughts troubled, miles away. There were other changes, too. At night, insomnia. Often she'd awaken to find him sitting up, smoking in the dark. Sometimes he dreamed and talked in his sleep, swore, called out and thrashed. But when she'd awaken him and encourage, "What is it, Will? Tell me," he'd only reply, "Nothing. Just a dream." Afterward he'd cling to her until sleep reclaimed him and his palms would be damp even after they finally fell open.

He needed time alone. Often he went down to the orchard

to ruminate, to sit watching the hives and work through whatever was haunting him.

The smallest sounds set him off. Lizzy knocked her milk glass off the high chair one day and he rocketed from his chair, exploded and left the house without finishing his meal. He returned thirty minutes later, apologetic, hugging and kissing Lizzy as if he'd struck her, bringing by way of apology a simple homemade toy called a bull-roarer which he'd made himself.

He spent a full hour with the three children that afternoon, out in the yard, spinning the simple wooden blade on the end of the long string until it whirled and made a sound like an engine revving up. And, as always, after being with the children, he seemed calmer.

Until the night they had a thunderstorm at three A.M. An immense clap of thunder shook the house, and Will sprang up, yelling as if to be heard above shelling, "Red! Jesus Christ, R-e-e-e-e-e-d!"

"Will, what is it?"

"Elly, oh God, hold me!"

Again, she became his lifeline, but though he trembled violently and sweated as if with a tropical fever, he held his horrors inside.

Physically, he continued healing. Within a week after his return he was restless to walk without crutches, and within a month, he followed his inclination. He loved the bathtub, took long epsom salts soaks that hastened the healing, and always eagerly accepted Elly's offers to scrub his back. Though he'd been ordered by Navy doctors to have checkups biweekly, he shunned the order and took over tending the bees even before he discarded the crutches, and went back to his library job in his sixth week home, without consulting a medic. His hours there were the same as before, leaving his days free, so he painted and posted a sign at the bottom of their driveway—USED AUTO PARTS & TIRES—and went into the junk business, which brought in a surprising amount of steady money. Coupled with his library salary, government disability check and the profit from the sale of eggs, milk and honey, which was constantly in demand now that sugar was heavily

rationed, it brought their income up to a level previously unheard of in either Will's or Elly's life.

The money was, for the most part, saved, for even though
Will still dreamed of buying Elly luxuries, the production of
most domestic commodities had been halted long ago by the
War Production Board. Necessities—clothing, food, house-
hold goods—were strictly rationed, at Purdy's store, their
point values posted on the shelves beside the prices. The
same at the gas station, though Will and Elly were classified
as farmers, so given more gas rationing coupons than they
needed.

The one place they could enjoy their money was at the theater in Calhoun. They went every Saturday night, though Will
refused to go if a war movie was showing.

Then one day a letter arrived from Lexington, Kentucky.
The return address said Cleo Atkins. Elly left it propped up
in the middle of the kitchen table and when Will came in,
pointed to it.

"Somethin' for you," she said simply, turning away.

"Oh . . ." He picked it up, read the return address and repeated, quieter, "Oh."

After a full minute of silence she turned to face him.
"Aren't you going to open it?"

"Sure." But he didn't, only stood rubbing his thumb over
the writing, staring at it.

"Why don't you take it down to the orchard and open it,
Will?"

He looked up with pain in his deep, dark eyes, swallowed
and said in a thick voice, "Yeah, I think I'll do that."

When he was gone, Elly sat down heavily on a kitchen
chair and covered her face with her hand, grieving for him,
for the death of his friend whom he couldn't forget. She remembered long ago how he'd told her of the only other
friend he'd ever had, the one who'd betrayed him and had
testified against him. How alone he must feel now, as if every
time he reached out toward another man, that friendship was
snatched away. Before the war she would not have guessed
the value of a friend. But now she had two—Miss Beasley
and Lydia. So she knew Will's pain at losing his buddy.

She gave him half an hour before going out to find him.
He was sitting beneath an aged, gnarled apple tree heavy with
unripe fruit, the letter on the ground at his hip. Knees up,
arms crossed, head lowered, he was the picture of dejection.
She approached silently on the soft grass and dropped to her
knees, putting her palms on his forearms, her face against his
shoulder. In ragged sobs, he wept. She moved her hands to
his heaving back and held him lovingly while he purged himself. At last he railed, "Jesus, Elly, I k–killed him. I
d–dragged him back to that f–foxhole and left him th–there
and the n–next thing I knew a b–bomb hit it d–dead center
and I t–t–turned around and s–saw his r–red h–hair flyin' in
ch–chunks and—"

"Shh . . ."

"And I was screamin, Red! . . . *Re-e-e-d!*" He lifted his
face and screamed it to a silent sky, screamed it so long and
loud the veins stood out like marble carvings along his temples, up his neck and above his clenched fists.

"You didn't kill him, you were trying to save him."

Rage replaced his grief. *"I killed my best friend and they
gave me a fucking Purple Heart for it!"*

She could have argued that the Purple Heart was justly
earned, in a different battle, but she could see this was no
time for reasoning. He needed to voice his rage, work it out
like pus from a festering wound. So she rubbed his shoulders,
swallowed her own tears and offered the silent abeyance she
knew he needed.

"Now his fiancée writes—God, how he loved her—and
says, It's okay, Corporal Parker, you mustn't blame yourself."
He dropped his head onto his arms again. "Well, doesn't she
see I got to blame myself? He was always talkin' about how
the four of us were g–gonna meet after the w–war and we'd
maybe buy a car and go on v–vacation someplace together,
maybe up in the Smoky Mountains where it's–it's c–cool in
the s–summer and him and me c–could go–go f–fish—" He
turned and threw himself into Elly's arms, propelled by the
force of anguish. He clasped her, burrowing, accepting her
consolation at last. She held him, rocked him, let his tears
wet her dress. "Aw, Elly—Elly—g–goddamn the war."

She held his head as if he were no older than Lizzy, closed her eyes and grieved with him, for him, and became once again the mother/wife he would always need her to be.

In time his breathing grew steadier, his embrace eased. "Red was a good friend."

"Tell me about him."

"You want to read the letter?"

"No. I read enough letters when you were gone. You tell me."

He did. Calmly this time, what it had *really* been like on the Canal. About the misery, the fear, the deaths and the carnage. About the "Last Supper" on board *The Argonaut*, steak and eggs in unlimited supply to fill a man's gut before he hit the beach expecting to have it shot out; about boarding a rubber raft in a pounding surf that roared so loud in the limber holes of the sub that no man could be heard above it; about that bobbing ride over deadly coral that threatened to slash the rubber boats and drown every man even before they reached the Japanese-infested shore; about arriving wet and staying so for the next three months; about watching your fleet chased off by the enemy, leaving you cut off from supplies indefinitely; about charging into a grass hut with your finger cocked and watching human beings fly backwards and drop with the surprise still on their faces; about learning what three species of ants are edible while you lay on your belly for two days with a sniper waiting in a tree, and the ants beneath your nose become your dinner; about the Battle of Bloody Ridge; about watching men lie in torment for days while flies laid eggs in their wounds; about eating coconuts until you wished the malaria would get you before the trots did; about the twitch of a human body even after it's dead. And finally, about Red, the Red he'd loved. The live Red, not the dead one.

And when Will had purged himself, when he felt drained and exhausted, Elly took his hand and they walked home together through the late-afternoon sun, through the orchard, through the flower-trimmed pergola, to begin the thankless job of forgetting.

CHAPTER
20

The war had been hard on Lula. It deprived her of everything she cared most about: nylon stockings, chocolate ice cream—and men. Especially men. The best ones, the healthy, young, virile ones were gone. Only shits like Harley were left, so what choice did she have but to keep on getting what she needed from the big ape? But she couldn't even blackmail him anymore. In the first place there was no gas to drive to Atlanta and window-shop the way she used to—who could go *anywhere* on three measly gallons a week!—and even if she could, there was nothing in the stores worth blackmailing for. That damn Roosevelt had control of everything—no cars, no bobby pins, no hair dryers. And *nothing,* absolutely *nothing* chocolate! It was beyond Lula why every GI in Europe got so many Hershey bars they were giving them away when folks back home had to do without! She'd put up with a lot, but it took the cake when Roosevelt handed down the order dictating what flavors of ice cream could be made! How the hell did he expect a restaurant to stay in business without chocolate ice cream? And without coffee?

Lula rested a foot on the toilet lid and spread brown leg makeup from toes to thigh, riled afresh by having to do without nylons. How the hell many parachutes did they need anyway? Well, never let it be said that Lula didn't look her best, no matter what inconveniences she had to put up with. When the makeup was applied, she carefully drew a black line up the back of her leg with a "seam pencil." Dressed in bra and panties, she scooted into her bedroom, leaped onto the high bed and turned her back to the dresser mirror to check the results.

Straight as a shot of Four Feathers blended, right from the bottle!

From her closet she chose the sexiest dress she owned, orange and white jersey with enormous shoulder pads, a diamond cutout above the breast, bared knees and nice, clingy hips. One more time she'd try it, just once, and if she didn't get results this time, the high and mighty Will Parker could cut holes in his pockets and play with himself for all she cared. After all, a woman had pride.

She squirmed into the dress, tugging it over her head, then returned to the bathroom to comb out her pincurls and fashion her hair into its usual whisked-up foreknot of curls. At least she had wave-set; the curls were hard as metal springs and bounced against her forehead gratifyingly.

All zipped, made-up and perfumed, she patted her hair, posed before the mirror with hands akimbo and calves pressed close, like Betty Grable, practiced her kittenish moue, bared her teeth to check for lipstick smudges, and decided the man'd have to be out of his mind to choose Crazy Elly See over *this*!

She licked her teeth, breathed into her cupped palm, smelled her breath and dug in her purse for a packet of Sen-Sen. Damn Wrigley's right along with Roosevelt, for supplying the entire U.S. military service with free gum for the duration of the war while people out here who were willing to pay for it had to suck this rotten Sen-Sen!

But her breath was sweet, her legs sexy and her cleavage showing as she set out to bag her prey. Hot diddly, that man set her to itchin' worse than ever! An ex-Marine now with a Purple Heart—imagine that!—with a bit of a hitch still detectable in his walk. It only made him more appealing to Lula.

She'd seen him from the window of the restaurant the day

in May when he returned from the war, and she'd nearly drowned in her own saliva watching him limp up those library steps to see that old biddy, Mizz Beasley. Before he'd reached the door Lula had pressed her pubis against the backside of the counter for a little relief, and it hadn't changed since. By August she was still watching the square incessantly for mere glimpses of him, and when he wasn't in town all she had to do was think of him to get the old juices flowing. Lord, the way he'd looked in that uniform, with those crutches, and that tan, and those sultry eyes beneath the visor of his Marine dress cap. He was the best piece of flesh this town had to offer, and Lula'd have him, by God, or wrinkle up trying!

The back door of the library was unlocked. She turned the knob soundlessly. Inside, a radio played softly and a dim fog of light showed at the far end of the narrow back hall. On tiptoe Lula crept its length, paused at the end to peer into the poorly lit main room of the library. He had only one light on, and the blackout curtains drawn. A stroke of luck—privacy!

He was working with his back to her, squatting down on one knee, peering up at the underside of a table with a screwdriver in his hand, whistling along with "I Had the Craziest Dream." Lula silently slipped off her shoes, left them beside the checkout desk and crossed the room on catfeet.

Stopping close behind him, she could smell his hair tonic. It set her nostrils quivering and her private muscles twitching. As usual, Lula followed the instincts of her body, not her brain. She didn't stop to figure that you don't blind-side a jumpy ex-Marine who's fought on Guadalcanal, whose reaction time is quick, whose instincts are deadly and who's been trained in the art of survival. He looked good, he smelled good, and he was going to feel good, she thought, as with a feminine, gliding motion she moved in and began slipping her hands around his trunk.

His elbow flew back and rammed her in the gut. He lurched to his feet, spun, knocked her off-kilter, landed a deadly blow on the side of her neck and slammed her to the floor, where she slid six feet before coming to a stop wrapped around the leg of a table.

"What the hell are you doing in here!" he exploded.

Lula couldn't talk, not with the breath knocked from her.

"Get up and get out of here!"

I can't, she tried to say, but her jaws flapped soundlessly. She curled up and hugged her stomach.

War had taught Will that life was too precious to squander in any way, even a few precious moments spent with people you didn't like. He stomped over and jerked Lula roughly to her feet. "What you got to learn, Lula, is that I'm a happily married man and I don't want what you're sellin'. So get out and leave me alone!"

Doubled over, she stumbled several steps. "You . . . hit . . . me . . . you bastard!" she managed between gulps.

He had her by the hair so fast he nearly left her leg makeup on the floor.

"Don't you ever call me that!" he warned from behind clenched teeth.

"Bastard, put me down!" she screamed as he held her aloft.

Instead he raised her higher. "Whore!"

"Bastard!"

"Whore!"

"Owww! Put me down!"

He opened his hand and she fell like a piece of wet laundry.

"Git out and never come sniffin' around me again, you hear? I had enough of your kind when I was too damn dumb to know the difference! Now I got a good woman, a *good* one, you hear?" He picked her up by the front of the dress, slammed her to her feet and nudged her roughly from behind—nine times—all the way to the back door, snatching up her shoes on the way. He fired the shoes like two orange grenades into the alley, pushed her outside and offered in parting, "If you're in heat, Lula, go yowl beneath somebody else's window!"

The door slammed and the lock clicked.

Lula glared at it and hollered, "Goddamn you, you peckerhead! Just who do you think you're knockin' around!" She kicked the door viciously and sprained her big toe. Clutching it, she screamed louder, "Peckerhead! Asshole!

Toad-suckin' Marine! Your dick prob'ly wouldn't fill my left ear anyway!"

With tears and black mascara streaking her face, Lula hobbled down the steps, retrieved her shoes and limped away.

She arrived back home enraged and marched straight to the telephone.

"Seven-J-ring-two!" she yelled, then waited impatiently with the black candlestick mouthpiece tapping against her chest, the earpiece pressed above her orange flamingo-feather earring.

After two rings she heard, "H'llo?"

"Harley, this is Lula."

"Lula," he whispered warily, "I told you never to call me at home."

"I don't give a large rat's ass what you told me, Harley, so shut up and listen! I got me a hard-on that's bigger'n any you ever had and I need you to do somethin' about it, so don't say yes or no, just get in your goddamn truck and be at my house in fifteen minutes or I'll be on my bike so fast I'll leave a trail like a cyclone. And when I'm done payin' your precious Mae a little social call she won't be left wonderin' what them yellow stains on your belly was from, *comprend-ay*? Now move, Harley!"

She slammed the receiver into the prongs and nearly loosened the table legs whacking the telephone down.

Harley had little choice. The older he got the less he needed Lula. But she was dumb and ornery enough to louse things up real good between him and Mae, and he had no intention of losing Mae over a two-bit whore. No sirree. When he retired from that mill with his pockets full after this lucrative war made him rich, he intended to have Mae to bring him iced tea on the porch and his boys to go fishing with and the girls—well, hell, girls weren't much use, but they were entertaining. The oldest one was sixteen already. Another couple years and she could be married, having his grandchildren. The thought held a curious appeal for Harley. Damn Lula, she could louse it up good if she started flappin' her trap.

When he opened her door he was already yelling.

"Lula, you got no brains or what? Where the hell are you, Lula?"

Lula was sprawled on the bed, wearing her orange high heels and her orange flamingo-feather earrings and a few black and blue marks from Will Parker's hands. An ingot of incense burned on the bedside table and her lacy underpants were draped over the lampshade to cut the light.

"Lula, what the hell you mean, callin' me up and givin' me orders like I was some—"

Harley rounded her doorway and stopped yelling as if a guillotine had dropped across his tongue. Lula was touching herself with one hand, reaching toward him with the other . . .

Two months later, on a bleak day in October, Harley got another call from Lula, this time at the mill.

"Harley, it's me."

"Jesus, what's the matter with you, callin' me here! You want the whole damn world to know about us?"

"I gotta see you."

"I'm working a shift and a half today."

"I gotta see you, I said! I got somethin' important to tell you."

"I can't tonight, maybe Thurs—"

"Tonight, or I'll blurt it out on this phone with Edna Mae Simms rubbering in down at central right now—you there, Edna Mae? You gettin' all of this?"

"All right, all right!"

"Eight-fifteen, my place."

"I don't get off till—"

The phone clicked dead in Harley's hands.

When he arrived at Lula's house she was dressed in a black sheeny dressing gown patterned with cerise orchids the size of cymbals. Her hair was neatly upswept and she wore high-heeled shoes to match the orchids. They reminded Harley of one time when his mother had made him eat beets and he'd vomited afterward. Lula opened the door and closed it behind Harley with a sober snap, then turned to face him with her hands on her hips.

"Well, I'm knocked up, Harley, and it's yours. I wanna know what you're gonna do about it."

Harley looked like a bazooka had just been fired three inches from his ear. For a moment he was too stunned to speak. Lula sauntered into the parlor, chin lowered while she pressed a bobby pin into its holding place high on her head.

Bug-eyed, breathless, Harley stammered, "Kn–knocked up?"

"Yup, all yours and mine, Harleykins." She patted her stomach and flashed a sarcastic smile. "Bun in the oven."

"B–but I ain't seen you for two months, Lula!"

"Exactly, and if you'll remember, you didn't use any rubber."

"How could I when I didn't have any! Goddamn rubbers're gettin' as scarce as tires these days. It's a wonder Roosevelt hasn't got the Boy Scouts out collectin' used ones like they collect everything else!" Harley dropped to the sofa and raked a hand through his hair, muttering, "Pregnant . . . Christ."

Lula braced a stiff arm on the back of an overstuffed chair, drumming paradiddles with her hot-pink nails.

"Oughta be here about next May."

"You seen a doctor already?"

"Yup. Went to Calhoun today."

Harley jumped to his feet and paced. "Dammit, Lula, why didn't you tell me you could've got pregnant that night! This is your fault, not mine!"

Lula came to life like a kicked cobra. "My fault! Why you cheap, sniveling penny-pincher, don't you blame this on me! You've always been a great one to hump first and ask second. And I know why! 'Cause all you think of is money-money-money! Up there at the mill haulin' it in hand over fist puttin' up government contracts at time and a half overtime, and too cheap to go to the drugstore and spend a quarter! Well, don't you point fingers at me, Harley Overmire! All you'da had to do that night was take ten seconds to put one on, but no, you had to leap on me like some tomcat sniffin' pussy!"

"Now you just wait a minute, Lula. I come in here and you were sprawled out like a tomato sandwich waitin' for salt and pepper and you expect *me* to back off and *think*! You could've shut your legs for just a minute, you know!"

"Me, me, always me!" Lula yowled. "You been layin' me for six years and how many times you ever thought about it before? Huh? Answer me that, Harley! I'm always the one got to think about it—well, I get sick of it! Just once I'd like you to do the thinkin' and treat me like the lady I am and take a little time first, instead of jumpin' on me and ruttin' like a boar!"

"A boar! So now I'm a boar!"

"Don't change the subject, Harley. I said I wanna know what you're gonna do about it and I want an answer!"

"Answer—hell, where'm I supposed to get an answer?"

Lula had done some reconsidering and had come to the conclusion that Harley Overmire was better than nothing. Besides, he wasn't really so bad in bed. And at least her kid would have an old man. Lula curled four fingers and studied her nail polish for chips while suggesting, "You could leave Mae and marry me."

"Leave Mae!"

Lula's nonchalance disappeared abruptly and her mouth grew sullen. "Well, what's she to you anyway—you never even do it with her. You told me so yourself!"

"She's the mother of my children, Lula."

"Oh." Lula tapped her chest. "And what am I?"

Harley couldn't think up a fast answer.

"What am I, huh, Harley? There's one of yours breedin' in me right now, but since Mae is the mother of your children, maybe she'd like to add it to her collection, huh? How about that? How about I pay Mae a call and just happen to mention, Oh by the way, Mae, I'll have another little monkey-faced brat to add to your brood next summer. How about that, Harley? Would that suit you?"

"Lula, be reasonable—"

"Be reasonable! Be reasonable, he says, when *I'm* the one faced with disgrace and he's off rockin' on his front veranda with Mae and his *legitimate* brats. Be reasonable? I'll give you reasonable, Harley. How's this for reasonable? Two months. Two months and I'll be starting to show, and by that time I want one of two things. Either your name on a wedding license beside mine so I'll know my kid'll be provided for for the rest of his life, or ten thousand dollars in the bank, in my name, Lula Peak."

"Ten thousand dollars!"

Turning to a bevel-edged mirror on the living room wall, Lula opened her lips and edged each corner with the side of a finger. She patted her varnished topknot and added as if in afterthought, "Or I could still offer it to Mae to raise and my worries'd be over." She swung to face Harley in a shimmer of black and cerise. "Oh, well . . . " She flipped her palms up. "I never cared much for monkey-faced brats anyway."

It was not a good autumn for Harley Overmire. Lula wouldn't leave off him. He earned good money at the mill—sure—but it'd be a cold day in hell before he'd hand over ten thousand dollars to a slut like her. And she'd almost torn his face off when he'd suggested looking for a doctor to get rid of it. But worst of all, she was beginning to pester him at home, calling him in the middle of the night, at breakfast time, asking for some trumped-up name if Mae happened to answer.

She showed up at the mill one night when he was getting off at nine o'clock, just to remind him he had only four weeks left to come up with the money or the marriage. When another week passed without any progress toward a solution, she actually called Mae, giving her correct name, and told him about it afterward.

"I talked to Mae today."

"You *what?*"

"I talked to Mae today. I called her up and said I was collecting for the Red Cross and wondered if she had any donations for Care packages. She said she had buttons and soap and tablets and pencils, and that I could come over there and pick them up anytime, so I did."

"You didn't!"

"Oh, but I did! I went right over and walked up to your front door and knocked and Mae answered and we had a pleasant little chat."

"Goddammit, Lula—"

Lula's expression turned serpentine. "You see how easy it is, Harley?"

Harley developed an ulcer. The stomach pains intensified one night when he came home and looked through the mail to find Lula had brazenly directed the doctor in Calhoun to send his bill directly to Harley's house. When Mae asked what the bill was for, he told her somebody had been hurt at the mill and the bill had come to the house accidentally.

But Lula's harassment continued daily. Harley began to detest her, wondering what he'd ever seen in her in the first place. She was hard and shallow and stump-dumb to boot. To think he'd actually jeopardized his marriage over a pussy like that.

At work Harley was distracted. At home, jumpy. Everyplace else, wary. The damn woman would show up anywhere, saying anything, doing any rash thing she took a mind to do.

The corker was when she stopped his oldest boy, Ned, coming home from school one day and talked him into Vickery's to give him a free ice cream cone. Afterward, she had the gall to tell Harley what she'd done and add in a sultry voice while fussing with the ugly yellow hair of hers, "You haven't been around much, Harley. And that boy of yours is gettin' better lookin' by the day. Losin' his monkey face and growin' tall. How old is he now, Harley? Fourteen? Fifteen maybe?"

The threat was clear as that varnish she spread on her pincurls and it was the last straw. When she started in on the kids, it was time to put a stop to Lula Peak.

Harley planned it out carefully in his mind. The gift he'd left under Lula's Christmas tree would shut her up temporarily, but he'd do it right after the holiday.

It'd work. He knew Lula and what Lula craved worse than anything, and it'd work. He hadn't been deaf, dumb and blind these last couple years. The men at the mill made ribald jokes about how Lula stalked Parker, how she ogled him out the window of the restaurant and even pursued him outright at the library. But word had it Parker had never given her a tumble, so Lula'd still be itchin' to get at him.

Parker. Even the name galled Harley yet. Parker and his goddamn Purple Heart. Parker, the town hero while people sneered at Harley Overmire behind his back and accused him of cutting off his finger on purpose to avoid the draft. Not one of them could even guess what kind of courage it took to run your finger through a sawblade! And besides, *somebody* had to stay behind and make crates for all those rifles and ammo.

So you think you're a hero, eh, Parker? Hobbling into town on those crutches and parading around the square in your fancy uniform so everybody'll fall on their knees and wave banners. Well, I didn't like you the first time I clapped eyes on you, whore-killer, and I don't like you any better now. It might not've worked when I tried to run you out of town the first time, but this time it will. And it'll be the law that'll do it for me.

It took Harley three nights of scouting the library trash cans in the back alley before finding the perfect garrote: a piece of discarded shop rag filled with easily identifiable dust and lemon cleaning oil.

Once it was in his possession, Harley prepared the note carefully, selecting oversize individual words and letters from newspapers which he glued perpendicular to the typesetting on an ordinary sheet of want ads from the *Atlanta Constitution*. No stationery to identify, no fingerprints left on the greasy newsprint.

MEET ME BACK DOOR LIBRARY 11 O'CLOCK TUESDAY NIGHT. W.P.

He mailed it in a used envelope from his electricity bill, addressing it by cutting away the old address with a razor blade and fitting a newsprint address in its place.

When Lula got the note in the mail she tore it in quarters and swore like a longshoreman. Fat chance, Parker, after you knocked me around and called me a whore! Go cut holes in your pockets!

But Lula was Lula. Undeniably hot-blooded. The longer

she thought about Will Parker, the hotter she got. Big bad boy. Big tough Marine. All shoulders and legs and sulk. She loved that sulkiness and the brooding silences, too. But she'd had a taste of his temper, and if he flared like that in the middle of a good piece of sex—oooo-ee! That'd be one to remember! And another thing she'd learned—men with long earlobes usually had peckers to match, and Parker's earlobes weren't exactly miniature.

By nine o'clock Tuesday night, Lula was taping together the torn note. By nine-thirty she felt like a piece of itchweed was stuck in her pants. By ten o'clock she was in a tub full of bubbles, getting ready.

Harley Overmire hunkered in the cold December drizzle, cursing it. One thing was lucky though: the blackout was still in effect in the coastal states. No streetlights. No window lights. Nobody on the streets after ten unless they had a permit.

Come on, Lula, come on. I'm cold and damp and I wanna get home to bed.

The rear door of the library was eight feet above his head, giving onto a set of high concrete steps with an iron handrail. He'd heard Parker lock the door and leave well over half an hour ago, had sat as still as a sniper in a tree, listening to Parker's footsteps scrape down the steps, to the sound of his car starting and driving away without lights on.

Now Harley hunkered in his black rubber jacket and old fedora hat, feeling the rain seep into a tear on his shoulder. He hugged himself with crossed arms, feeling the cold concrete pressed against his back, and listened to the rain drip from the library eaves onto the alley below. In his fist the oily dustrag formed a hard knot. Something solid to hold on to.

When he heard Lula's footsteps his heart hammered like that of a coon before a pack. High heels—click . . . click . . . click . . . probably toeless, because she stepped in a puddle and cursed. He waited till she'd reached the third step, then quickly slithered around the base of the steps and up behind her.

He'd planned to do it swift, clean, anonymously. But the

damn rag was old and rotten and tore and she struggled free, turned and saw his face.

"Harley ... don't ... pl—"

And he was forced to finish the job with his hands.

He hadn't planned to see the shock and horror on her face. Or the grotesqueness of the throes of death. But no blackout was total enough to hide it. And Lula struggled, fought longer and harder than he'd have thought a woman of her size could.

When she finally succumbed, Harley staggered down the steps and threw up against the north wall of the library.

CHAPTER
21

On a day in late December, Elly was working in the kitchen when she looked up and saw Reece Goodloe pull into the yard in a dusty black Plymouth with adjustable spotlights and the official word SHERIFF on the door. He'd held office for as long as Elly could remember, since before he'd come knocking on the door of Albert See's house, forcing him to let his granddaughter go to school.

Reece had grown fat over the years. His stomach bobbed like a water balloon as he hitched up his pants on his way up the walk. His hair was thin, his face florid, his nostrils as big as a pair of hoofprints in the mud. In spite of his unattractiveness, Elly liked him: he'd been the one responsible for breaking her out of that house.

"Mornin', Mr. Goodloe," she greeted from the porch, shrugging into a homemade sweater.

"Mornin', Mizz Parker. You have a nice Christmas?"

"Yessir. And you?"

"A fine Christmas, yes we did." Goodloe scanned the clearing, the gardens neatly cleared for the winter, the junk piles gone. Things sure looked different around here since Glendon Dinsmore died.

"Your place looks good."

"Why, thank you. Will done most of it."

Goodloe took his time gazing around before he inquired, "Is he here, Mizz Parker?"

"He's down yonder in the shed, painting up some supers for the hives, getting everything ready for spring."

Goodloe rested a boot on the bottom step. "You mind fetchin' him, Mizz Parker?"

Elly frowned. "Somethin' wrong, Sheriff?"

"I just need to talk to him about a little matter come up in town last night."

"Oh . . . well . . . well, sure." She brightened with an effort. "I'll get him."

On her way through the yard Elly felt the first ominous lump form in her belly. What did he want with Will? Some sheriffing business, she was sure. His homesy chitchat was too obvious to be anything but a cover for an official call. But what? By the time she reached the open shed door, her misgivings showed plainly on her face.

"Will?"

With paintbrush in hand, Will straightened and turned, his pleasure unmistakable. "Missed me, did ya?"

"Will, the sheriff is here lookin' for you."

His grin faded, then flattened. "About what?"

"I don't know. He wants you to come to the house."

Will went stone still for ten full seconds, then carefully laid the paintbrush across the top of the can, picked up a rag and dampened it with turpentine. "Let's go." Wiping his hands, he followed her.

With each step Elly felt the lump grow bigger, the apprehension build. "What could he want, Will?"

"I don't know. But we'll find out, I reckon."

Let it be nothing, she entreated silently, let it be a carburetor for that dusty black Plymouth, or maybe Will's got his road sign on county property or they need to borrow the library chairs for a dance. Let it be somethin' silly.

She glanced at Will. He walked unhurried but unhesitant, his face revealing nothing. It wore his don't-let-'em-know-what-you're-thinking expression, which worried Elly more than a frown.

Sheriff Goodloe was waiting beside the Plymouth, with his

arms crossed over his potbelly, leaning on the front fender. Will stopped before him, wiping his hands on the rag. "Mornin', Sheriff."

Goodloe nodded and boosted off the car. "Parker."

"Somethin' I can do for you?"

"A few questions."

"Somethin' wrong?"

Goodloe chose not to answer. "You work at the library last night?"

"Yessir."

"You close it up, as usual?"

"Yessir."

"What time?"

"Ten o'clock."

"What'd you do then?"

"Came home and went to bed, why?"

Goodloe glanced at Elly. "You were home then, Mizz Parker?"

"Of course I was. We got a family, Sheriff. What's this all about, anyway?"

Goodloe ignored their questions and uncrossed his arms, firming his stance before firing his next question at Will. "You know a woman named Lula Peak?"

Will felt the anxiety begin at the backs of his knees and crawl upward—sharp needles of creeping heat. Hiding his worry, he tucked the rag into his hind pocket. "Know who she is. Wouldn't exactly say I know her, no."

"You see her last night?"

"No."

"She didn't come in the library?"

"Nobody comes in the library when I'm there. It's after hours."

"She never came there . . . after hours?"

Will's lips compressed and a muscle ticked in his jaw, but he stared squarely at Goodloe. "A couple of times she did."

Elly glanced sharply at Will. *A couple times?* Her stomach seemed to lift to her throat while the sheriff repeated the words like an obscene litany.

"A couple o'times—when was that?"

Will crossed his arms and stood spraddle-footed. "A while ago."

"Could you be more specific?"

"A couple of times before I went in the service, once since I come home. Back in August or so."

"You invited her there?"

Again Will's jaw hardened and bulged, but he exercised firm control, answering quietly, "No, sir."

"Then what was she doing there?"

Will was fully aware of Elly staring at him, dumbfounded. His voice softened with self-consciousness. "I think you can prob'ly guess, bein' a man."

"It's not my job to guess, Parker. My job is to ask questions and get answers. What was Lula Peak doing at the library in August after hours?"

Will turned his gaze directly into his wife's shocked eyes while answering, "Lookin' to get laid, I guess."

"Will . . ." she admonished breathily, her eyes rounded in dismay.

Having expected circumvention, the sheriff was momentarily nonplussed by Will's bluntness. "Well . . ." He ran a hand around the back of his neck, wondering where to go from here. "So you admit it?"

Will pulled his eyes from Elly to answer, "I admit I knew that's what she was after, not that she got it. Hell, everybody in Whitney knows what she's like. That woman prowls like a she-cat and doesn't make any effort to hide it."

"She . . . prowled after you, did she?"

Will swallowed and took his time answering. The words came out low and reluctant. "I guess you'd call it that."

"Will," Elly repeated in dull surprise. "You never told me that." Her insides felt hot and shaky.

Again he turned his brown eyes directly on her, armed only with the truth. " 'Cause it meant nothin'. Ask Miss Beasley if I ever gave that woman any truck. She'll tell you I didn't."

The sheriff interjected, "Miss Beasley saw Lula . . . shall we say, ah . . . pursuin' you?"

Will's gaze snapped back to the uniformed man. "Am I bein' accused of somethin', Sheriff? 'Cause if I am I got a right to know. And if that woman's made any charges against me, they're a damn lie. I never laid a hand on her."

"According to the record, you did a stretch in Huntsville for manslaughter—that right?"

The sick feeling began to crawl up Will's innards but outwardly he remained stoic. "That's right. I did my time and I got out on full parole."

"For killing a known prostitute."

Will fit the edges of his teeth together and said nothing.

"You'll excuse me, ma'am." The sheriff quirked an eyebrow at Elly. "But there's no way to avoid these questions." Then, to Will, "Have you ever had sexual intercourse with Lula Peak?"

Will repressed his seething anger to answer, "No."

"Did you know she was four months pregnant?"

"No."

"The child she was expecting is not yours?"

"No!"

The sheriff reached into his car and came up with a cellophane packet. "You ever seen this before?"

Standing stiffly, Will let his glance drop, examined the contents of the transparent packet without touching it. "Looks like a dustrag from the library."

"You read the newspaper regular-like, do you?"

"Newspaper. What's the newspaper—"

"Just answer the question."

"Every night when I take a break at the library. Sometimes I bring 'em home when the library's done with 'em."

"Which one you read most often?"

"What the hell—"

"Which one, Parker?"

Will grew aggravated and temper colored his face. "I don't know. Hell . . ."

"The New York Times?"

"No."

"What then?"

"What is this, Goodloe?"

"Just answer."

"All right! The *Atlanta Constitution*, I guess."

"When's the last time you saw Lula Peak?"

"I don't remember."

"Well, try."

"Earlier this week ... no, it was last week, Wednesday maybe, Tuesday—Christ, I don't remember, but it was when I drove in to work, she was locking up Vickery's when I went past on my way to the library."

"And you haven't seen her since last week, Tuesday or Wednesday?"

"No."

"But you admit you went to your job as usual last night and left for home around ten P.M.?"

"Not *around*. At. I always leave exactly at ten."

Goodloe squared his stance, giving himself a clear shot of both Will's and Elly's faces. "Lula Peak was strangled last night on the rear steps of the library. The coroner puts the time of death at somewhere between nine and midnight."

The news hit Will like a fist in the solar plexus. Within seconds he went from hot to icy, red to white. *No, not me, not this time. I paid for my crime. Goddammit, leave me alone. Leave me and my family in peace.* While the tumult of sick fear built within him, he stood unmoving, wary of reacting the wrong way lest he be misread. His stomach trembled. His palms turned damp, his throat dry. In that quick black flash of time while the sheriff threw out his bombshell, a montage of impressions wafted through Will's head, of the things he valued most—Elly, the kids, the life they'd built, the good home, the financial stability, the future, the happiness. At the thought of losing them, and unjustly, despair threatened. *Aw, Jesus, what does a man have to do to win ... ever?* He was struck by the irony of having fought and survived that miserable war only to come home to this. He thought of all else he'd survived—being orphaned, the years of lone drifting, the time in prison, the hungry days afterward, the taunts, the jeers. For what? Rage and despair slewed through him, bringing the unholy wish to sink his fist into something hard, batter something, curse the uncaring fates who time after time turned thumbs down on Will Parker.

But none of what he felt or thought showed on his face.

Dry-throated, expressionless, he asked flatly, "And you think I did it?"

The sheriff produced a second cellophane packet matching the first, this one bearing the pieces of newsprint with the cryptic message. "I got some pretty convincing evidence, Parker, starting with this right here."

Will's eyes dropped to the incriminating note, then lifted again to Goodloe before he slowly reached to take the packet and read it. A rush of hatred poured through him. For Lula Peak, who just wouldn't take no for an answer. For the person who did her in and pinned the blame on him. For this potbellied vigilante who was too stupid to reason beyond the end of his horsey nostrils.

"A man'd have to be pretty damn dumb to leave a message that clear and expect to get away with it."

Elly had been listening with growing dread, standing like one mesmerized by the sight of a venomous snake slithering closer and closer. When Will began handing the packet to Goodloe she intercepted it. "Let me see that."

MEET ME BACK DOOR LIBRARY 11 O'CLOCK TUES-DAY NIGHT. W.P. While she stood reading it the kitchen door opened and Thomas called from the porch, "Mama, Lizzy wet her pants again!"

Elly heard nothing beyond the frantic thumping of her own heart, saw nothing beyond the note and the initials, W.P. Terror rushed through her. *Oh, God, no. Not Will, not my Will.*

"Mama! Come and change Lizzy's pants!"

She fixed her thumbs over the edge of the cellophane simply for something to hang on to, something to steady her careening world. From the recent past she heard again Will's voice admitting things that she wished now she had never heard ... *We used to go down to La Grange to the whorehouse there ... Me, I wasn't fussy, take any one that was free ... I picked up a bottle ... She went down like a tree and hardly even bled, she died so fast ...*

For a moment Elly closed her eyes, gulping, unable to swallow the lump of fear that suddenly congealed in her throat. Was it possible? Could he have done it again? She opened her eyes and stared at her thumbs; they felt weighty and thrice their size as shock controlled her system.

Will watched the reactions claim his wife. He watched her struggle for control, watched her momentarily lose and regain it. When she lifted her eyes they were like two dull stones in a face like bleached linen.

"Will . . . ?"

Though she spoke only his name, the single word was like a rusty blade in his heart.

Oh, Elly, Elly, not you, too. They could all think whatever they wanted, but she was his wife, the woman he loved, the one who'd given him reason to change, to fight, to live, to plan, to make something better of himself. She thought him *capable* of a thing like this?

After a life filled with disappointments, Will Parker should have been inured to them. But nothing—nothing had ever reduced him like this moment. He stood before her vanquished, wishing that he had been in that foxhole with Red, wishing he'd never walked into this clearing and met the woman before him and been given false hope.

On the porch a door slammed and Thomas called, "Mama, what's wrong?"

Elly didn't hear him. "W–Will?" she whispered again, her eyes wide, her throat hot and tight.

Aggrieved, he turned away.

The sheriff reached to the back of his belt for a pair of handcuffs and spoke authoritatively. "William Parker, it's my duty to inform you that you're under arrest for the murder of Lula Peak."

The awful reality hit Elly full force. Tears squirted into her wide, frightened eyes, and she pressed a fist to her lips. It was all happening so fast! The sheriff, the accusation, the handcuffs. The sight of them sent another sickening bolt through Elly.

At that moment Thomas eased up behind his mother. "Mama, what's the sheriff doing here?"

She could only stand gaping, unable to answer.

But Will knew all about hurtful childhood memories and wanted none for Thomas. As the sheriff pulled his left arm back and snapped the cuff on, Will ordered quietly, "Thomas, you go see after Lizzy P., son." He stood woodenly, waiting for the second metallic click, cringing inside, thinking, *Dammit, Goodloe, at least you could wait till the boy goes back in the house!*

But Thomas had seen too many cowboy movies to misinterpret what was happening. "Mama, is he takin' Will to jail?"

Taking Will to jail? Elly suddenly came out of her stupor, incensed. "You can't just . . . just take him!"

"He'll be in the county jail in Calhoun until bail is set."

"But what about—"

"He might need a jacket, ma'am."

A jacket? She could scarcely think beyond the frantic churning in her head that ordered, Stop him somehow! Stop him! But she didn't know how, didn't know her rights or Will's. Tears slid down Elly's cheeks as she stood by dumbly.

"Mama . . ." Thomas began crying, too. He ran to Will, clutched at his waist. "Will, don't go."

The sheriff pried the boy off. "Now, young man, you'd best go in the house."

Thomas swung on him, pummeling with both fists. "You can't take Will! I won't let you! Git away from him!"

"Take him in the house, Mizz Parker," the sheriff ordered in an undertone.

Thomas fought like a dervish, swinging, fending off their efforts to calm or remove him.

"Get in the car, Parker."

"Just a minute, sheriff, please . . ." Will went down on one knee and Thomas threw himself on the man's sturdy neck.

"Will . . . Will . . . he can't take you, can he? You're a good guy, like Hopalong."

Will swallowed and turned entreating eyes up to Goodloe. "Take the cuffs off for a minute—please." Goodloe drew in a deep, unsteady breath and glanced at Elly sheepishly. At his hesitation, Will's anger erupted. "I'm not runnin' anyplace, Goodloe, and you know it!" The sheriff's distraught gaze fell to the boy sobbing against Will's neck and he followed his gut instincts, freeing one of Will's wrists. Will's arms curled around Thomas, the metal cuff dangling down the boy's narrow back. Closing his eyes, Will clutched the small body and spoke softly against Thomas's hair. "Yeah, you're right, short stuff. I'm a good guy, like Hopalong. Now you remember that, okay? And just remember I love you. And when Donald Wade gets home from school tell him I love him, too, okay?"

He pushed Thomas back, wiped the child's streaming face with the knuckles of his uncuffed hand. "Now you be good and go in the house, and help your mother take care of Lizzy. You do that for old Will, all right?"

Thomas nodded meekly, studying the ground at Will's knee. Will turned him around and gave him a push on his backside. "Now, go on."

Thomas ran around his mother, sobbing, and a moment later the screen door slammed. Elly watched Will stretch to his feet, his image a blur beyond her streaming eyes. With a wooden face he willingly put both hands behind himself and allowed the sheriff to snap the cuffs in place once more.

"Will—oh, Will—what—oh, God . . ." Elly moved at last, but her speech and motion patterns had turned jerky. She cast her gaze around like a demented thing, reaching out a hand, pacing like a wild animal the first time it's caged, as if not fully comprehending its inability to change a situation. "Sheriff . . ." She touched his sleeve but he ignored her plea, tending his prisoner. Abruptly she veered to her husband. "Will . . ." She grasped him, clutching the back of his shirt, her wet cheek pressed to his dry one. "Will—they can't t–take you!"

Unbending he stared straight ahead, and ordered coldly, "Let's go."

"No, wait!" Elly cried, overwrought, turning beetlelike from one man to the other, "Sheriff—couldn't you—what's going to happen to him—wait—I'll get his jacket . . ." Belatedly she ran to the house, not knowing what else to do, returned panicked, to find both men already in the Plymouth. She tried the back door but it was locked, the windows up.

"Will!" she cried, pressing the jacket to the glass, already realizing what had caused his cold indifference, already repentant, needing to do something to show she'd been hasty and had reacted without conscious thought. "Here—here I b–brought your jacket! Please, take it!" But he wouldn't look at her as she pressed the denim against the glass.

The sheriff said, "Here, I'll take it," and hauled it in through his window and handed her, in exchange, the paint rag on which Will had earlier wiped his hands. "Best thing you can do, Mizz Parker, is get a lawyer." He put the car in gear.

"But I don't know no lawyers!"

"Then he'll get a public defender."

"But when can I see him?" she called as the Plymouth began to move.

"When you get a lawyer!"

The car pulled away, leaving Elly in a swirl of exhaust with her hand reaching entreatingly.

"Will!" she cried after the departing vehicle. She watched it carry him away, his head visible through the rear window. She twisted her fingers into the smelly rag and covered her mouth with it, hunched forward, breathing its turpentine fumes, fighting panic, staring aghast at the empty driveway.

The jail was in a stone building styled much like a Victorian house, situated just behind the courthouse where Will had gotten married. He held himself aloof from emotion during the booking procedure, the frisking, the walk down the echoing corridor, the cold metallic clang of the iron door.

He lay in his cell facing a gray wall, smelling the fetid odors of old urine and pine-scented disinfectant, on a stale-smelling pillow and a stained mattress, with ink on his fingertips and his belt confiscated and dullness in his eyes and the familiarity of his surroundings consciously shut out. He thought about hunkering in a ball but had no will to do so. He thought about crying but lacked the heart. He thought about asking for food, but hunger mattered little when life mattered not at all. His life had lost value in the moment when his wife looked at him with doubt in her eyes.

He thought about fighting the charges—but for what? He was tired of fighting, so damned tired. It seemed he'd been fighting his whole life, especially the last two years—for Elly, for a living, for respect, for his country, for his own dignity. And just when he'd gained them all, a single questioning stare had undone him. Again. When would he learn? When would he stop thinking he could ever matter to anyone the way some people mattered to him? Fool. Ass. Stupid *bastard*! He absorbed the word, with all its significance, rubbed it in like salt in a wound, willfully multiplying his hurt for some obscure reason he did not understand. Because he was unlovable after all, because his entire life had proved him so and it seemed the unlovable ones like himself were put on this world to accumulate all the hurts that the lucky, the loved, magically missed. She couldn't love him or she'd have jumped to his defense as thoughtlessly as Thomas had. Why? Why? What did he lack? What more must he prove? *Bastard*, Parker! When you gonna grow up and realize that you're alone in this world? Nobody fought for you when you were born, nobody'll fight for you now, so give up. Lay here in the stink of other men's piss and realize you're a loser. Forever.

In a clearing before a house on Rock Creek Road Eleanor Parker watched the law haul her husband off to jail and knew a terror greater than the fear of her own death, a desperation sharper than physical pain, and self-reproach more overpowering than the rantings of her own fire-and-brimstone grandfather.

She knew before the car disappeared into the trees that she had made one of the gravest mistakes in her life. It had lasted only a matter of seconds, but that's all it had taken to turn Will icy. She had seen and felt his withdrawal like a cold slap in the face. And it was entirely her fault. She could well imagine what he was suffering as he rode to town with his hands shackled: desolation and despair, all because of her.

Well, blast it, she was no saint nor seraph! So she'd reacted in shock. Who in tarnation wouldn't? Will Parker could no more kill Lula Peak than he could Lizzy P., and Elly knew it.

The fire-and-brimstone blood of Albert See suddenly leaped in her veins where it had been slogging since her birth, waiting a chance to flow hot for a cause. And what a cause—the love of her man. She'd spent too long finding it, had been too happy enjoying it, had changed too beneficially under its influence to lose it, and him, now.

So she straightened her spine, cursed roundly and turned her terror into energy, her despair into determination and her self-reproach into a promise.

I'll get you out of there, Will. And by the time I'm done you'll know that what you saw in my eyes for that piddly instant didn't mean nothing. It was human. I am human. So I made a mistake. Now watch me unmake it!

"Thomas, get your jacket!" Elly shouted, slamming into the house with yard-long strides. "And three extra diapers for Lizzy P. And run down in the cellar and fetch up six jars of honey—no, eight, just in case! We're goin' to town!"

She grabbed ration coupons, a peach crate for the honey, a tin of oatmeal cookies, a jar of leftover soup, Lizzy (wet pants and all), a skeleton key, and a pillow to help her see over the steering wheel. Within five minutes that wheel was shuddering in her hands, which were white-knuckled with fright. But fright wouldn't stop Elly now.

She had driven only a few times before, and those around the yard and down the orchard lane. She nearly broke three necks shifting for the first time, felt certain she'd kill herself and her two young ones before she reached the end of the driveway. But she reached it just fine and made a wide right turn, missed the far ditch and corrected her course without mishap. Sweat oozed from her pores, but she gripped the wheel harder and *drove*! She did it for Will, and for herself, and for the kids who loved Will better than popcorn or movie shows or Hopalong Cassidy. She did it because Lula Peak was a lying, laying, no-good whore, and a woman like that shouldn't have the power to drive a wedge between a husband and wife who'd spent damn near two years showing each other what they meant to one another. She did it because someplace in Whitney was a scum-suckin' skunk who'd done Lula in and wasn't going to get by with pinning the blame on *her* man! Nossir! Not if she had to drive this damned car clear to Washington, D.C., to see justice done.

She dropped Thomas, Lizzy P., the cookies and the soup at Lydia's house with only a terse explanation: "They've ar-

rested Will for the murder of Lula Peak and I'm goin' to hire
a lawyer!" She drove at fifty bone-rattling miles an hour the
rest of the way into town, past the square and out to the
schoolhouse on the south side, where she flattened ten yards
of grass before coming to a stop with the left front tire crushing a newly planted rosebush that the second-grade teacher,
Miss Natalie Pruitt, had brought from her mother's garden to
beautify the stark schoolground. Elly left word that Donald
Wade was to get off the bus at Lydia Marsh's place, then
backtracked to the library and accidentally drove the car up
onto the sidewalk, parking. There it stayed, blocking pedestri-
ans, while she ran inside and told the news to Miss Beasley.

"That piss-ant Reece Goodloe come out to the house and
arrested Will for killing Lula Peak. Will you help me find a
lawyer?"

What followed proved that if one woman in love can move
mountains, two can turn tides. Miss Beasley outright plucked
the books from the hands of two patrons, ordering, "The library's closing, you'll have to leave." Her coat flew out behind her like a flag in high wind as she followed Elly to the
door, already advising.

"He should have the best."

"Just tell me who."

"We'd need to get to Calhoun somehow."

"I drove to Whitney, I can drive to Calhoun."

Miss Beasley suffered a moment's pause when she observed the Model A with its radiator cap twelve inches from
the brick wall. The town constable came running down the
sidewalk at that moment, shaking his fist over his head.
"Who in the sam hell parked that thing up there!"

Miss Beasley poked ten fingers in his chest and pushed
him back. "Shut up, Mr. Harrington, and get out of our way
or I'll tell your wife how you ogle the naked aborigines in the
back issues of *National Geographic* every Thursday afternoon when she thinks you're downstairs checking the Ten
Most Wanted posters. Get in, Eleanor. We've wasted enough
time." When both women were in the car, bumping back
down the curb, Miss Beasley craned around and advised in
her usual unruffled, demogogic tone, "Careful for Norris and

Nat, Eleanor, they do a great service for this town, you know." Down the curb they went, across the street and up the opposite curb, nearly shearing the pair of octogenarians off their whittling bench before Elly gained control and put the car in first. Miss Beasley's breasts whupped in the air like a spaniel's ears as the car jerked forward, sped around a corner at twenty miles an hour and came to a lurching halt beside the White Eagle gas pump on the adjacent side of the square. Four ration coupons later Elly and Miss Beasley were on their way to Calhoun.

"Mr. Parker is innocent, of course," Miss Beasley stated unequivocally.

"Of course. But that woman came to the library chasin' him, didn't she? That's gonna look bad for him."

"Hmph! I got a thing or two to tell your lawyer about that!"

"Which lawyer we gettin'?"

"There *is* only one if you want to win. Robert Collins. He has a reputation for winning, and has had since the spring he was nineteen and brought in the wild turkey with the biggest spear and the longest beard taken that season. He hung them on the contest board at Haverty's drugstore beside two dozen others entered by the oldest and most experienced hunters in Whitney. As I recall, they'd given Robert short shrift, smiling out the sides of their mouths at the idea that a mere boy could outdo any one of them—big talkers, those turkey hunters, always practicing their disgusting gobbles when a girl walked by on the street, then laughing when she jumped half out of her skin. Well, Robert won that year—the prize, as I recall, being a twelve-gauge shotgun donated by the local merchants—and he's been winning ever since. At Dartmouth where he graduated top in his class. Two years later when he took on an unpopular case and won restitution for a young black boy who lost his legs when he was pushed into the paddlewheel of a gristmill where he worked, by the owner of the mill. The owner was white, and needless to say, an unbiased jury was hard to find. But Robert found one, and made a name for himself. After that he prosecuted a woman from Red Bud who killed her own son with a garden hoe to keep him from marrying a girl who wasn't Baptist. Of course, Robert had every Baptist in the county writing him poison pen letters declaring that he was maligning the entire religious sect. The church deacons were on his back, even his own minister—Robert is Baptist himself—because as it turned out, the murderess was a fervent churchgoer who'd almost single-handedly bulldozed the community into scraping up funds for a new stone church after a tornado blew the clapboard one down. A *do-goodah*," Miss Beasley added disparagingly. "You know the type." She paused for a brief breath and continued intoning, "In any event, Robert prosecuted her case and won, and ever since, he's been known as a man who won't knuckle under to social pressures, a defender of underdogs. An honorable man, Robert Collins."

Elly recognized him immediately. He was the one who'd come out of chambers in intense conversation with Judge Murdoch on Elly's wedding day. But she had little opportunity to nurse the memory before becoming distracted by the surprising opening exchange between the lawyer and Miss Beasley.

"Beasley, my secretary said, and I asked myself could it be Gladys Beasley?" He crossed the crowded, cluttered anteroom in an unhurried shuffle, extending a skinny hand.

"It could be and is. Hello, Robert."

Clasping her hand in both of his, he chuckled, showing yellowed teeth edged with gold in a wrinkled elf's face surrounded by springy hair the color of old cobwebs. "Forever formal, aren't you? The only girl in school who called me Robert instead of Bob. Are you still stamping books at the Carnegie Library?"

"I am. Are you still shooting turkeys on the Red Bone Ridge?"

Again he laughed, tipping back, still clasping her hand. "I am. Bagged a twenty-one-pound tom my last time out."

"With an eleven-inch beard, no doubt, and an inch-long spur, which you hung on the drugstore wall to put the old-timers in their places."

Once more his laughter punctuated their exchange. "With a memory like that you'd have made a good lawyer."

"I left that to you though, didn't I, because girls were not encouraged to take up law in those days."

"Now, Gladys, don't tell me you still hold a grudge because I was asked to give the valedictory speech?"

"Not at all. The best man won." Abruptly she grew serious. "Enough byplay, Robert. I've brought you a client, vastly in need of your expert services. I should take it as a personal favor if you'd help her, or more precisely, her husband. This is Eleanor Parker. Eleanor, meet Robert Collins."

Meeting his handshake with one of her own, Elly inquired, "You got a wife, Mr. Collins?"

"No, I don't, not anymore. She died a few years back."

"Oh. Well, then this is for you."

"For me," he repeated, pleased, accepting the quart of honey, holding it high.

"And there's more where that came from, plus milk and pork and chickens and eggs for the duration of this war and without rationing coupons, to go along with whatever money you need to clear Will's name."

He laughed again, examining the honey. "Might this be construed as bribery, do you think, Gladys?"

"Construe it any way you like, but try it on a bran muffin. It's indescribable."

He turned, carrying the honey into his messy office, inviting, "Come in, both of you, and close the door so we can talk. Mizz Parker, as for my fee, we'll get to that later after I decide whether or not I can take the case."

Seated in his office, Elly quickly assured Robert Collins, "Oh, I got money, Mr. Collins, never fear. And I know where I can get more."

"From me," put in Miss Beasley.

Elly's head snapped around. "From you!" she repeated, surprised.

"We're digressing, Eleanor, on Robert's valuable time," returned Miss Beasley didactically. "We'll discuss it later. Alone."

It didn't take fifteen minutes for Robert Collins to ascertain the few facts known by the women and inform them that he'd be at the jail as soon as possible to talk to Will and make his decision about defending him.

Before that hour was up, Elly herself was standing in Sheriff Goodloe's office with another jar of honey in her hand. He was deep in conversation with his deputy but looked up as she entered. Straightening, he began, "Now, Elly, I told you at your house you can't see him till you got a lawyer."

She set the jar of honey on his desk. "I came to apologize." She looked him soberly in the eyes. "About an hour ago I called you a piss-ant when actually I've always had a fair deal of respect for you. I always meant to thank you for gettin' me out of that house I grew up in, but this's the first chance I got." She gestured toward the honey. "That's for that. It's got nothin' to do with Will, but I want to see him."

"Elly, I told you—"

"I know what you told me, but I thought about what kind of laws they are that let you lock up a person without letting him explain to people what really happened. I know all about being locked up like that. It ain't fair, Mr. Goodloe, and you know it. You're a fair man. You were the only person ever stood up for me when they kept me in that house and let the whole town think I was crazy because of it. Well, I ain't. The crazy ones are the ones who make laws that keep a wife from seeing her husband when he's in the pit of despair, which is what my Will is right now. I'm not askin' you to open his door or put us in a private room. I'm not even askin' you to leave us alone. All I'm askin' is what's fair."

Goodloe glanced from her to the honey. He plopped tiredly into his chair and ran his hands over his face in frustration. "Now, dang it, Elly, I got regulations—"

"Aw, let her talk to him," the deputy interrupted, fixing a slight smile on Elly. "What's it gonna hurt?" Sheriff Goodloe swung a glance at the younger man, who shrugged and added, "She's right and you know it. It's not fair." Then, to Elly's surprise, the younger man came forward, extending a hand. "Remember me? Jimmy Ray Hess. We were in fifth grade together. Speaking of fair, I'm one of those who used to call you names, and if you can apologize, so can I."

Astounded, she shook his hand.

"Jimmy Ray Hess," she repeated in wonder. "Well, I'll be."

"That's right." He proudly thumbed the star on his shirt. "Deputy sheriff of Gordon County now." In friendly fashion he swung back to his superior. "What d'you say, Reece—can she see him?"

Reece Goodloe succumbed and flapped a hand. "Aw, hell, sometimes I wonder who's the boss around here. All right, take her in."

The deputy beamed and led the way from the office. "Come along, Elly, I'll show you the way."

Walking along beside Jimmy Ray, Elly felt her faith in mankind restored. She counted those who'd helped her today—Lydia, Miss Beasley, Robert Collins, and now Jimmy Ray Hess.

"Why are you doing this, Jimmy Ray?" she asked.

"Your husband—he was a Marine, wasn't he?"

"That's right—First Raiders."

Jimmy Ray flashed her a crooked grin oozing with latent pride. "Gunnery Sergeant Jimmy Ray Hess, Charlie Company, First Marines, at your service, ma'am." Giving her a smart salute, he opened the last door leading into the jail. "Third on the left," he advised, then closed the door, leaving her alone in the corridor fronting a long row of cells.

She had never been in a jail before. It was dank and dismal. It echoed and smelled bad. It dampened the spirits momentarily lifted by Jimmy Ray Hess.

Even before she reached Will her heart hurt. When she saw him, curled on his cot with his back to the bars, it was like looking at herself on her knees in that place, praying forgiveness for something she didn't do.

"Hello, Will," she said quietly.

Startled, he glanced over his shoulder, carefully schooling all reaction, then faced the wall again. "I thought they weren't gonna let you in here."

Elly felt as if her heart would break. "That what you wanted?" When he refused to answer, she added, "Reckon I know why."

Will swallowed and stared at the wall, feeling a clot of

emotion fill his throat. "Go on, get out of here. I don't want you to see me in here."

"Neither do I, but now that I have, I got some questions need asking."

Coldly he said to the wall, "Yeah, like did I kill that bitch. Was I carrying on with her." He laughed mirthlessly, then threw over his shoulder: "Well, you can just go on wondering, because if that's all the faith you have in me, I don't need your kind of wife."

Remorse spread its hot charges through Elly. With it came sudden, stinging tears. "Why didn't you tell me about her, Will, back when it happened, when she came to the library? If you had, it wouldn't've been such a surprise to me today."

Abruptly he swung to his feet and confronted her with fists balled and veins standing out sharply on his throat. "I shouldn't have to tell you I *didn't* do things! You should know by what I *do do* what kind of man I am! But all you had to hear was one word from that sheriff to think I was guilty, didn't you? I saw it in your eyes, Elly, so don't deny it."

"I won't," she whispered, ashamed, while he took up a frenzied pacing, driving a hand through his streaked yellow hair.

"Christ, you're my wife! Do you know what it did to me when you looked at me that way, like I was some—some murderer?"

She had never seen him angry before, nor so desolate. More than anything she wanted to touch him, reassure him, but he paced back and forth between the side walls like a penned animal, well out of reach. She closed her hand over a black iron bar. "Will, I'm sorry. But I'm human, ain't I? I make mistakes like anybody else. But I came here to unmake 'em and to tell you I'm sorry it crossed my mind you coulda done it 'cause it didn't take me three minutes after they took you away to realize you couldn't of. Not you—not my Will."

Coming to an abrupt halt, Will pinned her with damning brown eyes. His hair stood disheveled. His fists were still knotted as he and Elly faced off, doing silent battle while he fought the urge to rush across the cell and touch her, crush her hands beneath his on the iron bars, draw from her the sustenance he needed to face the night, and tomorrow, and whatever fight lay ahead. But the hurt within him was still too engulfing. So he returned in a cold, bitter voice, "Yeah, well, you were three minutes too late, Elly, cause I don't care what you think anymore." It was a lie which hurt him as badly as it hurt her. He saw the shock riffle across her face and steeled himself against rushing to her with an apology, taking her face between his hands and kissing her between the bars that separated them.

"You don't mean that, Will," she whispered through trembling lips.

"Don't I?" he shot back, telling himself to disregard the tears that made her wide green eyes look bright as dew-kissed grass. "I'll leave you to go home and wonder, just like I laid here and wondered if *you* meant it!"

For several inescapable seconds, while their hearts thundered, they stared at each other, hurting, loving, fearful. Then she swallowed and dropped her hand from the bar, stepped back and spoke levelly. "All right, Will, I'll leave if that's what you want. But first just answer me one question. Who do you think killed her?"

"I don't know." He stood like a ramrod, too stubborn to take the one step necessary to end this self-imposed hell. *Don't go, I didn't mean it, I don't know why I said it . . . oh, God, Elly, I love you so much.*

"If you wanna see me, tell Jimmy Ray Hess. He'll get word to me."

Only when she was gone did he relent. Tears came as he spun to the wall, pressing fists and forearms high against it, burying his thumb knuckles hard in his eyesockets. *Elly, Elly—don't believe me! I care so much what you think of me that I'd rather be dead than have you see me in this place.*

Miss Beasley had obligingly waited in the car. Returning to it, Elly looked pale and shaken.

"What is it, Eleanor?"

Elly stared woodenly out the windshield. "I did Will wrong," she answered dully.

"Did him wrong? Why, whatever are you talking about?"

"When the sheriff came out to our place and said Lula Peak was dead. You see, it crossed my mind for just a minute that Will might have done it. I didn't say so, but I didn't have to. Will saw it in my face, and now he won't talk to me." Elly tightened her lips to keep her chin from shaking.

"Won't talk to you, but—"

"Oh, he yelled some, got it off his chest how much I hurt him. But he stayed clear across the cell and wouldn't take my hand or smile or anything. He said it didn't matter to him anymore what I th–think." She covered her eyes and dropped her head.

Miss Beasley grew incensed at Will's callousness and took Elly's shoulder.

"Now you listen here, young woman. You didn't do anything that any normal human being wouldn't have done."

"But I should've trusted him better!"

"So you experienced a moment of doubt. Any woman would have done the same."

"But you didn't!"

"Don't be an imbecile, Eleanor. Of course I did."

Surprise brought Elly's head up. Though her eyes were streaming, she swiped at them with a sleeve. "You did?"

"Well, of course I did," Gladys lied. "Who wouldn't? Half of this town will. It means we shall only have to fight harder to prove they're wrong."

Miss Beasley's staunchness suddenly put starch in Elly's spine. She sniffed and mopped her eyes. "That durn husband of mine wouldn't even tell me if he suspected anybody." With the return of control, Elly began rationalizing. "Who could've done it, Miss Beasley? I got to find out somehow. That's the only way I know to get Will back. Who should I start with?"

"How about Norris and Nat? They've been sitting on that park bench for years, watching Lula Peak point her bodice at anything in pants that came along the sidewalk. I'm sure they'd know down to the exact second how long it took her to follow Mr. Parker into the library every time he brought me eggs, and also how long it took her to come back out looking like a singed cat."

"They would?"

"Of course they would."

Elly digested the idea, then had one of her own. "And they're in charge of the town guard, aren't they?"

Miss Beasley's face lit with excitement. "Prowling around town at night, listening for airplane engines, looking through binoculars and checking blackout curtains."

Elly tossed her a hopeful glance, tinged with anticipation. "And chasing curfew violators off the streets?"

"Exactly!"

Elly started the engine. "Let's go."

They found Norris and Nat MacReady soaking up the late afternoon sun on their usual bench in the square. Each received a quart jar of pure gold Georgia honey in exchange for which they gladly revealed the startling details of an overheard conversation behind the library one night last January. They had been together so long they might have had a single brain at work between them, for what one began, the other finished.

"Norris and I," Nat said, "were walking along Comfort Street and had turned up the alley behind the library—where the podocarpus bushes grow by the incinerator—"

"—when a high-heeled shoe sailed out and clunked me on the shoulder. Nat can testify to the fact—"

" 'Cause he had a purple bruise there for well over four weeks."

"Now, Nat," chided Norris, "you might be stretching it a bit. I don't think it was over three."

Nat bristled. "Three! Your memory is failing, boy. It was there a full four, 'cause if you'll recall, I commented on it the day we—"

"Gentlemen, gentlemen!" interrupted Miss Beasley. "The conversation you overheard."

"Oh, that. Well, first the shoe flew—"

"Then we heard young Parker beller loud enough to wake the entire town—"

" 'If you're in heat, Lula, go yowl beneath somebody else's window!' That's exactly what he said, wasn't it, Nat?"

"Sure was. Then the door slams and Miss Lula—"

"—madder than Cooter Brown—pounds on it and calls young Parker a name that you ladies are free to read from our logbook if you like but one that—"

"Logbook?"

"That's right. But neither Norris nor myself would care to repeat it, would we, Norris?"

"Most certainly not, not in the company of ladies. Tell 'em what happened next, Nat."

"Well, then Miss Lula yelled that young Will's—ahem—" Nat cleared his throat while searching for a genteel euphemism. But it was Norris who came up with it.

"—his, ahh, *male part*"—the words were whispered— "probably wouldn't fit into Lula's ear anyway."

Almost simultaneously, Miss Beasley and Elly demanded, "Did you tell this to the sheriff?"

"The sheriff didn't ask. Did he, Norris?"

"No, he didn't."

Which gave Elly the idea about running an ad in the newspaper. After all, running an ad had brought results before. Why wouldn't it again? But Miss Beasley's ankles were swollen, so Elly took her home before returning to the *Whitney Register* office to rid herself of another quart of honey as payment for the ad which stated simply that E. Parker, top of Rock Creek Road, would pay a reward for any information leading to the dropping of charges against her husband, William L. Parker, in the Lula Peak murder case. To her amazement, the editor, Michael Hanley, didn't bat an eye, only thanked her for the honey and wished her luck, ending, "That's a fine young man you married there, Mizz Parker. Went off and fought like a man instead of runnin' his finger through a buzzsaw like some in this town."

Which sparked the memory of Harley Overmire's long-ago antagonism toward Will and made Elly wonder briefly if it were worth mentioning to either Reece Goodloe or Robert Collins. But she hadn't time to dwell on it, for from the newspaper office Elly proceeded directly to the office of Pride Real Estate, where she unceremoniously slapped a heavy nickel skeleton key on the counter, followed by yet another quart of honey and announced to Hazel Pride, "I want to list some property." Hazel Pride's husband was fighting "somewhere in the south of France" and had left her to manage the paper while he was gone. She had typeset every word about Will Parker's heroism and his Purple Heart, so greeted Elly affably and said it was a shame about Mr. Parker, and if there was anything Hazel could do, just let her know. After all, Will Parker was a veteran with a Purple Heart, and no veteran who'd been through so much should be treated the way he'd been. Would Eleanor care to ride in Hazel's car out to the house?

Elly declined, following Hazel in her own car through the chill of a late-winter afternoon. The morning glory vines were dry and leafless around the front door, woven into a thick mesh of neglected growth. The grass was the color of twine. The two cars flattened it while pulling around to the back door.

Of all the things Elly had done that day, none was as difficult as entering that dreary house with Hazel Pride, walking into the murky shadows behind those hated green shades, past the spot in the front parlor where she'd prayed, past the corner where her grandmother had died on a hard kitchen chair, past the bedroom where her mother had gone slowly insane, smelling the dry bat droppings from the attic, mixed with dust and mildew and bad memories. It was hard, but Elly did it. Not just because she needed the money to pay Robert Collins but because she'd come so far in one day she figured she might as well go the rest of the way. Also, she knew it would please Will.

In the parlor she snapped up the shades, one after the other, letting them whirl and flap on their surprisingly tensile springs. The sunset poured in, revealing nothing more frightening than dust motes swimming through the stale air of an abandoned house with mouse leavings on the linoleum floor.

"Two thousand, three hundred," Hazel Pride announced, tapping her tablet. "Top listing price, considering the work that would be necessary to make the place livable again."

Twenty-three hundred dollars would more than pay Collins' bill, Elly figured, and leave extra for the rewards she hoped to pay. She insisted on signing the paper there, inside the house, so that when she walked out she'd be free of it forever.

And she was. As she climbed back into Will's car and drove through the hub-high grass of the deep twilit yard to the road, she felt relieved, absolved.

She thought about the day, the fears she had put to rout simply by attacking them head-on. She had driven a car clear to Calhoun for the first time, had confronted a town that seemed no longer intimidating but supportive, had set into motion the machinery of justice and had shed the ghosts of her past.

She was tired. So tired she wanted to pull the car into the next field-access road and drop off till morning.

But Will was still in jail and every minute there must seem like a year to him. So she drove clear back to Calhoun to find Sheriff Goodloe, give him hell about his slipshod methods of investigation and put him onto Norris and Nat MacReady's logbook. She forgot, however, to mention Harley Overmire.

CHAPTER
22

Will lay on his bunk in a cocoon of misery. From up the corridor came the chiming reverberations of a metal door opening and closing. He remained inert, staring at the wall. Footsteps came closer. One pair, two pair. Leather shoes on concrete, a familiar sound, too familiar.

"Parker?" It was the voice of Deputy Hess. "Your lawyer's here."

Will started. "My *lawyer*?" His head came off the pillow and he craned his neck around.

With young Hess stood an older man with flyaway gray hair and tanned skin; slightly stooped, dressed in a brown suit and a rumpled white shirt with a tie knotted at half-mast. "Your wife came to see me, asked me to come have a talk with you."

Will swung onto the edge of his bunk. "My wife?"

"And Gladys Beasley." The guard unlocked the door and the lawyer ambled inside, extending a hand. "Name's Bob Collins." He waited, peering at Will with gray eyes that appeared perennially amused, as if accustomed to introducing himself to surprised inmates.

"Will Parker." Rising, accepting the handshake, Will thought, *She not only came to Calhoun, she hired a lawyer, too?*

But what kind of lawyer? His suit looked as if it had been washed in a washing machine; his shirt looked as if it hadn't. His hair stood on end like a dandelion gone to seed, an occasional tuft lifted above the rest as if ready to fly at the smallest puff of wind. He was not only disheveled, but moved with a tired slowness that made Will wonder if he'd suddenly rusted up halfway onto his chair. There he hung, backside pointed in the right direction while Will counted the seconds—one, two, three—and finally the old duffer sat, expelling a breath and clasping one bony knee with an equally bony hand. When he finally spoke, his jocular tone of voice was one suited to a speech honoring the outgoing president of the lady's horticultural society. "I went to school with Gladys Beasley. There was a question for a while about which of us would be named valedictorian. It was always my opinion they should have named two that year." He chuckled as if to himself, resting a finger along his jaw. "Gladys Beasley, after all these years—can you beat that?" He glanced up with a hint of devilment in his eyes. "She was a damned fine-lookin' woman. And smart, too. Only one in the whole class who could discuss anything more intelligent than the length of hems and the height of heels. Used to scare the daylights out of me, she was so bright. Always wanted to ask her on a date, can't really say why I never did."

Will sat befuddled, wondering why Gladys Beasley would recommend a creaky old fart like this. In his dotage, smelling like the inside of a mummy's wrappings, and with a wandering, maundering mind. Will wondered if he might be better off defending himself.

But just when Will's opinions crystallized, Collins threw him a curveball.

"So, Will Parker, did you kill Lula Peak or not?"

Will fixed his brown eyes on Collins' faded gray ones and replied unequivocally, "No, sir."

Collins nodded thrice almost imperceptibly, studied Will silently for a full fifteen seconds before asking, "You got any idea who did?"

"Nossir."

Again came the lengthy silence that gave the impression

rusty machinery needed oiling inside Collins' scruffy head. But when he spoke, Will was somehow relieved. "Then we have work to do. The arraignment is set for tomorrow."

Collins took the case, promising to apply pressure to every possible quarter in an effort to get it through the courts fast. He was very good, he said, at applying pressure. Will didn't believe him. Yet in spite of his constant half-rumpled appearance and his surface slowness—he had a habit of tugging an earlobe, crossing his arms and pausing as if confused—he was bright, thorough, and totally unimpressed with the prosecution's case. Furthermore, he was convinced that he could gain a jury's sympathy by implying that the law had pounced on Will primarily because of his prison record when it was his war record they ought to bear in mind. He gave little credence to the note bearing Will's initials, even believed it might prove helpful since it would take one all-fired gullible fool to believe it wasn't a plant.

The arraignment was quick and predictable: the court refused bail due to Will's past record. But, true to his word, Collins arranged for a grand jury hearing within a week. Witnesses willing to testify for Will began piling up, but, as is the case with grand juries, the accused was not allowed counsel in the hearing room, thus the Solicitor General's evidence weighed more heavily than it would when rebutted: the grand jury handed down a true bill.

Disappointment crushed Will. He was removed from the hearing room through the back halls which led directly to the jail, so he had no chance to learn if Elly was waiting somewhere in the courthouse for word about the jury's decision. He had foolishly hoped for a glimpse of her, had fantasized about her approaching him with hands outstretched, saying, It's all right, Will, let's forgive and forget and put it behind us.

Instead he returned to his dismal cell to waste away more of his life, to wonder what would happen to him next, and if the shambling old attorney sent to him by Elly and Miss Beasley was senile after all. The confined space seemed suddenly claustrophobic, so he sat sideways on his bunk, his back pressed to the cold concrete blocks, and stared straight through the bars—the longest view—and thought of Texas, broad and flat, with wind blowing through the pungent sage, with an immense blue sky that turned hot pink and purple and yellow at sunset, with Indian paintbrush setting the plains afire just before the sun sank and stars appeared like gems on blue satin.

But imagination could rescue him only temporarily. In time he rolled onto his side and shut his eyes, swallowing hard. He'd lost again, and he hadn't seen Elly. God, how he needed to see her, how he'd banked on it. He didn't know which hurt worse, the fact that she hadn't been there, or that he'd lost the first round in court. But he'd hurt her so badly he'd been afraid to send word through Deputy Hess, afraid he didn't deserve her anymore, afraid that even if he called, she wouldn't come.

But she showed up even as he lay on his bunk, dejected.

"You got a visitor, Parker," announced Hess, opening the door. "Your wife. Follow me."

So she *had* been here all the time, waiting for word. His heart started klunking and he flew from his bunk. "Just a minute, Hess!" He dipped before the mirror and dragged a comb through his hair, four swift strokes. The mirror reflected his cheeks flushed with expectancy before he turned and hurried after Hess.

The visitors' room was a long, empty expanse totally devoid of trim. It held a bare window, a table and three chairs much like those in the Carnegie library. When Will entered, Elly was already seated at the table, wearing something new and yellow, clutching a purse on her lap. Hess motioned Will toward her, then took his place beside the door, crossing his arms as if planted for the duration.

Slipping into the chair opposite Elly's, Will wondered if she could feel the floor tremble from his thudding heart.

For a full ten seconds they stared.

"Hello, Will," Elly greeted with a sad smile in her eyes.

"Hello."

Their words, though softly spoken, echoed clearly through the room.

Will's palms were sweating and his neck felt hot as he

drank in the sight of her and suppressed the awful need to reach for her hands across the table.

"I'm sorry about the grand jury decision. I thought ... well, I hoped you'd be home today."

"So did I. But Collins warned me not to get my hopes up, especially when he couldn't be in there to tell our side of it."

"It don't seem fair, Will. I mean, how can they keep your lawyer out of the hearing room?"

"Collins says that's how the law works, and our chance will come when we go to trial by traverse jury."

"Traverse jury?" Her brow wrinkled.

"The big one, the one that lets us tell our side."

"Oh."

The thought of it shook them both as they gazed at each other, wishing futile wishes, regretting the harsh words of their last meeting. Elly kept a two-handed grip on her purse while Will dried his palms on his thighs.

"Elly, I ..." *Tell her you're sorry, fool.* But Hess stood guard, listening to every word, and apologizing was hard enough in private. The thought of baring his heart before an audience seemed to paralyze Will's tongue. So instead he told Elly, "I like Collins. He's a good one, I think. Thanks for hiring him."

"Don't be silly. Did you think I wouldn't hire a lawyer for my own husband?"

The words pressed up against Will's throat, and Hess or no Hess, he had to speak them. "I didn't know what to think after the way I talked to you last time."

Elly's eyes skittered aside. "I'd already hired him before I saw you."

"Oh." Will felt justly stung. His hands, only moments ago sweating, grew suddenly icy. *So what'd you expect, Parker, after the way you talked to her?* Again came the aching desire to ask her forgiveness, followed by the godawful fear that she wouldn't warm again, and if that happened, he'd have no reason to fight his way out of here. So he sat in misery, with his heart painfully clamoring and a lump in his throat that felt the size of a baseball.

"You okay?" Elly inquired, letting her glance waver back to him. "They feedin' you okay in here?"

Will swallowed the lump and managed to sound normal. "Pretty good. The sheriff's wife's got the cooking contract."

"Well . . . you look good." She flashed a nervous smile.

Silence again, made more awkward by the passing minutes and the fact that they spoke of everything except what was paramount on their minds.

"How did you get here?" He found himself obsessed with an irrational greed to know everything she'd done and thought since he'd been in here, to fill in the blanks of the time he was forced to forfeit. Life had grown so precious to him since she'd become part of it that he felt doubly robbed of his freedom.

"Oh, I caught a ride," she said evasively.

Distractedly, Elly scratched at the clasp of her purse and they both studied her hands until their eyes seemed to burn. Finally she opened the purse and told him quietly, "I know you told me not to come, Will, but I had to bring these presents from the kids." From the purse she withdrew two scrolled papers and handed them across the table.

"Wait!" Hess ordered sharply and leaped forward to confiscate them.

Elly glanced up, injured. "It's only greetings from the kids."

He examined them, rerolled them and handed them back, then returned to his post beside the door.

Again Elly offered the papers. "Here, Will."

He unrolled them to find a crude color-crayon drawing of flowers and stick people, and the message *I love you, Will* faithfully duplicated in nearly indecipherable printing, followed by their names: Donald Wade and Thomas. Will had never had to work so hard to keep tears from springing.

"Gosh," he remarked thickly, eyes downcast for fear she'd read how closely he treaded the borderline of control.

"They miss you," she whispered plaintively, thinking, *And I miss you. I ache without you. Home is terrible, work is pointless, living hurts.*

But she was afraid to say it, afraid of being rebuffed again.

"I miss 'em, too." Will's chin remained flattened to his chest. "How are they?"

"They're fine. They're at Lydia's house today, all three of 'em. Donald Wade, he gets off the schoolbus there. He loves it at Lydia's. Him and Sally're buildin' a fort."

Will cleared his throat and looked up, his heart still tripping in double-time, wishing futilely that she need not see him in this place that so reduced a man's self-respect, wishing for the hundredth time that he hadn't said what he had the last time he saw her, needing terribly to know if she, like the children, still loved him. *Tell her you're sorry, Parker! Just lay it out there and this misery will be over!*

He opened his lips to apologize but she spoke first. "Miss Beasley says Mr. Collins is the best."

"I trust her judgment." He cleared his throat and sat up straighter. "But I don't know where we're gonna get the money to pay him, Elly."

"Don't you worry about that. The honey run was good and we got money in the bank, and Miss Beasley's offered to help."

"She has?"

Elly nodded. "But I don't aim to take her up on it unless we have to."

"That's probably wise," he added.

Again came the oppressive silence and the swelling compulsion to touch fingertips. But he was afraid to reach and she was afraid Hess would jump all over her again, so neither of them moved.

"Well, listen." She lifted her face and smiled a big jack-o-lantern smile, as false as if it had been carved in a pumpkin by a knife. "I have to go 'cause I been leaving the kids at Lydia's an awful lot lately and I don't want to start takin' her for granted."

Panic swamped Will. He hadn't done any of the things he'd intended—he hadn't touched her, apologized, complimented her on her pretty new dress, told her he loved her, said any of the things crowding his heart. But it was probably best to let her off the hook. No matter what Collins said, the cards were stacked against him. He was a born loser. Innocent or not, he was bound to lose this trial, too, and when he did they'd lock him up for good. They did that on a second murder conviction, he knew. And no woman should have to wait for a man who'd be sixty—or seventy—when he got out. If he got out.

Elly edged forward on her chair.

"Well . . ." She rose uncertainly, still with a two-fisted grip on her small black purse. He didn't remember her ever carrying a purse before; it made him feel as if he'd been incarcerated for nine years instead of nine days, as if she were changing subtly while he wasn't there to see.

He, too, stood, tightening the roll of paper with both hands to keep from reaching out for her. "Thanks for coming, Elly. Say hi to the kids and tell the boys thanks for these pictures."

"I will."

"Kiss Lizzy P. for me."

"I w—" The word broke in half. Her chin began trembling and she forcibly tensed it.

They stared at each other until their eyes burned and their heartbeats hurt.

"Elly . . ." he whispered, and reached.

Their hands clung, flattening the scroll of paper—a tense, forlorn message of all that had not been said.

Tears glimmered on her lower eyelids. "I got to g-go, Will," she whispered and slowly pulled free. She backed up a step and he saw her chest began to heave as if she were already sobbing internally.

Desperate, he swung away and strode toward the door. "I'm ready, Hess!" The words resounded in the bare room as Will left Elly to shed her tears unobserved.

· She didn't come back again. But Miss Beasley did, the next day, with her mouth puckered like a two-day-old pudding and a look of stern reproof on her face.

"So, what have you done to that child?" she demanded before Will even touched his chair.

"What?" His eyes widened in surprise.

"What have you done to Eleanor? She came to my house crying her heart out last night and said you don't love her anymore."

"It's best if she believes that."

"*Bullwhacky!*" The word resounded from the walls, taking Will aback. He sat in silence while Miss Beasley raged on. "She's your wife, Mr. Parker! How dare you treat her like some passing acquaintance!"

"If you came here to give me hell, you can—"

"That's precisely why I came here, you young upstart! And don't speak to me in that tone of voice!"

Will let his weight drop to the chair and sat back in an insolent sprawl. "Y' know, you're just what I needed today, Miss Beasley."

"What you need, young man, is a good dressing down, and you're going to get it. Whatever you said to that young woman to put her in that state was untenable. If there was ever a time when you need to stand by her, this is it."

"Me stand by her!" Will stiffened and splayed two hands on his chest. "Ask her about standing by me!"

"Oh, I suppose you're sitting in here sulking because she had to take ten seconds to digest Reece Goodloe's accusation before coming to grips with it."

"Digest! She did more than digest!" He pointed toward Whitney. "She thought I *did* it! She actually thought I killed Lula Peak!"

"Oh, she did, did she? Then why is she running ads in the Whitney and Calhoun newspapers offering rewards for any information leading to your acquittal? Why has she single-handedly rounded up a dozen witnesses to testify on your behalf? Why has she learned how to drive a car and refused—"

"Drive a car!"

"—my financial help and run all over Gordon County passing out honey to make people forget all the nasty things they said about her years ago and badgering Sheriff Goodloe to find the real killer? And why has she contacted Hazel Pride and taken her into that deserted house that no woman who's suffered as Eleanor has should ever have to enter again?"

Will finally got a word in edgewise. "Who's Hazel Pride?"

"Our local realtor, that's who. Eleanor has put her grandfather's house up for sale to pay your lawyer's fee, to see that you get the best defense a man can possibly get in this state. But to do it she had to face that house, and a town full of despicable ... *horses' posteriors* who don't deserve to be groveled to. But grovel she did, and she did it for you, Mr. Parker! Because she loves you so much she would face anything in this world for you. And you pay her back by withholding your forgiveness for a reaction that would have been as natural to you had she been the one with the prison record who was being accused again." Miss Beasley collected herself and sat back self-righteously. "Perhaps I was mistaken about what kind of person you are."

Will was so dazed, he commented on the most incidental fact.

"She told me she caught a ride to Calhoun."

"Caught a ride—hmph! She drives that deplorable automobile you stuck together with spit and baling twine, and if she doesn't kill herself before this is over it'll be a miracle. She nearly killed Nat and Norris, to say nothing of the buildings she's bumped into and the sidewalks she's scaled. Why, a person's rosebushes aren't even safe on the front lawn anymore! She's scared to death of that thing, but she grips the wheel and drives, mind you! Clear up to Calhoun, sometimes twice a day, only to come home believing that you don't love her anymore. Well, shame on you, Mr. Parker!" Miss Beasley shook her finger at Will as if he were six years old. "Now I want you to consider how you've hurt her instead of sitting in here thinking only of yourself. And the next time she comes to visit you, you make amends!"

Like the grand jury, Miss Beasley offered Will no chance to rebut. She sailed out as gustily as she'd sailed in, leaving him feeling as if he'd just taken a ride on a tornado.

Back in his cell, Will experienced a curious reaction, a minute exhilaration. Elly ... driving the car? Elly ... rounding up witnesses? Elly ... going into that *house*?

For him!

It struck him fully what Miss Beasley had set out to do, and in her own inimitable way, she'd done it: made him realize how much Elly loved him. She must, to face all those apprehensions, all those fears that had held her prisoner on

Rock Creek Road for years, that had held her aloof from the townspeople, denying that she needed anybody.

In the wake of Miss Beasley's visit, Will's torpor disappeared, replaced by restlessness and a thrill of hope. He paced his cell, cracking his knuckles, wondering what witnesses Elly had found, smiling at the idea of her sweetening them up with honey. God, what a woman! He paced . . . and pondered . . . and thanked his lucky stars for both Elly and Gladys Beasley.

Within an hour after the departure of the latter, Will made a decision.

"Hess!" he bellowed. "Hess, get in here!" He clattered his dinner fork against the bars. "Hess, I want you to get a message to my wife!"

"Hold your horses, Parker!" came a voice from the distance.

"Hurry up, Hess!"

"I'm comin', I'm comin'!" The deputy appeared down the corridor. "What is it?"

"Can the sheriff drive out to my place and get word to Elly that I want to see her?"

"I guess so."

"Well, get him on the radio and tell him I'd appreciate it if he'd do it soon as possible."

"Will do." Hess turned away but stopped and flashed a crooked grin over his shoulder. "Miss Beasley can sure chew ass, can't she?"

"Whew!" Will replied, running a hand through his hair. "Can she ever! Tell you the truth, I was glad to be safe behind these bars."

Hess laughed, took two steps and turned back. "Everybody's talkin' about it. I'm surprised you didn't know."

"Know what?"

"About your wife drivin' that car like there was no rubber rationing, runnin' all over drummin' up witnesses for you, just like Miss Beasley said. You know, Elly and me went to school together and I was one of 'em who called her crazy. But people are sayin' now she's outwitting the Solicitor Gen-

eral. Drivin' *him* crazy, wonderin' what she and Collins will
unearth in court!"

Will's heart began to thunder with excitement.

"Could you tell Collins I want to see him, too?"

"Could if he wasn't out of town."

"Out of town. Where?"

"I don't know. That wife of yours has got him runnin' like
a fox in front of a pack of hounds, checkin' leads. I do know
one thing, though."

"What?"

"He got your trial on the docket for the first week in February."

"So fast?"

"Don't underestimate that old bird, especially not when
he's got your wife workin' with him." Hess sauntered away,
stopped and grinned back at Will. "There's a joke goin'
around, only it's not really a joke at all, it's—" Hess
scratched his head. "Well, you might say it's a sprinklin' of
respect that's about fifteen years late in comin'. Folks're
sayin', 'Look out, here comes Elly Parker with her honey!' "
Turning away, Hess added, "Nobody's sure if she really gave
a quart of it to Judge Murdoch or not, but word's out he's the
one who married you two and he's also the one scheduled to
preside at your trial." With a last chuckle drifting down the
corridor as he opened the far door, Hess added, "I'll get word
to your wife, Parker." Then the far door slammed.

CHAPTER
23

Elly didn't come back again. But she sent a brand-new Calcutta cloth suit and a striped tie and white shirt with cuff links and Will's military dress shoes all spit-polished for him to wear the day of his trial. And a note: *We're gonna win Will. Love, Elly.*

He dressed early, taking great care with his hair, wishing it were shorter above the ears, returning to the mirror time and again to run his fingertips over his shaved jaw, to tighten the knot in his tie, adjust his cuffs, unbutton and rebutton his jacket. At the thought of seeing her again a wedge of expectation tightened deep within him. He paced, cracked his knuckles, checked his reflection once more. Again he ran his knuckles over the hair above his ears, worried that it didn't look trim enough—not for a jury, but for her.

Staring at his own eyes, he thought of hers. *Hang on, Green Eyes, don't give up on me yet. I'm not the horse's ass I've been acting like lately. After we've won this thing I'll show you.*

Elly, too, had taken great care dressing. Yellow. It had to be yellow, her color of affirmation. The color of sunlight and freedom. She'd made a tailored suit in gabardine as pale as whipped butter, its shoulders built up, its pocket flaps buttoned down. She, too, returned apprehensively to check her reflection in the mirror: she'd had her hair sheared so that when she appeared in public Will would have no cause to feel ashamed. Staring at her shaped eyebrows and coral lips, she saw a woman as sleek and modish as the pictures on the coffee table at Erma's Beauty Nook. *Just wait, Will, when this is over we're gonna be the happiest two people on the face of the earth.*

Sitting in the courtroom waiting, she kept her eyes fixed on the door by which she knew he'd enter.

When he did their eyes met and their hearts leaped. She had never seen him in a civilian suit before. He looked stunning, his hair combed with hair oil that made it appear darker than usual, his tie crisp, his dark face a sharp contrast to the white shirt collar.

He lifted his eyes as he entered and his collar felt suddenly tight. He knew she'd wear yellow. He knew it! As if to point it out, the nine A.M. sun had seen fit to slash through a high window and fall directly across her. God, how he loved her, wanted to be free for her, with her. As he moved across the varnished floor their gazes remained locked. Her hair, what had she done to her hair? She'd had most of it cut off! It was sheared up high on the neck and above the ears, with a side part and a fluffy top. It brought her cheekbones into prominence in a wholly attractive way. He wanted to go to her, tell her how pretty she looked, thank her for the suit and the note and tell her he loved her, too. But Jimmy Ray Hess was at his side, so he could only walk and gawk. She smiled and discreetly waggled two fingers. The sun seemed to turn its warming rays on him. He felt a great rush much like that he'd experienced in the Augusta train station when he'd seen her approaching through the crowd. He smiled in reply.

The woman to Elly's left nudged her and leaned over to say something. For the first time he noticed it was Lydia Marsh. And on Elly's right sat Miss Beasley, stern-faced and sober as ever. Her eyes caught Will's and he nodded, his heart in his throat.

She gave a barely perceptible nod and a tight moue, releasing him to breathe again.

Friends. True friends. Gratitude swamped him but again he

had no way to convey it but to nod to Lydia, too, and cast a last lingering gaze over Elly as he reached the defense table and turned his back on them.

Collins was already there, dressed like a dotty museum curator in crinkled puce wool, smelly yellowed cotton, and a silk tie decorated with ... pink flamingos! When the handcuffs were removed, Collins rose and shook Will's hand.

"Things are looking good. I see you've got a cheering section."

"I don't want my wife on the stand, Collins, remember that."

"Only if necessary, I told you."

"No! They'll tear her apart. They'll dredge up all that stuff about her being crazy. You can put me on but not her."

"That *won't* be necessary. You'll see."

"Where were you yesterday? I sent word I wanted to see you."

"Pipe down and have a chair, Parker. I've been out saving your hide, chasing down witnesses your wife dug up."

"You mean it's true? She's been—"

"All rise, please," the bailiff called dryly. "The Gordon County Court is now in session, the honorable Aldon P. Murdoch presiding."

Will gaped as Murdoch entered, garbed in black, but he resisted the urge to glance over his shoulder to see Elly's reaction. Murdoch's eyes scanned the courtroom, paused on Will and moved on. Though his expression was inscrutable, Will had one thought: by whatever miracle, he'd been delivered into the hands of a fair man. The conviction stemmed from the picture of two little boys in a swivel chair sharing a cigar box of jelly beans.

"All be seated, please," ordered Murdoch.

Seating himself, Will leaned toward Collins and whispered, "She didn't really bribe him, did she?"

A pair of half-glasses hung on Collins' porous nose. He peered over them at the papers he was withdrawing from a scuffed briefcase. "Are you kidding? He's unimpressible. He'd've had charges brought against her so fast it would've spun her honey."

The trial began.

Opening statements were given by both attorneys. Collins' was delivered in a slow drawl that gave the impression he hadn't had enough sleep the previous night.

Solicitor General Edward Slocum's was delivered with fire and flourish.

He was half Collins' age and nearly twice his height. In a neat blue serge suit, freshly laundered shirt and crisp tie, he made Bob Collins look dowdy by comparison. With his ringing baritone voice and upright stature, he made Collins look ready for the boneyard. Slocum's eyes were black, intense, direct, and the wave standing along the top of his dark head gave the appearance of a cocky rooster who dared anyone in his roost to cluck without his approval. Vocally eloquent and physically imposing, Slocum promised, through undisputable evidence, to show the jury beyond a glimmer of a doubt that Will Parker had cold-bloodedly, and with malice aforethought, murdered Lula Peak.

Listening to the two men, Will couldn't help but think that if he were a member of the jury, he'd believe anything Slocum said and would wonder if the attorney for the defense was as senile as he appeared.

"The prosecution calls Sheriff Reece Goodloe."

While questioning his witness, Slocum stood foursquare to him, often with his feet widespread, knees locked. He knew how to use his eyes, to pierce the witness as if each answer were a fulcrum on which the outcome of the trial hinged, then to pass them over the jury at the appropriate moment to inculcate upon them the most incriminating portions of the testimony.

From Sheriff Goodloe the jury learned of Will's criminal record, the existence of the torn dustcloth and a note bearing the accused's initials, and his own admission that he often read the *Atlanta Constitution*.

When Bob Collins shuffled to his feet, half the people in the courtroom suppressed a grunt of help. He spent so much time pondering each question that the jury shifted restlessly. When he finally drew it forth, their shoulders seemed to sag with relief. His eyes avoided everything in the room except the floor and the toes of his scuffed brown oxfords. His mouth wore a half-smile, as if he knew an amusing secret which he would, in his own good time, share with them.

His cross-examination of Sheriff Goodloe revealed that Will Parker had served his time in prison, been a model prisoner and been released with a full parole. It also revealed that Sheriff Goodloe himself read the *Atlanta Constitution* daily.

From a gaunt, bespectacled woman named Barbara Murphy, who identified herself as a typesetter for the *Atlanta Constitution*, came unassailable verification that the note was cut from a copy or copies of that newspaper. Upon cross-examination Miss Murphy revealed that the circulation of the newspaper was 143,261 and that it was conceivable that since Calhoun was one of 158 counties in the state, roughly nine hundred copies of the *Atlanta Constitution* flooded into it daily.

From a tired-looking elderly county coroner named Elliot Mobridge the jury learned the time and cause of death and that Lula Peak was carrying a four-month-old fetus when she died. Cross-examination established that there was no way to determine who had sired a four-month-old fetus of a dead woman.

From a brusque female medical examiner who identified herself as Leslie McCooms came the fact that remnants of dust and lemon oil matching those on the torn dustcloth had been found on Lula Peak's neck, along with bruises caused by human hands—probably a man's.

Defense counsel released the witness without questions, reserving the right to cross-examine her later.

From Gladys Beasley, long-standing lioness of estimable repute, came the concession that the dustcloth and lemon oil (exhibit A) could possibly have come from the Carnegie Municipal Library of Whitney, where Will Parker was employed and on duty the night of Lula Peak's murder. Miss Beasley admitted, too, that the library did indeed carry two subscriptions to the *Atlanta Constitution* and she had given Will Parker permission to take home one of the two copies when it was three days old or more.

It was all testimony that Will had expected, yet he felt

shaken at how incriminating it sounded when stated by witnesses under oath, from a hard wooden chair on a raised platform beside the judge's dais.

But the tide subtly turned when Robert Collins cross-examined Miss Beasley.

"Did Lula Peak ever visit the library when Will Parker was there?"

"She most certainly did."

"And did she speak to Mr. Parker?"

"Yes."

"How do you know?"

"I could hear their conversation plainly from the checkout desk. The library is U-shaped, with the desk situated in the crossbar so that I can see and often hear everything that's going on. The ceilings are high and everything echoes."

"When did you hear the first such conversation between Peak and Parker?"

"On September second, 1941."

"How can you be sure of that date?"

"Because Mr. Parker asked for a borrower's card and I began to fill one out before realizing he had not established residency in Whitney. The card was filled out in ink, thus I couldn't erase and reuse it for another patron. Abiding by the motto, *Waste not, want not*, I filed Mr. Parker's card in a separate place to reuse when he came back in with proof of residency, as I was sure he would. He still uses that original card, with the date of September second crossed off."

Miss Beasley presented Will's borrower's card, which was entered as exhibit B.

"So," Collins went on, "on the day of September second, you overheard a conversation between Lula Peak and William Parker. Would you repeat that conversation, to the best of your recollection?"

Miss Beasley, prim and well-packed and indubitably accurate, repeated verbatim what she had overheard that first day when Lula sat down across from Will and stuck her foot between his thighs, when she trapped him between the shelves and attempted to seduce him, when she vindictively accused his wife of being crazy from the time Elly was a child, a time

when Miss Beasley herself remembered Eleanor See as a
bright, inquisitive student with a talent for drawing. She told
of Will's polite but hasty exit on that day and others when
Lula followed him into the library under the pretext of "bettering herself" with books which she never bothered to check
out.

Listening to her testimony, Will sat tense. After the dressing down she'd given him he'd feared her antipathy on the
witness stand. He should have known better. He had no better
friend than Gladys Beasley. When she was excused she
marched past his chair with her typical drill sergeant bearing,
without a glance in his direction, but he knew beyond a doubt
that her faith in him was unassailable.

Miss Beasley was the prosecution's last witness. Then it
was Collins' turn.

He spent thirty seconds boosting himself from his chair,
sixty gazing out over the gallery and fifteen removing his
glasses. He chuckled, nodded at his toes and called, "Defense
calls Mrs. Lydia Marsh."

Lydia Marsh, looking pretty as a madonna with her coal
black hair and pale blue dress spoke her oath and stated that
she was a housewife and mother of two whose husband was
fighting "somewhere in Italy." A careful observer might have
seen the almost imperceptible approval in the softening of the
jurors' mouths and the relaxing of their hands over their
stomachs. Certainly Robert Collins saw and set out to capital-
ize on the sense of patriotism running rife through every
American in that jurors' box.

"How long have you known Will Parker, Mrs. Marsh?"

The questions were routine until Collins asked Lydia to re-
late a story about what happened the day Will Parker left for
Parris Island to be inducted into the United States Marines.

"He came by the house," Lydia recalled, "and called from
down by the gate. He acted slightly nervous and maybe a little embarrassed—"

"Objection, your honor. Witness is drawing a conclusion."
"Sustained."

When Lydia Marsh continued it was with the avid determination to paint things accurately. "Mr. Parker refused to meet

my eyes at first, and he wiped his hands nervously on his thighs. When I went down to wish him goodbye, he gave me a green towel and a fruit jar full of honey. He told me he'd stolen them from me nearly a year and a half before, when he was down and out and had no money. At the time he stole the fruit jar it had been filled with buttermilk—he'd taken it from our well. And the green towel he'd taken from the clothesline along with a set of my husband's clothes, which had, of course, been worn out long before that day. He apologized and said it had bothered him all that time, stealing from us, and before he went off to war, he wanted to make it right. So he was bringing me the honey, which was all he had to repay us with."

"Because he thought he might not get the chance again? He feared he might die in the war?"

"He didn't say that—no. He wasn't that kind. He was the kind who knew he had to fight and went to do it without complaint, just like my own husband did."

"And more recently, Mrs. Marsh, since William Parker's return from the Pacific, have you been aware of any marital discord between him and his wife?"

"Quite the opposite. They're extremely happy. I believe I would have known if he'd had any reason to seek the company of a woman like Lula Peak."

"And what makes you believe he didn't?"

Lydia's eyes swerved to Elly's and took on a glow. "Because Elly—Mrs. Parker, that is—recently confided in me that she's expecting their first baby."

The shock hit Will as if he'd been poleaxed. He twisted around in his chair and his eyes collided with Elly's. He half-rose, but his attorney pressed him down gently. A rush of joy warmed his face as his glance swept down to his wife's stomach, then lifted once more to her blushing cheeks. *Is it true, Elly?* The words went unsaid but everyone in the courtroom sensed them with their hearts instead of their ears. And every person present saw Elly's answering smile and the merest nod of her head. They watched Will's dazzling, jubilant hosanna of a smile. And twelve out of twelve in the jury who were mothers and fathers felt their heartstrings tugged.

A murmur spread through the gallery and was silenced only when Collins excused the witness and announced the reading by the bailiff of Will Parker's military record into evidence. The bailiff, a small, effeminate man with a high voice, read from a file with eyebrows raised in approval. The records of the United States Marine Corps characterized William L. Parker as a tough recruit who knew how to follow orders and command men, thus earning him the honor of being named squad leader in basic training and in combat, and promotion to the rank of corporal before his medical discharge in May of 1943. Also on record was a citation from Colonel Merritt A. Edson, Commander of the First Marine Raiders, commending Will's bravery in battle and delineating the courageous acts that had won him the Purple Heart in what by now the war correspondents had dubbed "the bloodiest battle of the Coral Sea, the Battle of Bloody Ridge."

The courtroom was respectfully silent when the bailiff closed his file. Collins had the jury in his hand and he knew it. He'd gotten them with respectability, honesty and military valor. Now he'd get them with a bit of levity.

"Defense calls Nat MacReady to the stand."

Nat left his place beside Norris and hustled forward. Though his shoulders were stooped, he walked with amazing agility for one of his age. Nat looked spiffy, dressed in the woolen blouse of his World War I army uniform with its tarnished gold stars and lieutenant's stripes. It was obvious at a glance that Nat was proud to be called upon to help justice prevail. When asked if he would tell the truth, the whole truth and nothing but, he replied, "You bet your boots, sonny."

Judge Murdoch scowled but allowed the chuckles from the gallery as Nat, eager-eyed, seated himself on the edge of his chair.

"State your name."

"Nathaniel MacReady."

"And your occupation."

"I'm a retired businessman. Ran the icehouse out south of town since I was twenty-six, along with my brother, Norris."

"What town is that?"

"Why, Whitney, of course."

"You've lived there all your life, have you?"

"I most certainly have. All except for them fourteen months back in '17 and '18 when Uncle Sam give me a free trip to Europe."

Titters of appreciation sounded. Collins stood back and let the uniform speak for itself; not a soul in the place could mistake Nat's pride in wearing it again.

"So you've been retired now for how many years?"

"Fifteen years."

"Fifteen years . . ." Collins scratched his head and studied the floor. "You must get a little bored after fifteen years of doing nothing."

"Doing nothing! Why, sonny, I'll have you know my brother and I organized the Civilian Guard, and we're out there every night enforcing the curfew and watching for Japanese planes, aren't we, Norris?"

"We sure are," Norris answered from the gallery to another ripple of laughter that had to be silenced by Murdoch's gavel.

"Defense counsel will instruct his witness to direct his responses to the court and not the gallery," Murdoch ordered.

"Yes, your honor," replied Collins meekly before scratching his head again and waiting for the room to still. "Now before we get into your duties as a volunteer guard, I wonder if you'd take a look at something for me." From his baggy pocket Collins withdrew a small wooden carving and handed it to Nat. "Did you make this?"

Nat took it, replying, "Looks like mine." Turning it bottom-side up, he examined it myopically and added, "Yup, it is. Got my initials on the bottom."

"Tell the court what it is."

"It's a wood carving of a wild turkey. Where'd you get it?"

"At the drugstore in Whitney. Paid twenty-nine cents for it off their souvenir counter."

"Did you tell Haverty to mark it in his books so I get credit?"

The judged rapped his gavel.

"I certainly did, Mr. MacReady," Collins answered to the accompaniment of soft laughter from the spectators, then rushed on before drawing further wrath from the sober-faced Murdoch. "And where did you make it?"

"In the square."

"What square?"

"Why, the Town Square in Whitney. That's where me and my brother spend most days, on the bench under the magnolia tree."

"Whittling?"

"Naturally, whittling. Show me an old man with idle hands and I'll show you the subject of next year's obituary."

"And while you whittle, you see a lot of what goes on around the square, is that right?"

Nat scratched his temple. "Well, I guess you could say we don't miss much, do we, Norris?" He chuckled, raising a matching sound from those in the room who knew precisely how little the pair missed.

This time Norris smiled and restrained himself from replying.

Collins took out a pocket knife and began cleaning his nails as if the following question were of little consequence. "Have you ever seen Lula Peak coming and going around the square?"

"Pret' near every day. She was a waitress at Vickery's, you know, and our bench sets right there where we got a clear shot of it and the library and pretty much everything that moves around that square."

"So over the years you saw a lot of Lula Peak's comings and goings?"

"You bet."

"Did you ever see her coming and going with any men?"

Nat burst out laughing and slapped his knee. "Hoo! Hoo! That's a good one, isn't it, Norris!" The whole courtroom burst into laughter.

The judge interjected, "Answer the question, Mr. MacReady."

"She come and go with more men than the Pacific fleet!"

Laughter burst forth and Murdoch had to sound his gavel again.

"Tell us about some you saw her with," Collins prompted.

"How far back?"

"As far back as you can remember."

"Well . . ." Nat scratched his chin, dropped his gaze to the tip of his brown high-top shoe. "Let's see now, that goes back quite a ways. She always did like the men. Guess I can't rightly say which one I saw her with first, but somewhere along when she was just barely old enough to grow body hair there was that dusky-skinned carnie who ran the ferris wheel during Whitney Days. Might've been back in twenty-four—"

"Twenty-five," Norris interrupted from the floor.

Slocum leaped to his feet—"Objection!" just as the judge rapped his gavel. "Lula Peak is not on trial here!" put in the Solicitor General. "William Parker is!"

Collins pointed out calmly, "Your honor, the reputation of the deceased is of utmost importance here. My intent is to establish that because of her promiscuity, Lula Peak might have gotten pregnant by any one of a dozen men she's been known to have consorted with."

"By implying her fetus was sired in 1925?" retorted Slocum irately. "Your honor, this line of questioning is ludicrous!"

"I'm attempting to show a sexual pattern in the deceased's life, your honor, if you'll allow me."

The objection was overruled, but with a warning to Collins to control his witness's penchant for speaking to the gallery and soliciting answers from them.

"Did you ever see Lula Peak coming and going with Will Parker?"

"I seen her try. Whoo—ee, that little gal sure did try, starting with the first day he come into town and went in there where she was workin'."

"In there, meaning in Vickery's Cafe."

"Yessir. And every day after that when she saw him come to town and cross the square, she'd make sure she was out front sweeping, and when he didn't pay her any mind, she'd follow him wherever he went."

"Such as . . ." encouraged Collins.

"Well, such as the library when he came in to borrow books or to sell milk and eggs to Miss Beasley. It wouldn't take Lula two minutes before she took off her apron and hot-footed it after young Parker. I'm an old man, Mr. Collins, but I'm not too old to recognize a woman in heat, nor one that's been refused by a man—"

"Objection!"

"—and when Lula came spittin' out of that library—"

"Objection!"

"—she didn't have no matted fur that I could see—"

"Objection!"

It took a full minute for the din to die down. Though the judge ordered Nat's opinions stricken from the record, Collins knew they could not be stricken from the minds of the jury. Lula Peak was a slut and before he was done they'd all recognize the fact and indict her instead of Will Parker.

"Mr. MacReady," Collins explained quietly, "you under-stand we have to deal with facts here, only facts, not opin-ions."

"Sure—sure enough."

"Facts, Mr. MacReady. Now, do you know for a fact that Lula Peak had licentious affairs with more than one man around Whitney?"

"Yes, sir. At least if Orlan Nettles can be believed. He told me once he nabbed her underneath the grandstand at the ball-park during the seventh-inning stretch of the game between the Whitney Hornets and the Grove City Tigers."

"Nabbed her. Could you be more specific?"

"Well, I could except there's ladies present."

"Was *nabbed* the word Orlan himself used?"

"No, sir."

"What word did he use?"

Nat blushed and turned to the judge. "Do I have to say it, your honor?"

"You're under oath, Mr. MacReady."

"All right, then—screwed, your honor. Orlan said he screwed Lula Peak underneath the grandstand at Skeets Hol-low Park during the seventh-inning stretch of a game between the Whitney Hornets and the Grove City Tigers."

In the rear gallery a gasp was heard from Alma Nettles,

Orlan's wife. Collins noted the eyes of the jurors swerve her way and waited until he'd regained their full attention.

"How long ago did he claim to do this?"

"It was the night the Hornets won seven to six in the top of the ninth when Willie Pounds caught a grounder stretched out on his belly and threw a scorcher into home for the last out. Norris and me never miss a game, and we keep the scorecards, don't we, Norris?" Norris nodded as Nat handed Collins a scrap of white paper. "Here it is, last summer, July eleventh, though I don't know why it was necessary to bring this. Half the men in Whitney know the date 'cause Orlan he told a whole bunch of us about it, didn't he, Norris?"

"Strike that last question," Judge Murdoch ordered as the weeping Alma was escorted from the room in the arms of a solicitous matron.

Above the murmurs from the gallery, Collins inquired of Nat, "Did you ever *see* Lula Peak with a man, under . . . shall we say, a compromising position?"

"Yessir, there was an engineer on the L and N Railroad who used to lay over at Miss Bernadette Werm's boarding-house. I'm not sure of his name, but he had a bushy red beard and a tattoo of a serpent on his arm—Miss Werm would remember his name. Anyway, I caught 'em one day, in the act you might say, down by Oak Creek where I was fishin'. Naked as jaybirds they were, and when I come upon 'em, Lula she throws back her head and laughs and says to me, 'Don't look so shocked, Mr. MacReady. Why don't y'all come and join us?'"

From the gallery came a chorus of shocked female *ohhs*.

"Just for clarification, Mr. MacReady, when you say they were in the act, you mean in the act of copulation?"

"Yes, sir, I do."

Collins took an inordinate amount of time extracting a wrinkled handkerchief from his pocket, blowing his nose, letting the last bit of testimony sink into every brain that mattered and many that didn't. Finally he pocketed his hanky and approached the witness again.

"Now, let's go back again, if we may, to your very important job as a member of the Civilian Patrol. When you've been on patrol at night during recent months and weeks, is it true that you've repeatedly seen one particular car parked behind Lula Peak's house?"

"Yessir."

"Do you know whose car it is?"

"Yessir, it's Harley Overmire's. Black Ford licence number PV628. He parks it behind the juniper bushes in the alley. I've seen it there a lot, couple nights a week anyway, during the past year. Also seen Harley goin' to Lula Peak's house sometimes in the middle of the day when she ain't workin'. Parks his car on the square, goes in the restaurant as if he's havin' lunch and hits out the back door and takes the alley to her house, which is just around the corner."

"And you've seen Lula Peak with someone else lately."

"Yessir, I have, and truth to tell, I hate to say it in public. Nobody wants to hurt a boy that age, but he's probably too young to realize—"

"Just tell us what you've seen, Mr. MacReady," Collins interrupted.

"Harley's young son, Ned."

"That's Harley Overmire's son, Ned Overmire?"

"Yes, sir."

"Tell us how old you'd guess Ned Overmire is."

"Oh, I'd say fourteen or so. Not over fifteen, that's for sure. He's in the ninth grade anyway, I know that cause my niece, Delwyn Jean Potts, is his teacher this year."

"And have you seen Lula Peak with Ned Overmire?"

"Yessir. Right in front of Vickery's. She was sweepin' again—she always sweeps when she wants to ... well ... you know ... latch herself a man, you might say. Anyhow, young Ned comes along the sidewalk one day a couple weeks ago and she stops him like I've seen her stop dozens of others, stickin' that long fingernail of hers into his shirtfront and tickling his chest. She said it was hot, he should come on inside and she'd give him some free ice cream. I could hear it plain as day—heck, I think she wanted me to hear it. She always sort of taunted me, too, after that time I found her with that railroad man. Ice cream—humph!"

"And did the boy follow her inside?"

"He did. Thank heavens he came out again in just a couple minutes with a strawberry ice cream cone and Lula follows him to the door and calls after him, 'Come back now, hear?' "

"And did he?"

"Not that I saw, no."

"Well, thank the lord for that," muttered Collins, drawing a rap from the gavel but the approval of the jury for his reaction.

"But you're sure about Lula having sexual encounters with these others you've named."

"Yessir."

"And to the best of your knowledge, did Lula Peak ever succeed in drawing the attention of Will Parker?"

"No, sir, she never did, not that I knew about, no."

"Your witness."

Slocum's attempt to discredit Nat MacReady as senile, hard of hearing or short of sight proved futile. MacReady had an intimidating memory, and embellished his recollections with anecdotes that were so obviously real that his cross-examination proved more advantageous for the defense than for the prosecution.

When Nat stepped down from the witness stand, Collins stood to announce, "Defense calls Norris MacReady."

Norris stepped up, wearing, like his brother, his scratchy World War I uniform with the collar fitting loosely around his wrinkled throat. His high forehead shone from a recent scrubbing, setting off the liver spots like brown polka dots. Slocum squeezed his lips and cursed beneath his hand, then ran a hand through his hair, wrecking his rooster comb.

"State your name."

"Norris MacReady."

"Occupation?"

"I retired from the icehouse the same year as Nat."

There followed a series of questions regarding the establishment of the Whitney Civilian Town Guard and its function before Collins got down to the meatier inquiries.

"On the night of August 17, 1943, while making a curfew check, did you overhear a conversation at the back door of the Carnegie Municipal Library of Whitney?"

"I did."

"Would you tell us about it, please."

Norris's eyes widened and he glanced from the attorney to the judge. "Do you think I ought to repeat it just like Lula said it?"

The judge answered, "Exactly as you heard it, yes."

"Well, all right, judge . . . but the ladies in the courtroom ain't gonna like it."

"You're under oath, Mr. MacReady."

"Very well . . ." As a gentleman of the old order, Norris hesitated. Then he asked another question, "You think it'd be okay if I read it instead?"

Slocum leaped to his feet, spouting objections.

"Allow me, your honor, to establish the allowability of the reading material," Collins interjected quickly.

"Objection overruled, but establish it with a single question, is that understood, Mr. Collins?"

"It is." Collins turned to Norris. "From what would you like to read?"

"Why, from our log. Nat and me, we keep a log faithfully, don't we, Nat?"

"We sure do," answered Nat from the gallery.

Nobody raised an objection this time. The place was as still as outer space.

"You keep a log while you're on patrol?" Collins prompted.

"Oh, we got to. The government says. Got to record every plane sighting and every person who breaks curfew. This war is different than the Great War. In that one we never had to worry about spies in our own backyard like we have to this time, that's why we got to keep such close records."

"You may read your entry for August seventeenth, Mr. MacReady."

From an inside pocket of his uniform Norris withdrew a green-covered book with worn edges. He settled a pair of wire-rimmed spectacles over his nose, taking long moments to hook the springy bows behind his ears. Then he tipped back his head, licked a finger and turned pages so slowly that titters began in the room before he finally found the correct spot.

" 'August 17, 1943,' " he began in a crackly voice, then cleared his throat. " 'Nat and me went on patrol at nine. All quiet except for Carl and Julie Draith returning from bridge game at the Nelsons' house next door. Ten o'clock—coming up along Comfort Street heard someone entering back door of library. I stayed at the edge of the building while Norris reconnoitered behind the hedge to see who it was. Norris signaled me over and we waited. Less than 5 minutes later the door flew open and a high-heeled shoe came flying out and hit Nat on the shoulder causing a purple lump to form later. Big fight going on between Will Parker and Lula Peak. Parker pushes her out the back door of library and yells, "If you're in heat Lula go yowl beneath somebody else's window." He slams the door in her face and she bangs it with her fist a few times and calls him a goddamn peckerhead and an asshole and a toad-sucking Marine. Then she screams (loud enough to wake the dead) "Your dick probably wouldn't fill my left ear anyway." Such language for a woman.' "

Norris blushed. Nat blushed. Will blushed. Elly blushed. Collins politely took the MacReadys' logbook and entered it as exhibit C before turning his witness over for cross-examination.

This time Slocum used his head and excused Norris without further questions. Throughout the courtroom a restlessness had begun. Murmurs sounded continuously from the gallery and spectators edged forward on their seats as Collins called his next witness.

"Defense calls Dr. Justin Kendall."

Kendall strode down the center aisle, an imposing man of well over six feet, wearing a sharply tailored suit of brown serge, his receding hairline framing a polished forehead that looked as if he'd just scrubbed it with a surgical brush, and his frameless glasses giving him the appearance of a scholar. His fingers were long and clean as they pointed toward heaven while he repeated the oath. Collins was already firing questions as Kendall tugged at his trouser creases and took the witness chair.

"State your name and occupation, please."

"Justin Ferris Kendall, medical doctor."

"You practice medicine here in Calhoun, is that correct?"

"It is."

"And did you recently examine the deceased, Lula Peak?"

"Yessir, on October twentieth last year."

"And did you at the time confirm that she was approximately two months pregnant?"

"I did."

"Two months after Will Parker was heard telling her that if she was in heat she should go yowl beneath somebody else's window, you diagnosed her as two months pregnant?"

"Yessir."

"And do you employ a registered nurse named Miriam Gaultier who also acts as your receptionist?"

"I do."

"Thank you. Your witness."

Slocum obviously couldn't divine a reason for this line of questioning and glanced around, confused by the abrupt turnover of the defense's witness.

He half-rose from his chair and replied, "No questions, your honor."

"Defense calls Miriam Gaultier to the stand."

Heads turned as a thin gray wisp of a woman passed through the spindled gate, smiling hello to Dr. Kendall, who held it open for her.

"State your name and occupation, please."

"Miriam Gaultier. I'm a nurse and receptionist for Dr. Justin Kendall."

"You've just heard Dr. Kendall testify that he was visited by the deceased, Lula Peak, on October twentieth last year. Were you working at the doctor's office that day?"

"Yes, I was."

"And did you talk with Lula Peak?"

"Yes, I did."

"And what was the gist of that conversation?"

"I asked Miss Peak for her mailing address for billing purposes."

"Did she give it to you?"

"No, sir, she didn't."

"Why not?"

"Because she advised me to send the bill to Harley Overmire, of Whitney, Georgia."

Nobody heard Collins turn the witness over to Solicitor General Slocum, but they could hear the sweat ooze from Harley Overmire's pores as the prosecution cross-examined Miriam Gaultier in the silent room.

"Was Miss Peak's bill ever paid, Mrs. Gaultier?"

"Yes, it was."

"Can you, beyond a shadow of a doubt, state that it was not paid by Miss Peak herself?"

"Well . . ."

"Beyond a shadow of a doubt, Mrs. Gaultier," Slocum reiterated, skewering her with his dark eyes.

"It was paid in cash."

"In person?"

"No, it was mailed in."

"Thank you, you may step down."

"But it was sent in an envelope from—"

"You may step down, Mrs. Gaultier!"

"—the electric company, as if whoever sent it—"

Clakk! Clakk! Murdoch rapped his gavel. "That will be all, Mrs. Gaultier!"

Things were going even better than Collins had hoped for. He hurriedly called his next witness while the tide was rolling in the right direction.

"Defense recalls Leslie McCooms."

The medical examiner was reminded that she was still under oath and Collins made his point without histrionics.

"When you examined the body of Lula Peak you found that her death had not been caused by the dustrag as first believed, but by human hands, probably a man's. Is this true?"

"Yes."

"Tell me, Miss McCooms, how many fingerprints were found on Lula Peak's neck?"

"Nine."

"And which fingerprint was missing?"

"The one from the index finger of the right hand."

"Thank you—your witness."

Will felt hope swell his chest, climb his arms and infuse

his head. With one hand balled around the other, he pressed his thumb knuckles to his lips and warned himself, it's not through yet. But he couldn't resist turning to glimpse Elly over his shoulder. Her face was pink with excitement. She made a fist and thumped it against her heart, causing his own to bang with intensified hope.

Slocum took his turn, overtly agitated.

"Is it true, Miss McCooms, that it's possible for a victim to be strangled by someone with ten good fingers, leaving less than ten fingerprints?"

"Yes, it is."

"Thank you. You're excused."

Will's brief hope extinguished but he had little time to grow despondent. The surprising Collins kept a brisk pace, recognizing the value of concentrated shock.

"Defense calls Harley Overmire."

Overmire, looking like a scared, hairy ape, puffed up the center aisle, stuffed into a light blue suit with sleeves six inches too long for his stubby arms, sleeves that nearly concealed his hands.

The bailiff held out his Bible and ordered, "Raise your right hand, please."

Harley's face was pale as a full moon. Beads of sweat stood out on his upper lip and two discs of dampness darkened the armpits of his suit.

"Raise your right hand, please," the bailiff repeated.

Harley had no choice but to do as ordered. Haltingly he lifted his arm, and as he did so his sleeve slipped down. Every eye in the room fixed upon that meaty hand, silhouetted against the white plastered wall of the courtroom, with its index finger missing.

"Do you swear to tell the truth, the whole truth and nothing but the truth, so help you God?"

Harley's voice sounded like the squeak of a mouse when the trap trips.

"I do."

The bailiff droned his questions while Collins scanned the eyes of the jurors, finding every one fixed upon Overmire's trembling, four-fingered hand.

"State your name and occupation, please."

"Harley Overmire, superintendent at the Whitney Saw-mill."

"You may be seated."

Collins pretended to read over his notes for a full thirty seconds while Harley quickly sat and hid his right hand at his side. The air felt electric, charged with opinion. Collins let the voltage build while glancing pointedly over the tops of his half-glasses at Harley's hidden hand, the infamous hand that had already gained him a countywide reputation as a military shirker. Collins removed his glasses, stretched to his feet as if his rheumatism was acting up and approached the witness stand. Putting a finger to his chin, he paused thoughtfully, then turned back toward his table as if he'd forgotten something. Halfway there, he did an about-face and stood silently studying Overmire. The courtroom was so silent a spider could have been heard spinning its web. Collins scanned every face in the jury before resting his gaze on its chairman. In a voice rich with innuendo, he said, "No questions."

It was four-twenty P.M. Stomachs were rumbling but not a person thought about supper. Neither did Judge Murdoch check his watch. Instead, he called for closing summations.

They were, to Collins' delight, anticlimactic. Exactly as he would have it. A hungry jury, a judge and gallery in thrall, and a witness sweating on the sidelines.

The jury filed out leaving behind something unheard of: motionlessness.

As if everyone in the room knew the wait would be brief, they all stayed. Including Judge Murdoch. Reverently silent, too warm, hungry, but unwilling to miss the sound of the first returning footstep.

It came in exactly seven minutes.

Twelve pairs of shoes clattered across the raised wooden platform where twelve chairs waited. When the shuffle of bodies stilled, a question vaulted from the high ceiling.

"Ladies and gentlemen of the jury, have you reached your verdict?"

"We have, your honor."

"Would you give it to the bailiff, please?"

The bailiff accepted it, handed it to Murdoch, who opened the small white paper, silently read it, then handed it back to the jury chairman.

"You may read your verdict to the court."

Elly's hands clutched those of Lydia and Miss Beasley. Will stopped breathing.

"We, the jury, find the defendant, William Lee Parker, not guilty."

Pandemonium broke loose. Will spun. Elly clapped her hands over her mouth and started crying. Miss Beasley and Lydia tried to hug her. Collins tried to congratulate him. But they had a single thought: to reach each other. Through the crowd they lunged while hands patted their shoulders but went unheeded. Voices offered congratulations but went unheard. Smiles followed but they saw only each other . . . Will . . . and Elly. In the middle of the throng they collided and clung. They kissed, hard and hasty. They buried their faces in the coves of one another, harboring, holding.

"Elly . . . oh, God . . ."

"Will . . . my darling Will . . ."

He heard her sob.

She heard him swallow.

With eyes sealed tightly, they rocked, smelled each other, felt each other, shutting out all else.

"I love you," he managed with his mouth pressed against her ear. "I never stopped."

"I know that." She kissed his jaw.

"And I'm so damn sorry."

"I know that, too." She laughed but the sound was broken by a sob.

People bumped against them. A reporter called Will's name. Witnesses waited to congratulate them.

"Don't go away," Will's voice boomed at Elly's ear before he tucked her securely beneath his arm. She wrapped her arms around him and pressed close while he performed the rituals expected of him.

He shook Collins' hand and got a firm clap on the back.

"Well, young fellow, it's been a pleasure all the way."

Will laughed. "Maybe for you."

"There was never a doubt in my mind that you'd win."

"We'd win, you mean."

Collins put his free hand on Elly's shoulder, including her. "Yes, I guess you're right. We." He chuckled and added, "Anytime you want a job, young woman, I know a good half dozen lawyers who'd pay you handsome money to ply your wiles on behalf of their clients. You've got a nose and a knack."

Elly laughed and lifted her cheek from Will's lapel long enough to look up into his happy brown eyes.

"Sorry, Mr. Collins, but I got a job, and I wouldn't trade it for the world."

Will kissed her nose and the three of them shared a hearty pileup of hands that passed for a shake until it was interrupted by Lydia Marsh, who caught Elly around the neck. "Oh, Elly, I'm so happy for you." They pressed cheeks. "You, too, Will." On tiptoe she reached up to offer him an impetuous hug.

His heart felt full to bursting. "I don't know how to thank you, Mrs. Marsh."

She shook her head, battling tears, unable to express her fondness in any way but to touch his cheek, then kiss Elly and promise, "I'll see you both soon," before she slipped away.

A second reporter called, "Mr. Parker, may I have a minute?" But there were Nat and Norris MacReady, smiling like liver-spotted bookends, standing proud in their military uniforms which smelled of mothballs.

"Nat . . . Norris . . ." Will gave them each a hand-pump and a bluff squeeze on the neck. "Was I glad to have you two on my side! What can I say? Without you it might've gone the other way."

"Anything for a veteran," Nat replied.

"Say you'll keep a supply of that honey comin'," Norris put in.

While they laughed Mrs. Gaultier and Dr. Kendall brushed past, touching Will's shoulders, smiling.

"Congratulations, Mr. Parker."

The reporter snapped a picture while Will shook their hands and thanked them.

Feeling as if he was caught in a millrace, Will was forced to give himself over to strangers and friends alike while the reporters continued firing questions.

"Mr. Parker, is it true that you were once fired from the mill by Harley Overmire?"

"Yes."

"Because of your prison record?"

"Yes."

"Is it true he cut his finger off to avoid the draft?"

"I really couldn't speculate on that. Listen, it's been a long day and—"

He tried to ease toward the door but the well-meaning crowd swarmed like gnats around a damp brow.

"Mr. Parker . . ."

"Congratulations, Will . . ."

"Eleanor, you too . . ."

"Congratulations, young man, you don't know me but I'm—"

"Hey, Mr. Parker, can I have your autograph?" (This from a youth in a baseball cap.)

"Nice goin', Will . . ."

"Elly, we're so happy for you both."

"Congratulations, Parker, you and the missus come by the cafe and have a free meal on me . . ."

Will had no wish to be the center act of a three-ring circus, but these were his fellow townspeople, welcoming him and Elly into their fold at last. He accepted their handshakes, returned their smiles and acted duly appreciative. Until he simply had to escape and be alone with Elly. In response to someone's humorous banter he squeezed Elly tighter, tipped her till one of her feet left the ground and pressed a kiss to her temple, whispering, "Let's get out of here." She hugged his waist as they turned toward the door.

And there stood Miss Beasley, patiently waiting her turn.

The reporter hounded Will and Elly as they moved toward the librarian. "Mr. Parker, Mrs. Parker, could either of you make a comment on the arrest of Harley Overmire?"

They ignored the question.

Miss Beasley was dressed in drab bile green and held her purse handle over the wrists crossed militantly beneath her superfluous breasts. Will propelled Elly forward until the two of them stood within two feet of Miss Beasley. Only then did he release his wife.

A male voice intruded. "Mr. Parker, I'm from the *Atlanta Constitution.* Could you—"

Elly ran interference for him. "He's busy right now. Why don't you wait outside?"

Yes, Will was busy. Fighting a losing battle against deep, swamping emotions as he stepped close to Gladys Beasley and folded her in his arms, hooked his chin on her tight blue curls and held her firmly, choking in the scent of carnations but loving every second of it.

Unbelievably, she returned the caress, planting her palms on his back.

"You gave me one hell of a scare, you know that?" Will's voice was gruff with emotion.

"You needed it, you stubborn thing."

"I know. But I thought I'd lost you and Elly too."

"Oh, bosh, Mr. Parker. You'll have to do more than act like a complete fool to lose either one of us."

He chuckled, the sound reluctantly escaping his taut throat. They rocked for several seconds.

"Thank you," he whispered and kissed her ear.

She patted his hard back, her purse rapping his hip, then blinked forcefully, pulled away and donned her didactic façade again. "I'll expect you back at work next Monday, as usual."

With his hands resting on her shoulders, Will's attractive brown eyes fell to her face. A crooked smile lifted a corner of his mouth. "Yes, ma'am," he drawled.

Collins interrupted.

"You gonna hold that woman all day or let somebody else have a crack at her?"

Surprised, Will stepped back. "She's all yours."

"Well, good, because I thought I might take her over to my house and feed her a little brandy—see what develops. What do you say, Gladys?" Miss Beasley was already blushing as Collins commandeered her. "You know, when we were in high school I always wanted to ask you on a date, but you were so smart you scared the hell out of me. Do you remember when—"

His voice faded as he marshaled her toward the door. Elly slipped her arm through Will's and together they watched the pair leave.

"Looks like Miss Beasley's got herself an admirer at last."

"Two of them." Elly grinned up at him.

He covered her hand, squeezed it tightly against his arm and let his eyes linger in hers. "Three."

"Mr. Parker, I'm from the *Atlanta Constitution*—"

On tiptoe, Elly whispered in Will's ear, "Answer him, please, so we can get rid of him. I'll wait in the car."

"No, you don't!" He tightened his hold. "You're staying right here with me."

They weathered the questions together, begrudging every moment that kept them from privacy but learning that a warrant had already been issued for the arrest of Harley Overmire and he was already in custody. When asked to comment, Will only replied, "He'll need a good lawyer and I know a damned fine one I could recommend."

It was nearing dusk when Elly and Will escaped to their car at last. The sun glowed low along the rough stone building they left behind, lighting it to a pale copper. On the grounds of the courthouse the camellias were in full bloom, though the branches of the ash trees were bare, casting long thin shadows along the hood of their ramshackle automobile which sported a wrinkled front bumper and one blue fender on a black body.

When Elly headed for the passenger side, Will tugged her in the opposite direction. "You drive," he ordered.

"Me!"

"I hear you learned how."

"I don't know if Miss Beasley would agree with that."

He glanced at the bumper and the fender. "Banged 'er up a little, did you?"

"A little."

"Who put the new fender on?"

"Me'n Donald Wade."

Will regarded his wife with glowing eyes. "You're some woman, you know that, Mrs. Parker?"

A glow kindled deep within Elly. "Since I met you," she answered quietly.

They let their eyes linger for another devout moment before he ordered, "Get in. Show me what you learned."

He clambered in the passenger side and left her no choice. When the engine was revved she clutched the wheel, manhandled the stubborn shift, took a deep breath—"Okay ... here goes"—and promptly drove onto the sidewalk, hitting the brakes in a panic, jouncing them till their heads hit the roof and rebounded toward the windshield.

"Dammit, Will, I'm scared to death of this thing!" She socked the steering wheel. "It never goes where I want it to!"

He laughed, rubbing the crown of his head. "It brought you to Calhoun to hire a lawyer, didn't it?"

She felt herself blush, wanting to appear competent and prove how worldly she'd become in his absence. "Don't tease me, Will, not when this—this piece of junk is acting up."

His voice softened and lost its teasing note. "And it brought you to Calhoun to visit your husband."

Their eyes met—sober, yearning eyes. His hand took hers from the wheel, his thumb rubbed her knuckles.

"Elly—is it true? Are you pregnant?"

She nodded, a trembling smile tilting her lips. "We're gonna have us a baby, Will. Yours and mine this time."

Words eluded him. Emotion clotted his throat. He reached for the back of her neck and her belly, placing a hand on each, drawing her across the seat to rest his lips against her forehead. She closed her eyes and put both hands over his widespread right hand, covering the life within her body.

"A baby," he breathed at last. "Imagine that."

She pulled away to see his eyes. For infinite seconds they gazed, then suddenly both laughed.

"A baby!" he cheered.

"Yes, a baby!" She took his head in both hands and ruffled his hair. "With shaggy blond hair and big brown eyes and a beautiful mouth like yours." She kissed it and his lips opened to taste her, possess her, gratify her. His hand moved on her stomach, slid lower and made her shiver.

Against her lips he said, "When this one's born you'll have a doctor."

"All right, Will," she answered meekly.

He deepened his kiss and his caress until she was forced to remind him, "Will, there are still people going by."

Drawing a tortured breath he released her and said, "Maybe I'd better drive after all. We'll get there faster." The door slammed behind him and he jogged around the hood while she slid over. As he put the car in reverse he warned, "Hang on to that young one. We don't want to shake her loose." He backed down the curb, bouncing them a second time, while Elly clutched her stomach and they both laughed.

They drove around the courthouse square and out onto Highway 53, headed southeast. Behind them the sun sank lower. Before them the road climbed out of the valley, lifting them through rolling woodland that soon would burgeon with green. Will rolled down the window and breathed deep of the fresh winter air. He locked his elbows, caught the wheel with his thumbs and thrust his wrists forward, tasting freedom, drinking it like one parched.

Free. And loved. And soon to be a father. And befriended. And accepted—even admired—by a town that sprang to his defense. And all because of one woman.

It overwhelmed Will. *She* overwhelmed him.

Abruptly he pulled off the highway, bumped along a field access and pulled up behind a clump of leafless willows. In one motion he killed the engine and turned to his wife.

"Come here, Green Eyes," he whispered, loosening the knot of his tie. Like heat lightning she moved into his embrace. Their lips and breasts met and their tongues, cautious no longer, made reckless sweeps. Crushed together, they healed.

He broke away to hold her head and gaze into her eyes. "I missed you so damn much."

"Not as much as I missed you."

"You cut your hair." He scraped it back with both hands, freeing her face for his adoring gaze.

"So I'd look up-to-date for you."

He scanned her countenance, hairline to chin, and wondered aloud, "What did I ever do to deserve you?"

"Don't thank me, Will, I—"

He cut her off with a kiss. As it lengthened they grew breathless, feeling the bond strengthen between them. At last he freed his mouth. "I know everything you did. I know about the honey, and the ads, and the witnesses you found, and the car you had to learn to drive and the town you had to face. But the house, Elly. My God, you faced that house, didn't you?"

"What else could I do, Will? I had to prove to you that it wasn't true what you saw on my face the day you were arrested. I never meant it, Will . . . I . . ." She began crying. He caught her tears with his lips, moving across her face as if taking sustenance.

"You didn't have to prove anything to me. I was scared and stubborn and I acted like a fool, just like Miss Beasley said. When you came to visit me the first time I was hurt, and I—I wanted to hurt you back. But I didn't mean what I said, Elly, honest I didn't." He kissed her eyes, murmuring softly, "I didn't mean it, Elly, I'm sorry."

"I know, Will, I know."

Again he held her face, searching her pale eyes. "And when you came the second time, I kept telling myself to apologize but Hess was there listening, so I talked about stupid things instead. Men can be such fools."

"It doesn't matter now, Will, it doesn't—"

"I love you." He held her possessively.

"I love you, too."

When they'd held each other a while he said, "Let's go home."

Home. They pictured it, felt it beckon.

He took a lock of her short brown hair between his fingers, rubbing it. "To the kids, and our own house, and our own bed. I've missed it."

She touched his throat and said, "Let's go."

* * *

They drove on home through the purple twilight, through the brown Georgia hills, past cataracts and piney woods and through a quiet town with a library and a magnolia tree and a square where an empty bench awaited two old men and the sunshine. Past a house whose picket fence and morning glories and green shades were gone, replaced by a mowed yard, scraped siding and gleaming windows reflecting a newly risen moon. As they passed it, Elly snuggled close to Will, an arm around his shoulders, her free hand on his thigh.

He turned his head to watch her eyes follow the place as the car pulled abreast of it, then past.

She felt his gaze and lifted her smile to him.

You all right? his eyes asked.

I'm all right, hers answered.

He kissed her nose and linked his fingers with those hanging over his left shoulder.

Content, they continued through the night, to a steep, rocky road that led them past a sourwood tree, into a clearing where blue flowers would soon tap against a skewed white house. Where three children slept—soon to be four. Where a bed waited . . . and forever waited . . . and the bees would soon make the honey run again.